Stitched Up

D. A. MacCuish

Michael Terence
Publishing

First published in paperback by
Michael Terence Publishing in 2017
www.mtp.agency

Copyright © 2017 D. A. MacCuish

D. A. MacCuish has asserted his right to be identified as
the author of this work in accordance with the
Copyright, Designs and Patents Act 1988

This book is a work of fiction. Neither the words spoken by the
characters nor the actions taken by them should be attributed
to any real-life persons, living or dead. Any resemblance is
purely coincidental

ISBN 9781549843341

All rights reserved. No part of this publication may be
reproduced, stored in a retrieval system, or transmitted, in any
form or by any means, electronic, mechanical, photocopying,
recording or otherwise, without the prior permission of the
publishers

Cover image
Copyright © Allan Swart

Cover design
Copyright © 2017 Michael Terence Publishing

For big sis, always there for me.

Stitched Up

D. A. MacCuish

Stitch Up: *An act of placing someone in a position in which they will be wrongly blamed for something, or of manipulating a situation to one's advantage.*

There are many phrases to term a chance meeting. Divine intervention *seems too holy, godly even; should one only use it when the outcome is of that ilk?* Fate *is rather final and the ending often fatal, while* a collision of stars *is best placed to describe an unintentional act of nature that colludes to produce something of wonderment, of natural beauty. Often I'll hear someone say, romantically or thoughtfully, "it was meant to be" or "it was supposed to happen."*

But what happened to me wasn't supposed to happen, it wasn't meant to be. But it did, and therefore you could say that it was; it was *divine intervention, the stars* did *collide. I was to become the King in a game of chess, everyone coming at me from all angles with the same intention: to bring me down.*

Fate.

Because had I arrived just a minute later, my life would have turned out very different...

ONE: TOMFOOLERY

The place reeked of weed. Smoke hung in the air, the lounge no more than a blanket of haze you get from an ethereal springtime dawn. I could just about make out the silhouette belonging to Tom's brother Miles - the windows would have surely been ajar had it not been brutally cold outside and absolutely bucketing down. Miles had just stubbed out a joint and made no attempt to hide the bag of green that was resting on the coffee table.

'Oh, shit. Erm, oops?' he said after a few seconds before a smoker's cough busted my eardrums. Some smoke twisted upwards and folded itself between the patterns on the walls and ceiling, clearing the room a fraction. He'd seen me looking straight at the huge, cellophane wrapped bud that was lying next to a large clear glass ashtray supporting a burning roach, its end browned with sticky streaks of unfiltered tar. The bud reminded me of a massive green turd, the kind of shit a vegan would do, I imagined.

'Oh...that?' I said, casually nodding to it. 'Don't be silly...bit of weed. What's wrong with some puff in this day and age?'

'Phew. You never know...it's *mine* though' he said, tapping his chest. 'Tom here doesn't get involved in that stuff.'

'Not my business if you do pal,' I said turning to Tom and slapping him on the back. 'As long as you don't get out of your tree at work, then what you do at home is no concern of mine.'

The last sentence was lightly coated with sarcasm, as you'll find out.

Tom stumbled out of the room with a grunt, presumably to free himself from his suit which had, in just six hours, plummeted down from the heights of a stylish and well-tailored pristine light grey Hugo Boss number and into a montage of smelly yeast, sticky Sambuca and crusts of dry vomit. Even his shirt had abandoned all hope of ever seeing the light of day again and there was a generous patch of something sinister still lurking around his groin area.

My gaze followed him until he fell through his bedroom door and shouted something at his own carpet. I tried to work out just how much Tom had drank all afternoon but was interrupted by an angry mule braying violently from somewhere in the room, or rather Miles coughed again and then delivered something black and deadly into a tissue, forcing me to fill the embarrassing gap of silence that had unfolded between us.

'Erm look, I've been there many times myself, it's no big deal. It *was* an early start. Totally my fault,' I said.

'Sure. And thanks...you know. Getting him back without drama? He was making no sense earlier, it was quite funny,' reported Miles, as if I was oblivious to the gibbering wreck his younger brother had been since two o'clock. 'I think I got the lion's share of tolerance levels out of the two of us.'

No shit, Sherlock.

'Don't worry. It'll be tomorrow's chip paper anyway. I value him a lot, so it's not an issue if once in a blue moon he...well, you know.' I trailed off, knowing Miles would repeat back the bit about valuing him whenever Tom regained the power of speech, providing Miles hadn't choked to death on his own mucus.

That's the thing about being in charge of a company – you've got to make the odd allowance here and there for your top employees to let loose and make a prick of themselves once in a while. Show them you understand they're only human - no need to chastise them for it. Empathise with them a bit and give them the benefit of the doubt, etcetera. If Tom had a brain bigger than a black olive he'd probably work out that he'd be on a warning if he behaved like that again. But anyway, the events of the afternoon were largely down to me, and went as follows:

The last Thursday of the calendar month. Usually the

busiest time, when everyone frantically dials their base of customers and tries to flog them an advertising banner, or a subscription to our database of intelligence. Any one of thousands of companies who really *will not* want the proclaimed premium exposure through our online trade subscription e-zines will be hounded no end by the hunting young sales reps I employ. Poor Marketing Directors just trying to get on with whatever crap they have to do are relentlessly pursued on landlines, mobiles, email and even Facebook, by a pack of ravenous wide-boy sales reps hungry for commission that'll keep them in rent, beer, drugs and food – in that order – for the next three weeks. (Week four is breadline territory: bumping up credit card and overdraft limits, getting drugs on tick from trusting dealers, fare dodging, dabbling in a bit of shoplifting, begging etc.) We sell a database of all the latest news and deals going on in the solar energy markets; a massive topic these days. Sustainable, solar, green, eco-friendly energy yadda yadda. All the movers and shakers, deals and takeovers, mergers and acquisitions, big executive appointments, open bids for tender, company closures and company start-ups, industry shows and more. You name it and we'll report on it. It's classified as *Business Intelligence* and anyone operating in those aforementioned markets will - no questions - have to make a necessary purchase of our database. If they don't, then we sell them advertising banners on the system. Whether the ads yield anything of value is up for debate.

This is part of the song and dance my sales guys are trained to do on the phone when pitching for those said banners:

"*...therefore Mr Prospect your service/solution/product, if advertised on our database – a database that has a subscription base of fifty thousand senior executives* (five thousand is more accurate here) – *you will be seen as the leading player, the number one, the messiah in your marketplace, the 'go-to' vendor. It's a no-brainer. Now, how much have you set aside for this premium exposure?*"

It's a load of *BS* to be honest, but as with most businesses, if we don't take their ridiculously unnecessary marketing budgets, then some other bunch of cowboys will.

This afternoon had not been like that, however. *No one* was on the phone after 1 pm. At the start of the month, I had set a stretch target for the business, that when achieved, we'd down tools at lunchtime and the company plastic would be going for an inevitable spanking behind the bar next door at The Castle. So at half twelve, Tom closed a deal worth eighteen grand, taking the sales floor over the magic target of a quarter-of-a-million in new business. He was the hero - no doubt about that - and so true to my word I took the team for an early drink and declared with pride that we'd not be returning, although some of the useless gibbons who work for me didn't deserve anything more than a P45 and glass of room temperature toilet water. Un-flushed. The announcement was met with appreciative cheers and wide smiles in my direction, the new girl – Stephanie, French or German I think - seemed ecstatic at the news, so I made a mental note to offer her some champagne in isolation at some point later on when she was suitably oiled and her reaction time had waned.

Back to Tom: he started off *powerful*. By that I mean he had finished his pint of premium strength Dutch lager before I'd even completed ordering a round of drinks from barmaid Vicki (complete chav but very doable with a handy rack on her. I rattled it last year). I told my twelve sales guys that they could have any draft beer, house wine or soft drinks *on the tab*. After a few painfully awkward conversations with some guys I didn't know the names of, my attention level had strayed from mildly conscious to *why did Bungle off Rainbow wear pyjamas in bed when he was naked during the day?* I noticed Tom hovering about in the background willing me to engage with him, desperate to talk me through his big deal like he was a proud boy telling mummy about his winning goal at play time. Not what I wanted to do, but Stephanie seemed in awe of him, which would draw her nearer to me if she was clinging on to his coat tail. After closing that deal, Tom had been elevated high onto a pedestal in the last hour and had become *The Big Dog* of the sales floor, scoring an automatic increase of at least two points in the eyes of the females I employ. It really is like that - do some serious numbers and you become a local celebrity and all the minky looks up to you like you're monarchy or something and, more importantly, much more likely to open their legs for you without having to be drugged. It's the same principle with anything. Power is attractive. The stupid cows love it. My last top biller was a guy called Rory and his confidence was *off the scale*, outselling everyone, every month. The reason? The person he was selling to couldn't *see* what he looked like because it was over the phone, which gave him a form of super confidence I'd rarely come across before. That's because if anyone *was* unfortunate enough to actually lay eyes on him, they would do one of three things:

1. Run away – quickly - as bowels develop a mind of their own and deliver some warm punishment.

2. Look for a film crew under the assumption Rory was, in fact, a science-experiment-gone-wrong character from a horror flick.

3. Simply dial the police and inform them there's an escaped exhibit from Zippo's on the loose.

When Rory walked in for his interview, the first thing I wondered was whether he was an animal, a vegetable or a mineral.

But remarkably, Rory's dominance on the sales floor saw a mind-boggling metamorphosis from a downgraded version of John Merrick into Brad fucking Pitt; the ugly bastard worked his way through every female in the company (none at the time were worth my attention so I let him get on with it.) I guess it was nice, for him anyway – a character from the Beano having a taste of what he'd never be getting again if he left, which sadly he did to go and join the armed forces. The rumour was that he was scouted as a new form of a secret weapon designed to frighten the hell out of enemy lines within a ten-mile radius.

Anyway, half-an-hour later and four pints in, Tom was

giving it the biggun as Stephanie lapped it up like a greedy kitten; her girly flirting and encouragement at Tom to drink more irritated me. And for Tom, what better way to enhance his professional status and increase his chances of going home with a tidy French (German?) chick than to chew the fat with me - the owner - on sales strategy, territory, revenue forecasts and other crap I had no interest in discussing.

So being the noble chap I am, I gave into his attention seeking and finally acknowledged him, and in a heartbeat, he'd barged past a couple of other skivvy's and cornered me.

'Alright Sean?' he said, already dropping the first name familiarity and slapping my shoulder like he was a fucking yank soccer coach or something.

'Tom, buddy! Awesome result today…you got us over the line. You should let loose,' I replied, granting his wish of wanting to be on the soccer field. It was true though; he did close the deal that got us to the two-fifty mark. Stephanie seemed *very* impressed. Was I going to be outdone by someone twenty years younger? Quite possibly, yes, spurring me into action. Watch this you little punk.

'Tell me champ, what you gonna bring in next month? Gonna have to count on you now, right?' I said, making sure we held Stephanie's full attention.

'Phew…tough one,' he replied, blowing through his teeth as if he was thinking about it. Note: he was pissed by this time, so there was no way he was mapping out anything other than what to drink next and/or how to get Stephanie into the sack.

'I reckon I can double that, for sure. Thirty-six,' he said confidently. It took his tiny brain a minute of straining to work out what two times the eighteen grand he'd just closed amounted to.

Now then, a good tactic that all Sales Heads should use is that whatever someone commits to doing, in monetary terms or other, *always* push back and ask for more. The good ones will accept the challenge and likely still exceed all expectations. The other oxygen thieves will usually just frown and tell you it's not possible. What *is* possible is that you'll want to shoot them in the face.

'Thirty-six? Dude. You can do seventy plus you're *that* good. You just did, what, eighteen in a week? Once a week for a month, that's over seventy grand. Imagine the commission...it's-'

'Nearly eleven zousand,' Stephanie answered for me, thankfully. I was about to say nine.

'Yeah *exactly*. Eleven thousand in comms. Wow, that's serious money man. That's about what...one-fifty a year including your base? Nice money for a twenty-two-year-old.'

'Yeah, pretty decent,' said Tom nonchalantly.

Ungrateful little bugger. One swallow doesn't make a summer pal. If it wasn't for me poaching him from a dead-end temping job his dialogue wouldn't stretch much further than "Welcome to Burger King, can I take your order please?"

Let's see how you like these apples then:

While Tom tried to chat-up Stephanie, I turned away and beckoned Vicki over and told her to bring a bottle of Sambuca, giving the clear instructions to fill up *two* shot glasses of the liquid mayhem and a third with water (for me). Once the three shots were lined up on the bar, I grabbed the pair of them and thrust the glasses into their hands before they could protest.

'Bottoms up, chin chin and all that!' I shouted as our glasses met and we downed the shots. I screwed my face up at the harsh aniseed taste that I hadn't just endured.

'We drink zis at home all the time, or Pastis we call it, it's similar to Pernod. You know zis?' Stephanie said, licking her fingers clean of some of the thick syrup that had spilt over the edge of her glass. I noticed she had a pierced tongue and immediately felt my cock twitch at the thought of her licking another thick substance from my bell-end later on.

'Oh right, yeah it's one of *those* drinks. Yeah, I mean, I find I can drink it all night. Doesn't really get me pissed, just makes me quite...*happy*, you know?' That was a lie. It gets me *wrecked*, but more important, I recall Tom telling me one Monday morning how he'd gotten paralytic on the stuff at the weekend thanks to some mates forcing him to down shots of the stuff. Should never give anyone that kind of information.

'Oui, I mean yeah. We drink a lot of zis in France. It's in all ze bars. It give me no 'angovaire, really.' Her accent turned the small twitch in my pants I'd just had into something slightly more boisterous.

I did a *Columbo* and jabbed at thin air. 'Ah yes. I thought you were *French*,' I smiled, tapping my temple and wondering if being French meant that she had a shaved minge, or was *au natural*. 'Accent,' I said, still tapping.

The French. They know how to drink. They can elegantly sip on a couple of ten euro bottles of wine all night and not even flinch, and at that, it's a bottle that pisses all over the nonsense we get here. They can go to a bar and *take* Pastis, or Pernod, swill back magnums of exceptional value-for-money Champagne, demolish a delightful Fleurie sitting up until the crack of dawn in a narrow cobbled quaint Parisian side street, casually talking and smoking *Gitanes* until dawn and breeze into work without so much as a raised pulse. Over here? Not a chance pal. Us Brits are intent on filling our bladders up to a bursting point with cheap imported beer, radioactive warm white wine, neon coloured WKD, Jagerbombs, *Malibu* and Coke, and other hideous concoctions. So we cram in as much as possible before last orders, which are rarely later than eleven or twelve unless you're in the small minority of Londoners who belong to a members club like me. I'm well-off enough to just jump in a cab and slip into a private club or a hotel bar if I want to carry on; the hotels are also a good hunting ground for high-class hookers in case you're nuts are begging to be emptied, which for me is quite likely after a session. But the everyday Joes of this world? Nah, they have to make do with three or four hours power drinking once they've arrived at the pub, preparing in advance by having the obligatory bottle of schnapps before setting off out. These people are quite easy to spot whenever you pass a pub at, say, half past eleven in the evening (unless you're in Benidorm, where it's the same at half eleven in the morning). You'll often see a mass of piss-heads slouched on the pavement, chunder everywhere, grown men crying and/or scrapping, some of them pissing in the gutter while others have their hands up some kind of horror show's skirt and chewing its face off. "A pint and a fight for a Great British night!" my uncle once said to me through gaps in his teeth.

I decided to put this theory to the test and see what the outcome of a *Britain vs. France* Sambuca drinking competition would be. Well, Tom versus Stephanie anyway - I was happy to keep a clear head and adjudicate.

'Ok then yous twos, legend has it that the French can outdrink the English eh?' I said, looking to Tom for encouragement and setting the trap. He had no choice but to show me his loyalty, and furthermore to appear like he wasn't the pussy I knew he was in front of Stephanie, seeing as he blatantly wanted to end up taking it home like I did. It's that kind of scenario where a devious mind and abuse of power can really help secure a clinical victory.

'Pah,' he scoffed, taking the bait and walking bang into it. 'That's easy, boss.'

'I zink you will be surprised,' Stephanie said, cocksure of herself. I told her that as well - the *cocksure* part - emphasising the word *cock,* knowing that it would burrow itself into her memory undetected and stay there until she was hopefully feeling a bit loose.

Time for the elimination process.

'Righty-ho! Let's see about this claim then,' I said, before turning to Vicki and ordering another round.

'One two sree!' Stephanie shouted. They nailed their shots of aniseed liquor and I downed my h2O.

Tom's eyes lit up in terror at my suggestion of same again as soon as we'd slammed down our empties. Even Stephanie didn't look that keen. Fuck going easy on either of them, victory was in sight.

'Come on...don't tell me two shots each is all you can manage? What planet are you both on? Think that makes me the winner...' Great bit of reverse psychology right there.

'Ok,' said Stephanie, with that nonchalant shrug of the shoulders only the French can pull off. I looked at Vicki and told her to bring on another round. She knew what to do.

We did it twice more after that, a grand total of ten shots of Sambuca between Tom and Stephanie, and five shots of tap water for me. All in the space of twenty minutes.

What happened next was *tres amusement*: Tom retched. Doing that is basically waving the white flag, throwing the towel in. That's the same as dropping a bar of soap in the prison showers when Delroy and his six brothers – all from the same tribe in West Africa, starved of sex for the last decade – are taking a scrub in there too, i.e. you're going to get bummed into next week, and it's going to hurt.

Tom was *well* on the way. One more drink for him and my competition to deflower Stephanie was dead and buried. He'd lost the ability to stand up unassisted whilst trying to focus on Stephanie's chest, which had become subtly more exposed as another button on her blouse had popped open. She'd also let her hair down into a neat bob and her skin had a nice coating of shine. All in all a look that said she was at worst tipsy, but at best ripe for a good plucking.

Tom, on the other hand, could only muster up a response which sounded like Scooby-Doo on Valium when I offered him a pint of nail-in-the-coffin and so not wanting to give off the impression I was irresponsibly feeding him more alcohol, I answered the question for him and said it was probably wise to get him a large coke; something he appeared grateful for despite having just had a stroke. Also, a large coke meant I could get Vicki to put at least *three* shots of cheap house vodka in as well and finish him off properly.

I turned my attention to Stephanie. 'Some champagne?'

It was more of a statement than a question, and I'd already told Vicki to get us two glasses of Moet along with one triple vodka and coke. Stephanie liked that, it made her feel special.

'Is Pepsi ok?' asked Vicki automatically, as if I was worried about the brand of liquid caramel Tom was about to add to the litre of Sambuca already swirling about in his gut and about to induce the rapid onset of a neurological disorder. Why do bar staff ask that? Does anyone ever turn their nose up at such a suggestion and ask for something else, as if Pepsi is, in fact, the straining's of the Devil's ballbag, or a drink reserved for the black slaves of America, and therefore deemed unacceptable to the white, middle-class echelons of society who frequent public houses?

'Salut' I shouted, as we knocked back the bubbly, watching Tom gleefully drain his Pepsi and triple house vodka in one gulp, exhaling in an appreciation that lasted - by my calculations – all of two seconds before his relieved smile was betrayed by the confusing taste of surprise vodka ambushing his taste buds. Bingo! I could concentrate on Stephanie now that the thorn in my side was fast approaching being carted off in the back of an ambulance to have his stomach pumped.

'You smoke?' she asked, catching me looking at the carton of French fags she was fingering.

'Oui...er...*parfois*?' I said wincing like I had to think hard to remember the word for *sometimes* in her language.

'Ah ok. *Sometimes*. Very good,' she said, and smiled sweetly, no doubt admiring my bilingual skills. 'Shall we?'

Yes. I was nearly in.

Outside the pub, the conversation was going well. Subtle flirting, giggling, the odd touch on the forearm and whatnot. She was gently pulling down on her hair, a solid sign if ever there was one, which meant my mind had begun working towards the next steps I needed to achieve in order to bend her over later on. Another *Gitane* would acquire me some more time to keep her engaged.

'May I?' I asked, nodding at her pack. 'Sorry to ask...I'll

buy a pack in a bit but I *really* like these ones. They're just so...*smooth.*'

She pulled out her pocket dragon and sparked up another for me - the butt changing into a pink and waxy stub from her lip gloss. I was indirectly kissing her *already* I joked (to myself). Just as I was about to take the first drag, however, the *thwacking* sound of wooden furniture toppling over followed by glass smashing interrupted me, and then after a pause, some hysterical laughter. Stephanie's unlit fag dropped out of her mouth onto the pavement as she looked straight past me in horror.

'Oh. Wow!'

Something entertaining was happening at the back of the pub. I had a hunch it may involve him and I was right when I advanced over to where the noise had come from. Tom was standing on a table trying to balance a pint of beer on his head, whilst simultaneously attempting to piss into an empty glass, missing totally and spraying the onlookers as his urine, then a pint of beer, splashed onto the table and bounced off the surface. Quite forcefully.

Tom was pissing on the table in front of the entire pub. His tiny cock poking through his flies reminded me of Noddy's hat.

'Oh, Jesus,' I cried, not really expecting his degree of drunkenness to have reached Geordie stag-do level quite so easily.

Vicki shot me a slightly different look to the pleasant nodding she'd been directing at me half an hour ago as she willingly co-operated with my tomfoolery, a look that indicated she was far from over the moon at the inconvenience of fetching a bucket, mop, disinfectant, warm water and a yellow *WET FLOOR* sign - the not so nice part of the job that pays her a paltry five quid an hour or so, although she probably earns a bit more on the street corners of Luton on her days off.

'Ok, Tom that's enough. Get down from there!' I shouted. Several pairs of eyes followed me over to the court jester wobbling about on the table.

Rather than listening to me, he went one better and launched into an impression of Superman as given by a three-year-old, flinging his arms forward and roaring loudly before projectile vomiting everywhere. His breakfast, and quite possibly dinner from the night before, jetted out at a hundred miles an hour, splattering over a couple of colleagues who went from, within seconds, uncontrollable laughter and into horrified expressions more akin to a look you'd find on someone who's just sat through *Mexican Shit Eaters volume Five* (a real film, by the way). A few drops of his sick landed in one poor sod's open mouth, in turn causing him to hurl onto the steaming pile of puke that Tom had already delivered at his feet. There it was: a puke cocktail, split between the table and the pub floor. It was just before three in the afternoon, and it was my doing.

'Ok, Tom. Go and get yourself cleaned up,' I said, mouthing "large water" to Vicki straight after he'd fallen off the table. I refrained from the urge to get her to pour him half a pint of Smirnoff, there was no need to go beyond the call of duty after all.

'Perhaps you should take him home – he's in a bad way, no?' suggested Stephanie, the sentence giving me mild palpitations that she might actually be cock-blocking me and trying to get me out of the way. Or was she genuinely concerned about Tom? Either way, I had to keep things bubbling, she was within shooting range.

'Great idea. Listen, I've got a nice members bar nearby. We can go and have a drink there if you'd like?' I suggested quietly. 'Be interesting to find out what your plans are for hitting the ground running here now it's been what…a month?' I asked, pausing for her to nod. 'Plus they have a choice selection of wines we can get stuck into.' The wine part was true but the rest was a pack of lies.

'Sure, but what about everyone else?' she asked, less with concern but more to confirm that it would be exclusive to just the two of us. That's what I told myself anyway.

'Leave them here, they're enjoying themselves. I'll leave some cash behind the bar.'

Stephanie smiled, and I'd read it right.

Tom reappeared ten minutes later having salvaged about five percent of his dignity, so the three of us spilled out into the cold and an Uber was with us in two minutes. I caught Stephanie sending a few messages to someone on WhatsApp, which turned out to be *Mama*, which pleased me a lot. I was worried she was going to ditch me and I'd have to go on the prowl for a brass in Soho or something.

'Zis weather,' was all she managed to say as she looked out of the window and the rain began to tap at the windows of our Toyota something or other.

*

I shook hands with Miles and left him to deal with the mess that I'd made of his kid brother and as I skipped down the first flight of stairs, two females chattering away became audible. Eager to get on with the proceedings with Stephanie at Keystone Crescent - an impressive member's bar I take dates to - I breezed down and set eyes on the pair of girls the voices belonged to. One of them was fat, pale and frumpy, and worth about half a second of my attention, but the other one was truly incredible. Slim, blonde, full lips and a cute nose, with eyes that suggested she knew her way around the bedroom. A solid nine, no questions. As I got to the final stair, I caught her tits staring at my eyes, the cheeky monkey! She set down a letter on the ledge, and we exchanged smiles before they vanished through their front door, the big one resembled a human medicine ball and made tough work of it.

A split second before I went to exit, instinct took a hold of me.

It said her name was Rose Wilkins.

TWO: OFFER

Rose Wilkins shoes were a tragedy.

She'd debated whether to listen to Jimmy Choo's shameless vanity or trust the wisdom of Dorothy Perkins, who tried to keep her mindful of the weather. As she scanned the ashen November skyline through her Venetian blinds to evaluate the threat of rain and looked at the strips of orange light shining up from the glistening road, Jimmy's voice was louder.

Unfortunately he was showing-off.

It *had* rained, heavily, at precisely 3.04pm two minutes after she had left the trendy office block in Clerkenwell that she was temping in. Office block is an underwhelming description for the open plan converted tram-shed she found herself plugging in data and canvassing for new customers these last four months.

And it was Thursday; the day before pay day. Not good. Half-hour walks to and from work in the bitter cold all week having maxed out literally every penny in her overdraft. Times were bad. She'd painfully entered packed lunch territory as well, politely declining after work drinks twice this week between mouthfuls of night-before-leftovers spooned from Tupperware.

On her walk home, she passed rows and rows of cute, independent little deli's that commanded the best part of a tenner just for a bottle of olive oil. When she wasn't dreaming of being able to afford half-litre, triangular bottles made of dark green glass filled with extra virgin, she was passing the quaint little boutiques along Camden passage which sold one-off designer jackets that had hand-written price-tags displaying a tiny price of £750 in blue biro. Anything but tiny...

She stopped, looked and shed a few invisible tears.

Literally nothing could help her out, she was that broke. As she trudged along Essex road, wondering if she still had half a can of sweetcorn on *her* shelf of the fridge to go with the leftover chicken from Sunday (barely legal), she made a decision to empty her jar of five and ten pence pieces as soon as she got in. It would be a race to the post office to change up whatever she had, maybe enough for a £3.50 battered sausage and chips, or even better, if she had a fiver, she could skip dinner and get a bottle of wine on offer from Sainsbury's if she could 'borrow' a pound from Lucy's piggy bank and put it back tomorrow when she'd been paid. She double-checked how much she had on her. Seventy-six pence, plus whatever was in her piggy bank, definitely enough to buy something to eat *or* drink. She shut her purse. It was a Michael Kors and stood for little more than irony each time she looked inside two hundred quid's worth of leather only to find just a few lonely coppers rattling around between two exhausted credit cards.

She arrived at her front door and found the right key after a longer than usual rummage around in her bag. Well, it was pouring down, so everything took longer. It never rained but …you know. She scratched about until slotting the rogue key into the communal front door of the flats, her entrance coinciding with a sigh of relief as she pushed the round white timer on the wall in the porch. Intrusive light. Light that highlighted her current plight, not the ray of light she needed. It shone down for those ten or so seconds as the button popped out of its holder, revealing her special beige heels made of the finest suede now mimicked a drab pair of dark brown spaniel's ears.

She jumped a little as she caught a glimpse of someone standing next to her, but it turned out to be her reflection in the communal mirror. Rose stared at herself for a minute. A river of mascara trickled down a cheek as she touched her face with her fingertips and eyed herself up, realising she looked like a circus clown whose makeup had been applied by a five-year-old it ran so amok. A large pile of letters distracted her.

'Hmm…' she sighed, 'what have we got here?'

She scooped up the neat stack of inconvenience waiting to be opened, digested, and then binned. An energy bill, a phone bill, a card for one of the dudes upstairs, a handwritten letter for Lucy, and, hold on wait, now this was interesting - a letter for her with the *Foster Fisher Baker FFB* logo stamped at the top. A letter that would no doubt begin *Thank you for your recent application* and somewhere down the page the words *unfortunately, decline, good luck, future* etc.

Square one.

Drawing board.

She had reasoned with herself that she was under-qualified for the role of 'Business Development Executive' as she left the interview last Tuesday; the frustration of royally messing up blackened by having to exit the amazing offices she'd just interviewed in, never to return. Marble flooring, games room, immaculate toilets and flashy entrance gates by the lifts that worked like they were tube barriers. Offices that matched her vision of becoming a high-flying businesswoman in the city of London. Suits and Stilettos.

Much like her other recently graduated pals, the strategy was simple: to earn money in the city and enjoy a degree of independence trying to embrace all the tribulations that adulthood chucked her way, at least until some loaded and wide city-boy could be snapped up to cover the bar tabs and overpriced fancy restaurant bills. She always had boyfriends pay for her – one of her rules. Rose was a stunner after all. She needn't have even bothered looking for a job; she could've hung around in Essex and snared a Premiership footballer had she wanted life on Easy Street. She had the WAG look and then some, turning heads wherever she went. A young 23-year-old body toned to the max from marathon walks around the city and thrice weekly jogs and when she could afford them, Pilates classes. On top of that body was a face that wouldn't look out of place on a TV advert; huge brown eyes, olive skin, ridiculously white teeth sat perfectly arranged and sparkled under full and natural lips. All wrapped in wavy hair the colour of honey. But outside of those looks Rose embodied ambition. Bright, driven and determined to prove she was as much brains as anything else.

Tossing the rest of the post onto the ledge, she tore open the letter, keen to get the imminent disappointment left at the door and get inside for a hot bath. Had the last water bill even been settled? Probably not.

Without having to read a word, she noticed that it was definitely longer than a polite rejection letter. In the middle of the page sat a neat list of bullet points in bold type, a figure and a percentage somewhere, but before she did the maths on those, she drew her eyes back to the top of the page, her hopes of good news rose up from her chest and lodged somewhere in her throat. In a split second, the weeks packed lunches and walks to work were upgraded to hideously overpriced sushi and non-essential cab rides.

Offer of Employment.

Her heart skipped a beat. She blinked, and searched for missing words, like it was meant to read *Definitely Not an Offer of Employment* or something. But her eyes did not deceive her. Her pulse quickened and she broke into a smile, and right here right now, she didn't care much for her soaking wet body and smudged face paint. Starting salary offered was the upper end of the range they'd mentioned - twenty-eight thousand per annum plus quarterly bonus, twenty-*five* days annual leave, subsidised gym and a company pension scheme (although this pension thingy would only be something she'd mention when talking to older people). Immediately thoughts of living a superior life in the city flooded her like someone had popped open a champagne bottle in her head and let loose a million tiny bubbles to fizz around inside, each one representing a piece of the life a 23-year-old high-flying city-girl should get acquainted with. Essential new outfits to look the part would *have* to be purchased, via a short-term loan from the safety net of her mother, at least until her first proper pay cheque landed. The route from Essex Road to Bank meticulously mapped out. Timekeeping. She was in on time every day, period, no excuses, no hiding. Temping in the last few weeks had meant her timekeeping had waned and she was quite often late. Drinks with the older girls after work at least twice a week...heck, she may even treat herself to a new iPad in case she needed to work remotely. That's what people with real jobs did these days after all. The grown-ups who had important things to do, those ones who needed to be available 24/7 to close deals, negotiate terms, make overseas calls. She couldn't wait to find out. A city worker - she was going to be one of them very soon. In the last sixty seconds, Rose Wilkins had been unexpectedly thrust further into adulthood. Things were looking up. Scrap that, things were looking awesome.

I wonder what Lucy will make of all this thought Rose, just as the main door in the porch swung open and the chunky frame of her flatmate heaved its way in from the wet, shaking her umbrella without any consideration for Rose's tights. Hell, they were wet already.

'Another one today...fucking joke round here,' was Lucy's opening. Rose frowned, curled her lips downwards and shook her head, without a clue as to what garbage Lucy was yelling. 'Another bike? Gone from outside Sainsbury's. Fourth one in a week she said...that black woman on the till.' Lucy wiped her plain black Primark's on a doormat that Rose couldn't see.

It bugged Rose how Lucy always referred to the race or colour of anyone she spoke of as if she needed to feel superior. Lucy voted for Brexit, Lucy was full Brexit. Lucy bought a Make America Great Again T-shirt last summer when she was on holiday in Florida with her parents. Lucy was thirty-eight and still didn't own a property, and she hadn't had a steady boyfriend since the times when white dog poo formed patterns at the local park, and there were only four television channels to pick from. Rose wouldn't have chosen her as a living partner had she been aware of all of that prior to responding to her Gumtree advert.

'Mmm' said Rose, giving precisely no hoots about stolen cycling apparatus, but thinking that Lucy sure could do with one of the exercise variety. Rose's choice of a physical workout was somewhat more than her flatmate's, which was limited to the lifting of a package into a microwave oven and pressing a few buttons, or the strenuous task of pulling open a bag of jumbo-sized chocolate buttons twice a day. Lucy had once attempted a spin class a few months back but blamed an imaginary bad knee for having to leave the group after three minutes, getting booed as she limped out with cheeks resembling a pair of maroon Zeppelins, followed by a month of breathing aided by a ventilator.

'Good day?' Lucy asked, not sounding at all genuine.

'Well I got soaked to the bone on the way home and ruined these,' said Rose, nodding at the shoes that were still sodden and making her feet colder by the second. 'But, good news though.' She flicked the letter from FFB so it made a loud crack.

'What's that then?' Lucy asked with mild interest. Any good news for Rose was never such for Lucy and always received with a fake smile, sometimes even a wince. Whenever Rose shared bad news it was the polar opposite; genuine pleasure practically shone out of Lucy's planetoid face.

'Well, it's not massive really,' said Rose delightfully, knowing full well the sound of alarm bells would be quietly chiming somewhere in the far reaches of Lucy's massive head. She spiced things up and paused for a few seconds, an imaginary drumroll got steadily noisier, then she dropped the bomb. 'Got that job I went for at FFB. Look.'

The cymbals crashed.

Lucy's eyebrows rose in surprise as she looked at the letter Rose was holding inches from her nose, making sure she could see the good news as well as hear it. It wasn't pleasant surprise either. Had Lucy been a robot, she'd be on the verge of a short circuit even R2D2 would struggle to keep at bay.

Rose decided to take Lucy's disappointed expression as a sign of congratulations.

'I know! I can't believe it, really, but I must have done something right, right?' she said before Lucy could get a word in. 'I mean, they approached me.'

That much was true. The Talent Acquisition Manager for

FFB had invited her in to meet the Sales Head, and eight days later the results were in.

'Yeah, you sure must have. That's terrific…really chuffed for you,' Lucy said through gritted teeth, the word "really" was so OTT she might well have said, *"really not chuffed for you."*

'How much are they offering?' she continued, trying to sound like she wasn't concerned, like she was asking a normal, everyday question like what the time was, or if the chippy was still open. But they both knew that her thirty grand a year for a thirty-eight-year-old was in severe danger of being gazumped by someone fifteen years her junior.

'Twenty-eight smackers, two more than what I hoped for, so, can't complain really.' She pronounced smackers *SUR-MAK-ERS* for added effect, ensuring Lucy's bogus smile faded even more as she became practically incandescent with envy.

'Is that, erm like, enough for the role you're gonna be doing?' she asked, after five seconds of steadying herself; had she not been the same shape as a weeble she would have toppled over at the prospect of Rose being destined for better things than she would ever dream of.

'Absolutely. Increase to thirty-two after six month's successful probation. Start a week Monday hopefully. Can't wait.' Rose smugly looked at the letter once more. 'Now, I really must get out of these and run myself a hot bath before I get pneumonia. Think I've got a glass of chilled white left in the fridge, so I can enjoy a toast to new beginnings while I have a soak.'

And that was it. One nil to Rose.

As she turned to open their apartment door, a middle-aged man came down the stairs and into the porch, stopping to smile at Rose. He was easy on the eye and well-dressed with black hair swept off his face and bright green eyes, probably a Managing Director or similar. The sort of chap she'd be knocking around with very soon once she'd started her new job.

Lucy looked at him too and smiled hopefully, willing him to reciprocate. But he didn't.

THREE: CHAIN

The next morning I woke up harder than The Times crossword, so I rolled over and gave Stephanie a quick one before sending her packing in time for work. She'd told me she was 31 and not the 23 that I'd guessed she was, which was a trifle annoying if I'm honest. The danger there is that being ten years my junior, the age gap is *definitely* doable for something more than just a bunk-up, in her eyes at any rate. I really hoped that she wasn't going to pester me and try and turn last night's acrobatics into something meaningful that would require truly awful things like *date nights* consisting of dinner and the pictures, real conversations or even trips to flower markets, God forbid. Fuck that. I'd cross that bridge if we ever came to it, I told myself as I started to sweat a little at the thought of it.

The night before *was* seriously fun though. After a few cocktails at Keystone Crescent, we were both pissed by six, so when her flirt-o-meter had made its way round to the danger zone, I made my move and suggested we take a cab back to mine to enjoy some expensive French red I'd been keeping for special occasions, adding we could just hang out. By hang-out, I meant hanging out of the back of her, which I did to an acceptable standard judging by her moaning and bucking. She had the flexibility of a ballerina: strong and supple, enhanced by a cracking set of weapons dancing around on her chest - not massive, but firm and well-rounded – and a neat Brazilian too, which put to bed my earlier curiosity if her front garden was in need of management.

When I arrived in at ten, the normal busy hum of the sales reps pitching hard on the phones for that time of day, which is considered PST - *Prime Selling Time* - had been replaced by a bunch of the walking dead. Instead, I was welcomed by a sea of contrite expressions. They must have gone ballistic after I left them to it. Once the boss clears off they've the freedom to do what they please, and I bet no punches were pulled after raping the free drinks tab I left them. I dread to think what some of the kids in their early twenties get up to these days, it's scary. When I was, say 22, I was larking about at university going on all day benders every Saturday. Start at a pub and end up at some cheesy hotel 'nightclub' guzzling pints of watered down lager at subsidised prices, then taking home a Princess, sometimes a witch, for a bit of a drunken fumble aided by a diesel powered, fully functioning early-twenties erection made out of moon rock, waking up the next morning digging for gold in beer-soaked jeans for a bonus few quid that'd get me a dirty, budget breakfast. Student life, I loved it.

These days they don't even bother with the drinking bit. They're all shoving ketamine up their hooters and participating in foursomes, filming it all for good measure. Imagine what it will be like in another forty years? You'll likely have a generation of mutated, seven feet tall, mixed-race non-gender specifics dependent on a liquid mixture of meow-meow and sildenafil, unable to do anything unless someone's documenting it on a fucking smartphone.

Anyway, somewhat smartly, I'd already forecasted a grand total of zero pounds sterling to drop in all day, anticipating the whole team were going to be either hung-over to high heaven or still going. I knew at least one of the guys was still bang on it because when I got into the gents toilets some buffoon called Clarke, face covered in water or perspiration, was staring at himself in the mirror through pupils the size of large chocolate buttons, with a jaw into next week. I sent him home and then flagged it to the Old Bill, or HR as more commonly known.

In my office, I leaned back into my leather recliner and gulped down a mouthful of lukewarm latte and bit into my egg and 'roasted' tomato baguette. (Six-and-a-half quid for a coffee made by Piotr, a coffee a blind five-year-old could match in quality, a millimetre of egg mayonnaise spread thinly across a third of a stale baguette with a small sundried cherry tomato halved and shoved inside. It's no wonder Londoners arrive into work with faces like a reformed Phil Mitchell at Oktoberfest. Anywhere in the city that sells food and drink will fleece you for the best part of a tenner if you're dense enough to pay for it, not before you've alighted half an hour of misery with your face pushed up against some smelly Arab's armpit shitting yourself that he's going to detonate on a packed and delayed tube. You *should* have the right to a half-decent and value for money breakfast after the trauma of public transport.)

I looked down at the baguette and drifted off, re-running the session with Stephanie, I was definitely going to need some hand relief at some point later on. However, just as I tried to remember if her asshole was bleached or waxed, I was interrupted by some lively giggles coming from outside on the sales floor, prompting me to get up and look out at a few people hunched around a computer screen.

Louis. Louis is the office joker. His official title is *Social Media Manager* - he insisted on having the word *Manager* in place of *Executive* despite managing a grand total of no one. His real title should be *Dosser who* loves *to clown around and entertain people for thirty fucking grand a year,* but that wouldn't look too good on LinkedIn or on his business cards (he insisted on those, too). To be fair, he's not bad at what he does and never should be. He's got to promote the company via social media channels posting pictures of our occasional trade shows to Instagram and Facebook, tweeting links to articles we publish, and the odd bit of email campaign design. Then he assesses the response each campaign generates, which in turn provides a steady flow of warmer leads to dish out to the sales reps. However, being so active on social media means Louis will quite often come across those 'funny' viral video clips, memes, gifs, vines etc. and usually distract half, if not all, of the sales floor by sending them around on email. Or –if as suspected in this instance – it's too risky, he'll simply open it up on his screen and gather round an audience. With a hunch that whatever it was would be vile and graphic, unable to resist, I went to see.

'Alright mate?' asked Louis as I approached.

Louis usually calls me *mate*, sometimes *me old china* or just *china* or occasionally refers to me as *The Saint* with my initials being ST. He opted for Saint over Street once I'd told him there was no way he could justify calling me Station. On the rare occasion, he uses *Shergar* - after a famous racehorse – but that's only when we are peeing next to each other. Only once or twice have I ever heard him use my real name, and that's been when he's addressing me in front of other colleagues during meetings.

'Not bad sunbeam.,' I replied, edging closer to his desk and breaking into a sweat as to what awful clip I was about to be shown.

Louis is totally bald and of dual heritage, which I believe is the politically correct way of describing a half-caste, meaning he looks permanently tanned and his bald head shines like a cartoon version of the Sun. Crucial to his employment here, his dad also invested into the business in the early summertime and part of the agreement was that I gave Louis a full-time position. He promised me he was hard working and pretty nifty at all things tech, so I agreed to it, and voila, the funding came within a week. It was only after Louis had been with me a week that I realised he was an absolute unhinged maniac and capable of causing hourly mayhem, on a daily basis.

'What have we here then?' I asked as if I really didn't know what was coming.

'Oh jeez, mate...check this!'

He opened a still of the video clip that had just caused the few minutes of zero-productivity from the sales team. The title was German and read *Eine Kette von Hundert Homosexuellen* which I would soon come to learn the meaning of without needing Google translate.

It began with a fairly tame close-up shot of an erect penis steadily pumping in and out of a taut and shiny bum-hole.

'That's not that bad, mate,' I challenged, instantly realising there was much worse to come. Louis laughed dementedly just as the camera gradually panned out to reveal that the arse on the screen belonged to a man - a man who also had his own erect penis rhythmically sliding in and out of another man. The camera continued to move further out and across the arcade of buggery to fit in three...no four, actually five, six...hang on seven – ten...twelve? JESUS CHRIST. A couple of seconds later and we'd reached twenty: each one mechanically drilling in and out of the greedy dirt box in front. Louis sat there rocking back and forth in his chair, dribbling over his keyboard in hysterics watching me watching on, terrified.

Questions began to form in my head: *how did they get all those men to get hard at the same time?*

...up to thirty and still more, *did the men take Viagra before-hand?*

...at least thirty-five penises were in the chain, *are they all German?*

...there were *still* more, at least forty, *what's the currency is it still the Deutschmark?*

...no way that couldn't be half a century (yes it could), *what's the minimum penis length that was commissioned for this video nasty?*

...up to seventy-five...Jesus, *Jesus no?*

...yes,...fuck off no it couldn't be. *No more questions your honour.*

It reached a ton. A chain of a hundred cocks.

'That's enough now...turn it off, please,' I said, turning away to see that Tom, who was also watching, had gone from pale and tender to transparent and on the verge of death, nervously twisting the cap on his bottle of caramel flavoured sparkling soft drink that wasn't Pepsi. Louis, in between guffaws, shouted over at me as I left his desk, 'I bet Shergar would have split those poop shoots three ways if he had been there, eh sir?'

The translation of the video was *A Chain of a Hundred Homosexuals,* he informed me later on by very thoughtfully sending me a copy of the offending video on text, in case I wanted to watch it again, with a note attached that read *Stick that one in your wank bank Shergar.*

Back in my office, once I'd managed to eradicate the disgraceful last images of gay German pornography, I opened my inbox and quickly flicked over the twenty-three unread emails inconveniencing me, deciding that only one of them deserved my time – a request from Tom to approve a discounted deal he had sent out, which to my pleasant surprise was for ten grand, two grand below rate card (production cost is no more than fifty pence.)

I clicked the *approve* button and checked my calendar, very happy to learn that I had a couple of hours to kill - enough time to take a stroll around the city and go and look at St. Paul's, or go for a coffee at Ozone, so that's what I did. Kind of.

Outside the sun was teasing the steady flow of city workers that it was about to make an appearance from behind the bed of lead that carpeted the sky as I walked down to Moorgate. I'd listen to some music whilst doing nothing much except leer at anything in a skirt, so I double clicked my earphones to launch into the library of over a thousand tracks, just as a small sign that read *Genuine Thai Massage* sitting above a well-hidden doorway caught my attention. The first tune to play was a Chas 'n' Dave track entitled *Massage Parlour*.

It *was* a sign, in more ways than one.

Jo-Jo's massage was exceptional for twenty-seven minutes; the final three even better as she gave me a practical demonstration of how a cow with a solid seven-inch udder should be milked. Ferociously. Nice, I even got Jo-Jo to write out a receipt for *stress-related consultation* which I'd file in my accounts and whack in the expenses column. *Whack it in after being whacked off,* I thought as the yellow cutie innocently partook in my tax avoidance capers. After that, I picked up some sushi and went back to the office to run down the clock.

*

'Anything happen?' I asked my PA Melanie, who was busy filing. Filing her nails.

'Nope, nothing much. Just a couple of calls from unknown numbers that I didn't answer,' she replied, as if she'd been manning the direct line into the fucking NATO headquarters, 'but, I think you have a couple of hours clear now. How was your meeting at St Paul's?'

'Very satisfying,' I replied. It was the most truthful answer I'd given her all day.

Even though I'd not long ejaculated into a tissue cradled by Jo-Jo, I was still mildly hung-over and incapable of anything taxing on the brain, so I went onto the Spurs website and watched the highlights of the recent demolition of Arsenal. My concentration was disrupted by a knock at the door as Louis's grinning face appeared and entered without my nod. He sat down opposite me, again without being invited to. Like me, Louis is a Spurs fan, so I swivelled the screen on my PC so we could both enjoy watching highlights of our team tearing Arsenal a new one, his eyes glowing even more than usual, if that was possible, as Jan Vertonghen smashed a shot against the crossbar. *Vertonghen* is pronounced *Ver-tong-un*. Louis gave me a deafening rendition of a song he'd made up:

"*Jan Vertonghen...does his missus...up the wrong-un!*"

He sang it with such pride that Melanie got up and slammed shut the office door, narrowing her eyes and shooting an icy glare at the back of his head.

'Anyway, what can I do you for?' I asked, once the clip had finished.

'Well listen China, got an idea for a new Twitter strategy...wanted to pick your brains on it. Made some notes,' he said plonking a notepad on my desk like he was my boss.

The first page he stopped on had no words, instead there was a drawing of a giant felt tip erect penis covering one side, complete with a few hairs on the balls and a couple of drops of what I assumed to be semen shooting out of the end. I held back the laughter and told him to get on with it. But it was

Louis. He got on with it alright; the next page revealed that the artist responsible for the illustrated interpretation of a spunking cock had also tried their hand at more vulgar anatomy. This time Picasso had drawn a bum with its crack shooting out a jet of air down onto a cloud wrapped around the word *QUACK!* I tried not to laugh, but couldn't contain a snigger. Sat in front of me was a 37-year-old married father-of-one, with a semi-responsible job, who had earlier on proudly played me a video clip of a hundred cocks bumming a hundred arseholes, and was now taking up more of my time to talk about *Twitter strategy* with notes from a pad containing the cartoons of an ejaculating penis and a farting bum hole. Incredible.

'Impressive Louis. So do you have *any* notes of worth, or am I going to be looking at a pair of tits in a moment?' I asked, hoping that there was something of at least small value on the horizon outside of the earlier hand-job.

'Sure, hold on let me just find them,' said Louis, thumbing through the pad and stopping on a pair of tits complete with erect nipples, and underneath a scribbled mass of green pubic hair sitting over the letter V.

'Louis?' I said, speaking to him, but addressing my computer screen.

'Mmm?'

'Go back to your desk please.'

'But hang on a sec I've go—'

I raised my hand up and waved him out, still fixated on the email I wasn't looking at properly.

'What do we think of Arsenal? SHIT! What do we think of Shit? ARSENAL!' he shouted, all the way back to his desk, disrupting the whole floor.

I shook my head and flicked open the notes app on my iPhone to check if there was anything urgent I'd forgotten about. It turned out there was. I launched open LinkedIn and keyed the name *Rose Wilkins* in the search bar.

FOUR: PAYDAY

At last pay day had arrived. Had Rose been desperate for cash she could have stayed up until midnight and been able to withdraw a few notes from the machine at the twenty-four-hour garage at the top of her road, something she'd done in the past if she couldn't wait until morning to feel liquid again. There was the odd occasion she went out and met her friends late on in a bar or club after midnight, power drinking for a couple of hours.

None of that last night though; she'd resisted the urge and settled on a TV dinner of cold chicken salad and black tea. It turned out that there was neither half a tin of sweetcorn nor any milk on her shelf of the fridge.

'Thank crunchie it's Friday,' said Lucy.

Rose walked into the smell of burnt toast and a rattling kettle. 'Fancy a cuppa?'

'Go on then,' Rose nodded, instantly wondering why Lucy was so chipper at such a depressingly dark hour. She wasn't going to give her the pleasure though, she'd need to graft for it. Lucy scraped a kilo of margarine across a piece of cremated bread and pulled some ghastly long-life milk from the fridge, her shelf the usual jumble of orange and white packages that had *Basics* scribbled over them.

'Off out tonight?' asked Lucy, fiddling about with a loaf of bread, pondering whether to pluck out another pair. Rose did have plans to go and meet her best pal Zoe around Old Street way for a few drinks after work. Nothing major - just a catch-up - but there was always that danger of it turning into salary destroying festival of cocaine, cock and Prosecco.

'Say that again,' requested Rose, buying some time to think of a suitable lie to throw Lucy off-scent. Lucy had often in the past gate-crashed Rose's Friday night plans. She didn't really have many friends in London and had to go back to her hometown of Peterborough if she wanted to see any real ones.

Admittedly, Lucy was fairly light on the friend front, and Rose could understand why. She never had anything positive to say, other than to the TV when reality shows hogged primetime, and even then it was rarely more than "I wonder who's going to be evicted *this* week."

The first time Rose invited Lucy out for drinks, solely out of politeness, she found herself imprisoned in a world of embarrassment for two whole hours. She had to give a thousand apologies following Lucy's departure from the pub. "Fuck me I wanted to slit my wrists," had been the first words to leave Zoe's lips, in block capitals, as soon as the walking space hopper had squeezed her way out of the pub.

'Tonight...plans? Payday isn't it?' she confirmed, before crunching into a slice. Rose always wondered just how conscious Lucy was when it came to the policing calories, the piece of toast she had just bitten into had enough yellow gunge on it to fill a paddling pool.

Lucy poured some boiling water into her pink *Queen of Awesomeness* mug. Such was the chirpiness of her humming it was embarrassingly obvious that she was hanging on for Rose to ask s*omething* about her plans for later.

She thrust a cup of tea at Rose. Lucy did tea *all* wrong. She made a diabolically weak brew, the same colour as that awful, light brown atomic pandemonium that sprays out of you without warning at the tail end of a week's binge drinking somewhere foreign. On top of that, she only made half a cup. It baffled Rose no end; if a cup of tea is going to be half-full then you'd expect it to be strong, not weak. Another example of her pure laziness.

Rose took it anyway. She turned round to cross the hall and escape to the bathroom to pour it away and get showered. She'd almost made it as well.

'Oh, Rose?' called Lucy. The words made her close her eyes and grimace. She composed herself and turned back on the balls of her feet against her own free will.

'Where's good to go later on...for a *first date*?'

And then it all became clear. In a split second the last couple of minutes all became transparent. Lucy had a *date*. You could liken dates for Lucy to say, a frequent and fully functioning, comfortable and uncomplicated journey on the Northern line. Absolutely rare, almost extinct. The kind of event that makes headline news:

Page 1- WORLD EXCLUSIVE! Lucy Harper has a Date

Page 2 – Alien Sex Dolls on Saturn start Nuclear War

Phone calls to distant relatives, at the top of *trending now* lists, and so on.

Dates were rare for a library of reasons. Frumpy, overweight, negative, bitter, ill-mannered, unhygienic, fussy eater (anything green was a no-go except Chicken and Mushroom Pot Noodles), only drank cheap white wine…a bottomless pit of sadness. Lucy could quite easily fall into a bucket of cocks and still emerge sucking her thumb. Once when she was thirteen she'd been in the audience on *Rolf's Cartoon Club* and even Mr Harris didn't try and molest her. "Can you guess what it is yet?" No.

Yet here she was gulping down a tea after spooning three sugars into it, promoting 'margarine addicts anonymous', proudly bragging to Rose that she had somehow managed to hoodwink some poor lad into thinking she was half decent. A quarter decent, even.

Here we go, thought Rose. *Fuck sake*. 'Erm, depends on what you want to do. Just drinks, or you having food?' Rose asked, stupidly, already knowing that at some point food would indeed feature. Whether dining alone or at the expense of her victim, Lucy would definitely be eating.

'Dunno yet, start with drinks and then see what happens?' she said through a pound of glistening white dough. 'Always risky to arrange dinner. You know…in case he's not all that in the flesh.'

Fuck me! Rose almost laughed out loud…*Risky?*

Risky for him, that's for sure. The bill would comfortably

exceed three figures. Even in McDonalds Lucy ate for a family of four, and the golden arches share price went into orbit whenever she was hung-over. Risky for Lucy's cholesterol levels as well. But the thing that struck Rose the most was the audacity of her last nine words. Even if this chap was twice her size, which would practically be impossible, had three eyes and was at the end of a six-month sabbatical from genital cleansing, he'd still be a catch for her.

They stood in silence for a minute as an interlude of chewing noises filled up the kitchen.

Rose couldn't take anymore. 'There must be loads of bars around your office, no?' she said.

'Well, he works in the city and wants me to come his way. Somewhere round near you, actually.'

That statement was designed to subtly let Rose know that there was a slim chance that a couple of hours into the date, should things not work out (cast iron), then she'd be in the vicinity and hanker for an invite to join them. Rose concluded that Lucy's original question wasn't really meant to be taken seriously, it was merely an excuse to brag that the twenty stone Ghostbusters extra stood in front of her had miraculously gotten a date, and on a *Friday* no less. In an attempt to finish off the painful chit-chat and get ready for work, Rose suggested that Prince Charming choose the venue, a suggestion which Lucy emphatically received by nodding frantically in appreciation as if Rose had in fact delivered a Nobel Prize-winning piece of prose. Hyped up at the prospect of getting some action, for once.

'Yeah...*Yeah!* Fuck it, let him work for it eh?' Lucy said, straight up. Rose almost spat her tea out.

'Met him on Tinder,' added Lucy, with a wink and cock of the head before Rose could escape. 'He seems nice enough...from his profile.'

She said it like she was an active ambassador for the application as if it should have been blatantly obvious that this poor lad, unaware of what horrors awaited him, of course, would have swiped right. Lucy should be downloading an app called *Overfed and Underfucked,* or maybe *Starved of Sex but not of Bacon.*

Rose had always maintained Tinder was an efficient concept. Instant gratification or immediate disappointment. Left or right. Yes or no. Hot or not. In fact, she'd never known anything other than those types of dating applications. Since leaving school in 2012, she'd only ever been on dates with guys from Tinder, Plenty of Fish, match.com or e-harmony; the latter two actually requiring a degree of thought and the rigmarole of a registration process that involved answering ludicrous questions such as *do you have any pets?* or *describe your ideal first date.* That's why both sites boasted of a 75% female to 25% male ratio. Of course they did. Why on earth would any man give a toss about pets, after all? Rose did, however, go through with the irritating procedure, merely out of curiosity and the end result netted her a steady stream of wet farts. She'd wanted to write in the 'Ideal first date' section *Get pissed for free before getting a good panning all night by some six foot plus model hung like an Arab's Stallion, that'll do for starters,* but went against instinct and played it safe with *dinner drinks then a romantic stroll in the park while we plan the second LOL.* It was incredible the number of messages she received that all began with something along the lines of *Hey gorgeous/lovely so which park are we going to be strolling in lol x.* Yep, she actually got many, many emails like that, figuring that the *Match* or *E-harmony* concept was reserved for people who valued conversation but were less pleasing to look at, those poor souls who had to work hard on personality. Rose was lucky to have both looks and personality. Rose always won at Tinder.

She'd seen Lucy's profile a couple of times when she proudly showed off her five pictures as if they were in fact works of art and not a massive pile of fraud. What was she so proud of? Her heaven-sent ability to trick the million single guys using the app into believing that she wasn't an extra from the new Star Trek movies? Or was it to inform Rose that she *wasn't* a twenty stone munter, that the pictures she was staring at did, in fact, represent the real Lucy? Five pictures, all at least three years old, three of them edited into black and white (*everyone* knows that black and whites are by far the most flattering if you have dark hair), four of the five simple head and shoulders shots taken from above with a selfie stick. The final one was a full body shot of her in the distance on a beach, resembling a giant rugby ball with arms and legs. It was removed after one week and zero matches.

'Right, best go and put my makeup on,' Lucy said, finally leaving the kitchen as if Rose had been holding her up.

Aye, you'll need more than makeup if you've got even a whisker of hope of getting laid, thought Rose as she poured away half-a-cup and flicked the kettle back on.

*

The number seventy-eight bus went from the top of Essex Road to the junction of Upper Street, where it took a left and passed Angel tube, carrying on over the lights and down St John Street before making a right onto Roseberry Avenue. It stopped almost opposite the offices where Rose was temping. It was a twenty-three-minute journey minus any tube strikes or bad weather, meaning to get there for nine she could leave at half eight and have a few minutes to settle in and make a coffee. She worked nine til five with an hour lunch, seven hours a day in total at an hourly rate of twelve-and-a-half quid, Monday to Friday. Full-time hours but just over twenty grand p.a. for work in central London, anything but acceptable for someone living in Islington.

Because she'd been paid overnight, she left a bit earlier and jumped off the bus at Angel, dropping into an independent little deli and treating herself to a large mocha to wash down a salmon and cream cheese bagel. *Bit cliché* she thought as she tapped her contactless, relieved that *Approved* flashed at her, finally.

*

'Oi oi,' said Mark, another temp who sat opposite her. 'Nice!

Gotta luv a bagel, innit' he said, as if the bagel was really a bank holiday. Mark was a bit of a twat.

'Mmm.' Rose smiled politely back, feeling like chucking the piping hot drink she was nursing into his face, then ramming what was left of the bagel up his...you know.

Mark was the *epitome* of wide-boy chav, trying hard but failing to be the cheeky cockney. Buttoned up Ralph Lauren polo shirt, jeans tighter than Linford Christie's lycra, a whole tub of gel slapped over his ginger hair, 'trendy' beard that wouldn't look out of place on a homeless Viking, tattoos on both forearms - one was a British Bulldog - pristine white Fred Perry slip-ons and a mockney accent like he was an extra from a Krays movie. To top it all off the kid actually thought he was a bit of a player, using those exact words to describe himself when they were chatting in the pub one afternoon early into their employment. His level of banter was a notch below sixteen-year-old labourer, i.e. the odd "cor blimey guv'nor look at the pins on that!"

There *was* one other thing about Mark that caused her a crumb of guilt every time she found herself wanting to hurl him out of the window, and that was that he was unfortunately in the confines of a wheelchair. Something to do with falling on his back and damaging his spinal cord so much that he could never use his legs again. She hadn't noticed the handlebars attached to his chair the first time she sat down opposite him, and so formed an opinion of him purely based on the awful banter and misogynistic drivel that followed for the next hour. He was quite capable of doing most things anyway, except walking or running, he informed her with a wink when he noticed Rose had clocked on.

Rose logged on to her PC and watched Mark sink his jaws into a donut like it was his last meal. A dollop of strawberry jam shaped like a pear drop squirted out of the side and jumped down onto his white polo. 'Oh for fu-'

'Rose, Mark. Got a tick?' a familiar voice interrupted.

Jason Willey. "Willey with an 'e'," he'd said to them when he introduced himself on day one. Rose had the feeling that he'd had to say that before, from about the age of five, whenever spelling his name. Mark had laughed out loud when he said *Willey*, and to this day it was the only thing he'd done that she'd found funny.

Jason Willey was half of the firm Aspinall-Willey Management Consultants, his partner Jane Aspinall was based in New York and looked after their US operations. From what Rose could make out, they were a slick and sizeable management consultancy providing advisory services and bespoke reports on various vertical industry topics, such as healthcare and technology. She was surprised Jason actually mingled with his temps, but, as they had no official line manager, he spared her and Mark a few minutes once a week.

They followed him into his office, which was the size of a squash court, and he stood over the pair of them. He was friendly on the outside; charismatic and charming, handsome and dapper, but on the inside, you just knew he had the wit and killer instinct of a pack of starved wolves.

'Next week, Wednesday and Thursday. Big project coming up so gonna need you to work until seven,' he said. It definitely wasn't a question. 'I'll brief you towards the end of your day around half four.' And that was it. Class dismissed.

But Mark spoke anyway.

'Fine wiv me, bit of extra dosh'll come in handy for the weekend...beer money for the Arsenal,' he said as if anyone actually gave a monkeys where his extra...what was it...fifty quid would go. Rose knew that hers, if she worked the overtime, would be spent on a bonus gram. Wednesday was her last day though.

'Well, actually Mr Willey, I can work late Wednesday but I'm not sure I'll be in on Thursday,' she said, rightly assuming that the news of her decision hadn't left HR yet.

'Ah, ok. You can do extra on Friday.' Again it wasn't a question.

'Or Friday. Probably.' A look of confusion spread across the two men in the room with her.

'Sorry, I haven't seen the holiday sheet...' said Jason, twiddling what was probably a solid silver pen.

'Oh, sorry. I've got something permanent...'

Jason didn't need to go any further. 'Ah ok, so Wednesday is your last day then, very well. What are you doing?' he asked. Mark was still trying to work out what was going on. Mark was good with numbers but had the intuition of a flip-flop.

'BD for a company called FFB...based in Bank, actually,' said Rose.

'Ah yes, I know them well. Come and see me on that before you go then, would you?' said Jason.

'Good on ya gal, ave to ave a leaving drink for ya, wottdyareckon?' suggested Mark, with over-the-top enthusiasm.

Jason could only give an embarrassed smile after Rose simply replied "no" and left the room.

*

On her lunch break, she checked LinkedIn: sixty-four connection requests, seventeen messages and three figures lurking over the network notifications thingy. A quick scan down the list of connection requests revealed that most of them were from recruiters, with the odd random Indian man thrown in for good measure. The messages, again, were largely from the recruitment industry asking her what sort of exciting opportunity she was looking to move into. Her profile read *Rose Wilkins - seeking next exciting opportunity*.

The first message to capture her attention was from Sean Thomas, CEO and Owner of STI Limited:

Dear Rose. Apologies for the method of communication but I thought I'd drop you a note. Your profile says you are looking for new opportunities? STI is a leading media trade information company that specialises in Business Intelligence and trade journals. We are keen to expand our Business Development focus following our best ever year, and as such always looking for new talent to come and join us. If you are open to five minutes regarding this, then do please let me know and we can set up a chat. Best, Sean.

With no harm in seeing what they were offering, she hit reply and requested some more info, just as Mark wheeled himself back to his desk and resumed with the half-eaten donut that was glazed in sugar and looking like it was about to get up and walk off. Rose closed down LinkedIn, and Mark's phone vibrated twice.

'Good good...me date confirming time and venue for later,' he said to no one while beaming down at it, just loud enough so Rose could hear him. 'Good job I've got a spare shirt wiv me.'

That twat would be a good match for Lucy.

When five o'clock thankfully arrived, Rose downed tools and thought about how she could kill the couple of hours she had to wait to before meeting Zoe in the Magic Roundabout at Old Street station. Her options weren't particularly oozing with an appeal: stay in the office and surf social media sites, robotically clicking the *like* button on Twitter, Instagram, Facebook and Snapchat. Maybe shoot home and unwind for an hour, get changed and tuck into some wine? An option that would require bus travel and run the risk of being swallowed by the sofa. She *was* tired after all. Or lastly, she *could* actually accept Mark's imminent suggestion of going for a couple of jars next door at The Horseshoe, probably the worst pub she'd ever had the misfortune of setting foot in, and if not the worst it was definitely in the top five.

Settling for option one, she logged into Facebook, counting the seconds between the jingle of Mark's PC shutting down and an invitation to join him at the pub. Mark placed his telephone headset on the table next to his Arsenal mouse mat.

Five...four...three...two...o–

'Fancy a quick one?' he asked, half a second early and not disappointing. He tipped an imaginary pint glass in his right hand backwards and forwards. Maybe it wouldn't be so bad, she reasoned as she sized up the office. The permanent staff were sitting about chained to their desks, most of them looking like Belsen would be a preferable location to where they were. Jason made them work until six, even on a Friday. Fuck it. She may as well get that clown to buy her a drink or two.

It really was a blessing Mark was in a wheelchair at that moment in time, because had his legs functioned properly and he was standing up, he'd have collapsed in shock the moment Rose accepted his offer.

*

'Old Street, innit?' was Mark's first sentence once he'd ordered the drinks; his head just about reaching the bar. For him a pint of *Nelson,* as he called it to the confused barmaid, and a large G&T for Rose. They found a table in the corner of The Crown pub, already busy with a few guys standing around one of the elevated tables and necking shots though raucous laughter and handing round a small envelope of something she strongly suspected was cocaine. She wanted to be with them, too.

'Going to meet my bestie Zoe for a catch-up, nothing large...but famous last words and all that,' she replied, taking a welcome swig of ice cold gin and tonic. 'What about you?'

'Going on a date actually. Gotta meet this girl in a pub down near the station. She looks pretty dirty, an all,' he said.

Of course he was. He'd been itching to get that out all day. First Lucy and now him. Rose had wondered how Mark would fare in the dating game, this self-proclaimed player that would wolf-whistle any female that walked within a twenty-metre radius.

'Ah ok, nice. So, erm, I hope you don't think I'm prying like, but do you have *special* websites you use? You know...to date other people in wheelchairs?'

Marks expression went from happy and simple to something less happy and simple. He sipped his pint and banged it down on the table, signalling the start of a speech.

Stitched Up

'Facking hell luv, what do you mean? I use Tinder like everyone else. Just because I'm in the *wheels of steel,* it don't mean I can't date normal chicks' he said. Using the word chick was something else to add to the long list of things that influenced Rose's opinion of him.

'Right, sorry....yeah. Didn't mean to...' she trailed off, shrugging apologetically. He continued with his parody of a sex God anyway.

'Trust me I've had loads fitties! They love a bit of paralysis, can jump all over me and grind 'emselves silly. Gives 'em a right power trip' he said, with complete sincerity. 'One slag even handcuffed me to the chair and force fed me a blue smarty with half a pint of rum. Fucked the shit out me all night. I kid you not.'

The words literally left Rose speechless for a few seconds. The last sentence went in, but came straight back out, making her process it again.

'Sorry...*sorry,*' she said, sort of meaning it once she'd taken a deep breath and another glug of gin, still getting her head around what he'd just said. 'So who is the lucky lady then? Let's have a look.'

Mark grabbed his phone, pressed a few buttons and slapped it down proudly in front of Rose.

*

It was ten past one and the floorboards in the St Paul's branch of Dirty Martini were glistening with a toxic concoction of payday cocktails. Rose was sitting alone gazing at the spilt wine, Prosecco, beer, spirits and mixers that swam all over the floor to form multi-coloured lakes, when Zoe reappeared from the toilets led by a female bouncer who had a firm grip on her arm. She'd been caught red-handed racking up a monstrous line, made worse because she'd waited at least ten minutes queuing up to get into the toilet, *and* there was a generous amount still to get through. Guaranteed that little gem was nestling in the safety of the bouncer's blazer pocket waiting to be sold on. Those things happened to Rose and her pals occasionally. One of the shortcomings attached to draining a few bottles of Prosecco is the inability to be discreet in drug ingestion. They never learned, it seemed.

Without having to say anything, Rose grabbed their jackets and they staggered out into the freezing cold nighttime onto Poultry, flagging a black cab as they did.

Payday. Black cab drivers were probably just as grateful when it arrived as everyone else, where the usual convenience of tapping the Uber app is replaced by an even less taxing raise of the arm, or wave of the hand for that instant ride home, regardless of the fare. Look for the orange light and you're sorted.

Not wanting to finish the night so early, they decided to go back to Rose's and tuck into the bottle of gin that was sat on top of the fridge and get another gram delivered. It had a five o'clock finish written all over it, and in the ten minute journey from St Paul's to Essex Road, still very busy on the roads despite it technically being Saturday morning, Rose had enough time to call her dealer *and* reply to the message Sean had sent on LinkedIn, confirming she was happy to go and meet him on Monday. She'd always been efficient.

*

'Right then' said Zoe, scooping up four of the five pound coins left in the black saucer. 'Let's just get on it…no work tomorrow. Where's your man then?'

'Right here,' answered Rose. A man on the back of a scooter rummaged around in his pocket and produced a wrap and exchanged it for a bunch of notes. Zoe paid for the cab after all, and it was Rose's turn to get the next bottle of Prosecco in at Dirty Martini's - which never happened - so they were square. When they stumbled through the front door, they noticed that all the lights were still off and Lucy's jacket was missing from the usual hook. She was still out past 1 am with her date.

'She must have either drugged him or been carted off to London Zoo by a load of conservationists,' said Zoe.

*

Two candles gently flickered and two basins of gin and tonic sat on the glass coffee table, beyond that was an open wrap of coke with half its contents demolished already. They'd done well in the forty minutes since getting in, and as the clock reached two, just as an episode of *Black Mirror* was ending, they didn't hear the commotion outside the living room window, at first.

A huge bang made the pair of them jump out of their skins. Rose hit pause.

'What the fuck!' cried Zoe as she turned around, just in time to catch Lucy falling through the front door supported by something that looked like a...looked like a bearded man in a wheelchair. A bearded man in a wheelchair who had inked sketches running up his forearms. And ginger hair. It was moments after that, that Zoe heard the thick cockney accent on the man in the chair shouting. "Facking ell luv, mind the crown jewels!"

Lucy wheeled him straight into her bedroom door, slumping forward onto his lap and just managing to yank the door handle down. Mark's wheels scraped against the door and made a hideous scratching noise as it sabotaged her month's rental deposit and magnolia paintwork in the space of three seconds.

'Oh hi, Mark. Fancy seeing you here?' Rose called up the hallway, catching a glimpse of Mark's confused expression disappearing into the abyss of Lucy's chamber. She'd not let on to him earlier that he had somehow managed to match with her flatmate, figuring that on the off-chance Lucy brought him home, it would be too good an event to miss first thing in the morning. But Christmas had come early.

Mark's chorus of "Arsenal til I die!" vibrated off the walls and echoed down into the lounge a second after the door slammed shut. Payday.

FIVE: MACHINE

Monday morning really didn't get off to a good start thanks to the train operator deciding that it made no sense to put on a reliable service of punctual trains with functioning doors. The entire contents of my usual train into work were asked to leave at Alexandra Palace and wait for another. Without wanting to chance that and risk being cooped up with a million other miserable sods, I walked to a nearby bus stop and was greeted by Louis. I'd forgotten he was local.

While we were sat down making small talk, a woman with a large lower belly approached the bus stop. Louis greeted her like this:

'Morning, love. When's it due?'

'Excuse me?' she replied.

'When's it due?' repeated Louis.

The woman looked at him with a half-snarl half-frown and told him that she wasn't pregnant. I stared lovingly into the eyes of my coffee lid and wished I was somewhere else.

'I meant the bus, you fat bastard!' said Louis, and laughed in her face having just massively mugged her off. I didn't just want to be somewhere else, I wanted to be on another planet. The poor woman walked away and made a call. I panicked, thinking she was going to call a husband or boyfriend and get Louis a pasting. Either that or she was ordering a pizza. She was quite rotund, in Louis's defence.

Thankfully one of those stupid accordion buses appeared, and we jumped on it before any repercussions chased after us.

*

Come the afternoon and it was as warm inside as it was cold outside; the floor vibrant from the energy coming from the sales team toiling away doing their best to smash the arse out of the month and finish the year on a high.

December is usually as big a month as any, and during a meeting to kick things off, I told the sales and marketing guys we needed to have a "monster month," so Louis put his hand up and offered to arrange for Jonathan Ross to bring in a pack of pickled onion ones. It took a while for most of the plebs to get the joke, but I found it bloody hilarious, he should be on TV that one. Admittedly, sometimes he does go too far, but you can't fault the guy's sense of humour.

Anyway, most marketing directors that get pitched will have to spend whatever is left in their advertising and business intelligence budgets before year end, or risk having it cut come January, so the deals drop in thick and fast. The top guys across both sales teams qualify to go on the January ski trip as well, so there's added incentive for the reps to go beyond the call of duty and start the month off on the front foot. Tom was closing a whopping fifty grand multi-year deal with BP and much of my day, maybe forty minutes, had been taken up working with him on the terms of the deal: invoicing needed right away to get rid of leftover budget, exclusivity rights across two of our four energy journals and all the rest of it. Bells and Whistles. I didn't give a shit what they wanted. I'd have agreed to anything for fifty grand coming into the bank by the end of the year, literally. They could have asked us to post a picture of a man balls deep in a Range Rover exhaust pipe on the front cover, with their logo slapped all over it, and I'd have agreed. Louis would've sorted that out for me, no doubt.

Later in the afternoon, Melanie called me and interrupted my enjoyment of a clip of two lesbians fisting one another (*xhamster.com* really does help fill up those gaps in the diary), which was probably a blessing, because my curiosity at wondering if any places in the immediate area would recreate the scene was getting the better of me, and I was dangerously close to doing some of my own fieldwork.

'Mel, what's up?' I said hitting pause. The young actress currently in view deserved the Romanian equivalent of a BAFTA (a RAFTA?) she was doing such an authentic job of looking traumatised.

'Sorry to interrupt,' said Mel, tugging down on her skirt, as though just being in my presence meant it would automatically start to lift itself up. 'Hope it's not important?'

Although it was, I told her to carry on.

'Your three-thirty is here. Rose Wilkins?' she announced, reminding me that the absolute mega from the flats where Tom lived who I'd been tracking closely on LinkedIn and Facebook had arrived for a quick chat. I checked that my Breitling Bentley was polished and on display and told Melanie to go and fetch her, then I went to the bogs to check I was looking dapper. No food in teeth, check. No rogue nostril hairs in view, check. Chewing gum, check. It was all good, and I was already planning ahead that should the interview go well, I'd get this Rose babe out for a long lunch in the next week and ply her with alcohol. It was a bit embryonic in our relationship for Rohypnol.

Before the interview took a monumental nosedive, Rose did a great job. I loved her attitude once we'd got past the chit-chat (degree subject, living arrangements, hobbies, how she travelled to the office, what she's doing for fun, relationship status etc.), and on top of being the absolute doll I remembered her to be – and I mean *doll* – she had balls of steel. Far from guarded, she was confident, driven, ambitious and sharp; able to tell me exactly what she wanted to do with the commission she could earn and easily negated her way around the objections I served at full pelt. She convinced me of her determination to be a winner, and to cap it all off I felt like someone had injected my veins with a gallon of liquid Viagra because whatever was hanging down between my legs was pitching up like a fucking ten-man tent. So, half-an-hour in and she was thriving, seemingly already bought into the company culture I invented - "really lively young team, sociable, work hard play hard, loads of incentives etc." half of which I reeled off the top of my head along with a load of other yarns I'd been spinning.

Then, as per most interviews I conduct, I got to the point where I ask the candidate what they would like to know about us. I was a nanosecond away from ejaculating on the spot when she picked up and sucked on the end of a biro, deep in thought. My blood was pumping its way up from my groin and into my face, making me flushed, forcing me to think of the 2003/2004 Spurs back four to fend off the stiffy that was in danger of climbing out of my pants and gate-crash the interview.

'Well,' she began, 'I think the burning question is what kind of progression do y- '

Before she finished the sentence an almighty fart echoed around the room. I'm not talking a small and discreet squeak either; this was the mother-ship, the sort of noise you hear on the Comedy Channel, summoned from the rotten bowels of a ten-ton beast lurking in the swamps of Africa. And it didn't come from me. She returned my embarrassed look with one of her own, and then we fell silent for a second. I couldn't believe she had *farted* in the middle of an interview! The least she could do was apologise. But she didn't, so I braced myself for a whiff of rotten egg but nothing arrived, even her farts didn't smell. I found that confusingly attractive, like I might do with a pre-op transsexual.

'Go on, don't worry,' I said after a couple more seconds of silent hell thankfully passed.

'Sure, where were we...oh yes. Progression, what sort of- '

Fuck! Another humungous fart blasted out - prolonged, wet and high-pitched, like one of those excited squeals you get from teenage girls the moment Bieber runs onto the stage. I couldn't ignore it.

'Are you ok? Do you need the toilet?' I asked as my cheeks turned into baked tomatoes.

'Erm, *excuse me*? That wasn't *me*?' she boomed, looking pretty angry and jabbing her chest on the second "me".

'Well, it wasn't *me*, so...' I said, just as another one belted out from somewhere. Had it taken visible form it would have looked like a giant chocolate muffin.

'Jesus *Christ*,' she cried, looking the wrong side of

unsettled and making to leave, but not before a fourth one screamed out - a short, sharp, high-pitched burp as opposed to the earthquake moments before.

'What the fu-' I said, again completely innocent and trying to work out what in God's name was going on. The fifth one was as I said "fu-" and sounded like a balloon flying around the room losing air, screeching like a banshee. I swear it was laughing at me.

'I'm really not sure about this interview anymore,' Rose said, standing up as a sixth announced its arrival to the party with a deep squelch. I was mortified. Either she was doing them and didn't realise it, some kind of nervous disposition that happened now and again (it *was* possible, I supposed), or...or something else was making the noises.

'Really, Rose, I have no idea what's going on. Honestly.' Something prompted me to look under my desk and check there wasn't a fucking dwarf sitting there with clenched fists, mischievously thumping down on a trail of inflated whoopee cushions.

Then it all became clear. Louis.

Stuck to the underside of my desk was a plain black speaker the size of a small shoe, complete with flashing red LED light. It emitted another as I tried to prise it away, but it wouldn't budge. The harder I strained and kept on trying, the more the machine kept farting. It must have been triggered off by detecting close movement, or someone had a fucking remote control.

'I'm so sorry Rose. Someone's planted a fart machine to the desk it seems. Here look,' I said after reappearing from under the desk, red in the face and pointing to exhibit A.

But Rose declined my offer of explanation, instead letting me know that she would be in touch with me in due course, the whole time the machine carried on bleeping, trumping and burping as she slid on her coat and walked out of the office, not slowly. As I watched her walk out, my gaze ruptured when I got to Louis, standing in the middle of the sales floor wielding a small black box, laughing his head off and pointing straight at me.

Louis.

SIX: INTERVIEW

'But you know, he *was* really sweet! The wheelchair didn't prove a problem at all, I was really surprised.'

Rose ran her little finger under the cold tap in the kitchen before filling up a pint glass holding two Berocca such was her hangover. It needed to be cold. Lucy looked on with raised eyebrows, seeking approval from Rose for her misdemeanours with Mark.

'Yeah, sure. I mean, if you got on well enough and the chemistry was there, then why not just run with it? He's a nice chap...really genuine,' said Rose, choosing to withhold the pile of disturbing information she had about Mark's character, and avoid the defamation he deserved. 'I still can't believe how random it is! You ending up shagging a guy I work with!'

The night before was far from dull. Zoe and Rose knew something peculiar was about to occur the moment Lucy slammed shut her bedroom door, so they kept the TV on mute and sat there listening to all manner of grunting, banging and thumping. It was just too funny to ignore, their hands were glued to their mouths stifling their childish snorting. To kick things off, Lucy exclaimed in frustration that she couldn't get Mark's pants down and that he needed to give her a hand, which was quickly counteracted with "come on gal, give it some wellie and yank those bad boys off!" A few seconds of straining - with the odd comical "oomph" thrown in the mix - was followed by the same voice joyously hollering a sentence that sounded like "there you go lav, get yer laughing gear round that!" and then muffled groaning from Lucy as something other than the usual fistful of chips was stuffed into her mouth. *That* only lasted for a few seconds, as Mark requested her to "slow down a minute I'm close to spunkin' me 'ole barrel," at which point more banging vibrated through the whole flat following Mark's next demand ("go on gal git on that then"). A pause of ten seconds built up to a chorus of high-pitched moans and deeper "oofs", the frequency and volume increasing over a hilariously awkward couple of minutes, as the grand finale of the bedhead smashing against the wall approached, getting quicker and quicker, and Mark's hollering of "WA-HEY!" tried but couldn't succeed in drowning out Lucy's "OHMYGODYESYESYES!" before she finished with "OH COME ON THEN YOU FUCKING WHEELIE!"

Remarkably, Mark held on until Lucy was done, singing out "FORTY-NINE FORTY-NINE UNDEFEATED, PLAYING FOOTBALL THE ARSENAL WAY!" bringing it all to a close. Rose and Zoe could just about make out some self-congratulatory heavy panting coming from Lucy, who must have been extremely pleased the wait was over, albeit from someone who couldn't run away.

*

The rest of the weekend wasn't as entertaining. Due to the five-fifteen finish on Saturday morning, the whole next day was a write-off, so she took to hibernating on her couch, gorging on the original Star Wars trilogy accompanied by Domino's and making the most of the vacant flat. Lucy had gone back home to for the night, something that always pleased Rose to the extent that she just slouched around all day in her underwear with complete authority over the remote. Sunday followed much the same pattern: Narcos season one and a massive Chinese.

As soon as it had started, the weekend was over, and by ten o'clock Rose found herself wrapped up in bed having a lazy wank with her electric toothbrush.

*

When she walked into the office on Monday, the first of her final three days at Aspinall-Willey, Mark didn't appear until eleven but got straight into his probing as soon as he did.

'Sorry about all the noise on Friday, couldn't 'elp meself. Told ya I was a playa, innit,' he crowed, unwrapping something from tin foil to reveal a breakfast item that looked like it had come from a vending machine. 'So anyway, what does she think about me, reckon I'm in there?'

'Lucy...oh, yeah. Think she'd be up for another date. For sure,' said Rose, hoping that she was right and she'd be given another episode of *Spastics in Bed*.

'Knew she would be,' he said triumphantly. 'Not many tarts that survive the old wheels of steel and his foot long.' He clearly believed in his own mantra.

Rose clicked 'checkout' on the ASOS website and left her desk to go for a pee, and to seek shelter from Mark's rubbish.

*

December rain continued to lightly slap against the windows of the offices when Rose stared out and prepared to leave to go and meet Sean. She closed down her computer and fed her makeup mirror into her bag, noticing she was a little ahead of schedule.

There was no way she was going to get herself soaked before a meeting with Sean, so she went down and ordered a cab and waited in the foyer of her building and questioned the sky. A few clouds parted and a tiny ray of light peeped through, making for an infantile rainbow she could just about make out, and it made her smile. Perhaps it was an omen that things were going to brighten up even more.

The reception area at the office block that housed STI was shiny and clean, the front of house manned by an old and cheerful looking fellow who must have been pushing seventy. He took an age to sign her in, spending an eternity focusing on her blouse and doing little else. Eventually, after giving her a flimsy plastic visitor's pass, Rose went and settled down in a chair and picked up one of the glossy trade magazines, skimming through it for a couple of minutes before a young blonde and friendly looking girl about the same age as Rose emerged from the lifts.

'Hi, Rose?' she said extending a hand. 'Melanie Green...this way, please.'

The offices of STI were situated on the fourth and fifth floors of Farringdon Place. Once the old KPMG building on the corner of Farringdon Road and Cowcross Street, it housed a few different companies and STI chose the top two floors. It was nice enough, she thought. Not as much pizazz as the FFB HQ, but it seemed quite modern. She walked onto the main floor and took in the sales teams buzzing away: a few guys were on their feet talking animatedly on telephone headsets, gesticulating and hollering to the poor buggers on the other end, and the walls were lined with whiteboards which had tables and figures next to names in what looked like some form of leader boards.

She followed Melanie to a large glass-fronted office and caught a glimpse of a bald, tanned chap giggling away to himself in the corner.

Sean's office was quite bare and his desk was twice as wide as the ones out on the floor; the only other furniture of note was a bookcase with some trade magazines piled high and a few books on sales techniques. A whiteboard nailed to one side of the wall showed a graph with the years 2014 to 2016 next to some figures she had no idea what they meant, making a note to ask him during the chat.

Sean stood up and shook her hand firmly. Rose was aware that her palm was sweaty, and she felt a slight quiver somewhere inside as he looked her straight in the eye. There was something about him. She knew she'd seen him before. She knew who he was, vaguely.

'Rose hi...Sean Thomas,' he said, flashing perfect white teeth. She felt at ease in his presence, too. 'Thanks for being early, really helps. Got a bucket load on today. Anyway, have a seat, please,' he invited, before getting to it. 'So, tell me a bit about you – keep it free from vocational stuff. Tell me about...*Rose*.'

It was far from the informal chat they had arranged, but

none-the-less it went well for the first half hour and Rose sold herself well, giving examples of all her best achievements whether academic or other, and handling any kind of curveball (that was the term right?) he threw at her and asking him smart questions throughout the interview. Safe to say that it was going well - too well, perhaps - and she figured she quite possibly had another offer coming her way.

'So, what would you like to know about us, then?' Sean asked. Rose paused for a minute and took her time. She'd asked many questions about the company products, the working hours, average deal size, targets etc. but no focus on what they could offer her in terms of development, as yet.

'Well...I think the burning question is what kind of progression do y - '

Sean farted! It stopped her in her tracks and she sat there, terrified. They looked at each other for a moment in embarrassing silence. She didn't know what to do, so looked down at the desk, until he told her not to worry and go on.

'Sure, where were we...oh yes. Progression, what sort of - '

He did it again! Another huge one echoed around the office. Rose was totally put off by the whole scenario. This man was, despite being extremely handsome, rapidly losing every spec of charisma and literally breaking wind in an interview, in front of her.

Maybe it's a tactic to see how I handle unexpected situations.

'Are you ok? Do you need the toilet?' said Sean, incredibly. Fucking hell, was he really trying to pin the blame on her for his flatulence in a one-on-one interview?

'Erm *excuse me*? That wasn't *me*?' cried Rose, cheeks glowing and unable to stave off the urge to jab herself defiantly.

'Well...it wasn't *me*,' he said, just as he broke wind *again*. The cheek. *Time to cut loose.*

'Jesus *Christ*!' screamed Rose, still terrified.

'What the fu -' he said, precisely the same time as farting once more. This was getting out of hand, and she wanted out, quick sharp.

Rose stood up and grabbed her coat from the back of the chair, stifling the barrage of insults that were knocking about beneath her skull and dangerously close to spilling out.

'I'm really not sure about this interview anymore,' she said, putting on her coat. Waste of time it was proving to be.

'Really Rose, I have no idea what's going on, honestly.' He tried to fib his way out of it, still farting. She wasn't stupid, for God's sake. He even went so far as to look under his desk and try and tell her there was a fart machine or something stuck to it - one that he couldn't remove!

As she left the office, without shaking Sean's hand, she also left a composition of more farting. She couldn't get out quick enough. She hurried over to the doors and out to where the lifts were. The same bald bloke she'd seen on the way in was standing a few feet away from Sean's office with his arms flailing about and keeled over in hysterics.

The lift doors opened and it took her precisely three seconds to work out that the drawing on the side of the lift by the buttons, in felt green marker, was that of a giant penis. What a bunch of jokers.

SEVEN: SESSION

'Louis, get in here. Now, please.' I shouted at him, catching one final look at Rose's butt wiggling out of the office and, quite possibly, my life, for good. I did have her number however, perhaps a message apologising in a day or two might help rebuild the bridges that Louis had just spectacularly incinerated. She was just too sexy and smart to let slip away that easily. That arse as well. Jesus.

Louis breezed in like nothing was wrong.

'Shut the door, please,' I said, resembling a head-teacher and popping my head under the desk, still battling to get my head round what had just gone on. I came back up and was greeted by Louis's feet on my desk, and he was wearing a pair of my Prada shades that had been missing for at least three months.

'Alright me old china? Bit stuffy in here isn't it?' he said, twitching his nose and sniffing animatedly. 'What's that smell?'

'Louis…' I said sternly, indicating it wasn't the time for anymore nonsense. But it was too late. He clicked the button on the small black controller he was hiding under his notepad, and another noise echoed out from beneath us.

'Phwoar deary me mate, that you? Beans on toast was it?' he said. I still had a perfect view of the sole of his brogues and he was still kind enough to make sure my sunglasses had a home resting on the top of his head.

'Ok enough now. What on *earth* is that thing?' I said.

'What thing?'

'You know full we -' I said, just as he hit it again, this time raising a leg in the air making out he'd actually broken wind.

'Oh sorry mate, your bum-burps are contagious I reckon!' he cried, again clicking the remote and then wafting his hand in front of his nose and frowning.

The trouble with this whole scenario – like the many others I've found myself in since employing him - is that Louis never fails to amuse me. I have a childlike sense of humour too and will generally crack up at some point during one of his pranks; therefore he keeps on pushing the boundaries. Sometimes it is a little too much, as I tried to advocate during this episode, but it would prove to be fruitless.

'Right, seriously now. You've got work to do and so have I, so remove that thing from my desk and leave both the speaker and the control with me. You may have it back at the end of term young man.'

'Ah, well, slight issue with that Saint. I super glued it,' he said, laughing once more.

He found it genuinely funny that he was responsible for me essentially having to call out a fucking handyman to drill the damn thing away, ruining my own desk. 'But there's an off-switch. No need to worry about it making any more noises,' he said, as if that would somehow appease the whole fiasco he'd created.

'Well then switch it off and leave the control here then. Go on,' I said, not just sounding like a headmaster.

It turned out later on that a) there wasn't an off-switch, just a volume dial, and b) there was another remote control.

Twenty minutes after Louis had said he'd turned it off and left my office, he was at it again. Whilst in the middle of a monthly review with Phil and Mo - *Mo the Mad Muslim from Indo* as Louis called him on day one of his employment - a chorus of farts echoed around my office, again. The first one was so loud that all three of us actually jolted in shock. Louis had not switched it off at all, he had turned the volume *up* full whack and had another remote control. Of course he had, how could I even assume anything else?

'For fuck sake!' I dialled Melanie. 'Chuck me through to Louis please. I don't remember his extension.'

He answered after one ring. That was how busy he was.

'Wanking anonymous...how can I help?' he boomed through

the speaker. Phil and Mo sniggered like schoolboys already.

'Louis can you bring in everything you have regarding that fart machine, and I mean *everything*. Box, batteries, remotes…even the fucking receipt, if you have it. And do it now, I am n   ot in the mood for this right now!'

Louis's voice leapt out through the speaker, and he was now from Texas.

'I'm sorry y'all but this aint Looo-eeee…you've called Doctor Monkey Spanker at *Wanking Anonymous*, we're with you every step of the way in your battle to give up the – '

That did it, the battle my insides were having with my face ended as I cracked up, and so did Mo and Phil as Louis's laughter blurted out. Phil was keeled over and looked like he was having a very violent epileptic seizure, Mo was grinning and his face had turned the same colour as a plumb, and I felt like I was a stoned teenager gasping for air. Four grown men with a combined age of 135 all laughing at the sort of toilet humour reserved for teenage boys.

"So y'all wanna make an appointment then?" I heard at some point between our howling.

Never a dull moment. Ever.

*

After a painful presentation from Phil on his team's numbers, finally it got to my favourite time of the day: pub time. Even on a Monday, as soon as it gets to one minute past five, I stop whatever I'm doing and make a sharp exit before anyone can stop me with a question or something just as pointless.

The general plan most Mondays:

Flip open WhatsApp and confirm on the group chat '*Crown or Pig Posse*' which pub my pals and I are meeting in for our post-work pints, or *PWP* as we refer to them.

The Crown was my preference - and my local - but The Pig and Fiddle was Bob and Carl's. Steve, Leon and Andy didn't care either way. The Pig would mean I needed to stay on the train three more stops and get off at Hatfield rather than Potters Bar, and then get a cab home later, so if just going for a couple of pints the effort to go to The Pig is a bit far-fetched, plus a tenner in a cab, turning a twenty pound drink into thirty based on the assumption that I would be buying a round of four pints, sometimes more. We do this twice a week usually, pretty much every Monday and then one other day depending on who has escaped from the ball and chain – apparently some of my pals have this thing called a 'wife' at home who saps them of all their joy and keeps them prisoner, denies them sex and constantly watches their every move. Never heard of such pain.

An average of four participants means four pints will be consumed, at least, going on the ratio of one round each, unless someone is only literally flying in for just one. Under those circumstances the chap is expected to either buy a whole round or just get his own in. Little, unwritten rules for our PWPs. The other unwritten rule we have is that at some point, usually after pint number three – *The Devil's Whisper* named as such because it's the pint that whispers things like: "Go on, call your dealer," or "that boiler over there *isn't that bad"* – someone will always call it on, meaning a quick buzz to our dealer **** to get a couple of packets dropped off. Split four ways that's £25 each, unless someone's holding leftovers from the weekend which is an almost extinct possibility. So four pints turns into another four, because as soon as the fifth round is bought, you're effectively in the next round of rounds. Then after the eighth pint someone, usually Carl, will move onto Sauvignon Blanc with a pint of ice cubes on the side. We'll have two bottles between four of us, £21 a bottle or a tenner each, and then it might be time to call it a night. When it does get called on, Carl will demolish his in a maximum of three trips to the toilet. Common sense will tell you that it isn't the cleverest of ideas to leave him alone with your shared packet for *any* length of time. Being an onlooker, it's always quite amusing watching everyone try and avoid sharing with Carl when it gets called on. It basically becomes a race – loser shares with Carl. After The Devil's Whisper, a conversation usually takes this direction:

Carl: 'Anyone holding?'

Me: 'Nope.'

Carl: 'Wanna get some?'

Bob: 'Yeah shall we? Go halves on a couple from ****'

Me: 'Cool'

Andy (pulling out his wallet quietly and firing the gun to signal the start of the race): 'Sorted'

Me (to Andy): 'Here give me thirty and I'll give you five back, we'll go halves on one then?'

Bob: 'Hang on wait a minute, Andy owes me twenty-five from last week so he can just pay for ours and we'll go halves.'

Carl (to a petrified me): 'Ok so we'll go halves then, Sean?'

Me (changing tactic in desperate attempt to avoid Carl): 'Andy, are out for a bit longer?'

Andy: 'Yeah, why?'

Me: 'Same here. You, Carl?'

Carl: 'Probably off home not too long after we get sorted, better get back soon - the missus is giving me grief.'

Me: 'Bob?'

Bob: 'Soon-ish, I'd imagine. Get home roll a joint and have some munch.'

Me: 'Ok so it makes sense for me and Andy to split one, and for you two to split the other.'

Bob: 'Yeah but I'm going halves with Andy. He owes me from last week.'

Carl (to me): 'That's fine we'll just split it before I go.'

The scenario, as it stands, is worrying. Allowing Carl to make the call *and* organise the gear also means he'll be responsible for division and distribution. Weights and measures. What that means is that he'll go to divide it, in the pub toilets, but only after hoovering a massive line *before*, making sure that he gets the bigger half. Carl is totally blind to the fact that the rest of us share in this turmoil.

This is how my Plan B should go:

Me: 'Actually, grab me a whole one, got a few things on this week.'

Carl (to Andy and Bob): 'Jesus. Ok so we'll go three ways then?'

Bob: 'No fuck that.'

Andy: 'Can't you just go halves with Carl, be much easier?'

By this point the concern has left me and now sits with Andy and Bob who both know that Carl's gonna batter theirs before splitting it *three* ways, which will no doubt result in probably half a line each, at best. But then another spanner gets wedged into the works as Andy clocks on to my idea.

Andy: 'In fact, I'll have a whole one too.'

Carl: 'Make your minds up, for fuck sake! What am I asking for?'

This royally fucks Bob over. First off because he has to share with Carl, and secondly it also means he doesn't get the twenty-five quid that is owed to him because Andy will only ever have fifty pounds on him, to make doubly sure he can't go overboard. Such discipline.

Carl: 'Right so we want three in total? One each for you two and then me and Bob split one?'

Me (thrusting fifty into Carl's hand): 'Yep fine,'

Andy: 'Yeah here you go.'

Now Bob will go all out to sabotage the whole thing and suggest we chuck in another fifty quid, collectively, to make two hundred, so we can get an eighth of the stuff (3.5 grams or just under a gram each - much more for our money), instead of the usual packet we've ordered (half-a-gram each for fifty, or quarter-of-a-gram for twenty-five if splitting). Call it buying in bulk, but **** knows that it's quite likely that once three have been discussed, his punters will talk each other round into such a wise and shrewd business transaction. So Bob's suggestion does make sense, and we usually agree and give in. Everyone's happy. Then we repeat this whole show the next time, unless there are more people and/or someone is already holding. It's complex.

Carl: 'Shall we do that then? Better value all round.'

Bob: 'Happy with that.'

So, when you do the maths on it all, a typical Monday night PWP ends up at around £100, possibly £110 if it's at The Pig. A Monday PWP.

*

At The Pig, the recent, atrocious weather showed no signs of disappearing with Christmas around the corner, but it felt cosy inside. This time of year should be cold, freezing even, but without the torrential rain that was knocking at the windows beside us as we sat around a huge round table drinking. An arrangement of empty glasses was scattered about and we were well on the way.

The Pig's a warm and friendly pub on one side, with a dining area on the other, and the huge fireplace next to where we were sitting was smoking and cracking away nicely as Bob chucked on another log. (It's Bob's local pub and he insists on sitting by the fireplace in winter months and literally won't leave the thing alone; chucking chunks of wood on it, fanning it or shutting the door, poking away at it.)

We had a full house. December is party month, after work drinks are licensed out by girlfriends or wives in a free for all. Anything goes. All you do is add the words "it's our Christmas drink" at the end of any sentence and it buys you a late finish, empty wallet and hefty hangover. The whole of the *Crown or Pig posse* group members had made it out which was really pleasing, and we found ourselves onto pint number three by just after seven. It was going to be one of *those* Monday nights.

Bang on cue, just as we finished the first gulps of round four of our pints of Foster's/Peroni/Amstel/IPA/Foster's Top/Camden Hells Top, the Devil whispered something to Steve, and not Carl as usual. I had a bit left from the weekend

Stitched Up

so was ok; in fact I'd already had a cheeky pinch fifteen minutes earlier, chuffed that I would be able to sit back and enjoy the complex equations and imminent panic from the others as they decided what they wanted to do. The race was about to begin. Carl took the lead once Steve had opened the bidding.

'Ok who wants what then? May as well get three between the six of us?' he said, opening his phone and jabbing the screen, about to dial ****.

I raised a finger and stopped him. He knew exactly why.

'You holding?' he asked.

'Got a couple left over from the weekend, count me out,' I replied.

'Weigh me in then,' he said, his standard response when he knows someone is holding.

'Yeah in a min, I haven't been yet,' I lied. Situation tricky. I had about half left, so a good few lines. In the tremendously likely event that Carl wanted a line from me while waiting for **** to arrive, then he'd find out I had a good deal more than the couple of lines I pretended to have. This gave me a mild heart attack at what kind of complications his discovery would mean for the forthcoming drug acquisition pantomime.

'Ok, anyone else holding, or shall we get, what, two between the five of us?' he continued, clearly anxious to get the show on the road. This increased my pulse rate even more, his anxiousness to get the gear would without a doubt mean he'd definitely ask me again to sort him out while they waited for ****.

I had three options. First, and the easiest, was to just simply keep up the lie and tell him I really did only have a couple of lines leftover, but he could counteract that and try and persuade me to join in with them, then I'd have to pretend I didn't want to get that heavily involved, and he'd laugh at me as if I was in fact doing stand-up. Second option, and the riskiest, was to go into the toilets and split what I had left into a couple of wraps and make sure one of them only had a few crumbs left, therefore should Carl pursue his quest to tax some from me, I could give him the small wrap knowing at least I'd only be a couple of lines down, then I could muller a massive one of his when it arrived (payback). The third option was to keep stalling him until **** turned up, the most unpredictable of the three, and one that if it didn't work out, would mean a cast iron guarantee he'd pester me and I'd have to give in. Then I'd be rumbled. That is why the next phone call was a point of paramount significance:

Carl: 'Ok so, what's it to be?'

Andy: 'Half for me and Leon?'

Leon (immediately): 'Yes bruvva, you know it!'

Steve: 'Ok. Bob, wanna split one?'

Bob (relieved): 'Yep for sure

Carl: 'Why don't three of us split one? Or get three between us five...that's...thirty quid each. I'll see if **** can split them five ways?'

General agreement from the others followed. What Carl had suggested actually made financial sense. It was time for the phone call which we all had a vested interest in. Me because I wanted **** to be as quick as possible for reasons explained and fend off Carl's demented mission at pilfering all of mine before it'd touched the sides, Bob, Andy, Leon and Steve would all be praying that **** would indeed be able to split three packets five ways instead of trusting Carl to do it, and Carl obviously, because, well you know what I mean by now. He dialled the number.

'Straight to voicemail...' he said clicking off and pushing my pulse up by another twenty percent. It was coming, indicated by a nudge under the table from Carl.

'Oi, gimme that thing then?'

Option two it was.

When I got into the cubicle I fished around in my wallet for any kind of piece of paper that I could make a wrap out of, eventually pulling out the solitary receipt I had on me, and opening it out to reveal it was from *Jester's Jokes and Games*. Half-way down next to a price tag of £15.99 were the words *Fart Machine Dlx*. I couldn't escape Louis, wherever I went.

Then, something really good happened. Carl came into the toilet and shouted over the cubicle door not to worry, just before I was going to unnecessarily split up what I had left. Luckily, **** called straight back and was only ten minutes away. A nice, early Christmas gift. Maintaining the entire contents of my packet, instead of surrendering half of it to Carl.

*

Three empty bottles of Sauvignon Blanc sat on the table, and the clock was showing ten past eleven. Each of us had sunk nine pints prior to a half bottle of wine, and all six of us were pretty mangled. I'd given the group a full-blown account of Louis and the fart machine which went down well, then we'd had the usual rowdy debates of football while the Monday night late kick off between Liverpool and Watford played on the solitary television above the bar. Only Bob was genuinely interested in watching as he pretended to be a Liverpool fan, but was also fairly mute he was so twisted. As it passed eleven, we were all well-oiled and considering our routes home. Bob and Carl could walk, Leon and Steve could share a cab back, I would Uber it, and Andy would be hoping for an invite somewhere...

'Back to yours for a bit?' he asked me.

'Early start dude, gotta meeting at nine,' I said immediately. I did have a meeting. Well, my right hand did, so I wasn't strictly lying.

'Boo...come on. I'll be out of your hair by one, latest,' he said picking up a glass and emptying the last inch of white wine and melted ice. 'Grab a bottle and chew the fat for a bit?'

Andy was a year my junior at the same school so I've literally known him since I was twelve. He is also self-employed, some kind of chartered accounts work he does on a contract basis, and also single, so no boiler to bust his balls about a late one on a school night. Multiple reasons to go wrong on a Monday. I crumbled.

'One AM ripcord. Latest.'

'Yeah ok, for sure.'

I really wanted to believe him.

*

It was gone six when his cab to take him home arrived. Six on a Tuesday morning. My living room was a bombsite: two empty bottles of some atrocity called Isla Negra were spoiling what is usually a very nice solid oak dining room table and a duvet was spread across the floor where Andy had *intended* to sleep. But there was no sleeping until he left. Best laid plans and all that. One AM turned to three, by five all of the wine and drugs had been mercilessly destroyed, and come six the early morning commuters were de-icing windscreens as engines chugged away. Definitely home time for Andy.

I was just about capable of keying in a message to Melanie reminding her I was out for the day at meetings, but funnily enough she replied *Oh yeah,* pretending she remembered. A liar lying to a liar. I went back to sleep until about eleven, during which time I had a lucid dream about Spurs losing at home 5-1 to Everton. The relief I felt when I woke up realising it wasn't true gave me the motivation to open up Pornhub and have a quick five-knuckle shuffle. (Something that always gets a laugh from me is the various words and phrases used to describe wanking: fapping, strumming the banjo, beating the meat, spanking the monkey, shaking hands with the unemployed, tossing off, jerking off , Yankee doodle handy, masturbation, pumping the python, whacking the wotsit, bashing one out, bashing the bishop, five-knuckle shuffle, five-knuckle *shovel* – that one is when you've had far too much shovel aka cocaine and have to spend ages with your fist clamped around your knob when it's the same strength as a lump of Play-Doh, - self-abuse, milking the one-eyed messiah, choking the chicken. I could go on.)

After spanking the monkey twice in succession, I flipped open WhatsApp to see I'd got a message from Rose at half-eight in the morning; it simply said *sure why not you were up late lol* in response to a message I'd sent at one in the morning. A message that had given a lengthy apology and explanation about Louis and his antics, that then went on to say I had been impressed with her in the interview, and that if it was ok with her, we should reconvene over lunch one day later this week. I replied with *Thursday?* which is always a good day to go for a boozy lunch as it can turn into a session, and it's practically the weekend. Rose had mentioned that her last day of work was Wednesday, so there was more chance of a longer affair, meaning I would have an excuse to ply her with booze, in turn increasing my chances of getting her naked from the current level of less than two percent, up to maybe twenty.

Half a glass of wine and a cornetto for breakfast, in bed, followed my masturbation. Life doesn't get much better than that. #winning.

EIGHT: EXIT

The day had arrived, finally. Getting off the bus on Roseberry Avenue at just after nine, Rose made her final trip into the offices of Aspinall-Willey with the intention to do as little as possible. She was tired. Sean had sent her a few messages late in the night; the last one was at 00:53 and woke her up as it vibrated through, and she'd struggled to get back to sleep.

'Oi oi!' came the usual greeting from the *Wheels of Steel*, at least that's what Rose thought he said. It was hard to decipher as his gob was full of...*something*. Mystery meat and mashed potato, or was it white bread? Yes, white bread actually. *Logic*. It appeared as if Mark had been recommended to try the cherry Tango to go with his main. Half a litre of Tango and a meat bap to start the day...Rose let it sink in. Seeing as he wasn't really in the best of shape, Rose often wondered why Mark didn't pay more attention to his diet. Surely he'd be extra vigilant when deciding what to pump into his body if his body wasn't as physically able? But no, he seemed to stick two fingers up at any kind of questions asked by his arteries, instead choosing to gobble a broad spectrum of diabolical items for breakfast and lunch. What must it have been like for him at dinnertime? He'd go out to grab lunch and return twenty minutes later with a giant minced 'beef' crispy pancake, aka the ground up carcass of poor old Dobbin, large bag of chips all washed down with half a litre of any drink that has held the world record for having the most number of chemicals per millilitre. He would happily wheel past a place that could provide him with a decent salad and some lean meat or fish in a box for under a fiver, in favour of a fried chicken franchise or Greggs. Another one of those things Rose didn't...well, warm to.

She remained silent and chose to switch her eyes and ears away from his mechanical chewing, and launched into her emails. Sean just didn't let up, he'd sent her a confirmation email about where they were meeting for lunch, suggesting they go for a drink a bit earlier in the pub next door at 1 pm, and then eat for half past. Was it a sort of date? Or is this how busy and successful business owners act when they want to attract people to join them? Either way, she was going to roll with it.

*

Her last day of data entry. She'd taken the job in August, and here she was at the end of the year having worked thirty-five hours a week at £12.50 an hour. £437.50 per week over fifteen weeks, so around £6500 she'd earned, before tax, since the summer. She literally had nothing to show for it except depleted brain cells and a couple of mild urinary infections. The new position at FFB couldn't come sooner. In the meantime, she needed an older man to spoil her...

The hours were swallowed up by plenty of social media surfing, and as it approached five, she found herself shutting down her computer and gathering the bits and bobs thrown across her desk. Nothing of real value to be frank. Some lip gloss, her purse, and a book called *The Wrong Heaven* she was halfway through (the first words that came out of Mark when she plopped it down on her desk a few weeks back were "up the wrong un").

'Fancy a quick one then, say goodbye and all that?' Mark asked hopefully, his intention surely to a) drink, and b) get more Lucy info out of Rose. *Why not?*

*

Mark bought a whole bottle of red wine when Rose said she wanted a glass of something *wintery*. Apparently, his accumulator had come in on Sunday and he was "seven-ton better off," surely a massive exaggeration, but the chance of a free session saw her hold her tongue on that one. Approximately three minutes into their conversation, the subject matter of Lucy cropped up. Mark's strategy was simple and blatant: ask Rose if *she* was on Tinder – which she told him she was – leading to further discussion led by Mark about Tinder and the constraints of being an active wheelchair user, which in turn led to him praising Lucy for not being fussed about the fact that he was disabled, then swiftly on to the inevitable plugging of himself, trying to squeeze some more out of Rose about his chances. He was genuinely enthused by Friday nights stop-out. She rode it out for a while in return for free alcohol.

'So what's the job all about, sweet feet?' asked Mark as he poured them another glass of deep purple Malbec. It was already finished less than an hour after it was opened. That's what twenty-odd quid got you these days in central; one-and-a-half large glasses of wine parked on a wooden seat in an old man's pub.

'It's for a business development position. The company's called FFB. Big in the business info space. Decent money, too,' replied Rose, getting chilly.

'They got anything else going there? Could do with a change into permanent.'

Over her dead body, there was no way she was going to get him an interview and risk the management there thinking she was trying to sabotage their respectable brand by planting a dickhead on wheels into the business. He'd be better off somewhere that was full of other jokers like…hold on. A penny dropped.

'You know what, I interviewed the other day for a place up the road in Farringdon, STI they're called. Really good place, nice offices and paying decent salary. Monthly commission, quarterly bonus, good location and a pension scheme. All the trimmings. The owner is buying me lunch tomorrow. I'll put in a good word for you if you like? He said they were always on the sniff for new talent.'

Mark was so taken aback at Rose's suggestion of help that he scooted over to the bar and returned with another bottle.

'Don't mention it,' he said, coinciding with a raise of his hand as Rose went to reach for her purse. Pissed for free on a Wednesday.

By half-six The Castle was a busy hum of post work drinkers. Some of the people were in there seeking reprieve from the cold, a quick one before the journey home and all that. The Castle was opposite the recently completed new tube and train station entrance and exit and was serving those ridiculous Christmas type drinks mulled wine or hot spiced cider, and a festive pale ale that was for a limited time only. It was beginning to feel a lot like Christmas, and Rose felt good. A chilly breeze gusted in from outside as a group of office workers charged through the bar just as Mark returned to their table with some G&T chasers.

'Rose?'

'Yep?'

'Lucy, like. D'ya reckon she's hundred percent up for it?' asked Mark, probably for the fifth time since they'd arrived.

'Yes, I think so. I mean, actually, I *know* she is. Drop her a text and suggest another date – put your mind at rest.'

He raised his glass, and they downed their drinks in one sitting. He wasn't *that* bad, she found herself thinking.

'One for the road?' he said.

*

Lucy belched and blew it out slowly, catching the whiff of ham toasty, ketchup and Mars Milk – the sum total of her evening meal. As she sat there on the couch, the empty food wrappers surrounding a plate with a good dollop of ketchup blobbed on the side of it, she had a strange urge to message Mark but didn't, concluding that he should be the one to chase. She was in a dressing gown having had a hot bath. It was a cold night and she'd walked home from Angel tube, stopping off to pick up some Christmas presents. Because of the unexpected exercise, she rewarded herself with a trip to Sainsbury's local and purchased white bread, wafer thin ham and a 500ml chocolate drink. Of course, the long walk back home in the cold also meant a hot bubble bath, the only thing missing was a crane to hoist her in and out of the tub, but miraculously she managed. Where was Rose? It was pushing nine and she hadn't mentioned anything. She picked up her phone to send a message and saw Rose had sent one to her around half eight, asking if she was at home. She must have forgotten her keys.

Ten minutes later and the front door burst open. Rose had been shopping and was struggling with something, but Lucy couldn't be bothered to turn round and look, running the risk of being asked to get up off her backside.

Then shuffling and clanging continued.

'Hello...?' she shouted, again without moving an inch, feet still up on the coffee table and pushing a dirty cereal bowl further away from her. A trip to the kitchen to put it into the sink was an unnecessary waste of energy when she could do it on her way to bed.

'Hiya,' shouted Rose. She sounded drunk, animated. 'Guess who I've brought?'

It was too late to ask who. Bursting through the lounge door was Mark, startling Lucy so much that she kicked over the bowl of brown milk and Coco Pops, jumping up and screaming. Her dressing gown flew open and her bits and pieces made a run for it, swinging like a pendulum. It was quite a picture: Lucy, hand over mouth and displaying a pair of flabby and offensive knockers that had escaped from the tent that had been encasing them, Mark's moronic beam, fist clamped around a bunch of cheap flowers and Rose standing behind him, mouthing the words "Sorry...he insisted."

Rose's phone pinged with a message from Sean again. *Does he not give in?* she asked herself, finding it hard to read the words with double vision.

NINE: LATE

Melanie looked at me with a kind of expression I don't often see. A look that, had anyone been with her, would have preceded the furtive whisperings of "are you gonna tell him, or shall I?"

A look that told me something was up.

Melanie Green. My P.A. That was what we'd advertised last year when I decided I needed someone to open post, knock up invoices, send the reps offers out to prospects, compile spreadsheets of phone activity etc. General dogsbody by definition, or even something bland like *Administrative Assistant*. But why use those descriptions when there is much more glamour in the words *Personal Assistant?* Imagine how much fun I had interviewing for that position last summer. In the three years of owning the business, I have never had such a glorious and fulfilling stretch of rinsing out the tidal wave of absolute *megas* that applied for the position. We advertised on a couple of recruitment websites that specialise in secretarial and administrative positions. No previous experience necessary, the basic requirements were being able to use Word, Excel and PowerPoint to a decent level, along with walking, talking and being able to give skilful head etc.

Give it a day or two of the odd early bird dropping by, and then whoosh, it was floodgates. My office turned into the Playboy mansion from the volume of sorts aged between eighteen and twenty-three who all seemed to want to work for the *CEO and Owner of a Business Information Trade Journal company*. Some of the applicants were, of course, stupid enough to only skim through the basic job description, arriving under the assumption that the word 'trade' meant the trading floor of a big bank, and P.A. to some multi-millionaire Richard Branson type fellow surrounded by young men making a packet every day selling stocks and shares. A welcome by-product of such ignorance, for me anyway, was that a steady flow of gold-digging Barbie doll look-a-likes made it to the first interview stage. LinkedIn, Facebook, Twitter and particularly Instagram really do come in handy during the vetting process. A few minutes of snooping, stalking and whatnot can give you a great insight into each and every applicant. Is it fit? *Always* the first thing you ask yourself. If her Instagram profile has some great shots of her in a bikini from her last holiday, swigging out of a champagne bottle, then get her in, and double pronto. Facebook shows a few pictures of her with the same guy? No invite. Retweet after retweet of Jay-Z, Lemar or Drake allows you to come to the conclusion that the applicant is *that* sort of girl, loves a big one. That's a cast iron same day job. Oh yes, social media can really add value to the hiring process. It was an absolute joy to be doing all the perving I was, and given the temperature that summer was pushing thirty most days, I found myself opposite miles of bare legs stretching out of tiny skirts. Girls wearing dental floss around their waists, and heels you'd expect to see in a torture dungeon.

But you have to make that work for you. So I did. Quite often I'd arrange for the interview to happen at four in the afternoon on Tuesdays and Thursdays, deliberately turning up fifteen minutes late, so come five o'clock when Phil and Mo had their half-hour review together, minus me (to brainstorm with freedom, of course) I'd need to leave them to it and loan them the use of my office. If I hadn't finished the interview by five – guaranteed - then we could always go and finish it in the pub next to the station over a drink. "What the hell, it is *after* five now, live a little," I reasoned with them, leading them out of the office. That numbers game meant I managed to get eight of them into the pub, purposely making sure they were all total sorts with an average age, from memory, of 22. Of those eight, three of them became friends, one of them I actually took home that night after three bottles of wine, and the other two were invited out at a later date with the same result. I still kick myself at a missed opportunity; why didn't I scale up this efficient and effective business model to fit into Friday's agenda as well? I lost sleep wondering what my strike-rate could have been. Not wanting to be left in the dark and always wondering 'what if?', I went for round two a few weeks later and completely fabricated a position in PR with the same requirements, adding that the successful candidate would also be the *Face of the Company* needed for phantom photo shoots. Friday afternoons for a whole month became a hotbed of carnality, each and every candidate accompanied me to the pub, or Keystone Crescent, which impressed the dozy cows no end. I got through six of the ten I hoodwinked into actually believing they were applying for a real job, before getting Melanie, who was new, to send the usual short, polite rejection email about the position being taken by someone who's experience was a better fit, and bingo, job done and plenty of material to bash the bishop over. Thanks for the memories you dumb bitches!

But Melanie. Melanie is decent and well worth a wipe, for sure. However, the moment she went on the payroll as someone working so closely for me, I made a conscious decision to keep it in my pants. She was only 19 at the time, and definitely the most impressive of the bunch in terms of qualifications; i.e. her vocab stretched beyond chavvy words such as peng, fam and innit. Yes, some of the girls I interviewed spoke in some weird ghetto talk like it was something they were taught in English lessons.

But Mel. I liked her, and getting her into bed so soon into her career would have probably upset the apple cart. Plenty of fish and all that. Speaking of which, as I nodded to Melanie on my way past her to my office, I remembered I had to meet Rose in the pub before lunch up at *The Grill on the Square*, near St Barts, instantly putting me in a good mood. A morning of Pornhub, and then an afternoon having lunch with an absolute cracker.

'Check your email,' Melanie said to me after I nodded hello. She'd forwarded on an email that had been sent to our general inbox. One which had *Complaint* in the subject bar and sent with high importance:

Dear sir/madam.

I am writing to complain about one of your 'sales' team and the manner in which he spoke to me when I called in to enquire about a report we are considering purchasing, in regards to the green energy market in Scandinavia.

The main switchboard put me through to someone who identified himself as 'Mister Chicken McNugget.' He then said I had called through to the McDonalds report centre and that they had a special offer on where buying any reports meant you'd get a 'free large fries or something equally as stupid' (the exact words as I remember).

Assuming I'd called a wrong number, I called again, and your switchboard put me through to this McNugget chap once more, who after listening to my request, politely told me that you were unable to do any reports for a month because the whole office was having a nap.

I had heard good things about your journals and online information, however, this experience has left me questioning your company's integrity, and how you treat prospective customers in general. I will not be using or recommending your company to anyone in the future.

Sincerely,

Keith Newton

Head of Research

Research Times

My sales guys do like a laugh. They need to be able to as it's a stressful job. But no one would throw away the chance to make a sale. An inbound lead like that is a) rare and b) pretty much guaranteed commission. This left a couple of possibilities: Louis or Sandra, from Marketing; there is no way Hannah in HR would have done anything like that. In fact, there really was only one culprit.

'Hiya, Mel can you bring up the call logger for a tick and-'

'Already done it. Only two calls came through to sales yesterday and both were diverted to Louis. Everyone else was at lunch,' she informed me.

'Ok. Can you print-'

'Already done that too,' she cut in, knowing full well where I was going. 'Check your desk. Want me to send him in?'

I took a deep breath and wondered how much money Louis had cost the business.

Two things of note happened after giving Louis a bollocking: firstly and most importantly, I gave the complainant, Keith Newton, a call and apologised. The cover story that the whole sales floor was out on a special lunch when he called, and someone from another company we share the open planned floor with had answered the phone for a joke, was bought hook, line and sinker. This resulted in a nice juicy ten grand deal that I closed myself, saving a commission payout to one of the guys. It's always handy having a zero cost of sale with a deal that size. Sometimes you - and only you - have to take ownership of those situations. After a few emails and diary filling meetings with general people about boring stuff, it got to twelve, so I went to find Louis and tell him to *never* answer an inbound call again. But I arrived to find an empty desk; he was causing mayhem somewhere else no doubt. The image of a cat playing the banjo looked at me from his computer. I stared for a moment in disbelief - his choice of screensaver wasn't his child and or wife, or a tasteful image of a mountain or anything semi-normal. It was a domestic pet playing a musical instrument.

The next thing of note to happen an hour later was this:

Back in my office, I heard what sounded like a very loud hooter going off outside on the sales floor, followed by some hysterical laughter. It happened again, so I wandered over to see what, presumably Louis, was getting up to, and making sure the fart machine was still locked away in my draw. The noise was coinciding with Mo sitting down on his chair. Louis had brought in a hooter – or a foghorn, as he corrected me later on in a meeting with HR - and attached it to the bottom of Mo's chair, so that whenever Mo sat down, his chair would press down on the top of the fog horn, resulting in an almighty roar. It happened six times before Mo actually worked out what was happening, and where/what the source of the din was. To be fair he is good at his job, but really not the sharpest tool. Not content with just the one, admittedly quite amusing prank, Louis had somehow managed to change Mo's screensaver to a still shot of two female and two male dwarves indulging in what appeared to be some form of a gang-bang scene from a questionable website. On top of that, Louis had literally hidden every single file on Mo's desktop in a folder that he then put into the recycle bin, minimising the taskbar so Mo was unable to change his display back and was under the illusion that all his work was lost. Whether Mo was under a lot of stress or not (it was the first week of December sales month and his team were a bit off their annual target, so it was highly probable) it didn't go down well at all, despite entertaining half the floor. When it all got too much for Mo, he raced over to Louis.

Mo: 'Ok mate, sort my computer out. It's not funny.'

Louis: 'Oh hey Mo! I thought you'd love that awesome dwarfsome foursome?'

Mo: 'No really, I don't. So you'll just sort it out for me and get back all my files, ok. And you can remove that hooter why you're at it.'

Louis: 'Technically it's a foghorn buddy. But anyway, I'm sorry dude, I just work here, I have no idea who you are?'

Mo (rag slipping out of sight): 'Look - seriously you *prick* - just do it and stop pratting around or I'll...'

Louis (cutting off Mo in a Chinese / Japanese accent): 'Would you like flies with that...egg flied lice, chicken chow main, number fifty-five...'

Mo (removing his suit jacket and rolling his sleeves up): 'I'm Indonesian you prick. You have ten seconds to sort this out.'

Louis (standing up): 'Alright alright, keep yer knickers on pal don't blow up on me...oops sorry!'

That did it. Louis went to walk past Mo, but instead went flying as Mo stuck out a leg, tripping him over so he fell onto the desk of one of the new guys, Josh, knocking over an open litre bottle of Coke, half of it spilling all over his desk and keyboard, the other half soaking Josh's light grey trousers and white shirt - an outfit, that I would later learn in the previously mentioned meeting with HR, he had put on especially for a meal out with his girlfriend and her parents that evening. Josh was livid. And he's not small, either. Once he'd managed to stop all the Coke spraying everywhere, he rose to his feet and shoved Louis so hard that Louis knocked straight back into Mo, knocking Mo off balance so that he fell into Sandra, who was having a bite to eat at her desk and filing her nails with a steel file; steel that stabbed Mo in his anus and drew blood. Mo yelped in pain as Louis looked on laughing, but that was short lived as Mo charged back at Louis and rugby tackled him, the pair of them ending up on the floor and wrestling around like a pair of amateur UFC contestants. They had an audience of the whole sales team bar Stephanie, who was on the phone looking pretty pissed off she was missing the action. I got another big lad, Robbie, along with Phil and Josh, to help me split them up - Robbie and Josh wrenched Mo away, while Phil and I grabbed the cause of it all. Had it been the other way round, I feared Josh may still have put a boot into Louis for good measure.

Thankfully the fighting stopped, but a few minutes later I still had to contend with - in no particular order - a marketing executive in tears with the blood of Mo's backside on her nail file, a Coke soaked Josh demanding Louis pay for his suit and replace his ruined keyboard, a sales manager who's rectum had been pierced and was citing racism, a distracted sales floor, and of course the trio of grown men sat in my office with Hannah from HR. It took a while to get that all dealt with. Mo and Josh were given a verbal, and Louis received a written one for persistent misbehaving which he seemed proud to receive. 'Can I get that framed, me old china?' he asked me once we both signed it. I was just going through the formalities of it all with Hannah when my phone buzzed. I had two missed calls from Rose. Fearing I'd be too late, I called her immediately.

'I'm so sorry, had an emergency on the sales floor involving, well, blood amongst other things. Head to the restaurant and I'll be with you in five,' I said after she thankfully answered.

Hannah stopped me on my way out. 'Sean, this latest thing with Louis, we need to review the HR policy as soon as.'

'Sure, don't panic. Let it blow over,' I said.

'And he's been drawing giant felt tip cocks all over the place...' she said before I could move away. I was getting anxious Rose would be kept waiting too long and shift off.

'Yeah yeah ok. Just...just wait for me to come back,' I said, still distracted. Bloody Louis.

'And Tom pissing in public. It's going to earn us a bad rep,' she said, speaking sense. 'Will you be back in later on, so we can sit down and go over things?'

'Possibly.'

TEN: MEAT

Rose took a cab from hers to the pub next door to The Grill on the Square, the venue for the lunch interview with Sean. She got there just after one and waited for a few minutes before going ahead with a glass of red. Red seemed more appropriate around Christmas time, and, as they were going to a steak restaurant, she figured it was the right way to go, despite having just started to feel normal again after the impromptu session with Mark. It had taken her a while to shrug off the hangover and required a shrine of discipline to drag herself out of bed given that she didn't have work, although she was woken up around half six to some harrowing noises coming from Lucy's bedroom followed by the thumping and banging of Mark's departure.

The pub was bubbly and there was a rabble in the restaurant section upstairs having a Christmas lunch, and as she took her first sip of Rioja, she imagined herself in a years' time with her colleagues doing the same, and then laughed remembering Lucy's tits spilling out of her dressing gown just as Mark had handed the flowers over. Remarkably, once the shock of her quiet Wednesday night being mortar bombed by a drunk cripple, Lucy had welcomed the company, so Rose left them to it in the lounge, thankful that she was smashed and going to pass out the moment her head hit the pillow. Just before she passed out, she heard some faint groaning and Mark shouting something along the lines of "good job my cock ain't paralysed an all!"

It got to twenty-five past and just before she was about to leave, Sean called to say he was on the way and apologised. There was some sort of office emergency. Probably quite the norm, what with being a CEO. She made the short walk across St Bart's square to the restaurant after a quick check in the toilet mirrors.

The Gill on the Market looked pretty nice from the website

when she'd checked, and she wasn't disappointed. Lighting was nice and dim with a line of tasteful Christmas lights softly glowing along the ceiling, and a small and well-pruned tree sat in the corner of the bar and subtly blended in.

'Good afternoon Madame,' said a Hispanic looking waitress called Maria, 'do you have a reservation with us this afternoon?'

'It may be under Sean Thomas or STI. For half-one,' she replied.

Sean breezed in looking flustered.

'Rose. Hi again. Really sorry about this…I'll tell you over a drink, I could really use one,' he said offering his hand as they were ushered through to the restaurant. He smelled nice, again.

*

Thankfully, no large groups on Christmas lunches or jollies were able to disturb the quiet corner of the restaurant they were set down in. The place was lively enough to make sure it wasn't awkwardly intimate, but not too rowdy so they'd have to use sign language to communicate through mouthfuls of steak. That's what it was all about, after all, to continue the interview.

'To begin with,' Sean started as he beckoned Maria over, 'let me just apologise for the awful prank one of my staff played on me the day you came in. It was a shock to me. He was disciplined for it,' he said. 'I know I've since explained it but really…pff, you know?'

'Don't mention it. It was a tad embarrassing and I really didn't know what else to do. Let's just forget it…' she said, waiting for him to take the lead on the drinks.

'Are you drinking? I fancy red if we're having steak? But you have whatever you want,' he said, tracing his finger up and down a wine list Rose had no idea about. She noticed he didn't wear a wedding ring.

'Sure, I'll have some too.' And she caught him on the verge

of smiling, ever so slightly.

An hour later and they'd ploughed through a couple of *fantastic* steaks; a filet for Rose – she struggled to think if she'd ever had one before – and Sean had what was known as a Porterhouse cooked medium rare. Some triple fat chips that had gone soggy from the bloody juice remained on Sean's plate. Rose didn't like blood, so she ordered hers medium well, which disappointed the waitress, but she really wasn't going to lose any sleep worrying about what some tourist thought about how she liked her steak cooked – she was the punter having an important business lunch, after all. After talking Rose through the reason he was late - something involving one of his guys having an accident and falling onto a desk - Sean explained, again, that he was impressed with her interview and wanted to get to know more about her as a person and the kind of things that really motivated her, to try and understand what made her tick. He told her that if she was open to a sales role with the business then he'd offer her more than the thirty thousand offered from FFB. Rose had lied when he asked her what the basic was. She may not be all that clued up on the various cuts of steak or unable to navigate her way around a wine list, but she knew how to squeeze things out of men fairly easily. She was by no means a gold-digger, but still, she could play the game.

'So tell me, Rose, what *motivates* you…really?' Sean said, holding her gaze. He was growing on her. Maybe it was the wine, maybe it was something else, but whatever it was, she found herself becoming a little attracted to him without being able to do a thing about it. He sat back and folded his arms.

She thought for a minute. 'Erm, the usual I guess. Money, lifestyle, independence,' she answered, truthfully.

'In what order?'

'Lifestyle, I would say.'

'Why's that so important to you?' he asked.

'Just is, I think…I mean, like, who doesn't want a nice

lifestyle?'

'Lots of people. Lots of people, they just want as much money in the bank. Retire as early as possible, sail off into the sunset once they've banked enough. Lifestyle goes out of the window while they save up the money.'

He was good.

'I agree to a degree, but you say that some people give up the nice stuff so they can save up and retire early? Isn't that the point - so they can have a longer retirement and a better lifestyle?' she said, with confidence.

'Could be, but I also interview kids who are from filthy rich backgrounds right...daddy's a multi-millionaire banker, they still live at home in a seven-bed mansion, girls have a horse, boys have a Porsche and all that. Kitty and Tarquin, and a load of other toffs come through our doors looking for a job that pays a helluva lot less than what you've been offered for FFB. Those kids are definitely *not* driven by lifestyle. They have what they want when they want, right?' he said, his stare getting a little more intense, reminding her of something else she liked about him; his dark features and green eyes.

'So...what *are* they motivated by then? Surely if they don't need money then they're not gonna be ambitious?' asked Rose.

'Well, you'd think so. But no, they are. Tell me what you think they are motivated by?' he asked.

She felt herself struggle to answer. Whatever confidence the last minute had given her, the next minute took it back.

Sean waited thirty seconds. 'The rich ones born into wealth simply want to prove they can do it on their own, without the help of daddy or mummy. They have points to prove. It's amazing what motivates people. So, back to you, why is lifestyle important to *you*?' he asked. 'Take your time.'

He signalled for another bottle.

'Hmm...it's hard to sum up. I dunno...I'm young, single, practically live in zone one, and don't want to go without.'

'Go on,' encouraged Sean.

'I mean...I want to earn good money and enjoy myself and go on holidays and drink in the best bars and buy the good things in life and not worry about bank balance. All of it. Neon lights, the whole shebang. Surely you get that?' she said, believing every word more and more. What was he getting at?

'Did you lack all that, growing up?' asked Sean.

'How do you mean...was I poor?'

'No, I asked if you lacked the quality of life you just described now, growing up? Not if you were poor.'

Rose thought some more and pushed some spinach around her plate. 'Thinking about it...yeah, I guess. We weren't that well off really, most of my friends had the new gadgets and stuff and I went without a lot of the time. Had to make do with big brothers cast-offs. Didn't think it bothered me, but maybe...' She stared down at her plate as she trailed off, unable to shrug off the one Christmas she went without a main present because her dad had been made redundant; something she didn't want to tell Sean about. She was guarded when it came to family affairs if not much else.

Sean looked at his glass of wine and twisted the stem.

'Stands to reason. They often say what you lacked as a child is something you strive for as an adult. That's why I was curious to know,' he said, his voice softening a little. He finished his glass of wine just as Maria appeared with another bottle.

'I hope you don't think you're in a shrink's office!' he laughed, closing off the conversation. He must have picked up on something in Rose's demeanour. Clearly, the lunch meeting was going to run into the late afternoon, thought Rose, caught in a dilemma between the sticky toffee pudding and Tiramisu.

*

By the time they left it was nearly four and already getting dark outside. Rose was a trifle lightheaded, but the mountain of food she'd eaten made sure there was enough to soak up the alcohol and keep being really drunk at arm's length. She was tired, mind.

St Bart's Square's cobbled pavement was glistening under the recent downpour; the full beams on taxis projected out across the road both ways and lit up the entrance to Smithfield's meat market, still fully operational as scores of men in white hauled carcasses in and out of the gigantic air-conditioned stores. The rain looked like it was about to turn into a light snow and dust the pavement. Maybe they'd have a white Christmas this year.

Sean had closed proceedings by informing Rose that an offer would come if she was interested; Rose was frank and said that anything less than thirty-two would not fly, plus the offer at FFB included pension, subsidised gym and a few other bits and bobs. Sean went on to explain that there was a scheme in place to earn equity in the business which would result in a very attractive lump sum upon selling the company, something he said he was aiming to do within three years. All of it seemed to work, however, and she wanted to get a feel for the culture of the company and people before making a decision. Sean's response was to invite her back to the offices an hour or so to meet some of the team and ask as many questions as she liked. "Do some of your own due dil."

After she'd agreed to that, he made a quick call out of earshot and then they made their way through the market, the smell of leather wafting through them and then out onto Cowcross Street.

Hopefully no remote controlled fart machines were on the horizon this time.

ELEVEN: MEET

I almost broke a sweat racing up through Smithfield's to get there. Thankfully she was already hovering around the entrance and talking to some young Latino-looking thing with a bloody tidy arse on it – the first thing I noticed as she led us through to our table. An arse almost as useful as Rose's I thought, admiring her Mexican cheeks bobbing up and down next to the English Rose petals. I wasn't sure it was Mexican, but I placed it to a movie I'd seen recently. But which one would I choose given the choice? Phew, tough one that, but the effort I'd put into meeting Rose meant only one answer could be the right one, and she was sitting opposite me for the second time in four days. And this time I was safe from the threat of Louis.

Things went well. Very well. Firstly she allowed me to choose the wine – I opted for the cheaper of the two Malbecs, knowing that a girl of her age wouldn't be a red wine connoisseur, and anything half decent could be paraded as a quality purchase, something that I wouldn't be able to do with Stephanie (when was I going to fit her in for round two, I thought, as I was drawn to the New World Wines).

On to the food. I ordered a Porterhouse, medium rare, and Rose had a 250g filet, to be cooked *medium well*, which the waitress and I didn't seem to understand, or like. She should have had the 'House Burger' as it would've saved me about thirty quid. The damn thing was the second most expensive cut on the menu and she wanted it cremated. I nearly wept, it broke my heart. To complement the meat we had the triple-cooked duck fat chips and I ordered the pan-fried field mushroom, and Rose went for the wilted spinach. *Pan-fried*? What else are you going to use to fry something in, if not a pan? "Well, I'd like my field mushroom deep fried in a vase of pressed coconut oil thank-you." And spinach...*wilted?* You fucking what? Wilted? No, actually I want it frozen with mashed plantains on the side. How else is it supposed to be delivered, other than wilted, or creamed? It's not a deal breaker. Come to The Grill on the Square because we'll pan fry your field mushroom and make sure your spinach is wilted to perfection. What next, describing a portion of cauliflower as sesame seed infused albino broccoli? The real top draw restaurants I go to, of which there have been many, have no such obvious hawking. As if people actually need to know every exact syllable scrawled down a menu that's too big anyway; words like *drizzled* or *fused/fusion* even *infused*, or *medley* or *pulled* or *slow*, it riles me. *Paired with* – that's another one. Chicken paired with a tarragon sauce/Laurel paired with Hardy etc. Oh yeah, I see the connection now, glad that's cleared up for all of us dummies who can't work out a fucking list of food on offer.

None of that if you're sat in J Sheekey, Daphne's, Clos Maggiore or L'Atelier. They tell you what it is, and if you don't like it then go to Frankie and Bennies.

To be fair, the food we had *was* good.

So for Rose, the plan from where I was sitting was fairly straightforward: get into her head and open up feelings as if she was sat in a reclining psychiatrist's chair, allowing me to dip inside her thoughts, relaxing her at the same time, so she lowered her guard. If you manage to get your subject to open up about life, feelings, daddy issues and so on, then after a few drinks when trust levels have reached the green zone, you're absolutely smashing the granny out of them.

That was the path I chose, and soon she was under my spell, lapping up the questions with a change in body language shifting from closed and formal into looking at me in fascination and buying into my tactics without realising it. That gave me the nod to order another bottle of the cheaper Malbec.

"Is the pope Catholic?" I said to the tidy waitress when she asked if we wanted to see the dessert menu. It took an age for her to work out, but Rose laughed.

Half an hour later, I decided that I wanted to offer Rose a job, but she started banging on about "thirty-two this, benefits that, right culture the other." That amount was going to stretch the budget. I thought about stretching something else following those words.

'The offer is good...but I just have one concern,' said Rose when I agreed to thirty-two being just about doable, 'I'm not sure the culture or environment will fit with my personality if I'm honest, you know? Not sure it's my *tribe*.'

Fuck I wanted to choke her on the spot, the ungrateful little sow, making me strangely more attracted to her. *Tribe?* She was playing me, and I couldn't help letting her. I decided to use the same course of action that I'd do if it was actually a sales call. Empathise, handle the objection, gain trust and then close. I went for it and gave an award-winning speech:

'Look, Rose, I understand you feel that way (*empathy*), I would feel the same way if I was in your position (*more empathy*), however, I believe the culture is suited to you as a person – I've come to realise that from getting to know you. My business is too important to take a punt on someone who I thought wasn't from the same *tribe* so please don't let one crazy incident impact your overall opinion of the company. Our profitability this year is *off the charts* (*handling her objection with a small lie*). So, if it's ok with you, why don't you come and spend some time with the sales guys...see how you get on (*trust*) and if that goes well then why not accept the improved offer and come and join us, you've got to look after number one, right?' (*Close*).

The importance of smart questioning. If done properly it really can add value and can get you over the line. Not just in business either; apply the same level of effort when you want to get your nuts in and you likely will.

*

I snapped the Amex down on the silver tray when the bill arrived, without me having to look at it. I had done the maths and calculated the cost to be around the £180 mark, including service.

'Shall we go halves?' Rose asked me, out of politeness, which I appreciated. Apart from ordering her steak medium-well and using the word *tribe*, she really could have done nothing wrong. Besides, I could educate her on the etiquette of steaks give it some time. March 14th is always a good day to (Google it).

*

I called Melanie and broke her good mood, informing her I would be back in five, putting an end to her online shopping and (nail) filing.

'Where's Louis?' I asked.

'At his desk. Nothing to see there, you'll be pleased to know. Think he's had his fill of trouble for one day.'

'Ok. I'm bringing in a candidate and I want her to sit with some of the guys, get a feel for the place. Can you check the demo sheet and see who's got what booked in til five, and let me know in a minute when I'm in...oh and tell Louis to make himself scarce. Ask him to go and buy some Christmas decorations or something.'

*

Walking into the revolving doors of Farringdon Place, Rose and I made our way into the warm reception area and left the freezing winter air that had viciously bitten into our faces on the short walk through the market. As the main door spun around, I caught a flash of a bald shiny head heading the other way. Thankfully.

Rose followed me up into the offices, the guys all gawping at her as she tailed me to the water cooler and then to my office. I told her to make notes and get her head around the sort of calls that were being made on a daily basis, ask them whatever she wanted to know and all the rest of it. I didn't quite care how she fared, my mind was made up, and it was down to her to evaluate if this was the place for her. I was really hoping Lady Fortune was smiling, and that Rose would accept.

'Melanie?' I called. In an instant, she appeared. 'Anyone got a demo booked in?'

A demo is when one of the sales team has a pre-arranged call to a prospective customer that usually lasts for thirty minutes, and consists of the said sales rep showing our offering to the decision maker they were meant to be pitching. I say meant to be pitching because a lot of the time they pitch fucking receptionists, resulting in fistfuls of my own hair landing on my desk. Phil's team take care of the advertising side of things, Mo and his lot sell subscriptions to companies wanting the intelligence. It's quite a clean segregation.

'Yeah, Stephanie has a demo coming up,' said Melanie. My panic button suddenly activated and flashed red at the thought of Stephanie and Rose conversing. There was an off-chance Stephanie would drop in some kind of subtle hint about our sexual history. Maybe I should hover around Tom in close proximity and keep an eye on things...or...

'Ok. Actually Mel? Just remembered something important, you got a min?' I said, apologetically turning to Rose and leaving her in my office. 'Two ticks.'

I let Melanie know the plan: she was to leave the floor and text me once she'd found a vacant meeting room, at which point I'd call her mobile from *my* office and close an imaginary deal that was on the cards. I briefed Melanie on the job title, company name and all the other relevant details. Her clear instructions were to haggle a bit with me and then accept the deal -ham it up as much as possible without going overboard. All of this in front of Rose. Risk aversion you might call it, keeping her away from Stephanie, and Louis if he returned back, strengthening the chance of getting her to come and join us.

My phone beeped ten minutes later and I grabbed Rose from hovering around Tom who was on his feet yelling at some poor German woman to spend twenty grand. So far so good.

She'd been sitting with him and asking questions and listening into his call. I told her I was about to make a quick call to a prospect and would she like to listen in.

Melanie answered on the speaker after two rings, and the show started:

Me: 'Hi there is that Jennifer?'

Mel: 'Speaking.'

Me: 'Hi, Sean Thomas. How are you?'

Mel/Jennifer: 'Oh…hi. How can I help?'

Me: 'Oh, sorry to call last thing. It's to do with the piece of consultancy on the solar energy markets you asked us to look into. We've sent the proposal last week…'

Mel/Jennifer: 'Erm, hold on, let me just open the email.'

Tapping on keyboard. Mel was doing well - she even took her laptop. Loyalty right there. At this point, I hit mute to tell Rose that the deal was worth fifty grand, and the salesperson, who had conveniently left the business, was due seven-and-a-half grand in commission if it dropped in. Easy money, wasn't it?

Mel/Jennifer: 'Yep. Got it here. Let me see now…you've quoted fifty all into commission the piece. Hmm…'

Me: 'Yep, half up front, and half on delivery. All in, as you say.'

Mel/Jennifer: 'Bit of a stretch…what can you do on that?'

At this point, I stood up. Showing balls.

Me: 'You can have money off if you want me to remove some of the components? Otherwise, that's the cost…we're not in the market to hike up unnecessarily, as I'm sure you aren't either?'

Rose was mesmerised, hooked.

Mel/Jennifer: 'Let me check my budget, I'll give you a call say Monday?'

Now was the time to show Rose what sort of outfit I was running (kind of).

Me: 'Negative. The offer submitted was conditional on signature of an order form by five today, or it goes up to sixty. I'm not bluffing, Jennifer. You're speaking to the owner and CEO. So, with the greatest respect, are we in a position to move ahead?'

There was a beautiful and long, tense, minute of nothing.

Mel/Jennifer: 'Ok...let's do it. Fifty it is. Can you send my P.A. an invoice for that, and date it for last week?'

Me: 'Absolutely...I'll get mine - her name's Melanie Green - to knock one up now and email it through. Just sign the attached order form and I'll get the R&A team on it right away as soon as it comes back. Pleasure doing business with you, and welcome on board.'

Mel/Jennifer: 'Great. And I must say, thanks for all your support recently, you guys really do provide great intel.'

Me: 'That's great to hear, thank-you. All the best. Bye.'

Click.

'*That's* how you close a deal!' I shouted with just enough energy to sound genuine. Rose was sat there in awe. She looked at me like I was some kind of Jordan Belfort. Done deal, in more ways than one.

'See how much money you can make here? That was...over seven grand in commission right, just for a proposal and a phone call,' I said without even lifting my head up from the notepad I'd been scribbling nothing on. 'You do that once every two weeks and you'll earn...hold on...*two ten* before tax. At your age? I'll have an offer over to you later this evening.'

Rose nodded confidently, and for the first time since I'd met her, I actually pictured her working for me and making me money. Soon after that, my thoughts turned to something less vocational.

TWELVE: CLOSED

Rose sat in Sean's office and stared at his strong, veiny hand as it slammed down the receiver into the cradle. Good hands. She always liked good, strong, manly hands.

'That's how you close a deal!' he almost shouted as the handle clicked into place. She had to admit she was impressed at the way he dealt with the call. Closing fifty grand on a call and the woman on the phone had been *thankful*?

Bloody good opportunity.

'I'll have an offer over to you later this evening,' he said, not really asking. He'd already mapped out how much Rose could earn working there versus the package that FFB had on the table. Over two-hundred-grand per year if she billed fifty every other week like he'd just shown was possible. That was...fuck what was the tax rate? At least a hundred and five take home anyway, maybe eight grand a month *after* tax. That was insane money for anyone, let alone a girl of her age. Lucy would probably hang herself.

'So what do you think Rose?' he asked, as she grabbed her coat and made to leave.

'Like I said...thirty-two plus the commission scheme you mentioned...and I'll think about it. I'm due to start at FFB on Monday, so if an offer is coming, it's got to be soon.' She was serious to a degree, but the opportunity was too good to walk away from. The urgency card was a good way to see how serious Sean was.

Plus there was another motive.

'Ok, you'll have an offer by six, latest. I've got another candidate who I quite like and they're only asking for twenty-five,' said Sean shuffling some papers. 'So, if we're good to go then let me know as soon as you can.'

Rose slipped on her jacket and shook Sean's hand before remembering she'd promised Mark to put in a good word for him.

'Oh...nearly forgot to mention. Another chap who I worked with at Aspinall-Willey - temp as well – *really* good with numbers. Qualified with some kind of financial stuff. Anyway, he's looking for something permanent. Said I'd have a word with you, in case you were in need of someone in finance or accounts?'

Sean smiled and nodded. He looked like he was already valuing her.

'Always in need of new talent. Send me his details and I'll get him in for a chat, and thanks. If we take him on there's a hundred quid bonus for you, too.'

Rose shook that firm hand of his and said goodbye.

'Actually Rose?' Sean called back after her as she waltzed out. 'I'm out all day playing in a damn golf day...tee off at ten I think. Any questions you got then email me and I'll call you after two when we're done. We can fine tune things. Cool?'

Fine tune things she laughed to herself. All this jargon she was going to have to get used to.

THIRTEEN: CLIVE
1952 - Present day

Clive Baker is a young sixty-five. Father of two – boys aged 40 and 37 – and once a loving husband until recently, still with a few shares here and there locked up within companies he's invested in over the last year since semi-retirement from his job as MD and co-owner at Foster Fisher Baker, or FFB as they were globally known, following his wife's quick death at the hands of heart failure. *A nice little nest egg for the boys when I finally go,* he often finds himself thinking when he checks the performance of his portfolio. Death didn't faze him so much these days, an inevitable change in mindset after the loss of his nearest and dearest.

Born in St Georges in Grenada, he was only ten when his parents immigrated over to the United Kingdom in 1962 when the sixties started to swing, eventually settling in Brixton and becoming part of the tight-knit Afro-Caribbean community that was already established and thriving: a community that despite the odd xenophobic sneer or *go home* insult, was welcomed with open arms. Brixton was their home, and they brought to it Caribbean music, food, dress, diversity, and more importantly, tolerance and understanding of other cultures.

He was educated in South London, and once he'd finished his A-levels began work as a teaching assistant in a primary school in Balham where he met the late Barbara. They married in 1975 and by 1980 had two boys to share the family home in Essex they'd moved into when Clive had moved on from his teaching post. Having two children in the space of three years - for Clive anyway - meant that he needed to make more money and give the boys the life he lacked growing up. By chance, during a temporary filing post for a bank in the city, he met Antoine Fisher, also working on a temporary contract, and, also looking for something that would pay the rent, bills, food for the family and more. Over the next months the two of them became close; Antoine, like Clive, lived in Brixton and was also a child to parents who had moved over to England from the Caribbean in the sixties. Their wives became close too, and the Baker and Fisher families became inseparable. Traditional Caribbean meals twice a week at each other's places, weekend trips around the country to get to know and love their new home, Church gatherings every Sunday. Life was good, but both men wanted more for their families.

Enter Peter Foster.

Foster had opened up a small law firm on Brixton High Street that specialised in representing Afro Caribbean families who sought equal rights once they had been accepted into the UK. The cause was stressful: legal battles with a whole battalion of authorities, intent on squeezing as much money from the community as they figured they could get away with. But Foster LLP kept going. They kept doing what, in their view, was right.

Peter Foster stumbled across Antoine and Clive in the summer of 1985 when they needed legal advice obtaining licenses to open up a couple of Caribbean restaurants, one in Brixton and one in Camden. They spent time going through the ins-and-outs of the proposed business models until eventually it looked like the proposal was doomed thanks to red tape and Thatcherite bureaucracy. Impressed by both Antoine and Clive's dedication and passion to their cause, coupled with a shrewd knowledge and understanding of how to grow small businesses, Peter asked them what kind of cash they had to invest into a small management consultancy he was in the process of setting up...after all, he needed at least one entrepreneur to work with him on setting up and providing guidance to the pool of clients he already had lined up. Conversations went well and between Peter Foster, Clive Fisher and Antoine Baker, they clubbed together and set up a boutique management consultancy with offices just outside Victoria.

Today, FFB is located in Bank, operate in seven countries,

and the balance sheet shows a figure just shy of thirty million.

FOURTEEN: CHAIR

The build-up to Christmas. The only time of year that makes the bastard weather just about bearable. It can be sub-zero – if you want specifics then let's say minus two – dark by half four in the afternoon and not light until nine the next day, front page news every fucking day going on about *potentially* the coldest December since records began and the usual closure of airports, motorways and gridlocked B-roads. Cancelled schools, grit machine deployment, local lakes are frozen over, kids on sledges in parks, weather warnings from the met office saying avoid non-essential travel and all the rest of the crap they're paid to report. Every spastic under the sun, metaphorically speaking, will pathetically put 'em up at the first dusting of winter snow. We are not Canada, we are not Alaska and we are not Sweden. If we were we would carry on as usual. We'd put on the duck feather duvets, we'd leave for work a bit earlier, we'd have a hot chocolate, we'd say hello to the postman as we leave the houses with roofs caked in a foot deep bed of white, waving a thermal mitt to the dustmen as they collect stiff bags of frozen waste, and we'd keep our country moving. But nope, not here. An inch of snow and we drop everything.

That is why Christmas in this country is such a lovely, lovely thing. No matter how fucked up things in December get, we have the Christmas period to enjoy: The Oxford Street lights – a thing of beauty, joyful carol singers knocking on doors, youngsters nativity plays, hot spicy mulled wine, Christingle and midnight mass for the religious people, the nostalgia of hanging stockings on the chimney, lots of family time, carrots and mince pies for Rudolph and Santa, Cliff Richard songs caressing your ears through the radio, tasty pigs in blankets, helping decorate the tree with mum or the kids, Christmas edition radio times, waking up at five, being woken up at five, dry turkey that no one likes, pretending to like the socks you get from some elderly relative, fucking Home Alone *again* on TV, Christmas pudding (seriously, are you fucking joking...who eats that garbage outside of grave-waiters?), not getting everything on your list, passing out at six so drunk you wet yourself, a board game you'd rather poke your own eyes out than play and inevitably lose, all of that washing up then that drying up, monstrous hangovers. Christmas.

It's down to me to organise the Christmas do, so I tell Melanie what the budget is and leave her to it. The rough plan this year? Book somewhere for lunch and make sure that we can stay there until six, then on somewhere else until we get ordered to leave. So long as I get a deal on it, I'll pay for all the food and drinks, and hopefully by the time we go on to the bar/pub I've trusted Melanie to book half the idiots who work for me will be well and truly mullered and fuck off elsewhere, leaving a much lighter bar tab. It's key to my plans in fact, and I'm sure that Stephanie will be ripe for another session…unless Rose surprises me. But no, play the longer game with that beauty.

I watch Melanie's tits, which are held together in a tight red number, jingle into my office so she can run me through the plans for next Friday. I simply agree to the first thing she proposes.

She's done well and organised a set menu at some ok-ish place nearby, and she's got the bar area with music from five until ten, so we don't actually have to bother getting up off our butts and go elsewhere. I can well imagine that by five, half the company will need scraping off the floor.

*

It was nearly three on Friday, and to be honest I'd been ultra-busy and neglected a lot of things. For example, I'd spent the first two hours of the morning responding to important emails in between watching some well-choreographed point-of-view pornography, taking me through to eleven. I decided to go for a stroll in the cold crisp air, somehow stumbling upon a massage parlour that happened to insist on a thirty-minute massage that – much to my dismay – included what they said was a *happy ending*. I've never heard of this happy ending thing before, so I asked them to elaborate. Damn inconvenient if you ask me, but I gave in seeing as it was approaching Christmas and I hadn't bought myself a present.

A reminder flashed up on the screen: *Mark Muir chat*

Damn it...Rose's pal. I'd had a quick chat with him over the phone and he said he'd be able to pop in and see me today just after three. Fuck. I was busting for a crap and about to go when Melanie alerted me he was waiting in reception.

'Can you go and grab him please, or get someone to? Just gotta go and send a fax to Japan.'

'Of course,' said Melanie, sucking on the tip of her pen. She looked doable today, very doable indeed. Maybe I'd have time for a quick...nope. Just a shit.

After my dump – a 'Ghost Poo' that was in and out in less than a minute, nothing on the tissue after one wipe and it had already disappeared round the u-bend and out of sight when I went to look what was there – I was surprised to see that my office was still empty, and Melanie still at her desk. She answered me before I asked.

'Sorry, had to take a call as soon as you left. Only person free to go and get the chap waiting was Louis.'

'Ok no bother, thanks,' I said, confident that Louis could behave himself for all of two minutes and perform a simple task like showing a candidate to my office less any buggering about.

I was wrong.

Louis smashed through the double doors to the sales floor making *broom-broom* and beeping and screeching noises, in between an impression of Murray Walker commentating on a formula one Grand Prix race. I was literally speechless as I, and the whole sales team, watched him running along the side of the office, pushing a chap in a wheelchair! The chap I was about to interview. When he was a few meters from my office he sped up and shouted at the top of his voice; 'and here comes Hamilton on the inside and into the final straight, Hamilton's going to win it! Hamilton wins the Farringdon Grand Prix!'

'Alright, china? Where shall I park Mister Hamilton then?' he asked, thoughtfully. Incredibly, Mark didn't seem too unsettled.

'Thank you, Louis, leave us now, please. Goodbye,' I said with closure. Mark extended his hand out and shook mine firmly. I was so embarrassed.

'Sorry about that, he's a bloody nightmare. Sean Thomas.'

'Mark Muir, nice to meet you. Don't worry, to be honest it makes a change from the usual pussyfooting about I get from most others. No 'arm done and all that,' he said, in a proper cockney voice.

*

Taking Mark on boosted my *social responsibility*. Hannah had told me that I had to employ a certain ratio of females, ethnic minorities and, if possible, someone who was technically (using that very word) either mentally or physically challenged. Seeing as what we do requires a degree of intelligence, except maybe Melanie's job, I figured it was better to choose physically challenged over mentally. In front of me was this chap who interviewed very well and was qualified in accounts work, and I could use someone to keep track of all my expenses and stuff, keep an eye on the cost of production and payroll and things. It would free up more time to focus on the core activities that drive the business forward, such as happy endings dished out by the odd nineteen-year-old illegal Romanian. Even more satisfying was that he wasn't too concerned about the money; his exact words to me were "as long as it keeps me in beers, bitches and bagels, then I'm 'appy."

He told me he got a decent disability benefit and lived at home with his folks, so the paltry sum of twenty-four grand a year would mean he can live like royalty. "The Prince of Wheels" I joked. He laughed, I offered, he accepted. Then it was time for the other offer I had to chase up.

FIFTEEN: DEAL
April 2016, Bleeding Heart Tavern, Farringdon

At 45, Jason Willey is the co-owner of Aspinall-Willey Management Consultants; a global advisory services firm that was formed in 1997, headquartered in Farringdon. He also holds shares in other companies dotted around London, and a couple in the States, investing his profits from the main business into companies who needed an injection of liquid to grow or develop new products and services. He was even shortlisted to become a dragon on the popular *Dragon's Den* television show.

Back in April, he had been approached by the owner and CEO of a smallish trade journal and business intelligence firm. Sean pitched him for a quarter-of-a-million quid in return for 5% of the business, which he estimated was worth £1.8 million at the time. Due diligence was practically second nature to a man like Jason, so he did some research and what he found after a few hours of digging was that the company, with the right leadership, could become a global leader in the solar energy intel market. They had a unique set of reports, both printed and online, offering data and analysis - a unique proposition that the market was lacking. Red hot topics equalled a potential goldmine if the information and data could be harnessed and turned into meaningful insights, with the correct leadership in place. But Jason didn't just want to invest. He wanted to buy the company outright, so the lunch meeting that had originally been scheduled to discuss a potential investment turned into a formal, structured proposal to buy STI Ltd.

The direction of the conversation didn't go as desired, from where Jason was sitting anyway. Sean was in no way, shape or form willing to be bought out, and appeared to be insulted at the half-million offer Jason made. For a company that had been trading for just two years, it was like a lottery win, but Sean didn't share that view. The dialogue turned a little salty after that, so they said their goodbyes and went in opposite directions. *Nothing lost*, thought Jason. He wasn't a fan anyway, not personally. Sean was going on about the perks of being the owner and how he had "pussy on tap all the time" as if he was trying to impress Jason. Jason found him obnoxious and slightly immature, and any buyout would see Jason manage Sean out of the business as quickly and cleanly as could be permitted.

But Jason wasn't used to being denied anything. In fact, he worked hard for everything he wanted. From the age of eleven, he took on a paper round, in order to earn enough money to buy the things he wanted. Spokey-dokeys slapped round the wheels of his BMX, Queen's new album played on a shiny personal cassette player when he was on his way to watch Chelsea, bag of penny sweets clutched in his spare hand as he jumped on the tube, and then after the football he got home and played with his radio-controlled Porsche or Scalextric set. At sixteen he spent £500 buying a second hand Ford Capri and another £100 cleaning it up before selling it on for £900 - the profit of £300 he used to go on his first lads holiday away from home with his older brother and his pals. It was only Mallorca, but it was a milestone. He was wired that way; making money was built-in to him. He was a proud man, too.

In the cab on the way to meet with the owners of a company he had some shares in, to crunch some numbers and generally catch up, a plan came to him.

SIXTEEN: MONEY
May 2016, Comptoir Gascon, St Barts Square

'I'll have my accountant arrange for the funds to be transferred as soon as the contract is reviewed by our legal team,' said Clive as he took Sean's hand and confirmed his words with a firm shake. Two-hundred-and-fifty-grand for fifteen percent of a business that showed a healthy balance sheet and an even healthier product was too good to let slip by the wayside. Sean said he wanted the products to be best-in-class, and Clive really believed that they could be over the next couple of years with the right captain steering, and over ten years, the money they turned over with a year-on-year 25% profit margin would make for a very nice retirement fund, or God forbid if he snuffed it, a couple of houses and a windfall of seven figures for each of the boys. Not that Louis needed anything. Louis, the younger, was in his own words a "stay at home husband", "a full-time daddy" or occasionally a "house-husband."

That boy needed something to occupy his mind. A proper job in the city, doing something that, well, just doing *something*. Not a patch on Nathan, the prodigal son who was a year into his life as a Managing Partner at Deloitte.

*

'What's he good at?' asked Sean, finishing a white beer.

'Good question. Lots of things, but you know, he really has a knack for picking up on new technologies quickly…always on one of those social media sites. He knows all about them before anyone, really,' promoted Clive, also finishing his beer and burping up a taste of white wine mixed with cream, from the mussels. 'Teaches me something new every time I see him, does that one.'

Sean scratched his temple and thought for a minute. 'Well, I do have the need for a Social Media Executive, actually. I'll have a word, and unless he's a total clown I'm sure we can come to an agreement.'

It wasn't strictly what Clive meant. He got his wallet out and beckoned the garçon over, so Sean knew he was serious about the offer by paying for lunch. Sean didn't pick up the subtle message, so after a few seconds, Clive broke it to him.

'I want a guarantee. Give my son a job, and I'll invest tomorrow. He's a good kid, after all, he won't let you down,' said Clive, unable to shed his thoughts of the word *clown*. He'd have to have words with him, mind; let him know he had to take the job seriously instead of all the larking about he knew he was capable of.

So that was it, Clive settled the bill, Sean agreed, and they shook on the spot. The deal, in principle, was done. Clive Baker was soon going to own fifteen percent of STI.

*

The funds came from his accountant in Grenada who took care of the small local businesses that were under the ownership of Clive and Antoine. Money they would recoup from the sale of one of their premises to Aspinall-Willey, who were going to open up an office in St Georges. It wasn't really an office per se, but if a shed could be listed as an asset in the asset column, then who cared?

Phase one, complete.

SEVENTEEN: PARTY

'Oi oi, get the pitchers in then, would ya?' shouted Mark to someone, as he downed another glass of toxic Long Island Iced Tea. It looked more like a jug of sewage water with white, plastic, debris bobbing about on the surface rather than a Tequila based drink.

Every Tom, Dick and Harry got informed that he was getting "legless," and didn't they know it. Even the odd stranger who walked past our mob on the way to the toilets was notified.

The routine was that Mark would spot someone who he hadn't introduced himself to, or at worst not spoken to properly and grab their attention with an "awite mate!" whilst holding his arm out to high-five the poor soul and then pick up the pitcher nearest to him, down half of its contents and shout out "Oi Oi, I'm getting legless!"

When I realised it was a standard performance, I started counting each time he did it. Eleven times. Pretty much every person in the company, and all of the other normal punters upstairs in the other bar got to see it.

On top of that, half the gimps sat around the table seemed to believe they were on a fucking beach in Hawaii and not the downstairs function room of a place called Coin Laundry which, I was informed by the slim, homosexual walking sperm-bank that was our 'host' for the night, used to be dry-cleaners. In Clerkenwell.

Clerkenwell.

Clerkenwell, Hoxton, Shoreditch, Angel, Farringdon. The cool part of the city. Not the EC1 of Liverpool Street, Moorgate, Bank, or the E1 of Canary Wharf, where stuff actually gets achieved. Nope, not round here. The place is a hive of agencies: recruitment, media, creative, advertising, full service, marketing, promotion, PR, digital, internet, branding, media planning or design. All of them with one common denominator;

the people they employ. To qualify for a job around Clerkenwell, you have to be a trendy hipster wearing jeans with turn-ups, sport a spiky multi-coloured hairstyle, claim to be a vegan and only drink *ethically sourced* coffee from a recycled paper, bi-sexual cup. I was at Old Street station the other morning, and there was a giant of a woman walking in front of me clutching what looked like a bag made out of Band-Aid plasters. As if that wasn't enough, half of her hair was missing and the other half was dyed green, and she wore a sheet with a couple of makeshift holes for the arms. Several piercings with enough silver pressed into her face to rival the Oxford Street branch of H. S. Samuel littered her coupon - at least ten earrings divided between two ears and four studs around her mouth and nose. Black lipstick was smeared all over a face whiter than a white thing, and across that, a pair of glasses stolen from Dame Edna Everidge. To top it all off, she was on stilts. She was on stilts. Say it out loud.

Honestly, I'm serious. She was walking on stilts. Ok, they were small ones, but wait, what? Stilts. All this at 8.50am on the way to work. Even more incredible was that no-one except me glanced twice. Not a soul. You see that kind of thing every day around the places I mentioned. A far cry from the tailor-made, pin-striped Zegna suits, William Hunt shirts and Hugo Boss silk ties that sit above three hundred quid pairs of Barker shoes housing Ralph Lauren socks. All of that's a *very* far cry from us, yet well within walking distance. The bankers - the ones who earn more than Libya's national debt in a year - they would stick out like a white man in Willesden if they came this way. EC1 is where I'd choose our offices to be if the monthly rent wasn't the equivalent of a whole street of townhouses in Mayfair.

So there we all were at the Christmas party in the grubby hipster paradise of Clerkenwell, and despite being surrounded by utter morons, Melanie had done well, surpassing herself in terms of value for money. For something like £25-a-pop, we got a thoroughly decent and safe three-course meal. I say safe because anything fancy would have been received with complete chaotic confusion from half the chavs who work for me. *Smoked salmon with a lemon mousse* on the menu would have read back as *something foreign sounding next to a pudding dish*, a no-go zone for sure. It was either winter vegetable soup or chicken liver pate – again the pate option confused half of the team - *we ain't in France though?* - followed by a traditional roast Turkey dinner with all the trimmings (or a nut roast if you were a fucking rabbit like half of the people round here seem to think they are), and then a choice of Fig pudding or Chocolate Torte. Imagine the dilemma there for those idiots; something disgusting vs. something else foreign sounding?

"Cor blimey guv'nor can't we just av apple pie n custard?"

All of that with a glass of Prosecco on arrival and one bottle of house wine between two. So for £25 a head it was a real bargain, and the quality surprised even me. We had a good sized group: eleven sales guys, Hannah from HR, Melanie, Mark, Louis, Phil and Mo, Sandra from marketing plus the five analysts who put together the databases, three from production who do all the printing of journals, some smelly contracted out Indian kid called Darminder who invited himself along, and yours truly. A mob of twenty-eight. Twenty-eight times £25 equals £840 including VAT, so I chucked another £500 behind the bar, totalling £1340. A whole afternoon of boozing for the whole company was, in my book, a bloody great deal. Well done Melanie, not just a cracking pair after all.

It was getting later and the afternoon was dragging on and everyone except Sandra was plastered, so we tried to go and see some new Syrian stand-up comedian called *Mo Saffaf* upstairs in the main bit of the pub, but he was sold out, which is a shame as he's literally the next big thing according to my sources who are ITK (*in the know*, but you'd know that if you were ITK).

Even Darminder was barely able to stand up and I didn't think his lot drank much except for that fucking piss awful mango juice or a tin cup of water that'll give you Cholera. The last I saw of him, he was leaning on the wall and trying to chat up Hannah, who looked over at me with desperation in her eyes and mouthed "help." Obviously I ignored her. It's always fun to pretend not to see/hear and turn your back and hope, pray even, for some kind of mild sexual assault to be dished out by a drunk, Indian I.T. creature. An assault on the leading authority for red tape and political correctness, aka HR. The fireworks that follow an accidental and drunken molestation are worth the entrance fee alone. It's almost enough to give me a riser thinking of all those HR boilers getting stern and reprimanding inebriated pests from the third world.

So, I turned my attention to laugh at the dunces who were jigging away on the small section of wooden flooring as a selection of songs from *NOW! That's what I Christmas volume 50* boomed out. Louis was spinning Mark round in his chair to *Rockin' around the Christmas tree*. Louis and Mark had, in just under two weeks, become best friends. I'd sat Mark opposite Louis and begged for him to not distract Mark for at least a week while he found his feet, something I instantly regretted saying as Louis pointed out that his feet were probably made of wood. The promise not to distract Mark for a week was short lived; it was approximately two hours in on Mark's first day when Louis played his first prank by sticking a note on the back of his chair: *Kick me, but not too hard becoz I can't run after you!* Thankfully no one actually kicked Mark, who bizarrely found it funny, giving Louis clearance to hurl all kinds of wheelchair-related banter in his direction all day, every day. One afternoon straight after a pub lunch, Louis dew a penis on the back of his chair and sellotaped a sheet of A4 next to it that said *I HAVE A THIRD LEG TRUST ME THAT ONE WORKS, ASK ALL DEM BITCHES!*

So yeah, the daily carnage in the office, usually only at the hands of Louis, was amplified somewhat. But it was nice to see Mark settling in well.

At about eight, people started drifting off. Rose, who had accepted my desperate offer of thirty-five grand and joined us last Wednesday, was becoming more and more flirtatious and she looked fucking rude. Her tits, by my reckoning, were probably 30D's – slender back but racked up to the eyeballs – and they seemed to jut out of her tight, red Santa jumper and into the New Year. She had given the bird to the near Baltic weather and put on a skirt so short that most people would have assumed it was a shoelace, but it complimented the knee-high leather boots she had no trouble bopping away in.

I was like a dog on heat.

Even though I'd probably had two litres of decent red wine, paying extra for my own, a few vodka sodas and at least four heart-stopping lines of decent gear, I actually got a semi from just talking to her. We'd spent a good half-hour chatting away about deals and things, and she seemed genuinely interested in the business, asking me really taxing questions about profit margins, cash flow, forecasted revenue and stuff. Really impressive for someone so young, and I think she was trying to impress me. I rolled with it, naturally. Anything to give me a chance at getting her on her back.

'Fancy a line?' she asked. 'Everyone else seems to be getting involved.'

'Nah you're ok, I've got a bit of my own, but thanks anyway,' I said, instantly becoming more attracted to her. There's a fair chance that an incredible, head-turning girl in her early twenties knows her way around the selection of class A drugs London has to offer, but until you're a hundred percent certain, well then you aren't.

'No, I mean, wanna go and do one...' she said nodding over at the toilet sign. 'Disabled ones are free.'

Fuck. Was it actually going to happen? Was I about to lock myself in the disabled bogs with her and get to do what I must have had at least twenty wanks over already? No, she was just being friendly, generous to her new boss...showing him she's not *that* prim and proper. Best to assume that, rather than expect the other, that way I wouldn't get let down. Expectations need to be kept in check, always.

Disabled toilets...thank God for the disabled. As Glenn

Hoddle famously said, "disabled people must have been bad people in their previous life." Well as far as it went for me, the disabled of today were fucking saints - their toilets are just perfect for a nice comfy shit thanks to foam padded seating and armrest, or more appropriately, ingesting drugs and potentially getting your nuts in.

'You go and I'll follow…I'll knock when the coast is clear' I said seconds before she disappeared out of my sight and down the corridor.

Rose let me in after one knock. She'd already chopped out a couple of sizeable lines, way more than I would have. That's the thing about girls and gear - they have no idea how to manage their packets. You can slip a wrap of coke to a bird in the pub, and an hour later she gives it back to you empty. They seem to gobble it up as if it's a gram of di Caprio's jizz.

Her eyes widened as I slid a fifty out of my wallet and handed it to her.

'Ladies first.' I stood back and admired her bent over the toilet to snort it up off the cistern, enjoying the view of her traffic-stopping arse which was less than a foot away from my face.

'Your turn…' said Rose, handing me the nifty. I wasted no time in demolishing it. It was good stuff as well; it had that chemically kind of tang to it, like brand new paper or a felt pen. As I surfaced, Rose was standing there totally silent, just smiling at me minus her jumper which was draped on the toilet door's handle.

I was dreaming surely…my heart went berserk and tried to explode its way through my jumper. But her tits? They just seemed to sit upright in a lacy red number, and I knew when it was removed that they'd be staying exactly where they were. And they were clearly fake, something I'd been dying to find out since the first time I saw her/them.

'Aren't you going to take your top off, too?' she asked, walking a few paces and putting her hands on my hips. That was it…that did it. My wotsit sprang up like an angry jack-in-the-box, and I traced my hands along and over the top of the bra and then inside, squeezing at the silicone and yanking at her erect nipples. Jesus Christ. A dream come true. She kissed me softly on the lips and I took in the mixture of lip gloss, JD and Coke she'd just had a sip of and a tiny hint of cocaine that she'd got on her lips after licking the credit card. A perfect combination; fruit, cola and gear. The soft kiss turned into a longer one, and before I knew it, I was trying hard to reach her tonsils with my tongue, and she was licking my lips and face and biting my bottom lip as I clinically removed her bra – sometimes it's a mission to get a bra off, but this time the God's were with me, and it jumped off and onto the floor, double quick. Oh yes, the God's were definitely with me, all but confirmed when they sprang out. It was like the unveiling of a brand new, gold-plated statue outside Buckingham Palace. A thousand gasps followed by a round of applause and whistling ringing out from all four corners of the Earth. "Ladies and Gentleman...I present to you...The Knockers of Rose" and whoosh, down comes the curtain to reveal the most amazing creation ever to grace the planet. I could hear a chorus of "*Hallelujahs*" vibrating around the toilet. In my twenty-four years of sexual antics, escapades, activity or what have you, I have rarely come across a set like that, not even in Vegas. Perfection doesn't see to do them justice. I clamped both hands on them and began to enjoy the eighth and ninth wonders of the world, hands at first, then with my mouth as she pushed my head down from hers, inviting me to have a nibble.

'Fucking hell,' I said out loud, coming up for air. She shook her head as I went to lift her skirt up and see what joy awaited me there.

'Uh-uh...wrong time of the month,' she said.

Plan B in that case.

'It isn't for me,' I said, half-joking, but curious to see how she'd react.

'Oh...is that so?' she said and turned around to sit on the toilet and unbuckle my jeans, greedily yanking them down. She looked at it for a moment, then at me.

'Wow. You're a big boy aren't you?' she whispered, before licking around the base and running her tongue up to the tip, with lots of eye contact and all. It all got too much and I guided her head down with my right hand and held on to the rail thing that the spastics have to hold on to when they're having a dump. She was comfortable on the foam seat, and I was holding onto a rail. Two more benefits of these toilets, thank you very much, Mr Hoddle. I lasted no more than a minute I was so worked up.

'How about in the ass?' I asked her half-way through (thirty seconds), but she shook her head as she carried on. I could hear heavy nasal breathing and a small 'mmm' indicating a decline to my suggestion, which was just as well because, by the time I'd registered it was a negative answer, I'd bolted my load, big time. I doubt she was expecting the pint of wallpaper paste that followed, for sure, but guzzled the whole lot anyway and didn't gag. Impressive, but did that mean she did this a lot?

'That was a nice fourth course,' she said with a slutty smile, even stretching as far as to put it back in my pants and pull my jeans up for me. I was in love. I actually fell in love right there.

We were broken by a knock at the door followed by Mark shouting something like "hurry up in there else I'll wet myself!" Talk about perfect timing!

I laughed. For an accountant Mark had a…well, he *had* a sense of humour.

'One minute…having a dump. Use the men's,' I shouted, as Rose packed herself back into the bra and made decent; swilling the rest of her drink around her mouth as the steel scraping of Mark's wheels disappeared.

We'd got away with it. Rose went to kiss me again, but I moved away so she landed on my cheek. One thing I won't do after a bird's swallowed is kiss them on the lips, I'll always pass on that one. She told me she had to go off somewhere and then sneaked out of the fire exit once the coast was clear. I got my breath back for a moment, and took a minute or so to just let what had just happened sink in, and celebrate. It was like I'd won Wimbledon or a Golf major, I had to stop and register it. A lottery win. And I wanted more.

Mark stopped me as I made my way back in and glided over to the bar.

'Nice dump mate?' he asked.

'Yep. One of the best I've ever had,' I said, as I caught Stephanie staring over at me as a pissed-up Tom jabbered away.

EIGHTEEN: SEVEN

There's never anything particularly nice about doing it, but Rose was switched on and headstrong. On her third day at FFB, she called her line manager - a Spanish guy called Paolo who she thought shouldn't really be as tall as he was – and told him she was off, and that she didn't expect to be paid. She thanked him for the one-and-half days of assistance he gave her by setting up email and a tour of the building, then packed up and popped in to see Jason very briefly, before walking out into the freezing cold smog that was blanketing the city. She had nearly a whole day to spend; some last minute Christmas shopping was probably a good shout.

The lights of Upper Street were already gleaming and the place was an animation of Christmas. Upper Street is always busy, regardless of the time of year. Busy in the mornings and late afternoons with commuters, and then shoppers, students and tourists who don't have such inconvenience potter around in between during the daytime, before the evenings flow with diners, drinkers and cinema-goers. As her heels clapped on the pavement by Angel tube, she took in the warm and comforting smell of hot and spicy mulled wine and meat cracking on a hot plate being served from a tiny stall that had twists of steam rising up and out into the rest of the world. A queue of punters lined up patiently to get their Christmas sausages and wash them down with mulled wine. That lot would cost a total of eight quid - five for the hotdog and three for the wine - two pounds change from a tenner. She joined the queue, and thought how she could well afford this sort of luxury now - just a couple of weeks ago it would have been unthinkable, the same money could have got her enough groceries to feed her for two days. She stared up at the menu board and watched her breath get in the way as it spilled out of her, curled upwards and then disappeared forever with everyone else's. Her phone pinged. It was a message from Sean detailing where the STI party was being held, and that he expected her to join them even though she would be only a few days in when they had it. It would be a good opportunity to meet the other departments, anyway. He signed off with just *S x*, which made her feel a bit rebellious, without really knowing why.

After an hour finishing off some shopping and acquiring a very cute little number for the party, she got home and went straight to the bathroom and turned on the hot tap, and then slid in for a hot, foamy soak.

She lathered six grand's worth of silicone liberally with the foam, sixty percent of the inheritance she got when her Nan passed away. Not a crumb of guilt that she spent the majority of it on transforming 30 A's into 30 DD's. Her *weapons* her close friends labelled them, her bazookas, wobbly warheads, cruise missiles and countless other nicknames they dreamed up for a few weeks after she'd returned from the surgeon's knife. And yes, they were weapons, absolutely. But not secret. She couldn't have kept them secret for love nor money - they stuck out like a librarian at a thrash metal concert. She used them to get most things she wanted, where men were involved. All men; she even caught her own dad looking at them a couple of times, which was awkward. She could go out for an evening wearing a low cut top, and guys would be queuing up to buy her drinks. She'd rarely have to pay for a drink all night each time she went out, thanks to her assets. Six grand well spent. She'd recouped at least half of that in free drinks over the past year.

She slid further into the bath and lost herself in bubbles and began to think about the nice young lads she'd occasionally allowed to see them for real in the past couple of years, the ones she'd taken home. And then Sean popped into her mind, unannounced.

And seeing as Lucy was out, she reached for the shower head, twisted it round to *massage*, opened her legs a little and closed her eyes.

*

The following Friday morning, with no regard for her own circulation and inviting the sort of frostbite reserved for explorers of the North Pole, Rose dressed her lower half like it was July on the Costa del Sol. She was going to put on a sexy G-string but had come on in the morning, so went for a pair of knickers that would be better suited to Lucy. The big, heavy-duty granny knickers that lurked at the back of her top drawer and only given an outing when she'd run out of smaller ones. *Sean may have to wait*, she thought, feeling naughty again. But then that wasn't necessarily a bad thing; it was always better to wait and let the anticipation reach boiling point – added to the intensity of it all. Anyway, she could still have a bit of fun if she wanted, she was certain he would be game at the Christmas do.

*

Although still a little disappointed with herself that she only accepted thirty-five, she was glad on the whole and enjoying her time at STI, getting on well with most. She had actually hinted to Sean that, despite being at FFB only for a couple of days, if an offer too good to refuse came her way, then who knew what would happen, then Sean sent over a simple message that read *would 35k do it?* so she keyed in *yes, send the contract and I'll be in tomorrow. What time do you want me?*

She was in for nine, and after two days of sales training with Phil, she was up and running. Mark was sat in the corner opposite Louis, who she saw messing about when she first went in to meet Sean. The noise coming from the pair of them took her back to her school days, but she didn't mind; it was nice to see a familiar face in the office.

Mark had interrupted Louis – who was tapping away dementedly on his phone - and introduced Rose as his drinking buddy. Louis looked up and shrugged his shoulders before rummaging around in his desk. Just as she turned around to go back to her desk, Louis called her.

'Sorry Rose, really rude of me. Louis Baker. Nice to meet you,' he said and shook her hand. Something buzzed and vibrated in her palm, causing her to jump in shock. *What an absolute tosser.*

*

Rose turned up dressed in a red Santa jumper and a tiny skirt with long leather boots, ready to let loose. It was a competition to see who had the worst Christmas jumper on, judging by her team members efforts: Tom was wearing a Star Wars themed one, Robbie had flashing lights on a tree, Phil had one with a Christmas pudding on it, Josh had a bland grey number with a few patterns on it, and Stephanie had on a dark blue one with Rudolph on the front, his nose a red stick on bobble. Nothing remarkable.

Enter Louis and Mark. Louis was pushing Mark who was cradling a pair of hot baguettes and a couple of cans of diet coke in a cardboard fresh fruit tray thing. Louis had obviously mistaken Sean's request for everyone to wear the worst Christmas jumper for "can everyone put on the rudest jumper you can find?"

He had on a dark blue pullover that had a giant penis – complete with two balls – wearing a red Santa hat. Not only that, the penis had eyes and a smiley mouth with a nose dangling free from the front of the jumper, and underneath it read *Bingle Jells*. Mark had gone one better with a t-shirt that depicted a naked Mrs Claus bending seductively over a log fire, Christmas pudding between her legs, while Santa - minus his hat which was on Mrs Claus - sat in a chair, looking on with rosy red cheeks and a massive bulge in his trousers. A speech bubble that hovered above him had *Tis the season to eat pu~~ssy~~ dding!* written in the middle of it. Incredible.

Luckily Rose's drinking partner, Sandra, was a bit of a square and only wanted half a glass of wine, so Rose smashed through practically the whole bottle on her own. *Winner winner, Turkey dinner.* Following that, Sean informed everyone that there was a bar tab to get through, so she punished the Jack and Coke's, and it wasn't long before she'd tucked into her Bolivian - always such joy after a few early drinks to be able to straighten out. She also got the major horn from it. Sean seemed to be fixated on her jumper for a while after dinner, and people were either dancing about or trying to remember how to speak English. No harm in suggesting a quick line and seeing what happens...

*

Rose had not seen anything that big for a while, not since her second year uni days when she briefly dated the captain of the University first fifteen rugby team, a Welsh lad who was hung like, how did she describe it... "hung like a shire horse on steroids." To be fair, Sean was probably about seven, and she could only fit half of it into her mouth. Anyway, it had been fun, and when they'd finished, she gave herself a pat on the back as she left via the back door and climbed into a cab, shooting off through a city pulsating with Christmas, to go and meet Zoe, who was having her own do. Another unlimited bar tab and more, fine young men to choose from, no doubt.

But Sean...something about him that stuck with her. She was becoming a bit hooked on him, and she hadn't even slept with him. Best keep her distance, but maybe it was that which was making her feelings start to rebel. The power of negative suggestion.

*

Later on in the evening around midnight, Rose got a message through on WhatsApp from a French number that read *mission accomplished.*

NINETEEN: PRIZE

I was woken by a strip of light that crept in through Stephanie's curtains. It was a clear and sunny morning, and it shone through the crack and straight onto my face. I sat up and looked around the room and got my bearings. The light painted her wooden dressing table with a single streak of honey and stretched across the mahogany. The first thing I noticed as I rolled over and patted the other side of the bed, keen for some form of relief, was that I had a mouth like sandals at mecca, and that ferocious type of boner you get when you wake up after a session, blood still pumping furiously. But alas, she was still out for the count and remained so, despite my sliding up to her and prodding her in the back with the tip of it.

It turns out Stephanie is also a massive bugle head; following a few more drinks at The Coin Laundry, we slipped off and jumped in a cab and went back to her place in Dalston. Dalston is a shit-hole, but her house was quite nice, and she shared it with two other French girls who were obviously clean and tidy. One of them was up when we got in, and the other one was home for the holidays. The flatmate who was up, Sophie I think she was called, was quite a plain looking girl-next-door sort, an innocent lass. In my state, the first thing I wondered was if she'd be up for a threesome, but that was short lived because as soon as we sat down and opened a bottle of wine purchased from one of those all-night Turkish supermarkets, she left us to it. I was fine with just Stephanie, and after literally smashing the whole bottle in about ten minutes, we retired to her bedroom and had that steamy brand of drug-fuelled sex. She proved to be far dirtier than the first time, thanks to hoovering up Pablo's dandruff half the night. I had her in front of a lengthways mirror whilst I pumped into her from behind, then her on top of me (official reverse cowgirl), then her legs up and over her ears (the wheelbarrow), and even at one point she was arched over her dressing table with her arse in the air as I stood on tiptoes and mounted her like a rutting stag (there is no name for that, so I call it the *Secretaries inkwell* – work it out.) A proper top session, and as I'd already bolted once thanks to Rose, I went on for at least forty-five minutes before I gratefully pulled out of her and peppered her arse. She was exhausted and looked at me like I was some kind of maniac. As she towelled herself down and passed me some toilet roll, somewhere in the distance of my head, I wondered if thinking about Rose so much had caused me to take such a long time to cum. I kind of wanted to be next to Rose and not Stephanie, but the feelings were diluted, slightly numb, thanks to the hard partying. So we stayed up until about three smoking, drinking and taking it in turns to chop out lines, and then at some point, we played some weird game where we had to guess each other's social media passwords. She wanted to prove a theory that whatever password you have, it always represents something in the past or present that is *really* important. We had to give each other clues, and she managed to guess my Twitter password after a process of elimination through questioning, and then we finally flopped down into bed and passed out. Something inside me told me to sleep because I remembered that I was due at The Crown at half eleven in the morning as Spurs were at home to Chelsea. It was the early kickoff, so a massive day lay ahead.

Chelsea at home: one of the biggest fixtures in the calendar, a fixture that when we saw the time and date, a collective groan rang out between me and the other Spurs boys in the knowledge that it would probably be on a Christmas party hangover. But anyway fuck it, it was Spurs, and nothing gets in the way of that. Ever. Plus it was the perfect excuse to crack on where I left off a few hours before. As with Arsenal and West Ham, it's one of the first fixtures you look out for once the schedule is released. We usually play them in November or December and then again in March or April. If there's one team I hate as much as Arsenal then its Chelsea - a club that was in mid-table obscurity until they were bought out by a Russian billionaire Oligarch, pumping money at everything. Within two years he had bought the league title, paying stupendous amounts of money for the best players and the best manager in the world. Money talks - and boy does it in football. That club though - buying their success. Their fans? Racist beyond belief. They played abroad not too long ago, and after the game they wouldn't let a black man get on the metro, hurling racist abuse at him. The fans epitomise the club. Chelsea FC, despise them.

*

The Crown was empty despite the whole pub being filled with visual noise. Sparkling tinsel, massive holly wreaths, staff in Santa hats and mistletoe dangled from the wooden beams. The other decorations were Carl and Steve who were sat by the fireplace, and all of a sudden it felt like Christmas was really close.

'Right boys, who wants what?' I asked them, both with about two inches of beer left in their glasses. Awful timing, on my part.

'Hello son,' said Steve cheerily. Carl looked up and nodded. He had a bit of a vacant look on him; he'd started on the gear already I reckoned. If anyone likes a London derby more than me, then it's Carl. He gets so up for it. West Ham, Arsenal, Palace, Chelsea or even Millwall if it's a cup game, he's just super powerful and not afraid of a tear up, either.

'Usual please,' said Steve. Carl nodded.

I got the round in.

'You look lively,' said Steve.

Our glasses met.

'Cheers,' Steve and I shouted. Carl nodded.

'Tell me about it. Three finish,' I reported.

'Oh yeah, what did you get up to?' asked Steve. Carl nodded.

'Work do last night. Ended up in Dalston with that French chick, nailing our packets and then having a bit of grime. Don't feel too clever to be fair but, fuck it, only one thing for it,' I said, draining about half a pint of Hells in one gulp. It slipped down very well, and I knew come kick off I'd be wonky again.

Carl nodded, and charged off to the toilets.

'Is he at it already?' I asked.

'Mate...he was at it before ten. Stayed in last night. *Proper* up for it. Gotta watch him.'

Steve is the elder of the two but Carl a lot more powerful. Big brother's usually quite busy on days like these.

We took a cab to Enfield and got the train to White Hart Lane, arriving at nineteen past twelve. The seven-minute walk to the South stand entrance where we sit was hasty and silent as we contemplated how we'd be feeling in less than two hours. When you're on the way to the ground before an important game, there's a kind of silence as you approach, aware that very soon the thing you've been talking about for the last couple of weeks will be underway, and all you've been hoping for will just be a cluster of nice thoughts because when reality kicks in, its eleven men versus eleven men. No amount of fantasising or dreaming can influence what is going to go down on the pitch. I liken it to the run-up to Christmas as a child. You look at all the presents under the tree and pick one out that a) looks big and b) you have no idea what's under the wrapping paper. You wonder about it every day until it's time to open. You may get something pretty decent, say a remote-controlled car. That would be a slim one-goal margin victory for Spurs. However, you might find it's just a big box used to keep something difficult to wrap up in, like a pair of bookends or a fucking paperweight. That would equal a Chelsea win, or at very least a draw that they didn't deserve. But, you may unwrap Darth Vader's fucking Tie-fighter, with batteries and all, so you can play with it straight away. That's a comprehensive win for Spurs, a good solid margin with no elements of luck involved. A victory that even the staunchest of Chelsea fans would have to admit to.

On our way to our seats, we pass the visiting supporters

section: a queue of geared up and boozed up chavs, protected by a line of police horses. The abuse that both sets of fans dish out to each other is quite basic but aggressive and frequent. As we breezed past a sea of Burberry, Stone Island and mouths on shaved heads snapping away, Carl decided to gesture the wanker sign, prompting a dictionary of intellectual and well thought-out replies such as "you fucking mug, your mum, you cunts, wankers," and so on.

But Carl does not do things by halves.

It dawned on me exactly what "just going for a slash" really meant when Carl ran ahead of us on the way to the ground, as he slid out a full bottle of something cloudy and yellow from his pocket.

After he'd twisted off the cap, he looked around and launched the open bottle over the line of police horses and into the set of braying hooligans waiting to get into the ground, the majority of them still hurling expletives in our direction. Not one copper saw him throw it, but a good ten Chelsea fans did, as the bottle twisted down on them showering them with 500 mils of Carl's urine.

It was one nil to Spurs before a ball had been kicked.

Going into the game, Chelsea were sat at the top of the Premiership, with us in third place and only two points behind, with Manchester City sandwiched in second and not playing until Sunday. A win would take us top.

Which is what happened after two goals from Dele Alli secured a two nil win. I got the Tie-Fighter with batteries.

Back at The Crown after a few more beers Carl stopped nodding and piped up, finally regaining the power of speech.

'Shall we make the call?' he said, having demolished all of his already.

'I'm still ok...got a couple left. But you two go ahead,' I said, regarding Steve's happy smile fade into panic.

TWENTY: FRUIT
September 2016, FFB boardroom, Bank

A bowl of fruit sat in the middle of the solid oak table - oval in shape - that was in the boardroom on the top floor of the offices of FFB.

Apples, almost mutant green in colour, nestled next to bright yellow bananas, while shiny oranges wobbled at the top of the pile waiting to roll off onto the table at the tiniest tremor. Clive moved his seat a foot to the left so he could reach the fruit and plucked out an apple, and looked across at Antoine, waiting for the meeting to begin.

The boardroom was big and airy and had a huge HD ready TV clipped to the wall at one end, opposite a floor-to-ceiling window that presented a magnificent view over the city and out to the jagged skyline of Canary Wharf. Sat there flanked by acting MD Peter Foster and Jason Willey, Clive felt a surge of pride flood through him. The boy from Grenada born to poor parents, sat on top of the world, with a twenty-five percent stake in a thirty million pound business he'd set up twenty years ago with Antoine and Peter. Barbara was always so proud of him.

Peter Foster clicked on the big screen. STI's logo came up next to a screenshot of Sean's LinkedIn profile.

'Right gentleman, let's get this meeting underway.' Foster addressed the other three, filling up a glass with sparkling water and plopping in a slice of lemon using tongs. He watched it sink to the bottom and waited for it to rise back to the top before he spoke again.

'We all know why we are here. Between the four of us, we have over a hundred years' experience in this game. So I anticipate that come…' he said checking his Rolex, '…that come three this afternoon, we'll have some sort of rough plan. Now then, does he have what you might call an *Achilles Heel?*'

TWENTY-ONE: FINALE

The end of the year was on us. Being the considerate boss I am, I allowed my staff the time between Christmas and New Year as holiday. That meant that the last week of the year was 19th to 23rd of December, although I was fucking off on the Wednesday. Most people get in for half-eight, and no one leaves until half five, earliest. They have targets to hit and so do I.

It was all hands on deck for a solid week as the guys hammered the phones and tried to take the remaining budgets of anyone willing to spend with us. It was an incredible sight; grown men on their knees hiding in the cubby hole under a desk trying to concentrate as they begged some poor marketing bod to spend three grand on a fucking banner that will yield nothing but timewasters enquiring about their God-knows-what rubbish service. It was like walking into a zoo full of orangutans or chimps swinging about and screaming down phone receivers.

The other guys, the subscriptions ones who sold the actual database of intelligence, don't have to work as hard because what they actually sell has some value and could almost be called necessary.

And I loved it. I loved to see those monkeys sweating blood and tears, trying to close a deal for the three grand that may make them three hundred quid commission at best. So satisfying. One thing I did need to get straightened out was the years' numbers to submit to HMRC so they could bill me for corporation tax. To be honest I don't have an issue paying taxes, but I do have an issue paying twenty percent of my profits to a government who want to spunk it all on fucking Trident, when local councils are happy to turf out old aged pensioners from their accommodation, should rent not have been paid over a couple of months. This was where Mark came in handy. His clear instruction from day one was to keep the profit margin looking as healthy as possible, for this year anyway, but ensuring the cost column had enough in it to avoid paying an unnecessarily large amount of tax, telling him I had every confidence in him to do this (the feel-good factor), being candid in my explanation that the better the balance sheet looked, then the higher his bonus would be. Definitely a good incentive to get him to fiddle some numbers.

A large coffee sat on my desk still piping hot and untouched as I added up all the revenue we had billed so far in December. We were at one-fifty, with the final week to go. Another hundred or so would drop in. Nice. Half-a-million, gross, in two months.

Back to the coffee, however. I had to tell the barista I wanted a *tall* one. Is it just me, or do you need an MA in the English language to order a basic morning bevvy? They had three options: *Regular, Grande and Tall*.

Ok, so *Regular* is the smallest in fact? Maybe call it *small* then. *Grande* is really medium although you're led to believe its *Grande*, or large, or big or whatever, which to most people means large or big. And *Tall*? What the fuck? How tall - Peter Crouch, Jaws from James Bond, that massive freakish beanpole with glasses from the Guinness book of records sort of tall? Is it tall and wide, and therefore bigger than the *Grande*, or is it tall with the same circumference as the *Regular*, making it slightly smaller? See what I mean?

One day, the torturous process of finding your way out of a labyrinth of language just to get a coffee is all going to be too much for me, and when in line and sweating over what words I need to pick, I'll end up pulling out my *Grande* penis to fire a few extra *shots* of vanilla, with *Regular* ferocity at the *Tall* barista who's unlucky enough to be in my way.

So while I was boiling over the coffee nonsense, I started to panic at the annoying part of my job that is the end of the year *performance reviews* I have to do, acting all responsible as a company director, conducting a series of one-on-ones with key staff. The key staff are Hannah from HR, Sandra from Marketing, Phil and Mo the sales managers, Louis, Melanie,

Nigel - who heads up the analysis team - and Belinda in charge of production. I had outlooked all of them for an hour-long review at convenient times but forgetting Mark. It was a quietish day for me anyhow. I arrived into the office for around ten and had a half-hour chat with Sandra about next years' focus. "Keep it up" was the vague conclusion, and I praised her for the work she'd done this year despite not having a clue what that was. She could have plastered the company logo all over a paedophile's chat room and Tweeted an encyclopaedia of racist, anti-semitic abuse to the Jewish community, and I'd have said the same thing.

Next up was Hannah. I was very pleased with her support this year, and in the New Year I was also going to bring in some support for her, and promote her to *HR Business partner* which would tie in with a performance related bonus come June. Well, that's what I said, anyway. By June she'd have forgotten all about the conversation anyway. I was impressed with how I just reeled all that off the top of my head, adding some shine by reading from imaginary notes on my pad.

Nigel's review lasted six minutes after I asked him how he felt he'd done this year, and he replied: "yeah ok" to which I replied, "Yeah, agreed. Keep it up champ" and then he left me alone.

That was it...almost.

Belinda was off the week, so there was no such timewasting with her, and Phil and Mo were too busy with their teams to come and have a review, which I said it would be, thus stalling them. "Let's park it until Jan, and do a proper 2017 review then" I said to them as they actually believed I was going to bother. I say almost done because as I snapped shut my notepad following Nigel's departure, I realised I needed Mark to sort the accounts out and to have a kind of mini-appraisal with him, keep him onside, and at least appear to value him. I kind of did anyway.

'Can you grab Mark? Bring him in here, please?' I said to Melanie on the phone. It was late on and I could see the back of

Mark twitching away as he entered some numbers into a spreadsheet. Two minutes later he appeared in my office.

'Yip, you rang m'lord' he said in a stupid voice.

'Take a seat...sorry. Hi. Need you to fill out the usual balance sheet and submit a tax return to HMRC. Need it done by this Friday as well. Can you do that?'

He looked at me like I was mad. 'Does a bear shit in the woods? Of course, I can...just need to access your accounts database and we're good to go.'

'Of course, I'll send you the username and password now. And thanks...the less tax we have to pay the higher your bonus will be, but keep the balance sheet nice and healthy, hide some things, do some moving about, if you catch my drift?' I said with a wink. He winked back and touched his nose.

He knew what I was getting at. Mark was alright.

TWENTY-TWO: HOLIDAY

I was booked onto the 13.35 London Kings Cross to Leeds train, arriving at 15.51.

Christmas time with my family. One of the only times of the year I genuinely look forward to outside of London derbies. I left behind a company in decent shape; it had been a solid year and even better was that I had abused my position to nail two sorts in the last few weeks.

The following week after the party, I purposely kept Rose late behind at work one night to talk about prospects, and we'd ended up going for a drink in Farringdon, and then I finally got to get her into bed...it was worth the wait, for sure. Tight, neat, shaved. I had hit the jackpot.

It does rank up there with the best sex I've ever had; an incredibly hot, twenty-three-year-old with fake Bristols going for it with me. All night. Fucking hell...if I said I was in love after the Christmas party then I was ready to get married on the spot, just a few days later. Age is just a number at the end of the day; Rose acts like she's at least thirty and I act like I'm thirty-five so actually, intellectually speaking, there is only a five-year age gap. Plus I don't look forty-one. She didn't tell me that yet, but I know she thinks it. She'd said she'd like to see me over Christmas if at all possible. I was on cloud nine. I was basically dating a girl who could pass as a porn star, and just to think, had I not taken Tom home that afternoon, I'd never have laid eyes on her. I kept telling myself it was fate, destiny, written in the stars and all the usual mumbo-jumbo more suited to a lovesick teen than a grown man like me. We arranged to meet up on the 29th when we were both back in London, and already I was planning on what to do: dinner somewhere cool, then a night in the W hotel and a good long session.

But until then I had Christmas to tackle.

*

I arrived at my sister and her family's house in the late afternoon, already steaming. Virgin first class is *the* best way to travel anywhere over an hour. Big comfy seats, two plug sockets and free food and booze all journey. Getting the train at half-one as well - off-peak so if you get on it early enough, you get a whole berth of four seats and big table to yourself. You can stretch out, eat loads of free food and get smashed on any drink you want. Maybe flip open the laptop and do some work, or more likely watch a film. Then you're always where you need to be on time. Bravo Mr Branson.

I walked into the kitchen and got cuddles from my sister and two nieces, probably the only three females on the planet who trust me, I reckon. Even my own mum doesn't. She told me so when I broke up with my last girlfriend; a long-term one that the family really liked, despite her being a narcissist.

'You're a bad bet. If I was a female I'd steer well clear of you,' my mum said to me, after finding out I'd broken it off with Jasmine following an accident, then an abortion.

'Well you raised me,' was my reply, and she soon came down from the moral high ground.

But Christmas was an *ocean* of booze, as usual. I went on a shop with my brother-in-law Keith and bought a case of Prosecco, twelve bottles of decent wine, and a couple of crates of beer. I always like to buy a load at Christmas when I go up north, pay my way and all that, plus my dad was arriving from Scotland the next day and he loves to take a drink. I found myself really looking forward to catching up with him and tucking into a fucking bathtub of grog.

*

Dad arrived on the twenty-second and remarkably his journey down from the Hebrides was free from any complications, which I told him I thought was positive, until he shot me down straight away with a "yes but who knows what the return leg will be like." He actually began to worry about a train and plane journey five days away, adding that he hoped his roof didn't lose any tiles in the storm that was headed to the island he wasn't on. Anyway, I put those thoughts to bed and we had a good catch up over dinner and when the kids went up, we absolutely smashed into the booze, so much so that I lost count of the bottles of wine we managed to empty over the course of the evening. I do recall at some point messaging Rose on WhatsApp, and she read it but didn't reply, which got me a wee bit miffed. It was just a polite *how's it going?*, but then in my desperation to get her attention, I sent another message, attached to a picture of me naked that read *this body is longing to see you again,* which again she read but didn't reply, even more annoying as it made me restless trying to get to sleep.

'Fucking whore!' I said out loud, and threw my phone on the bed aggressively making it bounce off the other side and crack the screen.

The next morning I woke up early to a trio of madness thumping away up and down the stairs. From seven o'clock. My youngest niece – Megan - entered my room without knocking, and asked me if I wanted a cup of fresh coffee that my sister Lily was busy making. It was hard to get cross at being woken up so early by the innocence of a child, even with a horrendous hangover. I asked her to pass my phone after accepting the offer of a cuppa and checked WhatsApp again and saw Rose had last been online at 2.03am, without reply, still!

Was she with someone else, or out partying, or in bed just flicking around? If so, then why the silence? A load of paranoid questions and various unpleasant potential outcomes started speaking to me from inside my head (which was pretty sore). I've had lengthy debates with people on that subject; some saying they didn't sweat over it, but I beg to differ. When you're really into someone, how can you not be? I've lost count of the number of boilers I've ignored in the past who have messaged me the moment they notice that I've read a previous one and caught me online, the dreaded *typing...* appearing next to their name as they frantically try and cajole you into a conversation as if it's the law. It's not nice when the boot is on the other foot, mind. Maybe it's payback for all the times I've ignored some poor Doris who wants a chat. Karma's only a bitch if you are, I suppose.

I slouched through to the kitchen and had my coffee, which was double nice - none of that *Tall or Grande* rubbish, just a straightforward mug of fresh caffeine. Lily makes great coffee. Rose would get back to me; it's rude to ignore your fucking boss.

After I'd showered and rid myself of the small hangover, which included a wank, we all went shopping to do some last minute bits. I bought my dad a *lot* of clothes because a subscription to the weather channel was a bit too tricky, and some other crap for the old people in the family; the usual patronising boxes of toffee, scarves and toiletries. What a waste of time and money. Another scarf to add to the twenty-odd Grandma had accumulated in the last five years and a gift-wrapped box of Toffee for Grandpa who is practically fed through a tube these days. What else can you do? They'd be better off with a one-way ticket to *Dignitas* in Switzerland, but that's not my call. Just as I was coming out of *Next* clutching two bags of clothing that looked like it was from *Next,* my phone vibrated in my pocket, and I hoped and prayed it was a message from Rose.

My heart skipped a beat when I opened it, wondering if it was good or bad. Maybe the silence so far had been because she was waiting to horribly inform me she didn't want to keep seeing me or something. The suspense was terrifying. I didn't even read it at first, I just looked at the end of it and saw a kiss.

It turned out I was, of course, being stupid. She informed me she was taking a break from WhatsApp for the moment because it did her head in, and that she'd be able to text now and again over the break. I thought I'd leave it for a while before replying and let her sweat for a bit, see how she liked it. I had the upper hand, the power. The ball was in my court, and

I was happy at that, so much so that I bought my nieces and nephew a big bag of sweets. Each.

TWENTY-THREE: TWIT

'If I hear the word *opinion* once more I'll throttle you. Now, if you have nothing of value to add to this meeting - which *I* consider to be closed - then I'll leave you to it.'

Inspector Diana Cornish showed Police Constable Pritesh Sharma the door. Sharma wasn't flimsy though, far from it. Thick skinned and a stubborn streak. Who did this obnoxious white woman think she was? He'd show her; he wasn't ready to leave.

'It wasn't *hate speech,* and you know it, Diana. You're just doing something to show you're doing *something*. Six words, count them. Six.'

Sharma was referring to a Tweet he'd sent two days ago, hastily and without thinking through the potential consequences. It was enough to cause a bit of a shit-storm, what with the rapid onset of social media, and how these things can go from zilch to a million views in a matter of hours. Chief Inspector Woodruff handed the matter down to Cornish to deal with once there was sufficient bad press.

The tweet simply read *women should know their place #sharia.*

He wasn't that accustomed to Twitter and thought he was replying privately to someone he followed who had shared an article about women's rights under Sharia law. But the journalist who shared the article has over fifty thousand followers, and within probably eight minutes, the tweet had been retweeted over a thousand times and posted to Facebook. Within another minute someone had discovered that Sharma was a police constable at Islington, and two minutes after that twelve tweets had hit the @metpoliceuk Twitter account. (The varying levels of criticism ranged from one user *tweeting @metpoliceuk do you plan to investigate this sexist member of staff?* to the candid *show some balls and fire this waste of skin but you won't because it would be 'racist' @metpoliceuk*). The associated press was all over it and the story made just about every mainstream newspaper's Twitter accounts, but as with all things social media, it old news a day later by the time Cornish had Sharma sat in her office asking for an explanation. The Directorate of Professional Standards had got hold of it and wanted answers, however.

Sharma's defence, at first, was to say it was one of his friends playing a prank on him, but then foolishly went on to contradict himself by arguing it "wasn't anything that bad." Cornish had replied that it was no better than hate speech. Typical woman, overreacting like that, that's all she was, he thought, as she dressed him down.

'Ok. I'll show you what I'm talking about. Let's see if the message sinks in. Stay where you are, Pritesh,' said Cornish tapping away on her brand new laptop – a recent *Thank-You* from the met for fifteen years' service. At least a grand of laptop just a few inches from him, yet light years away and out of sight, too. When would *he* ever get such recognition?

'Right, here we go. Come round.'

Cornish vacated her chair and invited Sharma to replace her. One day he'd be there for good, he thought, sliding into shiny leather. The screen showed a news article from *The New York Times* from 2015 and gave an account about how a racist taunt had turned into a bloodbath as some demented teenager went on the rampage in a Philadelphia mall and slashed his way through six unlucky shoppers. He took it all in but likened her reasoning to the butterfly effect.

'See what I'm getting at?' Cornish said, once he finished skimming over it.

'Yes, but I don't agree.' You had to give him credit for his balls and arrogance.

'Ok. You don't have to agree, but because of all this, you are being investigated by the DPS. I'll have a nice new assignment for you first thing, Pritesh. You may leave now,' said Cornish. This time he did.

TWENTY-FOUR: MINDS
September 2016, FFB Boardroom, Bank

'How long have you got?' said Clive, straight away in response to Peter Foster's opening question about the *Achilles Heel*.

'Go on,' said Foster, his eyes widening with intrigue. Jason's wry smile said he knew where this was going.

'The chap's a joker. Womaniser. As you all know part of the agreement we have is that Louis works for him – a condition of the money I fronted – and he agreed on the spot,' continued Clive. 'Anyone of sound mind wouldn't trust my son with their cup of tea, let alone give him the responsibility of handling the company's social media profile.'

'So how do we use Louis in all of this, or, would he even be open to participating?' asked Foster.

'Already on it, Pete…you underestimate this lazy man of Caribbean heritage. We do have brains, you know.'

Clive often accused Peter, with his tongue firmly poking his cheek, of never taking anything he said seriously since he'd been semi-retired and chose to spend half his life trying to get his handicap down into single figures.

'He feeds back to me about how the company is run, the way he's constantly in and out all day long, interviewing young and pretty girls every other day to suit his own – it would seem - *addiction* to sex.'

'So…' said Foster.

'Last I heard from Louis was that he'd interviewed three very cute girls for a non-existent job, just so he could give himself a chance of getting laid. He's not discreet about it, either.'

Jason looked up from his notepad as he finished writing something down. 'How is that going to help a takeover? What do we do, offer him unlimited access to high-class hookers as part of the deal?'

'He'd probably go for that, I suppose,' answered Clive, straight up.

'I think you forget the purpose of this meeting, gents. He won't *sell* the company to us, to Jason, or whoever...not for what we want to pay, anyway,' Foster said, his voice twitching with impatience. 'He's deluded. Thinks it's worth silly money. Between us we can figure something out, can't we?'

Antoine, generally mute during most meetings, piped up. 'It would be much easier if he was *forced* into it.'

'Oh, so you're going to press a gun to his temple?' said Clive, laughing.

'No...but let's do some research. Look at case studies of past, hostile takeovers. Forced hands, so to speak. That's gotta give us some ideas.'

'Good shout. Try and find any that involve women at the centre of it...honey traps. Sounds like it would be appropriate. Tax evasion's another good one,' said Foster.

'Yep, and I know someone who could be perfect for the honey trap thing,' said Willey.

'So do I, actually,' said Antoine, topping up his water.

TWENTY-FIVE: JOURNEY

Rose's journey home to Cambridge measured up abysmally. On top of a forty-two-minute delay leaving Kings Cross, she had to share the foursome of seats with a tattooed beast and it's two screaming brats, causing havoc for the entire journey. The mother must have said "oh ahm so sorry luv" at least twenty times over the course of the journey, a ghastly arrangement of apologies leaving her mouth thanks to the string of irritating mishaps happening at nice regular intervals, the pick of the bunch when brat number one spilled his fruit shoot all over Rose's copy of The Metro she was trying to occupy her mind with. But Christmas was around the corner and she'd be home soon enough, she thought, each time she had the strong desire to jab her clenched fist at someone nearby.

But she wasn't home soon. At Cambridge station, the queue for taxis was fifty strong by the time she'd struggled through the barriers with her holdall and three carrier bags brimming with presents. She could barely walk carting it all around. *The bus?* But the one and only bus going through the tiny village of Impington was cancelled and both parents were working late and they'd left a key out for her. *There's some lasagne in the fridge just microwave it when you get in x* her mum had texted her in the morning. Chance would be a fine thing. *What to do...?*

She tried Uber. None around for miles and it was cold. She was stranded, but called her mum and dad on the off-chance one of them may be able to help out. Unfortunately for Rose, her mum could do just that. Unfortunately, because it meant the saviour called into action by their neighbour who, although willing to pick her up, was driving in a very old Fiesta that three miles from home decided to snap its own fan belt; the hazardous weather and busy time of year took care of the recovery vehicle arriving twenty-seven minutes longer than *Guaranteed response within half-an-hour* that they lauded on their website. As Rose and neighbour Jack, a creepy old loner, sat in the car with the engine running to keep warm, she'd had to endure his bizarre dialogue surrounding political correctness and the word *Christmas*, harping on about a shopping centre in the city not having a tree because it was offensive to non-Christians. He did have a point, but she just wasn't in the mood to get into it. When the recovery van finally did arrive, the hooligan driving it didn't even apologise. Screw him, it was his *job*.

When she finally got home two hours later than planned, she dumped her bags, heated her food up and poured a large glass of wine.

'Finally, Christmas has arrived. Eh, boy?' she said, stroking Archie, who hadn't even bothered to nuzzle up to her and welcome her. He was more concerned with her plate of food, and just sat there beating his tail on the kitchen tiles and staring up hopefully. Her phone pinged up a notification on WhatsApp as she took a gulp of wine: a message from Sean on top of hundreds of others from the other group chats she was added on. WhatsApp was annoying.

Later that evening, after Rose had spent a good hour discussing her new job to her mum and dad - who both struggled to grasp what she actually did - she got a bit of life in her and went to the local to meet a couple of old school pals and say "Hello Happy Christmas" and all that. A quiet drink turned into bottomless Prosecco at some awful chrome and carpet type establishment in the centre, where for fifty minutes they abused the deal and quaffed as much as possible with minimal conversation, until midnight when the deal ended, when they staggered onto the dance floor and shamelessly danced away as a steady stream of drunk herberts bought them double vodkas, repaid with words of swift and harsh rejection.

Come one, she staggered out to the taxi rank that was mercifully quiet; her journey home made only a tad more interesting when she received a picture from Sean coupled with some words that appeared in double-vision.

*

The next morning, or technically speaking afternoon, she forced herself to get up and participate in some lunchtime drinks with her parent's friends. The Wilkins' impressive kitchen/utility room was awake with conversation and Christmas songs; the smell of spices coming from the mulled wine and nibbles welcomed her when she finally made an appearance. Two couples – friends of her parents - had descended upon the Wilkins' household and were sat there cheerily drinking and enjoying a selection of homemade mince pies and other little delights her mum had knocked up. Mrs Wilkins was dynamite in the kitchen. Unfortunately Rose really wasn't as up for the polite chit-chat directed at her as she was for the food and drink; explaining with a brave face exactly what she did, and what STI did. It was painful on a hangover having to run through it on four separate occasions no less, the ins-and-outs of what she was paid to do.

"Ooh that sounds really interesting" or "oh so you're a city high-flier now?"

"Well no not really, I'm basically a telephone monkey who's already shagged the owner," was what she wanted to answer, but as normal she held it in and nodded politely. That reminded her - she had best reply to Sean before he wonders if she's still alive, keep him sweet. On text though, or even better, a call.

She had to be careful, discreet.

TWENTY-SIX: ASSIGNMENT

"It's really not that *bad*, but it's essential we clamp down on it. I thought you could experience first-hand the damage it can cause, Pritesh.'

Sharma found himself digesting a three-page document detailing out specific instructions for his next assignment. He kept staring at the title: *Met Police to increase surveillance on social media abuse.*

Bollocks, he thought, running his eyes, again, over bullet points that were looking at him with narrow and vindictive eyes. *Hurtful and abusive messages concerning but not limited to: race, sex, disability, age, religious beliefs, hate speech, death threats and threats of violence, treason.*

'You are joking me...surely?' His first five words as he stepped into her office following a ten o'clock summons.

'Do I look like I am? It's there, in black and white,' said Cornish, trying to keep the laughter from escaping. 'The Directorate of Professional Standards, or DPS as you and I know them, are investigating your little Twitter misdemeanour at the moment and have requested that you be put on restricted duties. Hence, this nice little assignment for you working in the Community Safety Unit, monitoring racially motivated malicious communications.'

Sharma was dumbstruck. Being investigated by a load of job-worthy creatures was bad enough, but to restrict him by making him sit on fucking Facebook and Twitter all day?

'But, please. Diana, I'm beg-'

'From tomorrow, *you* are going to be handling all the complaints passed to us regarding the matter, *and* you'll be investigating the ones that could pose a risk to the safety of individuals or groups.'

She had stitched him up, properly. Fucking Draconian, that's what she was.

'This isn't what I do, Inspector. It's not what I'm good at.

You proved your point yesterday...I get it. Duly noted and all that.'

'But you *didn't* see the point yesterday. In fact, you were quite adamant about your position, I seem to recall, weren't you?' she said, her eyebrows rose in tandem with her pitch before she took a sip of a hot drink. The steam made her specs foggy.

'But I mean-'

She raised a finger and cut him off. 'Not open for discussion Pritesh. DPS and Woodruff have made their decision.' She was a stern woman alright, quite the bitch when she wanted to be.

'I don't need to explain myself to you, but I'll do the decent thing and give you it anyway,' she said, preparing herself with another gulp of what was something boring, probably green tea. 'We're taking a *very* serious stance on the issue in light of all the recent media attention surrounding it. We have to toe the line, to be seen tightening up on it. You know how this all works, Pritesh Your stupid, ignorant tweet the other day is what you might call *unfortunate* timing.'

Sharma felt himself shrink, but Cornish wasn't finished. 'Look at the last week alone. Two teenagers cyberbullied so badly they took their own lives. If your boy was a teenager you may be a tad softer in your mindset and actually see it as a necessity, rather than assume it's just me trying to...*inconvenience* you due to a personal vendetta.'

'Jesus. You are actually serious aren't you?'

'Deadly. Look, Pritesh...' she relaxed herself a notch.

Here comes the compliment...

'You're a good guy and I value you...the work won't go unnoticed. If it leads to arrests that we can shout about then it'll raise your profile. Try and look at it as something that will help your career, not least in Woodruff's book. So, are we all clear, now?'

She was a teacher dishing out a firm but fair bollocking to a pupil who'd argued about not doing his homework because he disagreed with the subject matter. He stayed silent for a minute, prompting Cornish to stab into the pocket of silence and repeat herself.

"Are. We. Clear?'

'Yes, Inspector. From tomorrow then?'

'From tomorrow. Now I'll let you go as I'm sure you've got things to be doing,' Cornish answered, without looking up.

For the second time in less than twenty-four hours, he left her office wanting to kill her.

TWENTY-SEVEN: CAPABLE
October 2016, FFB boardroom, Bank

The next time they met was two weeks later. Same quartet of shrewd businessmen in the same boardroom with the same agenda. The only difference was that Peter Foster entered carrying a pile of printouts. He sat down and divided four copies of *The Sydney Herald* from October 2014 between them.

'What I have here are some examples of how companies have, in the past, been forced into selling. Some of them make for good reading, if a little bizarre. Take a look at this one,' he said.

The printouts showed a detailed description of how a company called *AdA Trade* had been taken over by *Maddison Holdings*, a conglomerate of IT and FinTech companies, for ten percent of what the company was thought to be worth. Even better for Maddison was that the owner of AdA Trade was a self-made millionaire who had a history of tax evasion, and had been married and divorced three times thanks to a tendency to play away from home, always getting caught. Bad press for the chap. AdA Trade's name was mud, plastered all over social media and the news for a week, forcing the share price to plummet followed by a full-blown investigation into the previous three years of trading, which revealed that the accounts had been fiddled somewhat to avoid paying the right amount of tax. It resulted in the owner being sent to prison for a short while and forced into selling the company for a pittance. *Cutting his losses before serving his time,* the headline above two pictures of the owner, Andre di Agostino, read.

'Sean's not married, though? And how do we know he's been withholding tax? And even if we did, how on *earth* would we be able to expose him?' Antoine asked, the first to speak since they'd been handed the article.

'That is something we'll need to work out. Like I said to you all last week, there are four, brilliant, creative minds sat here around the table, so I'm sure we can think of something. Think of the end game.' Peter sounded as determined to make it happen as Jason first was. 'Now then...these girls you mentioned last week. How do we get them to agree to help out? Money talks, but, I dunno. Young women under extreme pressure? I think you're being optimistic.'

'I beg to differ on that. Who I have in mind is capable of helping out for the right incentive,' said Jason. 'Definitely.'

'And what about Louis, Clive? How can we use him in all of this?'

'That joker'll tuck anyone up if it provides him with a laugh. Throw some incentive in there and he'll likely go to town,' said Clive, laughing at the thought of his son doing some proper damage.

TWENTY-EIGHT: TURKEY

Christmas Eve arrived in a bit of a blur. Every morning the same sort of hangover woke me up, together with the chaotic jumping and thumping of three kids under the age of ten, the house was dancing with mayhem and breathing anticipation. Like most families do at Christmas, we have a list of traditional things to do: mulled wine and mince pie visits from friends is somewhere near the top of that list, and as usual I make a batch of venison sausage rolls to be enjoyed by everyone, which is surprisingly easy to make. First, you get a pack of good quality venison sausages, even better if you can get ones containing something extra, like blackcurrant, then you fry them up like you'd do if you were having them for tea and wait for them to cool down. Next get some mashed potato, pre-bought and easy to microwave, plain or the fancy stuff with cheese and chives in it – the ones from Waitrose or Marks and Sparks are your best bet. Once the sausages and mash are cool, coat each sausage with some mash, and then get your roll of puff pastry, wrap a circle of that round each sausage and brush with beaten egg, making sure there's enough pastry covering all the meat and potato. Whack in the oven at one-eighty for twenty minutes and you're done! Have that Nigella! I find it really satisfying that they are usually considered better than my mum's sausage rolls, and Keith's mother's efforts, too. It's basically a three-way *sausage-roll-off*. My mum always panics and says something along the lines of "but I'm making *a lot* this year, are you sure *you* need to as well?" because she knows my batch will be the most popular. It would be a closer contest if she put more effort into her lot, considering she no longer works. I also bribe my youngest niece and nephew with bags of sweets in exchange for a vote for mine over the other two batches. Even though I'd win outright, it's always fun to bend the rules a little.

Anyway, all that kick-started a monster session. This:

I cracked open a cold beer around two in the afternoon. No

one else wanted to join me which made me feel like a bit of a Gazza, to be honest. I don't know why this was because a pot of warm mulled wine was simmering away on the stove for anyone who stopped by, so technically I wasn't alone in drinking at such an early hour, although no one else was at the precise moment I spooned out a ladle's worth into a fishbowl, once I'd ended the beer's short lifespan. I ended up cracking on for the rest of the day and working my way through eight bottles of Corona with lime wedges. (Such a refreshing and crisp experience: holding up a cold bottle and admiring the droplets of condensation sliding down seductively, taking in the centimetre of froth sitting in the neck gently popping away under a wedge of fresh lime. It makes your mouth water, but that can't go on forever, and the first sip is a thing of true pleasure). That's why by five o'clock on Christmas Eve I was halfway to drunk having got back on the mulled wine once I'd dealt with the eight-pack. Time for some wrapping before things got out of hand.

Wrapping Christmas presents is possibly the biggest ballache of all the ones to pick from during the holidays. Trying to wrap a pair of socks is hard enough, but when you've got to contend with giant boxes that hold some fucking three foot high pink Unicorn, you sort of wish your life was over. I won't lose much sleep if the presents end up looking like they've been wrapped by a blind man with no hands though; there's always a mountain of the stuff to clear up by the time breakfast is over, and most of us only care what's underneath. But anyway, it's slightly less painstaking if you've had a beer or eight, and a gallon of mulled wine.

After some wrapping, dinner was helped along with a few glasses of red and I said goodnight to three balls of lunacy, who, for the one solitary night of the year, requested an *earlier* bedtime than normal. I remember doing that, too. Happy times. Then I ventured out into sub-zero Yorkshire and met an old pal from my uni days in a cosy little pub straight out of Emmerdale, where we worked our way through two bottles of good red. My pal, Ash, then called it on. He grabbed us some *doo-da* as he called it, which was a good idea seeing as I was entering the memory-loss stage of drinking and desperately needed straightening out. It didn't quite work out that way, unfortunately. We left the pub and ended up back at Ash's place, where the only drinks on offer were eight cans of Stella and something that had the petrifying title of *Californian White Wine* wrapped around it. Even in the current state I was in, I knew to steer well clear of that and went for the wife-beater. Here's the thing about Stella: hidden amongst its usual ingredients is a magic one where after four pints it triggers off the loopy switch. The type of loopiness varies from person to person depending on who's consuming it.

Example: A usually placid and reserved man drinks six pints of Stella on an empty stomach and returns home to a dinner that doesn't quite meet his expectations, turning him into a wild and abusive leading authority on domestic violence. I've seen many a fight started by a bunch of thugs who are sat around a cluster of empty glasses that all display the iconic red and gold logo. It's *dangerous* stuff. A drink doesn't earn a nickname *Wife-beater* for its fucking flavour, that's for sure. Thankfully with me, it doesn't make me aggressive. It does, however, give me a memory similar to something living in a goldfish tank. Which is why it didn't quite work out how I'd hoped. The doo-da Ash had got dropped off did bugger all to stop the Stella Express somehow steaming into my bloodstream at a rate the same as if I had injected the stuff into my eyeballs, and after a few (I found out from Ash I actually had *six* of the eight in his fridge), I lost control of all coherence and started babbling nonsense.

*

The next morning I woke up still drunk. Confused and disorientated, it took me a minute to work out my name, age, sex and location. The biggest clue was the stocking on the end of the bed, the next was the rabble of noise coming from the kitchen and *Hark the Herald Angels* blaring out from the kitchen. Miraculously, I had found my way back, and it was Christmas morning.

It was time for the fear. How had the evening ended, and what kind of mischief had I been up to? All would be revealed. I opened the investigation with what's known as *heart-attack on a screen* AKA checking my phone. Like I was holding an undetonated hydrogen bomb, I delicately opened up WhatsApp. A few *Merry Chrimbo Homos* messages to some group chats, with a load of responses back. Nothing to see here, move along. Then at 1.51, I'd pestered Stephanie with *looking forward to loads of dirty sex in 2017 LOL,* without delivery or reply – *phew*. She was probably in France, but still, it was a stupid message. It was time for the drum roll as I reluctantly hit the green SMS button, to see what news of damage awaited me. Four unanswered messages to Rose that went, in order: 1) *hey gorgeous x,* 2) *hey what's up?* 3) *evry thin ok xxx,* and 4) *real wanna get dopn and dirty with yoy ccc,* the last one was sent at 3.47am, and I couldn't even spell simple three letter words. Amidst hyperventilating at the shame I'd cast on myself, I managed to call Ash to get the lowdown, trying to prepare myself for what further stories were in store for me, but trying to prep for that is as about as useful as a one-legged cat trying to bury a turd on a frozen lake. I looked at the call records, and his number wasn't the most recent number dialled, it was third behind Stephanie who'd received two calls, both were cancelled after two seconds at 1.49 and 1.50 (ah, so *that's* why I sent the message at 1.51.)

But the champion was Rose, I didn't even bother counting the number of calls I made to her. There were a lot. The last one was at 4.15am. I had managed to lose a good four hours, and probably both bits of office pussy.

Thankfully Ash answered, and I felt some relief at last. 'Morning mate,' he said, giggling. 'How yer feelin'?'

'What happened?' I whispered. My mouth had decomposed overnight. If I spoke any louder the room would start melting.

'You just babbled nonsense for ages in between singing stupid Spurs songs, clattering about. Demolished six of my Stellas. Luckily you didn't wake the kids up, or I'd have got in the neck. Was good fun. No harm done.'

'Yeah, it was,' I said with genuine relief. 'What time did I leave?'

'Dunno mate must have been after three, I'd say,' said Ash. I felt a touch better to know that I couldn't have got up to much more nonsense if I was asleep by just after four, although that was an educated guess. 'You were going on and on about some bird called Rose you've said you're into, and I think you were trying to call her' he went on, pissing on my bonfire of relief with a swift reminder of the antics I'd already forgotten about.

The conversation alerted Spiderman, and then Wonder Woman, to me being awake, so they bounded into my room and offered to help me open my stocking, something I wholeheartedly did *not* want to do, except maybe to search for and open the can of gin and tonic that Santa always leaves. Santa knows alright. I hauled myself up and out of bed to the kitchen for round two of the investigation.

'Morning. Merry Christmas!' said Lily, cheerily. That was a decent sign, although my sis rarely gets angry at anything. 'You were late in, did you have a good night?' she asked. This part was going better than expected, so far.

'Yeah, from what I remember. I didn't wake you when I got in?'

'Well yeah, that's how I knew you were late in…lots of clanging about. Luckily Santa had been by then,' she smiled.

'Uncle Sean! Guess what?' cut in Megan, who had already changed from Wonder Woman and into a bear with glitter all over it.

'What darling?'

'Erm, Santa drinked his sherry *and* some of daddy's whisky too. We found the bottle on the table. And he *spilt* some!'

Lily looked at me and smiled.

I'd raided the whisky cabinet when I got in, but Santa took one for team Sean.

'Can we go and open your stocking now?' asked Megan. Spiderman followed. Ivy, the oldest looked tired and wasn't that fussed. Perhaps Santa had woken her up, banging around in the kitchen. My dad arrived downstairs clutching his iPad and was straight onto the weather app.

The kids followed me to my room and the three of us got under the covers and delved into my stocking.

'Have you spilt some water in your bed?' asked Hamish, innocently.

'No, why?'

And then it made sense. Panic stations again. 'Oh erm yes, I did actually,' I said, as it dawned on me I'd signed off my Christmas Eve bender by pissing the bed. Great form.

'Come on let's open this in the lounge,' and I scooped them up. 'Don't want to get all wet from that water I spilt.'

'Maybe Santa did that too,' said Megan. 'Clumsy old Santa.'

'Yeah, he's a nightmare, isn't he?'

Christmas Eve was made up of eight coronas, a few glasses of mulled wine, a few bottles of red, six cans of the wife-beater and a good few gulps of Single Malt, not to mention some lines to straighten me out, which never happened. Chuck in some telephone based harassment of two female employees, half the household woken up at four-ish, and cap it off by pissing the bed. I needed to take it really easy.

*

Of course, I didn't. Take it easy on Christmas day? No chance, that's like the whole calendar month of December absent of Noddy Holder, Wizzard or Mariah on the radio. The three adults plus my dad got stuck into some bucks fizz at breakfast and then headed out to the local while the Turkey roasted. Back home by two, we owned a few bottles of bubbly to wash down some nibbles. Not a venison sausage roll in sight, however.

We had fun opening presents: I think I did alright with some Star Wars T-shirts, a Stormtrooper lamp courtesy of the old man (what a hero), aftershave and shirt from my mum and step-dad, loads of stuff from my sister and Keith. In return I let the kids have theirs, the girls had asked me for a candyfloss maker and a chocolate fountain, but the boy doesn't get a choice. He gets the Spurs kit every year, and I've been doing that since he was three, so by the time he's old enough to work out that he's been supporting a team that probably won't win much, it'll be too late and he'll be committed to a life of pain. Just doing my bit for the club.

Dinner was scheduled for four, and I had pledged to do the starters this year – 'Posh Prawn Cocktail.' Such simplicity, a right touch considering half my liver had vanished and it was quite hard to do anything more than breathe. Luckily all I needed were some prawns, little gem lettuce, mayo, ketchup, tobacco, Worcester sauce and lemon juice thrown into some dessert glasses.

One thing I wasn't so keen on was the choice of meat - Turkey. What in God's name is that all about? Tasteless and dry, not even Heston Blumenthal on crack could make it palatable. Why not a couple of lovely, tender, corn-fed free-range chickens stuffed with lemons? Fuck that, we'll just crack on with the blandest and driest bird God created, and then use up half the fridge keeping it for the next month. Turkey.

*

Dinner was successful on the whole. The prawn cocktail went down well with the grown-ups but not with the kids – tasteless brats – and the Turkey wasn't really that dry. Keith had rolled his sleeves up and made sure it was as tender as possible; he did explain his method to me as I tucked in, although I was well on my way to inebriation by then and didn't take a word in. Come ten, I was exhausted. In all the fun and games and the monument of food, plus only about five hours kip, I was ready to hit the sack. We had to do it all again on Boxing Day over at Keith's parents. That one was going to be a proper tear-up. Sixteen drunks, mullering the booze all day long. My liver was taking a proper pasting, which made me think of Mo from work's brother – Mo number two - who has a franchise of *Reviv*, a place you can go and get sorted internally after a week-long bender and apparently this shit's nothing short of a miracle. The concept originated in Vegas when all of the rich dudes hammering five-day binge sessions needed get-out-of-jail cards before going back to work on high-profile lawsuits, performing stem cell surgery or shooting their latest film etc. Drink, drugs and hookers, all that you can eat, getting so out of it that they'd be broken for weeks. So some smart-arsed medical guys set up these travelling IV drip units to visit all the party animals in their hotel suites. Units that literally pump a load of essential vitamins and minerals straight into your blood, then Hey Presto! within thirty minutes you're as right as rain, literally brand new. I made a note to self to look into it on the second of Jan.

I went to bed, and in all the chaos of Christmas day had forgotten my phone, which was still lying on the side plugged in. Rose had called me around seven.

'Hey, Merry Christmas. How's it going?' I said.

'And to you too...bit merry, bit tired. You know how it is, but had a good day today...all things considered.'

'Ah. I take it you're referring to my antics. Yep, really sorry. Had a bit of a bender in the end. In my defence, I don't remember any of it.'

I made sure she knew the blame was firmly pinned on Stella and went so far as to say I'd wet the bed I was that tanked.

'Sure I get it...but erm...that's not the sort of behaviour you'd expect from a man of forty-one,' she said in a tone that made me think of her telling me off in the office one evening and spanking me. I assured her I'd make it up to her on the 29th when I was back, and she sounded pleased.

TWENTY-NINE: IMPROVED
Late October 2016, Oxo Tower, Blackfriars

The plan was taking shape. At least, that's what it felt like to Jason. Not the other three sat around a table that overlooked the Thames. Just a few weeks ago they'd have probably been sitting outside on the terrace with loosened ties and rolled-up sleeves, sluicing on ice cold water and enjoying a perfectly chilled, expensive Sancerre and hoping for a breeze to caress them over the blistering city heat. But the skies were dull, and the October drizzle was falling through single figure degrees.

An establishment such as The Oxo Tower is commonplace for a man like Willey; a sharp mind to go with his sharp suits, and, as many would say, his sharp looks. He still had it at 45 - *silver fox* was the description he got most of the time. Tall and handsome, every pore on his body bled charm and charisma, and once you'd spent a few minutes in his presence, you'd have to be brain-dead to not understand why he was as successful as he was.

When out dining, or at a social event, he was never tempted to play away and give in to the many offers he received from countless women, and the occasional man. He was a devoted family man, after all. Married for nineteen years and counting, with three children, his commitment to his family was what drove his success. The firm Aspinall-Willey went through peak growth when Jason's wife Marcia had their first child two years after tying the knot, and it wasn't a coincidence that Jason was the main driver of that growth. Since then, the company has continued on a steady rise to the top of the management consultancy world, making smart acquisitions and diversifying into new practice areas, which forms the business model outside of its core activities. The next acquisition would hopefully be that of STI Ltd, once the four of them had agreed on how to go about it. Jason had outlined his thoughts as they waited for their mains – thoughts that were off-centre with the others.

'To be honest Jason - and I think the other two here will probably agree with me on this – it's a little farfetched, and pretty tough on Sean,' said Clive. 'I think we'd prefer a slightly less, er, *devious* route. Above board, you hear what I'm saying?'

'I think so too. I like your creativity but have a big concern that if it's not executed to the last drop of detail, then we lose out and end up in court,' said Foster.

Antoine nodded as a plate of Dover Sole, two Filet Steaks and one Duck breast appeared on a silver trolley, tailed by a waiter carrying a selection of veg. Their lunch meetings...never disappointing.

'So what, then? Do you want me to go back and have another go?' said Jason, raising his hand in the direction of the sommelier, who hurried over. 'Bring a bottle of...that Riesling and...that Barolo,' he said, pointing at the wine list then looking to the others. 'I trust you'll all have a glass?'

'What's the max we'll go to? Literally a take it or leave it, no messing, shit or bust type thing?' Foster asked, ignoring the wine question.

'Remind me what the offer was last time,' said Clive.

'Half a mill, all the usual *stay on and run it for three years*, which of course would turn into six months, once we'd managed him out. Give him a percentage of the shares to live off. The guy's crackers for not taking that up.'

'Go to seven-fifty with five percent equity. Exit in two, for now?' Foster said.

'Sounds good to me, and if he doesn't bite at that then maybe we'll have to consider Jason's suggestion,' Antoine said, contributing the most sensible thing he'd said all meeting.

They all nodded; mouths full of overpriced mains and continued their expensive lunch in the heart of the city.

*

A week later Jason's phone vibrated for the sixth time in the hour-long conference call he'd been on that afternoon. He'd ignored all previous five email notifications. He could engineer three-way calls between the UK, Spain and New York if needed, the Americans started work at eight in the morning so technically, as long as Jason was present from 1 pm, he could link up New York to Madrid and be in the middle in London. The daily routine of needing a siesta was all but extinct in Spain these days, thanks to advances in air conditioning, but Jason made the option available to whoever wanted it from the months of May through to October when the heat was at its most oppressive. Besides, the guys in Madrid were all consultants working quietly on various briefs. No direct sales were made from the office, so as long as the staff did the contracted hours, then he was fine with how they chose to make the time up. He was a good boss like that. Jane Aspinall on the other hand, well, she was in and out of the States at least six times a year and he hardly ever saw her - Jason had sole ownership of the M&A strategy.

He closed off the call, thanking the participants for their time, and then pulled the phone from his pocket to open the six unread emails. The fourth one down caught his attention, the subject bar read *Re: Potential New Offer – Private and Confidential* and was from ***sthomas@sti.co.uk***.

Jason had emailed Sean the day after the lunch at The Oxo, suggesting a meeting to submit a new offer, but Sean had simply said to put what the thinking was in writing and he'd take it up from there. Incredibly, despite offering an extra quarter-of-a-million plus keeping hold of some equity, Sean again declined the offer, stressing that in a couple of years' time max (underlining the word *max*) the business would be within touching distance of three million. The tone of the email pissed off Jason: no word of thanks, no *keep in touch*, nothing. Instead of hitting reply, Jason forwarded it on.

THIRTY: CRUNCHING

Not much business was written in the week between Christmas and New Year, outside of the odd late order form that was due in before the break. Budget holders in prospective companies were never going to choose work over festivities, so Sean always encouraged using annual leave in that period for sales, marketing and Louis. Only a certain amount of analysts had the same privilege however. They had reports and journals to put together, ready for launch in January. It was the same for Mark - he was needed.

The Christmas decorations were still haphazardly strewn across the fifth floor of Farringdon Place. Bits of tinsel here, small desk-sized Christmas trees there, fairly lights that lined the boarding separated rows of desks. There was even some white foam sprayed on the windows, the one nearest the desk opposite Louis, unsurprisingly, had what he assumed to be a pair of women's breasts minus the nipples. Or was it someone's backside?

Mark switched on his PC and launched into the *ProSheet* accounts database Sean had gotten some I.T. intern to build for him. One which he maintained and updated himself. How he managed to do it all was a mystery, what with some of the outgoings Mark knew the business was committed to. Building rent, specialist databases, CV libraries, client entertainment, subsistence (Sean's choice of word for food and drink, although some of the receipts...), travel, marketing and digital services – all of those in one column while the other column showing credits kept down to *'advertisements/sponsorship' 'report sales' 'subscription' or 'bespoke consultancy.'*

Mark had clocked that Sean had been encouraging his teams to sell a lot of single reports and advertisements at the end of the year. That revenue hits the bottom line immediately, unlike the annual subscription services that are only recognised monthly, i.e. if someone sold a twelve thousand pound subscription, only one thousand of that appears on the bottom line each month. An easy way to make the balance sheet healthier and boost up the profit margin before a quarterly dividend could be drawn. Mark had a hunch that the volume of services sold in 2016 was much higher than the numbers he was staring numbly at, and the single report number was, therefore, in reality, much lower. Sean himself had been plugging all that data in. He was looking at a bit of a mess truthfully and it needed a shed load of digging and double-checking against each and every outgoing for it to make sense. He had access to Sean's files, so no need to bother him on his hols. The only frustration was he'd likely be working longer hours chained to his desk and shorter hours chained to Lucy's bed.

'All this number crunching, what a mess,' he sighed, scooping up a limp slice of *Pepperoni Passion* from a greasy Domino's box and biting half a slice clean off.

THIRTY-ONE: PREPPED

'All set?' said Mrs Wilkins as she grabbed two carrier bags and bunged them next to Rose's holdall in the back of the Q5.

Peter Wilkins was already prepped at the wheel as the engine's fumes steadily huffed and puffed out and rose up, joining the light evening fog that hadn't quite vanished. Thankfully, she was travelling back to London lighter than when she came up as most of the gifts she got this year were easy enough to carry back. Clothes, vouchers or just hard cash. *Hard cash* – she loved the term, it always made her attach a naughty thought whenever a load of notes fell out of a card. "Ooh some good, hard cash," her mum would say, with innocence, as Rose imagined taking a fistful of notes from a young punter paying her to strip.

By her reckoning she'd be back in the flat around nine latest, allowing for half-an-hour of hiccups - enough time to unpack, take a bath and have a cold glass before curling up in bed and drifting off. Tomorrow night might not be as quiet. That reminded her; she needed to call Sean on the way back. He'd been up to his usual on Boxing Day with a bunch of text messages that gradually got cruder and cruder and the spelling and grammar nosedived in line it.

She plotted down in First Class, prepared to pay an upgrade should an inspector actually be present for once. She wanted a quiet carriage and a nice big table to rest her arms on or spread a magazine over, support her iPad, or whatever. It was just nice to have all that space, a wider chair and a plug socket on hand. Life's little treats.

Although her insides were yearning for one by the time she'd pulled out of the station and departed for Kings Cross, accustomed to the copious amount she'd been guzzling since arriving home, she refrained from getting a wine. Her mind turned its attention to how much weight she'd probably gained over the holiday, so she made a vow not to weigh herself until the 2nd of January, where a month of hard dieting and hot yoga sessions could begin. Lucy wanted to join her at yoga, according to a message she sent over the holiday. Rose took it with a pinch of salt and thought that the only way to get Lucy into a yoga class would be to tell her there was free pizza before, during and after.

Ah, that's right, she's got to keep herself in shape for her new boyfriend, she thought, as if pushing Mark around all day long wasn't infinitely more than what she usually did. Lucy at hot yoga? Now that would be worth paying to see.

She called Sean five minutes into the journey.

'"Look I'm sorry about Boxing Day...always a massive one, and think I overdid it on the old messaging and calling, again.'

She needed to align a little to his ways and accept that being his age and all, he would be keener to speak and have human interaction over SMS.

'It's ok. It's Christmas, but please, try your best not to do that *every* time you're drunk. If I can answer, I will. If I'm asleep I won't, even if you wake me,' she said as if *she* was the forty-one-year-old, and he was a twenty-three-year-old sex pest. Once that was dealt with they had a couple of minute's small talk before he told her to meet him at Leicester Square tube tomorrow for six sharp. He was direct when it came laying out plans Rose had noticed. Something she liked.

THIRTY-TWO: SPICE

As I got into my waiting Uber, the immigrant driving told me that he was charging me extra because I'd kept him waiting, which I had, but he had arrived earlier than the app was showing me, which resulted in an immediate protest which he couldn't wrap his head around. In that case, I'd get dropped off at Holborn and *not* Leicester Square, shaving a few quid off the tariff. Fuck him. Play him at his own game, the fucking ungrateful tosser.

I live, and always have, in and around London: a diverse city full of all creeds and colours, races and religions, genders and sexual preferences etc. Everyone should, and largely does, just get on with things and get on with their business. But you can spot an immigrant a mile off. Just their general behaviour and apparent lack of basic communication (and hygiene), and that they seem to know they can take the piss, acting as if they are in their own cesspit where it's acceptable to behave like Neanderthals and beat their women and jump about like a pack of possessed baboons. The way I see it isn't too complex: we live in a country that has enough land and space to house and provide shelter for a quota of people who have fled their war-torn homeland to escape persecution, dictatorship and poverty - or worse still - daily mortar bombing and chemical weapon attacks. Half the countries that spew them out are usually all being bombed to fuck by the US and its coalition – us lot included - so it's only right we take in a number and look after them. What I would say to that then, is attach a set of simple fucking conditions, like *not* coming over here and rinsing the benefits that could go to the elderly, disabled or homeless. Come over here and *work* for a living, contribute positively to the economy and community. A lot do, granted. But, *don't* come and assemble your own little communities and isolate yourselves from everyone else. Don't march around in London with banners like *Death to Infidels*, or *British Police Burn in Hell* or sabotage Remembrance Day. Don't preach hate; integrate and keep communication channels open and accessible, with the people of the nation that provide you with refuge and a safe place to exist. *But*, if you so much as commit *one* fucking crime, however petty it may be, then you are straight back on the rubber dinghy with your six wives and eleven kids, and you *aint* coming back. Why can't it be that simple? It should be.

Perhaps I should run for Parliament.

*

I jumped out of the Prius, slamming the door without even saying "thanks", making sure he got one star and then trotted down Charing Cross Road, and checked my phone to see if Rose had messaged with an ETA. I was early and wanted to avoid loitering around the tube looking like a pimp in the freezing cold. But of course, she had. She'd called me without leaving a voicemail – a good tactic. Fucking women! They say when most girls are born they are born late, and I've had first-hand experience of that theory ever since I can remember, stemming back from my mum consistently being late to pick me up from school, cubs, or football - anything that required a degree of promptness and punctuality. Once when I was seven, I remember being so sick that I had to stay at home instead of going to school, but my mum had to go to work. Grandma was summoned over to look after me. I sat patiently in the lounge, shivering on the couch with a duvet over me from probably eight in the morning, watching television from the four channels we had back then waiting for her to arrive, but it was five in the *afternoon* before Grandma rocked up, armed with a tin of stale buns. In later years, every girl I dated, or those who I had to meet in a social capacity, were *always* late. Some of them even had the gall to excuse themselves stating it was a condition and that nothing could be done about it. I ask anyone to go down on day one of the *Selfridges January Sale* and see how many boilers turn up late for that. None.

I made my way to some skanky little pub opposite the tube and decided I'd go straight for the strong ale, what with it still technically being the holidays. The rabble of bodies that bounced about was made up of tourists or pissed up chavs on day release, that is to say, not a good mix. I grabbed a seat by the window and stared at my phone until Rose called and told me she was fifteen away, leaving me enough time to nail two cold pints on the basis she was at least half-an-hour from arrival. It would help me loosen up for a night of debauchery. I'd booked a room at the W Hotel in Leicester Square for some grimy sex once we'd had dinner at La Bodega Negra - a Mexican street food restaurant that's disguised as a sex show. One thing that's always fun when going on a date there, is seeing the bird's reaction when you've waltzed them down a seedy side street in Soho and approached a set of doors that are under a fake neon sign saying *'Peep Show.'* *Most* will follow you in, but I did take some bird called Becky there a while ago, and as we got to the double doors she'd pegged it off thinking I was a pervert. She was right, but I had to literally pelt it after her and drag her back, explaining in desperation that it really was just a gimmick (we stumbled at the first hurdle, and the evening declined, when after dinner and a few drinks, she insisted on seeing me again before coming over to study my ceiling).

I knew Rose had entered the pub - not from seeing her do so – but from the expressions on the pair of Albanian convicts sat in front of me. The pair of them had chins that needed leveraging up from the table they were perched over.

I looked at Rose, and then proudly scanned the bar area. All the men enjoying their five quid pints of wife-beater locked onto her and I could see them undressing her mentally as she made her way to me through the bunch of salivating perverts. Jesus I was going to finish her later on; the poor girl was going to get the rogering her mother warned her about, and no mistake. And she looked beautiful, almost too good to spoil. A red dress that just about hid her arse sat seductively over the pair of black boots complimenting the cute black fleece that draped over her shoulders. She looked like an X-rated Mrs Claus.

'Hey, sorry I'm late,' she said planting a kiss on me. I could feel the daggers coming at me from all angles and the whisperings of one man to the next. "How *did* he manage that, she's twenty years younger, he must have paid for it, he must be loaded, he must be hung like a horse etc." Pretty much all of that actually, buster!

'That's fine. Want one here or shall we go to the place and get a cocktail in the bar there?' I asked.

'Let's move on,' she said, surveying the horrible little saloon and probably feeling the same nauseous contempt for the clientele that I had.

'Good answer.'

We left the pub to twenty men still fixated on the stunner leading me out by the hand.

My stunner.

*

After a deliciously over-priced meal at La Bodega Negra, we took the short walk to the W. The room cost me just shy of a monkey – or five hundred quid if you're not from London. You might wonder what justifies spending nearly a grand all in for an evening between Christmas and New Year when not much is going on. Let me tell you. For the room rate of £459, dinner at £145, drinks in the hotel bar at £80, a bottle of bubbly to the room £145, a gram of gear £80, plus another £40 for breakfast. Altogether a total of around £950, you get to spend fourteen hours with Rose Wilkins. Rose Wilkins, dressed to kill and insanely superior to 99% of all the other girls in their early twenties who roam the capital. If you herded up all the babes from channel 901 upwards and stripped them down to just their basics, chucked Rose into the mix of silicone plastic wanking objects, well, she'd still steal the show. And what a show it was. I hadn't really noticed her holdall most of the evening; not until we checked in and scoped out the room and she tossed it onto our six-foot wide bed. She encouraged me to take a peek inside. I was reminded of that scene in *The Goonies* when they discover One-Eyed Willy's box of stolen treasure.

Inside she'd packed a couple of sets of lingerie, a schoolgirl uniform, a pink paddle, a massive black dildo (something that I wasn't sure how to react to), a choker that read *I'M A SLUT*, a few smaller vibrators and a string of anal beads to cap it all off. My mind was lost, wandering about deliriously in a whole forest of perversion, and it wasn't up for being found any time soon. Our bed turned from a comfortable place to sleep into an Amsterdam sex emporium, a banquet of debauchery more than enough to make my pecker's ignition fire-up and start to smoke.

But then I became a tad confused.

That's because I pictured her having the anal beads inserted into her as some young stud fed a foot-long punisher into the other entrance, while she greedily sucked his throbber - a vision that was strangely not as appealing as you may think. However, in her defence, most of the accessories looked like they had never been used.

'That's an interesting selection, where did you get all that?' I asked, trying to sound like it was an innocent and quite legitimate question.

'Went shopping earlier. Mum paid off my credit cards for me, so I whacked it all on the plastic...except this,' she said, holding up a black outfit of suspenders and PVC bra. 'Brought these along with me.'

I didn't probe any further, as no doubt *that* little number would have been enjoyed by some other lucky sod, so I kept schtum, not wanting to tarnish the immense relief that the rest of the clobber had not seen her insides. Yet.

'Let me see it on then.' I nodded to the bathroom. She didn't need any more encouragement than those six words. While she did that, I sniffed the paddle, beads and black dildo to check they were brand new and then my cock was wide awake and asking me where supper was as soon as I'd realised they were.

*

A pair of suspenders lay rolled up in a ball on the end of the bed. They'd managed to stay there all night despite tossing, turning and a couple of lazy ones that happened around half-four and again at six. My boner was made out of a graphite/steel mix thanks to the Viagra I dropped around eleven. We'd had a quickie when we arrived, then hit the bar and been allowed into the private resident's section where we were one of only two couples to enjoy the luxury on offer, soon smashing down cocktails and playing tonsil tennis like a couple of school kids. I had a whole gram of rocket-fuel as well, so we tucked into that after we were appropriately drunk, hence the necessary precaution of dropping a bluey. (I doubt I would have needed it, but I really wanted to make use of the hotel room and her selection of accessories.)

Once we'd racked up an impressive bar bill, I ordered a bottle of something – Laurent Perrier Rose, I think, for the room – and we made our way back along the fluorescent pink lined corridor to number 122, and the moment the door clicked shut I was yanking her dress off and she was yanking at my belt and within ten seconds she had my balls cupped in her mouth and was staring at me. She had the power.

Without giving a blow-by-blow account of the whole sordid three hours, the activities we participated in involved the following:

Hard spanking with a pink, wooden paddle on an arse that belongs on sands of Copacabana, small vibrators rubbed on her as I crept around the back, a set of anal beads fed into Copacabana's finest (once I'd sufficiently stretched it), a foot long dildo drilled in and out of - with the aid of some lube - her front door - there was no way *that* would've got in her arse, even if Geoff Capes had been on hand, a good forty-five of sixty-nine and then doggy-style in front of the mirror bringing proceedings to an earth-shattering climax. I even fed the end of the Laurent Perrier bottle into her before we finally collapsed around three, once the whole packet of gear had been demolished and the mini-bar had become nothing but a tiny, bare, lukewarm cupboard.

The only annoying bit was she didn't let me film *any* of it.

THIRTY-THREE: EXECUTE
Late October 2016, L'Anima, Broadgate

'Ok so let me get this totally straight, one last time,' said Foster, with a concentrated frown.

Four empty notepads lay in front of two empty bottles of Barbera standing amongst a quartet of clean plates dotted around a table in the main section of L'Anima. A story that tells you very little had been achieved outside of an education of how pasta is meant to be served. A really good Italian, top notch. Good enough to ensure the four of them were distracted from the task in hand, each mouthful justifying a few "mmms" and "oh wows" followed by a description of what had just been enjoyed, each man commentating on their plates of fine Italian cuisine and offering a forkful to the others to see for themselves. It was that good they almost forgot why they were there.

Once he'd finished his veal ribbons with farfalle, Foster hushed the other three and described what he understood to be the idea Jason briefly discussed with him when they both arrived a little earlier. Finally, their attention was cornered.

'So far there are going to be two honey traps and not the one that you'd think would be enough?' he began, 'and then one of them catches him in the act, so to speak. Films it and begins the persuasion process?'

'Essentially yes, but we need others to help with the peripheral stuff like the alarm going off, the books not adding up...what was the third...oh, and the chance meeting,' answered Jason.

'And...*you* think you have one of the two honeys who could easily get a job there with her languages, and her looks. *And* be willing to go along with it all?' asked Foster to Antoine.

'Sure. Debbie's niece is a greedy little madam, leave her to me. That side of things will be a piece of cake. From what Louis is saying to us about him, he won't be able to resist her. I'll put in a call later on.'

'Ok, so that leaves two more? Another honey, and then some bent accountant, which you say you can sort, right?' asked Foster to Jason.

'Actually, it's likely we may need one other for the chance meeting. I'm on that, plus, what, we're not even in November. The distraction of Christmas, remember.'

Clive: 'I still think if we're gonna go the whole hog then we need to put the boot in. *Really* hard. Anyone got any other ideas of how to execute some form of a smear campaign?'

The four of them fell silent for a couple of minutes and then Jason came alive with a tap of his spoon on the empty glass in front him.

'Twitter?'

THIRTY-FOUR: EVE

New Year's Eve. A couple of my local pubs wanted a score just to be allowed into the place. With that score, you get nothing of value, not even a complimentary tap water. You get a mile-long bar queue, humidity caused by all the sweaty bodies buggering about on a makeshift dance floor which could quite easily turn into an ice rink with all the spillage. You get awful music *all* night, you get overpriced drinks and you get double cab fares. Give me a house party over that any day of the week. Music chosen by the host and not some failure playing Mr Blobby and masking themselves as a 'DJ', no queue at the bar, an eight-pack of beers and a bottle of decent vodka for under thirty quid, most people you get on with or at least know and not a bunch of pissed up chavs in checked shirts and brogues *having it large*. But alas, after checking out of the W Hotel on the 30th December and then packing Rose off onto the tube, I noticed a message through from a couple of the *Crown/Pig Posse* group asking what the plan was. Bob had managed to persuade his other half to allow him out for the evening – given that he became a father for the first time in the summertime it was quite a surprise his keeper had given in and granted him a ticket. Not as surprising was Carl. His missus didn't care what he did, so he'd already started to make plans for the three of us for New Year's Eve. I kind of wanted to spend it with Rose as I was sure I'd fallen for her some more – despite lots of good fun in the sack we also had a very enjoyable meal and held a good conversation, she's so mature for 23. She told me she was going to a house party with close friends, anyway. Never mind, there's always next year.

Carl had bought us tickets for a pub called The Kings Arms a few miles up the road from us in Southgate; a *gastro*pub with clientele similar age to us lot – that is to say an older crowd and therefore free from any horrible little chavs intent on causing havoc. So there I was with Bob and Carl, all three of us tooled up with a gram of ****'s strong stuff *each,* at the bar gone half-nine, chatting nonsense in between staggering around on the heated outdoor decking smoking menthol fags on our way to and from the bogs, line after line after line, Carl ploughing through whole bottles of the usual New Zealand Sauvignon while Bob spanked pints of Peroni like they were going out of fashion in three gulps, meanwhile I was looking at breaking into the Vodka Soda and fresh lime record books. Powerful? To say we were powerful would be insulting to the word. We were fucking *dynamite,* the other two had a pass and were off the leash and all that, maximising the occasion to get as messy as possible in as short a time as possible. It meant I had to keep up with the pair of them, and by doing so, when it got to eleven, things had progressed into wide-eyed, lively-jawed ranting and raving tapping up the odd bit of skirt who passed our table, although I had half of my mind occupied on Rose and wondering if she'd get in touch at any point and invite me over, or even better invite herself over to mine. I really could use some sort of action later on, and Rose was in pole position if I had the luxury of choosing. Fuck it, I'd give her a buzz around eleven and wish her an early 'Happy New Year' and then see what she thought about meeting up later...

*

Back at mine at 2 am the three of us sat around all silently tapping away on respective devices; Carl and Bob were on Facebook or Twitter despite both being in a worse state than Oliver Reed at the end of a Bank Holiday weekend, and I had re-launched Tinder and was chatting to a couple of old boilers I'd matched with a few weeks ago and trying to get something out of the conversations. I did manage to speak to Rose just before midnight where we chatted for about a minute. I don't remember much except that she said she was going to hit home about 2 am and go to bed because she had a family lunch in Windsor that started at midday or something. I wondered if it was a lie because there were nicer younger men than me in her presence and I wondered it out loud which wasn't received well. So, I reverted to the next course of action, which was to see if any boilers were up, and after some perseverance, some old ripper called Paula who lives out in Watford was. And she was home, and more importantly, game. Now, I hadn't actually met Paula in person up to that point, although we'd swapped messages - pictures ones mainly - and she looked *filthy*. Big set of bells on it and although she was 45, they sat up nicely and weren't inches from her ankles like a lot of forty plus women of today, plus she had a real slutty look about her; heavy eye makeup and very bright red lipstick. But, I'd only seen headshots outside of the ones she sent me of her chest, which caused me a bit of concern - she may well be the wrong side of curvaceous. By that, I mean a real stonker.

So I weighed it all up with Carl and Bob when I informed them I had an offer to go round to hers, to which Carl made my mind up for me and sent me packing, adding that he would go and do it if I didn't. I was looking at just under fifty quid each way in travel due to Uber wanting surge pricing times three, fucking terrible of them to do that, no corporate responsibility skanking customers so blatantly.

Thirty minutes later I had arrived at a block of apartments and was standing outside a front door that had glass panels either side of it, enabling me to see into the main reception area and where the stairs were. My forehead was pressed against the window. Paula was on the first floor and told me to ring her, not buzz, because her daughter was in bed and she didn't want her woken. My heart was doing the salsa from the strong gear I'd been sniffing for the previous six hours, I also had that familiar feeling of adrenaline mixed with anticipation just before you get balls deep in some really dirty sex with a new bit. One of the best parts of it all is knowing that imminently you'll be experiencing something different, and as its pre-arranged, it's usually going to be mind-blowing because you both know exactly what you've signed up for. It's essentially just mutual prostitution without any money exchanging hands, although cab drivers must do rather well out of it.

I heard a door creak open slowly and then some footsteps

approach, and I was able to make out a shadow on the first floor, a shadow that belonged to Paula...but it couldn't have been. The shadow belonged to, I'm guessing, at least seventeen stone of pale and flabby council estate creature who had wandered off-piste and ended up somewhere nice. I was looking for Rob Zombie and a cast of extras filming a remake of *The Blob,* as the main character bounced down the stairs into full view, grinning at me through the glass panels and leaving me wondering if the grin was, in fact, masking the laughter that went with royally stitching me up, or she was genuinely beaming at the thought of some rare action. She looked more like Rod Hull than the Paula from her pictures. I would have preferred fucking Grotbags to Jabba the Hutt's twin sister.

What to do? I couldn't leg it as the Uber had long gone, even though I could have walked briskly away and left the thing standing there she was that monstrous and immobile. But it was too late to even wonder. She opened the door and beckoned me in, lifting her finger up to her mouth with a "hush" as if I was going to start screaming in terror (which I was, inside).

I followed her up to her flat and we talked quietly for a bit, but I couldn't concentrate much, because not only was she much larger in real life, she was also really thinning on top. Yep, as well as being a total fraud and twice the size I had imagined, she was going bald. And the icing on the cake – a cake she'd no doubt finish in record time – she looked 55, not the 45 she said she was. If she was 45 then fuck me, she must have had a bloody hard paper round.

A couple of minutes of chit-chat in, I was questioning myself; get out now or stay and get some kind of return and at least blow my muck and have something to show for nearly a ton in cab fares. Being the shrewd businessman I am, I of course opted for the latter, pushing her head down towards my groin (I couldn't even kiss her she was that bad) and then managing somehow to get hard as she gave me a pretty competent nosh. I suspected that she was extremely grateful for the opportunity and therefore decided to put in maximum effort. She had the audacity after a while to stop and try and remove her knickers, but I told her to keep using her mouth as I was close and I'd give her one in a bit. Instead of keeping my eyes open and looking at the top of her bald crown bobbing away, I thought about my favourite porn star as I unloaded a bucket load – she should have had a shower cap on, well actually, she probably didn't keep any. I pulled up my pants and trousers without even saying "thank-you."

Once she'd showed me to the bathroom and waddled back off to the lounge, I slipped out of the front door and hossed it as fast as I could, where back on the main road I ordered an Uber that was spectacularly only two minutes away, jumped in and then blocked her from my phonebook. As we pulled away, I nervously checked behind me to ensure she hadn't rolled herself out of the flats in pursuit.

And that was the last she ever saw of me, and my driver was over the moon at a job worth fifty quid, and I wanted to see Rose, but it was pushing 4am and I thought she wouldn't appreciate a phone call just after I'd technically cheated on her. And all of a sudden, I wished I hadn't, because I'd just cum, and all I felt now was remorseful and tired.

Yeah, New Year's Eve. Nice.

THIRTY-FIVE: TRIP

Neither Louis nor Mark answered when I called them to find out where they were, so I naturally feared the worst when nobody said they'd heard from either of them. It turned out they would join us later, two-hundred-and-fifty quid worse off. It cost them another flight and a 90€ cab fare from Geneva to Chamonix, the delay caused by Louis losing his son at the airport.

Two things here to note: firstly his son was never coming on the work jolly I'd organised for the sales guys, and therefore was *not* at the airport, and secondly, crucial to his release from the airport police, his son's name isn't *Allah Akbar*. But despite those two vital factors, he decided to run around departures shouting for his son as loudly as possible. And he'd forgotten to shave, so was sporting a decent sized beard, and also had a large rucksack clipped on to him. They spent four hours being held by the airport police and investigated/interrogated before they had finally believed his lie that he was a recent convert to Islam, and his shouts of "ALLAH AKHBAR!" were to calm himself down as he was a nervous flier. So nervous in fact, that once the pair of them had boarded their seats at the front of the plane and had started their climb, he turned to Mark and said very loudly "Just remember that we're doing this for Allah!" causing the passenger beside them to panic and ask for a seat change, explaining to the flight attendant what Louis had said, making it very difficult to find someone willing to take up the vacant seat, in turn disturbing the Captain, who had to leave his co-pilot in charge for ten minutes while he negotiated with the passenger who wouldn't sit back down. There really are no limits to the trouble he seems to conjure up. But, it made for a hilarious story when they finally charged through the door of our chalet as the rest of us finished our five-course supper.

We had two chalet-hosts Bas - short for Sebastian not Bastard - and Claire, a 19-year-old goth on a gap year, and weirdly sexy. Stephanie, Robbie, Tom and Phil had qualified for the trip, and of course, me and Louis - who had a knack of inviting himself to anything mildly exciting - and Mark, who I invited along because I didn't want him to feel excluded. Apparently, you could hire special sledge things for people who can't walk and he'd learned to use one at the Snow Dome before we came away. So a total of seven in an eight-man chalet. I allowed Stephanie to have her own room, and I shared with Phil. A few ideas of sneaking off in the middle of the night to give Stephanie one bounced around my mind. When in Rome...

The chalet was *fat*. Cinema room on the ground floor with heated leather reclining seats and a choice of a thousand films, hot tub, equipment room complete with boot warmer, huge open-plan lounge with stunning fire. Three delightful floors all under beautiful alpine timber beams and located at the heart of the town centre. People could see us in the hot tub as they trudged past after a hard days skiing followed by their après ski. When the guys who worked in the chalet weren't busying themselves getting breakfast ready for us from 7 am, they were making a cake for us for when we were back from the mountains at tea time. They re-appeared at six-ish to start prepping the five-course dinner of canapés, proper starter, main, dessert and a cheese course, all with as much booze as we pleased. All this while keeping the place spic and span with soft fresh towels and bed linen every day, ready to receive those tired and aching limbs. A grand a head including flights and transfer, but not equipment hire or the lift passes. Skiing trips don't come cheap, but boy, are they worth it. The whole experience is right up there when it comes to any vacation. Up and out on the mountain for about ten-ish, taking in postcard after postcard while your lungs fill up with the purest of alpine air, gliding between rows of deep green forest on fresh powder until you need a rest and stop-off for lunch at the summit, sitting out a sun deck armed with a plate of spag bol, chips, large beer and plenty of Kodak moments. Once that's done it's a couple more hours of easier, more leisurely afternoon skiing, coming off at half-three, maybe four, hit the bars and batter the après ski where you end up getting smashed until seven or eight then it's back to your chalet for a hot soak, freshen up and ready for your well-earned five-course munch and decent French plonk. By eleven you're ready to turn in, satisfied, exhausted and just about able to decide what breakfast you'd like to set you up for the next day's adventure, before a sound and unbroken kip.

*

On day three we certainly weren't ready to turn in by eleven.

Wednesday is the night off for the chalet hosts, so the town is heaving with seasonnaires letting loose and spending their €100 weekly wage on booze - the hundred euros that will get them approximately ten pints it's that expensive in ski resorts. Anyway, we booked into a restaurant called *Munchies* which is the best in Chamonix, spending a fortune on dinner and all the wine we could hold, then staggered out of the place at ten to jump next door into *Le Cave* - a swish little bar and nightclub with cosy stone alcoves dotted about the place. Louis then suggested we try and score some "bits and pieces" seeing as we were on a trip, but I couldn't be arsed to go on a mission, however he insisted.

An hour later he returned, armed with six grams of coke and two small bags of potent MDMA, half the contents of one of the ones holding the mandy ended up in Mark's beer when he was in the toilets, much to the amusement of everyone else. Had I known that was his plan, I'd have stopped him, but I didn't see him, apparently quite blatantly, tip it in and give it a good stir with a straw he'd taken from Stephanie's long drink, adding "I think it's time for Mark's medication don't you...this stuff makes him fly let alone walk!"

Louis informed Mark of his prank when Mark started hand dancing at the table to a house version of *Billie Jean*. The lyrics *the kid is not my son* were changed to *the spastics off his bun,* by Louis, of course, prompting an enquiry from Mark; Louis telling him that it meant off his nut/head and that there was a reason for it, at which point Mark grabbed his beer, poured the rest of the drugs into it and downed it - about a third of a pint - pulling a face as he swallowed the dregs of warm beer and chemicals. Mark did very well all things considered.

Back in the chalet, all of us were in a pickle but I didn't care; everyone was at it, banging massive lines off the dining table and dabbing the other bag of mandy. Mark was performing wheel spins with the help of Louis, every other time they attempted to the chair toppled over and three of us had to pick Mark back up and put him back in, but he didn't seem at all troubled by the constant injury. Then at around four, he demanded to be lifted into the hot tub and chill out he was so mangled. Louis and Stephanie joined him, pissing me off a tad because she was quite loved up and allowed both of them a grope of her knockers. I heard Louis refusing to believe she had real ones when she said they were, meaning he and Mark had to obtain the necessary proof to settle the dispute and prod them a few times. Oldest trick in the book and she fell for it.

Claire turned up to start making breakfast at half six, surprised at first at how early we were up before clocking on that there was a bunch of drug casualties yet to go to be and still climbing the walls. I told her to come back at eleven and make us all a brunch - no one was going to be going out skiing in the morning since we'd all drank a reservoir of wine, beer and spirits. She seemed grateful for that change in schedule, but also looked at us like the animals we were. I don't think she's used to hosting a bunch of wrong'uns who turn into bed after 6 am all chewing their faces off. Phil's snoring forced me to creep up to Stephanie's room and leap into her bed and shake her awake, trying very hard to get any sort of action, as my mind had entered that perverted stage only the last trails of drugs can induce. All I wanted to do was shoot my load and get to sleep, but I couldn't for love nor money get a stiffy, cursing myself inside about fifty times for forgetting to pack some blue helpers which would've come in *really* handy, despite probably giving me a heart attack as my pulse would've doubled. In the end, I had to just frig her off until she came, explaining that my pathetic, limp, portion of silly-putty was because I was still too wasted and that she'd have to wait until later on for my length, something she didn't seem fussed about. Maybe she was being extra nonchalant because she was in her home country, selfish bitch.

*

The morning after no one except Tom had gone out to ski, and I looked for some kind of vitamin C boost to try and not feel like I was going to die today. The conversation around the table at brunch was limited to the groaning, head-shaking and tutting that comes with the general self-loathing the day after a massive session, even Louis was pretty quiet by his standards, thankfully, and once we'd finished the food laid on for us by Claire, everyone decided a stroll around the town in the fresh air might at least provide a small amount of escape from the appalling state we found ourselves in. I opted to stay put - fuck shopping when I could stay in the warm chalet and snuggle up in the cinema room and watch a film, and I'd hoped Stephanie would hang back too as I could feel myself getting a bit worked up having had some sleep, spending an hour in bed imagining bending her over one of the chairs in the cinema room. I was keen to live it out, but she wanted to go out with the gang, which left me alone with Claire...

*

Claire told me what she was going to university after the summer. She was acting like an adult despite having only just turned 19, and the conversation was around literature and the classics, and not being too mad on some of the old rubbish people wank over, I held my own and we had quite a nice chat about various modern-day novelists/writers and what have you, and I got for her my copy of 'The Second Coming' by John Niven, probably my favourite book of recent times, and she seemed pretty grateful. On the surface she was a cold and typical goth, keen to fit in by not fitting in, however underneath that layer of moodiness was a fragile little thing and I noted a few scars on her arms, and no fingernails - sure signs of anxiety. It turned me on. Could I try it on since the place was empty? No, I found myself resisting and telling myself she was young enough to be my daughter, or younger sister, *either way, its incest*, to quote Partridge. The trouble was that *she* turned the conversation to relationship status and told me she was "having fun" while out in Chamonix. The season for her ran from early November to mid-April so no time for a relationship, just active on Tinder. Fuck me, everyone was at it. In my mind there are two lines of relationship statuses – in a relationship, or on Tinder. I then had to make a decision whether to suggest a quick one while everyone was out as she was giving me the look, definitely, or keep it in my pants and wait for Stephanie to return. But that decision was taken care of when Claire bent over to put some pans away under the sink and I caught a glimpse of the top of her black knickers peeping out of the top of her leggings and then visualised peeling them off to reveal a baldy, ready for a pounding. Fuck it, I went for it.

'So when did you last hook up with a guy, then? Plenty of men in this town – we all noticed how cock-heavy it is,' I said, getting proceedings underway.

'Last night. Usually get lucky on a Wednesday,' said Claire with a shy smile. 'Bit tired actually.'

Hmm, that wasn't an ideal start, but anyway, go in for the kill now, I told myself. After all, if you don't ask you don't get – that's always been one of my mottos. I had to. She had big brown eyes and a tiny nose stud. A few scars up the arm, moody Goth, *nineteen* and black knickers equals fantasy fuck. I got a semi there and then.

'Fancy getting in the hot tub for a bit?' I said, moving closer.

'What? Seriously?' she said, not in a way that suggested she couldn't believe her luck. More of a tone that actually should have translated as "Are you fucking insane?!"

'Yeah, why not? We could have a bit of fun...' I said, touching her lightly on the arm. She moved back a bit and then hit me with a sucker punch.

'Erm, no offence, but you're what, like forty-odd? That's the same as my *dad*.'

She laughed on the word "dad." I backtracked and made out I only meant go for a hot tub and chat, nothing else, a story she didn't buy one iota. Instead, she went up to tidy the bedrooms, clearing the coast for me to lock myself in my room where I knocked one out thinking about a foursome with her, Rose and Stephanie. Stephanie was going to get what for, later on, I thought, as I mopped up a gallon of hangover goo using a ski sock that was lying on the floor. Luckily for Phil, it was one of mine, and I had brought a spare pair.

Thank God for socks.

THIRTY-SIX: BRUNO

A week skiing for a few sales reps and a sales manager meant productivity across the floor was somewhere between five and six percent of its usual. Even Mo was kicking back, free from any harassment at the hands of Louis and the inconvenient micro-management from Phil (Phil was the senior sales manager and had the final say over Mo should Sean not be around). Mo had, in fact, emailed Sean on Monday asking for the Friday off at short notice, and Sean had replied saying that as long as he had the vacancy in his team filled by then, then it wasn't an issue. *Best get onto it then*, Mo had thought, launching into CV Library and looking through the latest uploads, searching keywords *business development, sales, intelligence, advertising, London*, and right away he had a list of over fifty potential candidates. Two days later and he'd met a couple of them: one of them was a guy from Brazil called Bruno Perreira - a dead ringer for Christiano Ronaldo. Six foot one, ripped to shreds, olive skinned and quite clearly a magnet. On top of that, Bruno had been working for another smaller business info and trade journal company - based in Paddington - and had just left because they capped his commission to ten percent on all new sales, meaning he was being vastly undervalued, if the figures he was quoting stacked up, which Mo believed they were based on the strength of the interview. Plus he was being paid twenty-five on the base, so plenty of wiggle room to get up to the thirty that Sean had said was in the budget. If Mo could get this guy signed sealed and delivered to start on Monday then he'd maybe earn himself the title of Senior Sales Manager.

Mo checked with Melanie – who looked quite horrified at being disturbed – if anyone had a demo for the Thursday afternoon which is when Bruno was due in for his second stage interview, and as luck would have it Rose had back-to-back ones booked in. Perfect. Mo sent Rose an outlook and told her that Bruno was going to be listening in to her demo, adding a note that this chap was good and needed impressing. Rose had noticed Bruno already when he was in for his first hour with Mo, as had Sandra, Melanie and Hannah. Melanie sent an email to the other three which read *FIT!!!!!!!!* in a huge pink font, starting off a chain of replies even Hannah got involved in, *yes, please! I would* and even a *fuck me who is that?*

Safe to say that if Bruno accepted an offer then he'd provide quite a distraction, not something Sean would be over the moon with. But the guy was a big hitter and Mo was sure he'd be billing a nice chunk of revenue for STI. Surely Sean would prefer that over childish jealousy.

*

Rose made sure her call was on point. Bruno listened in and nodded at many of the sound bites Rose was making as if he knew the whole process already and was being acquainted with a familiar old pal, and after a few questions around commission structure and territory division, he was in Sean's office sat opposite Mo finalising a basic salary. Start on Monday.

THIRTY-SEVEN: MISSING

Our last day and night in Chamonix. As if it was going to be without incident. The idea was to be up and ready for eight to enjoy a full cooked one and get the ski bus out of the town and through the Mont Blanc tunnel, arriving in Italy to be at the Courmayeur lifts and then get a morning of ski under our belts. I meticulously planned a route we could all enjoy in the morning before stopping off for a group lunch around midday where I would buy bottles of cheap Italian Prosecco and take some photos etc. Then we'd ski back and take the bus back into Chamonix and explore Brevent and Flegere for the final afternoon, before battering the après ski. Pulling no punches.

We eventually boarded the Gondola at Courmayeur at half past ten; the thirty-minute delay was general loose preparation of lost ski passes, masks, helmets. Oh and Louis, who decided that it would be amusing to ski all day long in fancy dress – changing into his Fred Flinstone ski costume took him twenty minutes longer than everyone else to get ready. Had he informed just one of us that was his plan then I'd have suggested a half seven wake up, but what was half an hour in the grand scheme of things?

The sun was shining all morning after a big dump overnight which meant near perfect conditions. Soft fluffy powder underfoot and beautiful scenery stretched out beneath clear blue skies making for one of those days where you truly appreciate the sport and realise we live on a beautiful planet. You really realise exactly why you spend so much money on a cold week in Europe in January.

Everyone in the group was competent on skis and Mark had come on leaps and bounds (no pun intended) with his SnoGo wheelchair sledge - the only thing that held us back from tearing around the mountain were groups of people wanting to take pictures of Fred Flinstone. It was quite amusing watching Fred gliding about as other skiers looked on in disbelief, some of them even losing balance as he rushed past them. By midday we'd found a cosy little mountain cabin serving pizza, pasta, beer and wine, so settled down for a nice long lunch sitting out on the decking in the sunshine and discussing the mornings ski runs. Although it was around minus ten, we were catching the sun, and life felt really good.

After a huge plate of pasta and a few portions of chips washed down with three bottles of Prosecco, we skied back down to base camp via a nice long blue run that was still conditionally on point despite busy pistes and the local's weekend skiing. There were no slushy or cut up parts of the run which can prove challenging - you end up with your thighs on fire as you do your best to navigate those bastard moguls.

Once we'd all convened at the bottom of the run, I did a head count as everyone unclipped their gear and helped put Mark into his chair. We were missing one person. Guess who?

'Where's Louis?' I asked, correctly predicting the row of blank looks and shrugged shoulders that came my way. 'Anyone see where he is?'

We all looked up at the mountain and then down to the end of the run, in the hope we'd see an orange and beige ski suit charging down, but after a minute it became clear he'd either had a fall or more likely, landed himself in trouble.

'For fuck sake...what now?' I said it quietly, but Phil read my mind and cracked up. I was reluctant to leave Louis on the off-chance he'd had a bad fall and needed assistance. Much as I wanted to, I couldn't risk abandoning the son of my only investor to leave him stranded on a fucking mountain in sub-zero temperatures. Five more minutes passed. I told the guys to go and relax in the bar next to the gondola, and that if we hadn't arrived down in another ten, they could jump on the bus and I'd wait about.

Whatever the conversation between the pair of us, it was engrossing enough for us to miss the pantomime at the top of the final stretch of piste down to where we were patiently hovering, because it was only when we spotted the couple standing behind us pointing up to the slope, that we were alerted to something. Upon turning round to see what the scenes were, it became clear why Louis was so late; in hindsight I should really not have been at all surprised. There, gliding proficiently across the piste, was Fred Flintstone leading a group of a dozen five-year-olds traversing across the mountain and getting the tiny child skiers to balance on one ski and then switch over to the other, at the same time smacking his ski helmet with one of his poles on each and every turn, which of course was copied. Somewhere in the melee was an *Ecole du Ski* instructor, all in red, cutting across the group and gesturing to Louis, probably not engaging in pleasant chit-chat judging by his colourful body language. The group of youngsters paid no attention to their official leader, mirroring their unofficial one instead. All the way to the bottom. It must have been fun, after all. As he got into earshot, I could hear him bellowing "YID ARMY!" a split second before the group of kids shouted it back, oblivious that they were shouting a pro-Tottenham chant the FA tried to ban a few years ago.

So that was the reason for his late arrival - he had hijacked a ski-school lesson dressed as Fred Flintstone and taught the kids to traverse down the mountain on one ski, all whilst shouting something offensive from the terraces of north London . As soon as he hit the bottom he ripped off his helmet and ditched his skis, pelting off to the bar to meet the others, waving his arms and still shouting. We both just stood there before bursting into hysterics.

*

Towards the end of the day, once we'd all recovered from the afternoon in Brevent and Flegere, we took our equipment back to the ski hire place and went to a bar in the main town and absolutely hammered the après ski: Jager Bombs, pints of continental lager and then shots of Sambuca (which I let Tom sit out), then come eight we all staggered back to the chalet for the last supper. Bas and Claire saved the best til last. Curried monkfish to kick-off then on to the mains - breast of duck with plumb sauce, washed down with plenty of bubbly and finished off with a chocolate torte that broke my heart. Then, just about all of us crammed into the hot tub and shared some more bubbly. I was next to Stephanie and had my right hand wedged between her legs and somehow it got possessed by a demon and slipped a finger into her before she pushed it away and whispered "stop!"

It became clear she was uncomfortable at being violated in the presence of others, which was a shame because I couldn't leave the tub with the raging hard-on that materialised, having to wait until I had the wrinkles of a granny before I could get out.

In my room I checked my emails for only the second time in the week, delighted to see that Mo had employed a big hitter from a competitor of ours, due to start Monday, alongside an email from Rose about a deal she wanted me to get involved in. All of a sudden, when I saw her name in bold type in my inbox, I felt like I missed her. A lot.

'Hey! Greetings from Chamonix...how goes it?' I opened.

'Sean...how is it? I was just thinking about you earlier, actually,' said Rose. I looked at myself in the mirror and pressed my fingers into my pecs. I still scrub up well for forty-one.

'Ah really, that's nice to know. I was thinking about you too,' I said, truthfully. 'How're things? Making money?'

'Trying to. The place is quiet without you and Tom and Louis and Mark, you know? When you back in?' asked Rose.

'Tuesday. We'll catch up properly when I'm back...keep yourself free one evening anyway, I've got you a souvenir.'

That was a lie, but it just came to me at the time. I figured it best to dangle a gift in front of her, to secure another evening with her when I was back. I'd get her something at the airport, something smelly. All birds love a bit of smelly from duty-free.

'Ooh...thank-you. Can't wait. Anyway, Lucy wants to know if Mark has behaved himself. Think she's a wee bit paranoid,' asked Rose.

I returned to the mirror and flexed my right bicep. My phone was in my left hand pressed to my ear. I looked like I was posing, but I felt powerful and attractive.

'Yeah, he's been awesome, loved every minute. Keeps talking about her, you can tell her that. Right, I'm being summoned so I'll speak tomorrow when I 'm home,' I said as I heard Robbie calling me through to the lounge seconds before some pumping house music came on.

'Bye. Mwah,' said Rose.

At that moment I decided that I would cut ties with Stephanie, once and for all. After tonight.

THIRTY-EIGHT: SPY

As soon as Louis got into the office on Monday, he let Clive know that Sean was working from home all day and the coast was clear. Clive had asked Sean if it was ok to pop in, and said Monday was the only day he could get there, and Sean had trustingly agreed and gave Clive use of his office.

*

'So, Mark, life treating you well? Sean informs me that you're really helping out with the books and things,' Clive said. Mark was disappointed when Clive produced a couple of pastries and a flat white, and not a polythene box holding something that had just jumped out of a frying pan and a cylinder of Red Bull.

The figures stacked up well enough - bottom line healthy with anticipated growth of 22%, seven more than forecasted.

After a long dissection of the books, Clive made his move.

'Between these four walls, Mark, if the books were to show a slightly *lower* margin on the balance sheet, then I would be more than happy to reward you with something that would enhance your...mobility. If you catch my drift?' he said.

The coffee was still piping hot and the smell of beans wafted around Sean's office along with Mark's curiosity.

Clive continued. 'How much is the top of the range wheelchair these days, anyway?'

Mark thought for a second. 'Blimey, guv...you're looking at a fair few bags and then some. What do you mean anyway?'

'Off the record, make the books show a smaller profit margin for 2016, then when the accounts are due I'll personally see to you getting the best you can buy, on top of a pay increase,' he said, casually. He answered Mark's next question before it left his mouth.

'It's not bribery; it's commonplace in this game. We just want the tax bill to be kept in check. But anyway, let's just say if you can *massage* numbers for the last trading year, to meet where we need to be from a Corporation Tax perspective, well then you'll be much better off. Physically and financially. Make sense?'

Clive was firm. It took Mark about ten seconds to agree and when he did, Clive produced a spreadsheet that explained everything.

'I have every faith in you, Mark. Sean – its best he's not involved at the moment – leave him to me, ok?'

'Erm, ok, if you say so,' said Mark, his voice higher than usual and a lump in his throat.

Clive slipped on his jacket and left Mark clutching the instructions to devalue STI.

THIRTY-NINE: TEMP
July 2016, Salter residence, Brookmans Park

Claire Salter kept a brave a face and ignored best friend Karen's uncomfortable demeanour when he arrived. Godson Tom had somehow stumbled upon her sixtieth birthday party minus long-term sweetheart Cindy. Not only that, he was a complete wreck with shoes decorated in mud and loud music from the V-festival in Chelmsford. His jacket was a display of grass stains and other bits of unsavoury artwork. He appeared around the side gate clutching a half-eaten bottle of wine picked up on the way. Mum Karen and dad Byron turned away embarrassingly as he concentrated hard on keeping his balance.

'That boy...I'm sorry. Bad idea, I know,' Karen said to a bowl of cold potatoes. A group of guests were under the marquee sheltering from the light drizzle that tried to dampen the celebrations.

She looked at her husband. 'Byron, have word with him, love. He's just a different person since he...moved into London. I've not seen him sober since-'

'Oh come on, Karen, he's young. At least he made it here, he's just a kid still,' interjected Claire, catching the conversation. 'What boy wants to come to a party with a load of old fogies on a Saturday?'

'Easy for you to say, you're a Godparent. He stays indoors *all day* playing that blasted Xbox or whatever it is and working part-time at a bloomin' golf club. That's not what we forked out *thirty* bloody grand for on university. Living in London as well, he can't afford to not get proper work.'

Karen mechanically picked up a strawberry tart from the selection of desserts laid out in front of her, and slapped on a dollop of cream.

'He'll be ok love. No boy at that age knows what to do with themselves – I didn't. Don't force the issue,' said Byron.

Jason Willey's sixth sense summoned him over. Jason and Marcia knew Karen and Byron through Clive and Barbara. Clive wasn't present – he'd not been to many social gatherings this last year. He didn't want to go on his own. He wasn't ready to.

'Tom? Overheard something about employment. *Part-time*. Sounded like a whinge as well, Karen,' said Jason playfully before immediately holding court.

'It was. Typical mother, fussing about-'

'Be quiet Byron, he needs to buck his ideas up. Look at him, he can hardly stand up. He's embarrassing us. Again!'

Karen was irritated. Jason picked up on it.

'If you want him to get a bit of work over the next few weeks, I do need some temps to do some canvassing stuff. Just dial through a few lists and see who bites. Easy enough,' Jason said calmly, taking over the conversation and relaxing the slice of tension that Tom's arrival had brought along. 'Decent money. Want me to have a word?'

'Oh would you, please?' said Karen, gratefully. 'Would be awfully kind if you could give him *something* to...I dunno, at least occupy his mind. There is a half decent brain in there somewhere.'

'More than happy to. Final say so has to come from his Godmother though. It is *her* sixtieth after all.' he said, pouring some wine out for him and Marcia, who had just appeared at his side.

'Well,' said Claire. 'If Karen's cool with it then so am I.'

'Good. Now where is he?' said Jason, just as Tom emerged from the house smiling indifferently, as if no one had been talking about him.

FORTY: POACH
August 2016, Aspinall-Willey HQ, Clerkenwell

The email came through at half one on a boiling hot Monday morning after the first weekend in August. Tom was thankful to be inside the spacious offices of Aspinall-Willey while the sun baked the city in 31 degrees. It had penned most of his colleagues inside it was so uncomfortable out.

Sweat was bleeding out of him. It trickled down his neck onto his collarbone and spine; a stream of it meandered down through to his sternum. Some more travelled down his back and landed at the base between his skin and his pants making him itch. Thank God there was a fan on his desk, even though his shirt was sticking to him.

He looked outside and everything had a wavy edge to it from the heat. He could see it.

The last mouthful of what had been two litres of water slipped down and kept his hydration levels safe. Tom clicked on his messages on LinkedIn. He always checked his LinkedIn and email accounts at lunch, he had to be the model employee seeing as a family friend was in charge of the company and gave him the chance to earn decent money albeit temporary.

It looked suspiciously like another one of those generic emails that he got spammed with every so often, he thought, as he scrolled down, but the content had an air of appeal about it. The sender – Phil Long – seemed clued-up and was offering a good package to essentially go and do an extension of what he was already doing for Aspinall-Willey, except on a permanent contract, and with it, he was offered a healthy increase on base. The promise of equity in the business, should he meet growth targets over two years, and a delicious commission scheme that seemed attainable was the cherry on top. He'd be mad to at least not speculate. Even at his young age and with a relatively infantile career history, instinct told him that a quick, off-the-record chat could do no harm.

And so despite Jason being a good pal of his parents, Tom went behind their backs and met Phil and Sean, to see what they had to say. They convinced Tom of the very real potential to earn six figures in his first year, and had boasted of a recent cash injection from an angel investor, enabling a significant drive in the product offering, all of which would aid expansion into new markets. That would require young talent like Tom to lead that growth. So after a couple of interviews, and a night out with the sales guys – Sean splashing the cash and treating Tom to a few hours in some swanky members bar surrounded by stunning and game young women – Tom was sold, and a day later he'd printed out and signed a contract to join STI Ltd the following week, having only two weeks at Aspinall-Willey under his belt. Thankfully, the conversation the next day with Jason wasn't as bad as he envisioned. Yes, Jason was a touch disappointed at Tom's haste, but said that at his age he had to make choices of his own accord and learn from experience and that he would hold no grudges. Good luck to him and all that. Tom, through a touch of guilt, had told Jason that his neighbour from the flat downstairs, Rose, was qualified in something business related, and that she had asked him recently if there were any vacancies going at Aspinall-Willey. Having just moved into the city, she was looking for a job that paid alright. At first, Tom brushed it aside and said he'd ask for her, but didn't bother. Despite Rose being a total babe, Tom *was* trying to patch things up with Cindy and didn't want to engage much with Rose at all since Cindy spent a lot of time at his place, and also demanded full and unrestricted access to his phone. Sure, he felt like a bit of coward because of all that, but he was prepared to overlook his insecurities and Cindy's control in order to offer Jason maybe a solution. At the very least it was a nice gesture.

Jason took up his offer and got Rose in for an interview, and then on a rolling temporary contract.

FORTY-ONE: MODEL

The third week of January and the Mondayest Tuesday ever. Week one had been pony. January is usually a write-off, anyway. In week one, no one wants to do anything with most still recovering from the holidays, suicidal and absolutely penniless, miserable and usually coughing spluttering and spreading germs all over the shop. Week two we have the ski trip for the top performers in the business, so again most people left behind do not bother straining their tiny brains with anything more than the journey to and from work, and instead take advantage of a nice easy week without a boss or two, instead of actually getting off to a decent start and having a crack at being in the running for next year's one – ironic really. Week three is a knock on effect from fuck all happening in weeks one and two, and then week four most people just think *oh well fuck it off, its February next week, I'll make it up then.*

We'd had a sturdy year; a massive November preceded a giant December, so I had mentally allowed for a crap January, plus those who came skiing seemed invigorated and bought into the company for at least the next few months, meaning genuine and enthusiastic activity that would drive up revenue. I arrived into work around ten to see the whole floor in and beavering away – half of Phil and Mo's teams looked like they were either feeling guilty at doing fuck all for the last two weeks, or the pair of them had somehow realised that they had some money to bring in in order to avoid being torpedoed out of the window. I made sure I was dapper and clean shaven for my first day back, and as I walked to my office, I received a variety of shallow and tedious greetings such as "back on land now then boss?" "how was it, any broken bones?" and something more colourful from Louis:

"Hey you over there, with the short black hair?

I say Thomas? You say ANUS!

Thomas? ANUS! Thomas? ANUS!"

I think he makes up half of his songs on the spot. A genuine talent, that one, I wish he'd channel it on our fucking Twitter account and generate some more money for me.

One thing that caught my attention immediately was this new chap Mo had hired, Bruno something from Brazil. I'd heard excellent things about his pedigree and apparently, his track record was formidable - this from Mo, anyway. I booked in an hour first thing to give him a company overview and explain what our mission statement was and some other useless things like that. The official lines. I was reminded when Mo knocked on my door before I'd even sipped my *Grande*.

'Send him in in fifteen, let me just get sorted,' I said, before looking at my screen and swerving the crap Mo was about to give. I wasn't in the mood for any lame excuses as to why there was dick-all on the board for his lot. Mo wore a sheepish look and I think he wanted to discuss something. I frowned at an imaginary email before he took the hint and buzzed off.

Fifteen minutes later there was a polite knock at the door, impeding my enjoyment of some video highlights of a Spurs match I missed last week when in France, a solid five nil obliteration of Swansea. This Bruno chap walked in. I don't know why, but I had imagined him to be a short and stumpy bald man with glasses and slightly overweight who spoke in one of those moronic accents the Dagos have where they lisp half the time. I hadn't seen him when I arrived in, but anyway, he was the exact opposite of what I imagined. He was a handsome fucker: six foot plus, black hair, clear blue eyes and shredded to fuck – he looked like a catwalk model with cheekbones that were closer to his fringe than his chin, and a jaw that looked like it could withstand Klitschko's hardest right hook. All of that with skin from a month on the beach. He was very good looking, so to speak. Seeing as we also had Rose out there – who was as pretty as this guy was handsome – it put me off my breakfast and made me anxious. I needed to find out *immediately* what his relationship status was before I could relax and get on with the thing I was supposed to be doing, which I'd already forgotten.

'Hello, you must be Bruno?' I said, standing up and shaking his hand firmly, trying to counteract his even firmer grip. It felt like a couple of dogs marking their territory. We might as well have lifted our legs up and pissed all over the floor and then ran around and sniffed each other's arseholes.

What was his game? Why would he shake my hand so firmly and stare me down? Maybe he wanted to make a statement that he was the new kid in town and going to replace Tom at the top of the leaderboard in a month's time – not such a bad thing. Healthy competition and whatnot.

'Hello, Mr Thomas. Pleased to meet with you,' he said, smiling and taking a seat. His accent wasn't the hotchpotch *Spanglish* I was expecting either; it was deep and crystal clear, and I could tell he would be able to speak better English than some of the pissants who sell advertising space for me.

'Please, call me Sean.'

'Okay then, pleased to meet you, *Sean*,' he laughed as if there was something funny about what he just said. Christ. So after that little intro, back to the task at hand; was this fucker going to be a threat to me and Rose?

'So, you're from Brazil, I understand?' I said before he nodded to confirm what I already knew. 'Lovely country, adorable people. And the *women*...' I kissed my thumb and forefinger like I was one of those pricks on *Masterchef*.

'Ah, you have been to Brazil, which part?' he asked me. I had to think quickly seeing as I have never set foot in the country. 'Oh Rio...to the carnival, you know that Mardi Gras thing. Long time ago when I was in my twenties...but dear me, I had some fun. So many lovely *women* out there, I bet you miss that?'

He looked a bit bashful, maybe my prayers would be answered and he was going to tell me he was a raving mincer.

'Well, I moved here when I finished my studies...but

London is a good city, good for women,' he said, my heart sinking an inch. 'And a lot of other things,' he added hastily. I see what he did there.

'It is. Love this city too. So tell me about *you,* seeing as I didn't meet you properly until now. Where do you live? Married, kids etcetera...'

'Hmm. Okay...well I just moved out of my girlfriends – we broke up – so now I live in Newington Green, do you know this?'

Of course I fucking did. It was a few hundred yards down the road from Rose. Fuck me could it have gotten any worse? He was newly single and a stone's throw away from her.

'Oh I know it alright, one of the girls here lives nearby,' I said, wondering if he already knew.

He did.

'Yes, er, Rose? I met with her already, she lives a few streets along funnily enough, and we got the same bus home yesterday.'

Jesus wept.

'So you live with friends now, or family, new girlfriend?' I went full blast, I couldn't stop the questioning; it was like I was standing in the corner of the room and enjoying watching myself get squashed with every answer he gave.

'Nope, I live alone. No girlfriend,' he said, as if he knew exactly what to say. I could feel my face nicely warming up aside the need for heart surgery.

'What about you?' he asked. Nosey bugger.

'Same as. No kids or wives and that, enjoy my freedom too much,' I said, instantly cursing myself for being so honest to someone I hardly knew. I should've told him I was seeing Rose.

'Sure, me too. I'm really enjoying London as a single man. I'm only twenty-six, so just having a little fun,' he laughed.

Great. A few years older than Rose and not the eighteen or so I had on her. This was charging into a disaster at a speed I couldn't halt.

'So what did you do in Brazil before you moved here?' I said, changing tactic because I felt like I had shrivelled into a five-foot pensioner in the presence *of Colossus the Male Model from Brazil.*

'I was a model.'

Oh for fuck sake.

*

I got through the rest of the chat relatively unscathed, the only other slight niggle was a bit conflicting: he took me through his deals and performance at his previous company, bragging to me that he would easily bill fifty grand a month, which if he did, would elevate him to number one sales person and therefore make him even more of a catch for the girls (as if he wasn't already). I was smiling falsely as he continued on, unable to stop the internal panicking that he may try it on with Rose at some point. Then I thought of the money the company, and more specifically, I would make, which turned my green eyes slightly less green.

After Bruno left me, Louis decided to come and hound me with some blurb for our Twitter account he'd been working on. This was his opening gambit:

'Alright, Shergar? I think I'll have to call you *Shergar Junior* from now on. Stood next to that new kid Bruno earlier as he had a piss...fuck me you've not seen anything like it. I asked him if it was all his he was packing so much. I had to laugh, it was ridiculous...a fucking murder weapon! It was like a circumcised Brazilian baseball ba - '

'Thank you, Louis, for that insight,' I said, feeling like hanging myself. 'I hope you kept that to yourself?'

'Nah of course not, it was the first thing I told the bitches out there as soon as I got the chance...imagine the scrap they'll have trying to get his schlong out!'

'Louis, can you come back in an hour or so, got something very important to do now,' I said, telling the truth.

I opened the middle draw on my desk and pulled out a bottle of vodka and took a massive swig. It made me retch violently.

FORTY-TWO: CAR
October 2016, Maidenhead Station

Antoine Fisher and his wife Debbie didn't really see much of their immediate families. Antoine was an only child and both parents had passed away by the time he was 50 and Debbie's sister lived in St Malo, so contact between the sisters was usually via Skype except for three times a year when Debbie and Antoine jumped on the ferry and went to visit in the summer, and her sister and brother-in-law would come over and stay for a week a couple of times a year. Debbie's niece, Stephanie, had been living and working in London since 2013. No car meant she had to spend two-and-a-half-hours trekking across East London to Paddington and then a train out to Maidenhead, finished off with a taxi to the village of White Waltham whenever she visited her aunt and uncle. It wasn't cheap, either. But when Debbie invited Stephanie over for Sunday lunch she offered to pick her up from Maidenhead and give her a bed for the night with the promise of a lift into West London the next morning, early enough for the M4 not to be congested with commuters driving into the big smoke for Monday morning, or holidaymakers going to and from Heathrow.

'You should get a car love,' Debbie had said to Stephanie as they pulled away from Maidenhead station. Stephanie had the weekend off from her job as a receptionist in the Swiss Cottage Mariott and was relieved of her duties until Tuesday afternoon, so a day with her aunt and uncle and a nice Sunday roast with some decent wine was a pleasant way to spend Sunday. How very *Thirties*.

'Well, you know, is not so important in London. Bus, tube. Zis is enough for me...plus it's too expensive,' said Stephanie. Debbie suspected the last reason was the important one, and so seized her chance.

'Well, you can pick up a cheap second hand one for nothing

these days. You really should think about it love? You could come and stay with us a lot more often if you had one.'

'Oui, I know...but...'

She trailed off, putting an end to the conversation and Debbie knew not to keep on. She didn't want it to seem too rehearsed later on when after dinner Antoine would take Stephanie through a very easy way for her to earn herself a brand new car of her choosing with a value up to £50,000.

*

A week later Stephanie had created a new LinkedIn profile with the help of Uncle Antoine, and then messaged the HR manager at STI asking if they were looking to take on any business development executives who were trilingual; on top of mother tongue French, Stephanie was fluent in English and Spanish. Hannah had passed the note onto the sales managers and Phil got Stephanie in for an interview, inviting Sean along, who showed his face for about ten minutes. Soon after that, Phil was offering Stephanie a position in his team. It really was that easy for Stephanie to get a job at STI: all she had to do was make up a LinkedIn profile, make sure she was dressed to kill, act a little flirtatious in front of both the men interviewing her, and she was in.

FORTY-THREE: CHANCE
Late October 2016, Lutyens Restaurant, Fleet Street

A couple of well-dressed businessmen with a pair of young, high-class hookers on their arms. Men away from home on business in London and treating themselves to a delicious lunch with a pair of beauties. But there was no such pleasure involved in this meeting, all the pleasure would come once everything had fallen into place, and Sean was cornered.

Jason sat opposite Rose, with Antoine next to her opposite Stephanie. She'd been briefed already on the concept, and was fine with it; Rose, however, would require a bit of work, and that is why Jason suggested to Antoine that all four of them should talk things through over lunch and a glass of wine or two. Jason would lie about Sean as much as possible if it meant getting Rose to see the light.

The idea was simple in principle, but needed intricate planning and a precision execution if it was to come off, and of course, one hundred percent buy-in from everyone outside of the four men behind it.

'Ok so that is how it happens - and we'll wait as long as we need to for the right moment,' Jason said as soon as lunch was finished and their stomachs needed a breather. 'But, *when* that moment comes, if anything is less than perfect we abort and get back to the drawing board. None of us want that, do we?'

He sounded like an army general. He looked at both girls.

'Stephanie will lead him to where Tom lives – as suggested it needs to be after work preferably, or at worst when he takes his guys out on one of those afternoon jollies, and Stephanie, you *have* to ensure Tom is trashed enough that Sean is obliged to see that he gets back safe, and if he doesn't then suggest it for him.'

Both girls nodded hypnotically and Jason went on. 'Stephanie you have to be there to make sure it doesn't go tits up. Remember Tom's mum is a family friend, so don't cross the line ok?'

Rose shifted uncomfortably, like she was going to be involved in a diamond heist or contract killing. Jason picked up on it.

'You have nothing to worry about, really Rose. All you need to do is keep in touch with Stephanie, then, when she gives the signal, make sure you enter your place seconds after Sean goes in with Tom. Hang about until he comes back out, flash him a cheeky smile and accidentally leave the letter on the floor, or anywhere that'll tempt him to look at it. Then sit back and wait.'

'Sure...but, what if he doesn't? What if he's in a rush and just leaves?' asked Rose. It was a sensible question, one that even Jason shared a touch of concern around. In order to calm Rose's uncertainty, Jason appeared to be fully convinced. A simple backup would ease her worries. He spoke slower and in a softer manner and rested his hand on hers. 'It won't come to that, trust me. Louis has told Clive what this chap's all about. There's no way he won't want to know who you are. Give him a smile and then just drop the letter right under his nose, go inside and then look through your spyhole. Make sure he hovers about and studies the letter. If he doesn't then Antoine thought of a backup...'

Antoine cleared his throat.

'Ok, so, Stephanie will ask the car they have been into drive a few yards down from yours to here,' he said, pointing to a junction at the top of Rose's road where the Sainsbury's was located. 'This will allow for some time before he gets back to the car and for you to chase after him with this,' he said, holding up a wallet. 'Story is that you went back to the porch to pick up your post and found *this* on the floor and chased him to see if it was his. Of course, it wasn't, but *that* way you initiate contact and flirt a little as Stephanie gets out of the car to get cigarettes from *here*, buying you more time to probe about his business and say you're looking for permanent work la-di-da. It *will* work. Whatever happens, he'll make contact with you - for professional reasons of course.'

But the backup plan that wet afternoon in late November day wasn't needed as Stephanie watched Tom getting drunk until Sean fell into the trap, far too easily. It was executed perfectly. Stephanie kept in touch with Rose, or *Mama,* as she was saved in her phone, to make sure the timing was bang on.

The chance meeting. The chain of events that kick-started the whole thing.

FORTY-FOUR: WASTE

'There's been nothing at all, Diana. Zilch. Zero. Nearly a month of this so-called crackdown on trolling, I could be doing a lot more valuable things with my time, rather than trying to catch some spotty dweebs who find it funny to hurl abuse at people on Twitter or Facebook or whatever. Take me off this project, before I go and see Woodruff myself. Please?'

Sharma was right. There had been literally four complaints made to Islington Police, well, four quoted tweets with some mild abuse open to interpretation as to whether it was *that* bad. Just over one investigation a week for Sharma and the less the complaints came in, the more he began to question his own sanity. Inspector Cornish, however, was having none of it. Instead of letting him get on with other things, she incredibly made the poor guy do more of his own investigations, suggesting he was proactive and looked between the cracks for any kind of trolling out there. "Assist other constabularies if you need to," she said. Not on his watch, which is why he found himself once again in her office.

'Well, go and see Woodruff then. In fact, call him now and put him on speaker, and you can talk to him directly? Be my guest,' said Cornish, gesturing to the phone and moving away from it.

'Look, come on. Give me a break...it's a waste of time. Can you have a word at least? See if he'll agree on something like...I dunno, a week more of this and then if nothing comes to close it all off?'

For once Sharma didn't sound too single-minded and unreasonable. Definitely not the whiney tenor Cornish was used to lambasting over the last month or so. She agreed to have a word with Woodruff and see if he would be in agreement on something; not just because deep down she saw Sharma's frustrations and point, but also to "get him off her back" which she told him, reproachfully.

Two days later Sharma's email pinged with a message from

Cornish saying that Woodruff had confirmed with the DPS to lift the restrictive duties punishment. After two more weeks.

'Thank fuck for that,' he said to himself, as he keyed in a one-word reply of *Thanks*.

Events were going to get busier in that said fortnight, however.

Bloody Twitter.

FORTY-FIVE: SNOOP

The rest of my week turned shite come Wednesday. Thanks to the IT kid, I gained immediate access to all staff's email accounts to check for any revenue emails that may drop in, out of hours. And to do as much snooping as humanely possible in the very tight schedule I faced, day in, day out.

I'd covertly checked on Rose's emails every half hour to make sure there'd been no flirting with Bruno. That's always the way these days – a 'cheeky' email to break the ice with a few smiley faces and *LOL* and all that other fucking pointless lazy talk the under thirties vomit out today. Seriously, I hardly ever use Facebook or Twitter, but sometimes some of the things people write leave me speechless. I genuinely worry for this country; the people who are going to be running it in twenty years' time are going to be this breed of mongs unable to look up at the sky because their necks will be so damaged from permanent staring at smartphones or tablets or whatever they're named these days. Throw in some ridiculous gangsta talk that those stupid rappers from America think is cool, spelling and grammar checks on *everything* and this Island will be as fucking dead as Arsenal's spirit. It won't have a heart or a cultural richness anymore. I can see the future now. You're in Sainsbury's, walking along the aisles ordering your bag of dolphin friendly kale, talking to an interactive screen that helps you pronounce things correctly. Example: "I'd like one pint of semi-skinned milk." A non-gender specific voice (how is that possible?) will pipe up with, "I'm sorry. I didn't quite understand that, did you mean *Give me a pint of that peng cow's juice innit blud?*" Then when you get to the check-out to pay for your basket of vegan-friendly tofu, some poor student who works sixteen-hour shifts to pay for their non-gender specific higher education will be so tired they won't even be able to point their phone at your phone to complete the transaction. Fuck that. As soon as I've got the company to where I want it to be, I'm off to...just off to somewhere better. And hot as well. A place with more than three seconds of plus twenty-degree heat a year.

Anyway, nothing between Rose and Bruno much to my appeasement, however from checking Bruno's emails, I'd seen he's already trying it with Stephanie, some French lingo going on, which I copy and paste into Google translate. Turns out it's just a bit of work stuff about a lead they both pitched and Stephanie telling him to leave it alone. I like her, she has balls, like Rose. Both of them literally have more front and balls than their male counterparts put together, beach balls between their legs, whereas some of the boys would be lucky to find a couple of fun-sized petit pois rolling about if they rummaged around in their empty hacky-sacks. They'd be dangerous as a team, those two.

I went through all of Rose's sent items, and literally, there were no personal emails to anyone. I love the commitment and focus she shows, but to be sure she was going in the right direction I did a spot check on some of her proposals – all of them take the same format. It's obvious she's getting into the whole 'tough businesswoman' mode with the language she chooses:

*"Dear so-and-so, I head up the Energy division/wanted to reach out to you/be good to communicate/do you have the resources/we have the bandwidth blah blah bla*h" and more.

How can anyone function writing that day in day out? Just talk straight. It's probably the only other thing I dislike about her apart from how a steak is cooked, and I excuse that because she's young and I'm really into her. Call it love, or lust, she has me weak at the knees every time I see her. That reminds me, I need to see her soon. I'm pining for her. Apart from a quick drink on Tuesday after work, I haven't spent any time with her since the first week of January when she stayed with me a couple of nights the week before I went skiing. Loads more kinky sex and then some cuddling up on the couch and films and stuff. It was nice and it made me feel young again, nothing else mattered at that moment in time. I was becoming softer inside, gradually feeling the horrible, womanising part of me that I know I have, slip away.

I sent her an e-mail and asked to see her in my office just before five. Despite PWP's being on the cards, I'd sooner spend time with her. *Hoes before bros.* As soon as I'd sent the e-mail, I launched into her inbox and waited for the bold type to change to normal, so I knew she'd opened it. As I waited, however, another email hit her inbox, from Bruno Perreira! The subject line was simply *Re:* and the content was just one line which read: *LOL...ok, you can show me around on Friday then* ☺

I had some mad rush of blood to the head and my heart decided not to beat for a moment. I looked down the chain and read the whole correspondence. It started with harmless chitchat but then Bruno went in for the kill pretty swift, asking Rose what the bars and pubs were like around the area, Rose returning that question and saying they were ok, then smooth old Bruno suggesting perhaps she show him about, and Rose saying yeah sure! Then the last one from Bruno was the one I'd stumbled upon. It was the exact same pattern I'd have followed had it been me. What a cunt! Plus his email changed from bold to normal before mine did – she prioritised him over me. I went to her sent items, as I did one popped up at the top of the screen, her instant reply to Bruno: *LOL sure why not!* ☺

FUCKING SMILEY FACES! I hate them.

And Friday? Even worse news then. No work Saturday so plenty of drinking to be done, the more drinking the more chance of...I didn't even want to think about it. Everyone knows if you arrange a date on a Friday or Saturday, your chances of getting laid jump from 50/50 to at least 80/20. Over my dead body.

I was seething with rage; I wanted to get a fucking machine gun and to hold it to his head while screaming at Rose "LOOK AT WHAT YOU'VE DRIVEN ME TO, YOU UNGRATEFUL LITTLE CUNT!" before emptying the magazine into his brains.

But I settled on just sitting there, taking another swig of vodka, and boiling.

As quickly as her reply had appeared in her sent items

folder, it had disappeared. My hunch that she was deleting everything between them was confirmed when I went back to her inbox and his email had vanished. I continued my detective work and went into the *deleted items* folder to find a stack of emails from him in between her replies. Fucking devious. Did she know I was monitoring her activity or was she just being careful? Either way, it made no difference; I'd caught her. I felt sick - I actually wanted to cry, my worst nightmare was coming true. Another massive rush of blood to the head nearly knocked me off my seat so I steadied myself with round three of vodka.

*

'Sorry it's so close to five, but I've barely had time breathe today.'

I started with an almighty whopper. Rose sat there obediently with a pad and was sucking on her pen again, and I already felt that very soon I'd have forgotten about most of the things that upset me and I'd be rogering her into oblivion.

'No worries. You looked super concentrated every time I looked in here, fixated on the screen,' she said.

Did she know what I was up to? I went red as I thought about it.

'I just wanted to run through a couple of proposals you have out there - sometimes it's good to get my view on them, you know?' I said, trying to sound calm. She seemed to buy it.

'Sure, no worries.'

'I trust Phil and Mo to go through the detail with their guys, but now and again I need to see that you're on it, if that makes sense?'

'What do you want to know?' she asked and I made up something or other. We chatted for few minutes. I wrapped it up and then hit her with a sucker punch.

'Listen, can I ask you something?' I said with an edge of panic in my voice. Not too much but just enough to intrigue her.

'Yeah go on,' said Rose, already curious.

'That new chap – Bruno - has he been, you know, hitting on you, or said anything cheeky?' I said lowering the volume. It was hush-hush after all.

'Hmmm nope, not really, just a couple of emails about work stuff. Why?'

Fucking liar!

'Ok, and this goes no further at all, understand?' I managed to channel my burning rage at her lying to me into a stern and concentrated glare. I was staring at her loudly.

'Okay, sure, I'll keep it between us,' she said, still intrigued. I knew why as well, the fucking slut.

'Well, a couple of the girls have already complained to me that he's been emailing them and asking them to *show him around the area* after work tomorrow, or Friday...hold on let me just read the email, where is it?' I said scrolling down to an imaginary email. 'Ah, here we go: *Sean can you make it clear to Bruno that it's not the done thing to pester girls for dates after two days of employment. Next time he does I'm going to HR.*'

I said it as if I was reading a real email word for word at a slower pace than usual, the sequence of words was monotone and I even winced at the word *pester* and leant into my screen. I think it was a decent performance, not Oscars but definitely Eastenders. I looked up from the screen and held on to my frown.

'I can't name names but both complainants have made me aware of it, *and* one of the *analysts* said something to Mel, as well, can you believe? I'm going to ask Stephanie, but it seems like he's on a mission. I'm sure it's only a matter of time before you get it, too,' I said, taking great pleasure at Rose's expression going from intrigue to disappointment as it sunk in that she was low down in the pecking order. Even one of the geeks in research, none of whom are remotely as nice as her.

'Oh...erm, ok well I'll let you know if he does,' she said. I could tell she was still pissed off, so I struck her with something to make her feel attractive once more.

'If he keeps it up I'll give him the bullet, this business is too important to have him trying to shag everything in a skirt after less than a week, however good he may be. And keep this between us, whatever you do. Anyway, enough of that, what are you up to Friday?'

She looked at me, doe-eyed like she was cornered by a wolf or something. It was a real turn on, as well. Whether or not she knew that I knew, or even had a hunch, this would tell me all I needed to know about if she was into me as much as I wanted her to be.

'Loose plans to see Zoe, but, she's not too sure either. Why...?'

'New restaurant in the Blackfriars that I'm keen on going to, and then a cocktail making class at Keystone Crescent. Need a co-pilot and it's been a while since we've had some fun. Get done up Friday and be ready to leave with me after work. Unless you'd rather see Zoe?'

'Sounds fun, yeah cool. I'd like that. Be nice to spend the night together and not have work in the morning,' she said, and like that, she was mine once again and I could not wait to read her email cancelling on Bruno. And then his face when she came in Friday morning looking like a ten out of ten supermodel.

She left the office, so I took a long swig of vodka and initiated some celebratory PWPs. This time I didn't retch.

FORTY-SIX: FALSE

Stephanie had called the meeting herself. She was concerned about her January performance and felt like Phil wasn't providing the best counsel for her to progress. Best pick Sean's brains for a while, but she left it late in the day, to be safe.

As she entered his office, Rose went in too, and asked Sean very apologetically if he could run out and listen in to a prospect she had on the line, one who wanted to negotiate on price. Sean agreed and left Stephanie who had just enough time to slide Sean's phone into her blazer pocket. What was about to happen would be pivotal in the whole operation:

Sean returned after a minute; apparently Rose's prospect hung-up and didn't answer when she hit redial. So ten minutes into the meeting Stephanie had called, the fire alarm sounded. It wasn't the short, thirty seconds test that happened now and then though, the bell kept screaming until it became apparent it was real and everyone started shuffling out and down the stairwells, except Mark who took the lift. It was at this point that both Stephanie and Sean left the office, hampered by Sean looking for his phone for ten seconds beforehand. As they left the floor and got to the stairs, Stephanie slowed down and waited back until Louis - who had set the alarm off - appeared next to her and took Sean's phone, in a move that looked like they were doing a drug deal on a street corner. Then Louis checked back, waited for everyone to go on ahead before slipping back up to the toilets and locking himself in a cubicle, where he tapped in the four-digit code Stephanie had managed to retrieve from careful observation of Sean's fingers at hers that night of the Christmas party. Once into the phone, he had the password for Twitter. Louis had fifteen, maybe twenty minutes, max, to go to town before plonking the phone back in Sean's office once he'd deleted the Twitter app to avoid alerting Sean to the imminent tidal wave of notifications that would inevitably come.

And he certainly went to town.

FORTY-SEVEN: VIRAL

'Well it looks like your big break might be here Pritesh, at the eleventh hour,' Cornish said smugly. *'Seek, and ye shall find.* Here, look.'

She handed over a report from the Metropolitan police with a list of racist and vile tweets made from the account of *@Thomas_Sean1976* directed to some of the nations most loved celebrities. The perpetrator had, within the space of a quarter-of-an-hour, sent as many tweets in as many minutes, opening up the investigation for Sharma to get his teeth into. The first one that caught his attention was to an old page three model called Flame, AKA Jade Smith, aimed at her son, Roman, who most people know is mixed race and overweight, and has been subjected to recent abuse on social media that had calmed down thanks to an anti-bullying campaign that got widespread media attention. The account Sharma found himself looking at had kicked off with a tweet that read *your son is a big fat black spastic & he should be put down* and was deleted a few minutes after, not before a few screen grabs were made and hundreds of retweets, one by Flame herself. In fact, Sharma soon found that all the tweets had been deleted a few minutes after being sent, indicating that either the person tweeting was so stupid and naïve that they did it for a laugh and then deleting them in the thinking there was no way to be caught – something Sharma would have probably done himself. Either that or the account had been hacked. That was easy enough to find out.

Tim Doyle the gay Olympic swimmer got it next: *I hope you drown in a swimming pool of your faggot husband's aids ridden semen you gay cunt* (Sharma had laughed out loud at that one). Then Jewish TV critic and celebrity Damien Gold was next, this time the troll had suggested that Gold himself should go to Auschwitz and *party on down with the million stinking Jews that perished.* It was incredible. Sharma had never seen anything that bad in the past month during his special assignment, or ever, for that matter. The account then went on a mission to go after various Paralympic athletes, sending all sorts of terrible messages, calling them a range of names like *god's rejects, the devils spawn, fucking spazmos, waste of skin, subhuman etc.* and one even said *Theresa should cut all your benefits and make you pay society for having to look at you LOL!* with the disabled icon/emoji. It was brutal. The outrage it caused was free-flowing and relentless, literally every minute, over a whole day. Tweets, retweets, quotes, messages to the police, with plenty from celebrities.

Sharma got to work and within four minutes found that the chap was the owner and CEO at a company based literally ten minutes away in Farringdon. Nik Nak Paddy Whack.

FORTY-EIGHT: HACKED

'Mark! Leave it for fuck sake, it's blatantly not him!'

That was from Melanie, in vain, as Mark's arms became a blur. He went full-pelt at Sean the moment he stepped into the office on Friday morning. Melanie's words didn't have the desired effect, and Mark continued his pursuit of Sean, who was totally oblivious to what was going on. Catching up with him and smashing his wheels on the back of Sean's ankles so hard that he spilt his coffee, Mark finally confronted him.

'What the fu-' cried Sean.

'You got a fucking problem, pal?' shouted Mark.

Sean was totally perplexed, as you'd imagine, but still smart enough to sense something was not quite right. He turned around and looked down at Mark, who was clutching a microwaved Ginsters something or other for when the showdown was over with.

Sean composed himself.

'Right, clearly you think I've done something to upset you, so if you want to talk about it, I suggest we go and do it in my office and not on the floor. Follow me,' said Sean, for once behaving like a man totally in charge. Everyone was still staring.

In the office he sat down and calmly asked Mark what the issue was, still unaware of the absolute mess from the night before.

'You pissed up yesterday was ya? Tweeting a load of abuse about disabled people? Blacks, Jews, anyone else? I can't believe it.'

'Wait...what? What the fuck are you on about?' asked Sean, rightly concerned.

Mark showed him: the colour in Sean's face disappeared in five seconds. Even though he knew it wasn't him, damage had been done. The company name was all over Twitter, his name, death threats and the like. It was bad. *Very* bad.

'Ok, Mark. That wasn't me – I don't use Twitter much. Clearly I was hacked, so can you just fuck off out of my office and let me deal with this because I'm rather insulted at *you* for actually believing this was something I would do.'

Mark went to leave, but Sean added a very valid point before he made it all the way out.

'Oh...and you seem to be ok for Louis to prank you every day, write things about you and slap on the back of your chair. So why the sudden shift in morals?'

Mark stayed silent.

'Thank you. Now go,' said Sean with finality.

Once he'd got his head round what had gone on, Sean went and got the whole floor's attention.

'Guys, just to let you know that some arsehole hacked my Twitter yesterday because those tweets were not made by me, but I'm sure you're all smart enough to work that out. So, get back to work, and if anyone mentions it then tell them what I just told you, or put them through to me. Thanks.'

Then he went down to get some fresh air and make a call to his solicitor, Chris. But he couldn't because there was a police officer in reception.

Then it dawned on him that somebody must hate him. So much.

FORTY-NINE: STITCHED

I got into the office later than usual on Friday. I had to get myself ready for the hijacked date with Rose. I wanted to pull out all the stops and get her to fall for me, or some more if she had started to already. If not, she was edging closer, I was sure of it. I must have been done up so well because the second I walked onto the floor, the whole place fell silent and gawped at me. It was weird, actually. I know I am well presented and stuff, but I don't usually get *that* kind of reception. Anyway, that pleasure was short-lived as it turned out to be something else. Mark came bounding over to me yelling something to my knees about being anti-disabled, so I took him inside the office and he showed me all these screen grabs of tweets I'd supposedly made late yesterday afternoon. It was fucking incredible! Even Louis wouldn't tweet awful stuff like that. Someone was really out to get me, and I had a good idea who. Bruno.

How the fuck had he found out I was monitoring his emails? And made up a lie to Rose about him harassing other birds on the floor? This was his revenge.

*

After I watched that stupid raspberry ripple disappear away from the office, my blood still boiling over the audacity of him actually believing they were made by me, I went out to get some air and call my solicitor Chris to brief him on the whole story. Chris is based up at Chapel Market and has helped me out no end a couple of times in the past, so I could just jump in a cab and go see him right away, but as I went to call him I noticed a bunch of missed calls I got late last night from Carl. Must have been in relation to all the drama going on with Twitter. Then I was stopped in my tracks by some dark policeman who wanted to interview me about the supposed *trolling* from my account. I surrendered my damn phone as well, requesting that they get on with it and trace the source of the abuse. I'd already thought that as part of the damage limitation process, I'd ask the police to do me a favour and tweet that it was a hacker, or release a statement or something and help clear my name. It was bad. All I wanted to do was go home and cuddle Rose and hear her tell me everything was going to be ok, and for that, I felt mildly ashamed at not being man enough to brush it aside and carry on. She was definitely changing something inside me, and I couldn't do anything to stop it.

*

It got to the end of the day and Rose hung back, long after Bruno had gone. I checked his emails and he'd left a reply she'd sent him earlier in the day saying she was busy this evening now, and that it wasn't a good idea to go out for a drink with someone she worked so closely with, and it looked like he didn't reply as there was nothing in his deleted items folder. Good, fuck you. All I had to do was prove it was him.

*

We had an awesome time over dinner. I let Rose in a bit; she wanted to know why I was still unmarried and had no kids, and I told her the truth. Perhaps it was the wine, perhaps it was because I felt like I could open up to her, perhaps I felt even close to her, maybe all of that. But I let her have a look inside.

I told her about my younger years, my engagement to Chloe, my first and last serious relationship. Chloe who had been in labour for eleven hours only to give birth to a stillborn baby boy, a child we said hello and then goodbye to in the space of a few minutes. It meant the collapse of us because of the trauma we went through. Since then I'd shied away from anything serious. I talked about my dad, and my mum and step-dad, and that although I knew they loved me, I didn't feel like they loved me unconditionally when I was growing up, the anxiety I got when mum and dad divorced, and then the turbulent relationship my mum had with my step-dad for the first few years of their marriage. I told her of my memories of standing at the top of the stairs and my sister holding my head against her tummy and covering my ears so I couldn't hear them as they fought downstairs, my tears wetting her pyjamas, feeling so scared there would be another divorce and it meant I wet the bed every other night. I looked at her and told her that maybe all of those things meant I was scared of commitment and long-lasting love I thought I craved but deep down all I wanted to do was be happy, laugh, enjoy life and share it with someone, and that it was just dawning on me now at 41.

And for the first time since my early twenties, I cried in front of a woman.

FIFTY: TREAT

'Yep, it worked a treat, Pa.'

Louis called Clive and informed him that his share of the plan had gone smoothly. 'Stephanie and Rose was dynamite, it was a breeze.'

'Were dynamite, Louis. Stephanie and Rose *were* dynamite. And what about the messages?' asked Clive.

'Yip. Deleted all the messages from both of them, all that was left was his ones.'

'Yep, well, let's just let the others sort it out from here. But you'll be rewarded nicely once it's sorted. And thanks, again.'

'Sure. Hey, Pa?

'Yes.'

'What does a dead 'phone sound like?'

'Eh? I du-'

Beep beep beep.

FIFTY-ONE: PUZZLE

They were so near to the final part of the plan. The part that, once executed, would mean that Sean was bang in trouble. No way around it, he'd *have* to sell. No choice, cornered from all angles, no way out, no escape. Nothing. The job would be done in a few days depending on how soon Rose could get him alone in the office after hours and act out their role-play. The role-play that would be filmed by Stephanie.

Since the Twitter fiasco, the business was suffering bad press. And those figures Mark had been busying himself with; bribed to massage into a very slim and measly bottom line. It all made for a pretty bleak future. How much would a company with an awful social responsibility image and a slim bottom line be worth? Not the millions Sean had told Jason it was worth, just a few months back. You're looking at a fraction of that. CEO and owner steps down after the buy-out, new owners rename the place and give it a revamp, keeping the happy customers who haven't run a mile, then some investing into the product. Within a year it's rocking. Aspinall-Willey and the FFB board have another high-performance company in their portfolio to add. And Sean? Who cares? Once it was all done and dusted, Foster would take care of all the legalities, ensuring any loopholes that needed to be open were open, and those that needed to be closed, closed. Stephanie would have her brand new company X6, Rose would have her Audi TT, Mark his state of the art chair and Louis would be taking a cut of equity and profit share. That was the mastermind plan.

But it all hinged on the final piece of the puzzle running smoothly.

FIFTY-TWO: ARREST

Diana Cornish sat next to Pritesh Sharma and opposite Chief Inspector Colin Woodruff, this time in his office, which was twice the size of Diana's. Chance would be a fine thing to get to that level. A brown man like him, getting to Chief Inspector? Yeah right. He'd often told himself that when he thought about long term. Not even Siddique Khan being voted in as Mayor gave him any hope. He had, what you might say, a chip on his shoulder. To be truthful, he was a British citizen, born in Whitechapel to parents from La Hoare, raised in the area until he joined the force at 24 after some travelling and time spent in the motherland. He was as much a Londoner as Alf Garnett, the only difference being his choice of religion and place of worship. Muhammad over Jesus, Mosque over Church. Yet he always felt, that in his line of work, he was overlooked for any kind of promotion opportunity that came up, or even a shift in unit. As he sat there with the two 'big dicks' of Islington Constabulary, something told him that a high profile and well-documented arrest would give him the break he needed, and at least make a good case to push for promotion or a changeover to domestic, or even the terror squad. Something new, anyway.

'So in essence what we've got here is one account belonging to a 41-year-old business owner – and quite a successful one at that, it would seem – who, according to the results from tracking the device, sent *fifteen* tweets, all of them racist, homophobic or extremely abusive between...let me look...' Woodruff held a piece of paper closer to him, '4.31pm and 4.50pm, and then in the next two minutes deleted each and every one, and logged out of his account. Is that what you are getting here, Pritesh, hmm?'

Cornish shifted a little. She felt uncomfortable for Sharma, the last word "hmm" hung in the air unnecessarily longer than it should have she could almost see it. She tried to interject.

'Well I think what we - '

Woodruff cut off Cornish with a simple raise of his index

finger and kept his eyes on Sharma. 'Pritesh?

'Sir, unless someone physically stole his mobile, managed to unlock it and then go into his Twitter and do all that - in the space of fifteen minutes and then clear all the evidence - then it is of my opinion that this...erm...*Sean Thomas* is behind it. He's a racist, he's anti-disabled, he hates fag...ah...gays. Classic case of someone trying to be funny, then deleting the tweets right away when they realise the scale of it all,' he said, feeling confident up until the last part about the "scale of what he's done", and knew both his colleagues were thinking about his own fuck up a few weeks back. The reason he was sat there now.

He continued nonetheless. 'No one hacking into an account would do that. They'd just leave the tweets where they were for as many people to see. That's what I think sir, and I think Diana is with me.'

That told him. Smug bastard sitting there with his stupid tash and massive belly. He reminded Sharma of those *Fast Show* characters *The Fat Sweaty Coppers*.

'You *think* do you...?' Woodruff didn't look like he agreed. 'Diana?'

'I'm with Pritesh on this, Colin.'

Woodruff looked up, finally and stared behind the pair of them. All his awards and certificates and framed newspaper clippings with headlines decorated the walls - a subtle hint that he was sat where he was for those reasons.

'So, you traced the device, and it all came from the phone you have in there?' he said, pointing a sealed, see-through bag that contained Sean's phone.

'Yes, everything. It was him. Probably pissed up on a jolly. Unless he can prove otherwise,' said Sharma.

'*Unless he can prove otherwise*, you think we – sorry, you - have enough *proof* beyond reasonable doubt that this man is guilty?'

Cornish and Sharma both replied "yes" in unison, Sharma

the louder.

'Very well. Go and do what you need to do, and once you bring him in we can release a statement we have arrested someone on suspicion of racially aggravated hate amongst other offences, including bullying and homophobic abuse. Pritesh you can go now. Diana stays here.'

'Yes sir, thank you.' And Pritesh left, feeling that the last few weeks were not given in vain. As soon as the door shut, Woodruff spoke.

'Diana, give a fool enough rope and he'll hang himself. Leave him to it, with your backing as well. He needs to learn from his mistakes, and you'll need to learn from yours too, I'd say.'

'What? Don't you think what we both believe to be true is really the case? We've been closer than you for the past month,' she said, belligerently.

'Let's just wait and see,' he replied. 'Thank you.'

And then Cornish left, right after her bubble burst.

FIFTY-THREE: TRIPLE

Clive had a strong gut feeling something was amiss, even though Mark said he was clear on the given instructions. He'd triple checked the balance sheet, but something told him it just didn't stack up well enough. A discreet meeting would be called, but at least time was on their side.

First things first, call the big man.

*

Jason stepped out of the luncheon to take the call from Clive; he'd called twice and then sent a text alerting him that words were needed.

'Excuse me, ladies and gentlemen, I must make a call. Please, go ahead and order some more wine, and I'll rejoin you as soon as I can.'

Those words happened to be the last words he spoke – for that afternoon anyway - to the board of directors of *The Informant* magazine and online business insider; a company Jason was in pursuit of. He'd worked out that the company's operating profit margin could be doubled in three years with the right leadership, and made no bones about wanting to buy them outright. The meeting hadn't gone so well but he still sniffed some kind of agreement. He usually would in times of doubt. Clive's messaging wasn't too much of a hindrance, as he came to the conclusion he'd need to bide his time with the guys he was entertaining at the Criterion.

'Clive, talk to me.' He was standing out in the cold and admiring the tourists taking pictures of Eros. London. What a city.

'Sorry to interrupt Jason, but...' Clive said, fading to reassure himself the reason for the call was justified.

'What...what is it?' said Jason.

'The accounts. Look way too good. I'm not sure Mark understood what I got at last week. I need you to have a look - bottom line seems boosted by all the immediately recognisable revenue.' Clive sounded frail, tired like he was facing a problem, absent of the patience needed to sort it.

'What do you mean, Clive? Spit it out. Talk straight because I don't follow – that was *your* task.'

'I mean, I think Sean's been fiddling the books with Mark's help, right? Asking Mark to fiddle them in the opposite direction has put Mark in a predicament. Mark is a problem.'

'Ok, I follow. Round up the other two and let's meet in your boardroom at...' Jason checked his watch, 'half two. I'll leave now. Bye.'

He hung up, made his way to the concierge of the Criterion, left his Amex details and told him to send over a bottle of Kristal with a note of apology.

*

'Oui allo?' Antoine answered after eight rings. Six vibrations on his arm and another two as he removed the phone from the left pocket of his duck down jacket. He had to take his gloves off, too – a real pain in the arse.

'Antoine? It's me, Clive. You're on speaker. I'm with Pete and Jason.'

'Yeah, right. 'Allo, erm, how are you all? This isn't a call to enquire about how much snow we've got here in Verbier, I assume? But I can tell you, it's 'eavenly right now,' replied Antoine. Debbie flew past him and spun round to a stop, and some snow flicked into his shins. She lifted up her ski mask to check it was her husband she'd just sprayed half-way down the glorious blue run they'd picked out to end the day.

'We're running through some accounts together. Clive has spotted something that puts it all at risk,' Jason said, 'I won't go into it now, but you have to let Stephanie know that it's gonna be in the next couple as soon as we've fixed this. Can you do that?'

'Roger Roger. When do you want me to make the call? Now? This evening?' Antoine asked, holding up his hand as Debbie protested at him being on the phone while they were supposed to be on holiday.

'On my signal. We'll sort Mark out, then prep Rose in the next day or two. Then, once that's done, call *Papa* and fill her in. D'accord?'

'Oui, d'accord. Au revoir.' Antoine hung up, put his gloves back on and kicked off down the mountain past Debbie, who had turned into a statue.

'Now, Mark? What do we do with him?'

Foster asked the first thing he'd said in over an hour of trying to work out just how the profitability of STI was so healthy, and how to reverse it, quickly.

'Clive. Are you totally sure he was clear of the *implications*? Seems like he's either sent you the wrong spreadsheet, or he's playing dumb,' said Jason.

'Or, perhaps he isn't comfortable doing it...that's my bet,' offered Clive.

'So what then? Can we just manually adjust these?' This was from Foster as he held up a copy of the accounts.

'No. As if...are you *crazy* Pete?' said Jason, genuinely shocked, 'if they differ from what Mark and Sean have on their own system then we could be looked into when he cottons on. We can investigate the books properly until the cows come home when it's done. That's always been the plan.'

'Ok. Let's hit Mark hard. Clive get Louis to keep him late on Monday, and to message you when Sean fucks off home, then we'll go in and work through the accounts line by fucking line with him until its set in stone, and we have the company barely running on fumes. I have a good idea what we need to fix, anyway. I'll tell Rose over the weekend. Antoine can deal with Stephanie, see if Rose can work it for Tuesday, strike as soon as possible. All agreed?' Jason was on his feet and those words were his last ones before he left the building.

FIFTY-FOUR: DINNER

My weekend was all but consumed by a darkness that hovered expectantly over me. Although I felt happy that Rose allowed me to be so open with her on Friday, I couldn't shrug off the worry that the whole Twitter hack had brought with it, and it still hadn't been resolved. It was a dark time, despite knowing it was at the hands of a hacker. Smashing into the drink and shovel all weekend didn't help with the aftermath either, even though at the time it seemed to help me forget about everything. The weather as well, still dark in the mornings and cold. Nothing to look forward to, except spending time with Rose. It just about kept me alive.

That policeman hadn't returned my calls and even though I had a second phone for the time-being, something niggled me about it being in custody. Paranoia sent me into a panic that they may trawl through my iCloud account and find all kinds of wrong porno clips various mates had sent to me over the years. I needed a clear head, so I sent Stephanie a text message to say that we couldn't have the casual sex thing anymore as she'd been giving it recently but I fucking well sent it to Rose instead! She replied with *what?*

I came clean and told her it was meant for someone else and she seemed remarkably ok with it, however, so on Saturday I asked her if she wanted to go for dinner on Sunday somewhere quiet and chic in Hampstead.

*

We met in The Flask pub in Highgate before driving to an Italian place on Haverstock Hill, where we shared the best Veal in North London and an insanely expensive bottle of Barolo, then a cheaper Valpolicella. We sat in the place until ten, talking like we had known each other for years and I mentioned to Rose what I was thinking and her face came over with a little blush at the suggestion, sidestepping a little, choosing to study her napkin in a cute and bashful way; as if she was on screen and acting. At that moment I wanted to just hold her and breathe her in and smell her hair and...not even fuck her. Crazy, but things change when you fall in love. You can't do anything about it, and you know you need to keep yourself in check and all that, but you just stick two fingers up at anything sensible and really do let your heart lead you, wherever that may be. I found myself being endeared towards the way she chose to use a spoon with her fork, and how she held her wine glass inches from her lips for a couple seconds before she took a sip. Little, simple things that no one else would bat an eyelid at. Little things that meant something big was happening to me, something that controlled me, and kept my heart a prisoner that couldn't escape. That was fine with me.

The conversation was largely about her. Childhood, upbringing, mum and dad and older brother and the role each of them played in her life, hopes and dreams and life ambitions, no pretence on her part. A far cry from the interview of a few weeks back. I let her tell me all of it without interjecting and she talked and talked and laughed and giggled and joked and put her hand on mine and squeezed it tight. And for the first time in a long time, I lost myself in the eyes of a woman, and didn't want to be found.

*

I suggested going to hers after as it was much closer and she had a few important calls to do in the morning, but she said Lucy had Mark over and that she really didn't want to pussyfoot about, plus she wanted to get down to it "without the shackles on" - my earlier take-it-or-leave-it of getting her into the sack had disappeared just as the second bottle of wine did to be replaced with the raging horn. Anyway, in my mind, I'd make love to her first, slowly and passionately and then we could get kinky. I think she'd packed a few toys into her overnight bag, and right enough, later on we enjoyed another very experimental session of whips, chains, dildos, paddles and collars. Then before we went to sleep, we had a longer, calmer and much more passionate time – I just about managed to stop myself saying *those* three words. She told me that on Tuesday she wanted to live out her fantasy role-play of me interviewing her and then "mock-raping" her - she had plans Monday.

'Are you sure you're comfortable with that?' she even asked me. *Bless.*

'Yep, never done it before. Anything for a bit of spice eh?' I said, cheerily, not really meaning it, although she could have asked me anything. She could have asked me to bend over and take a stiff one from a rampant, sex-starved African Elephant and I'd have touched my toes on the spot.

FIFTY-FIVE: COLUMN

There was nothing complex about what needed to be achieved to make it all fall into place. Clive had rightly predicted that Louis would be able to keep Mark behind later on the Monday, and when the coast was totally clear Jason and Clive would wait for them in the pub opposite, one that Sean wouldn't be seen dead in – a ghastly Wetherspoons - where they'd be waiting to reiterate the importance of the accuracy of accounts. There was also a much bigger incentive attached to his cooperation as well; not only the very best, top-of-the-range motorised wheelchair Davros himself would envy, but, if things went to plan, a small slice of equity in a few years' time was up for grabs, the *few years' time* bit nice and vague.

'Ok, Louis just text me. Be down in five,' said Clive. 'Go and get them in then, the boy said pints of Stella for both.'

Jason went to the bar and returned with a tray.

'Oi oi gents. Fancy bumping into you lot then eh?'

Louis pushed Mark into the pub and over to Clive and Jason. Of course, Mark had met Clive once but had no idea of the link between them.

'Ah Mark, we meet again. Good to see you,' said Clive.

'Nice to see you again, Mark. Hope STI are looking after you?' said Jason.

Clive spoke again before Mark could work out what was going on.

'Those numbers you gave me last week. Something isn't right here. Can you run me through *this* column please?' He was pointing to a line of numbers.

'Eh?' said Mark.

'This one? The one that has the words *report sales* next to it,' snapped Clive as the colour from Mark's face disappeared.

'Well erm,' Mark began. 'I-I-It's erm, open to interpretation what that means. So I believe.'

Mark was stammering and twitching in his chair. Clive pushed the air with raised palms and stopped Mark.

'Ok. Look, the way I've read this is that Sean has *maybe* asked you to code some service revenue, like subscriptions, as single reports. So as to impact the bottom line immediately and make the profit margin appear larger than it should be. I'm not saying that's definitely what's happened, but it *looks* like it. Certainly to someone looking in from the outside, an expert in these things, they may well have questions about the type of revenue STI is submitting. Now, you're the expert, you tell me what it is.'

Jason fixed his stare on Mark, Mark shrunk.

'Let me just have a look for a sec-'

Clive slid a copy of the accounts over to him. Some dregs of spilt pints dampened the paper. Mark picked it up and looked at it closely in a silence that Clive broke.

'Jason here, who you know well, is also an independent accountant as well as a business partner of mine - IFA and FS regulated and all that. He's here to run through what *you* need to do - as the accountant of STI Ltd - to clear *your* name. Because if these accounts are submitted to HMRC, not only will Sean be facing a hefty fine or worse, so will you. Get this right and we can discuss equity in the firm as well. Now then, I'll leave you to it. Gentlemen.'

*

Five pints later with closing time looming, Mark had converted two-thirds of the *report sales* revenue over to *subscription* revenue and enjoyed a good long chat with Jason about nothing much work related. The 2017 operating profit had gone down by a sizeable enough amount for the company's valuation to fall within the boundaries of the best and worst case prices Jason would offer Sean. That side of things was taken care of.

With Sean's phone still being dissected by the Old Bill, the coast was clearing for the finale.

FIFTY-SIX: LATIN

The scent of grilled meat was constantly mouth-watering. Winter had tried to sneak into the restaurant, but was quickly shooed away by the warm, Latin atmosphere of the place she was in. The sound of chefs talking away in Spanish amid plates clanging was just about audible through the salsa music that was jumping out of the speakers fixed to the wall, and it danced around the chic little Peruvian restaurant. Table for two, wine, cocktails and some very commendable grub. She had *The X Factor* on record, she'd watch it when she got home, and if Bruno was into it, then it was a good excuse to get him back to hers.

Stephanie had not been to a place like it since moving to London. Bruno had finally persuaded her to go for dinner on Saturday evening to some place in Hackney that he knew of. The restaurant was alive with Saturday night diners chattering away, mostly in Spanish - always a very promising sign. A guarantee the food would be quality.

'We'll have a couple more cocktails now, I think. Please, give us five minutes,' said Bruno politely to the waiter, as he swiped away their empty wine bottle and asked them with his eyes what they wanted next.

'Oh, wow,' said Stephanie, feeling the alcohol already.

'Excuse me,' said Bruno getting up. 'I must use the gents.'

He was well-mannered and charming, not that he needed to be. He could have been rude, arrogant and smelly; his looks still would have won over any straight female. Stephanie took it as a chance to check her phone. One thing she didn't like was fiddling about with it during drinks or dinner. Bad etiquette. She made a point of keeping it in her handbag if she was part of something intimate.

There was a message from Uncle Antoine: *Tuesday. Speak to Mama to finalise. Ax*

Bruno returned and clocked her sliding her phone quickly

back into her bag.

'Ah ok, telling everyone I'm not an axe murderer, and the date is going well?'

When the waiter returned to take their order, she ordered a Vodka Martini, all of a sudden feeling the need for a stiff drink.

*

Rose's Saturday night had been dull. The previous night she'd spent with Sean at some nice new place in Blackfriars and then to Sean's members bar for a lesson in mixology, rolling into bed late-ish after a lot of sex and chat, the next day and evening surrendered to Netflix and pretzels, again taking full advantage of a free flat.

She spread out on her leather sofa, arms above her head, arched her back and curled her toes up, binging on TV, good marks for her impression of a dozing cat. As she tried to decide on the thousands of films on offer, cursing herself that it always took so long to choose, her phone vibrated and the screen glowed in the living room, illuminating the coffee table in light green. Four words ran across the screen: *It is on Tuesday* and the message came from *Papa*. She responded back with *affirmative* and put it back down on the table, only for it to vibrate again. Why did Stephanie feel the need to reply back to that so quickly?

But the message came from an unknown number that said *I'm sorry, but I can't see you anymore. I know it's nothing serious but it's not right. Hope you understand xx"*

Then she realised it was from Sean on his other number.

Hello Sean, this is your other number the one on the end of your emails, what are you getting at? responded Rose.

Sean replied *oh fuck I'm sorry, I meant to send that to someone I was seeing before Xmas, just for a bit of fun but I kinda want to just be exclusive with you from now on xxx.*

Rose knew who it was meant for, and was happy in a way that Sean had decided he wanted exclusivity. Soon she'd have that new TT and she could sell it for a second-hand mini and bank forty grand, on top of a pay rise. All she had to do was get Sean to play the game.

FIFTY-SEVEN: TWIRLS

Sean had given her specific instructions to get to The Flask for six. Rose was only seven minutes late, by which time Sean was already relaxing in an arched, stone booth. A bottle of Rioja sat in the middle of the table. Under the soft light of two candles, the wine rippled in ever-decreasing circles having just been poured out. He knew how to treat a girl. They made light work of it, and once it was done they strolled down to a quaint little restaurant on the hill. Rose had never been out in the Hampstead before and was impressed; it seemed classy and cosmopolitan without the snobby vibe she'd felt in Chelsea or Mayfair. Small enough to have a nice and friendly close-knit community, but quiet and pretty to entice people to go and hang out in. She liked it from the moment she stepped off the tube.

They ordered some Veal to go along with a plain Arrabiata dish, following some authentic Italian bruschetta, arguing over which type of pasta was the best. Sean eventually gave in and they had the Fussili (or twirls as Rose called them) when he wanted linguini. Rose was enjoying his company and found herself, after another bottle, talking about a lot of things she didn't really think she would be capable of discussing with anyone she'd only known a couple of months. But she did, and like a person who experiences a drug for the first time, she was surfing a wave of something new.

They talked for at least three hours – mainly her – just life stuff in general. Hopes dreams fears regrets plans nightmares enemies passions hates and so on, and the time flashed past her without her even noticing it, and somewhere lurking deep within her conscience she was pleased it was time to go, because she couldn't allow herself to get too close. Not when everything was within touching distance.

FIFTY-EIGHT: ATTENTION

An early morning arrest next Tuesday at the offices of STI would not work. Sharma would be tucked up in bed, and nothing would get in the way of his duty as a father to collect his boy from nursery school once he was up and about. Nothing was more important than his son and heir.

He clocked into work at ten o'clock on the Monday evening, surprised to see the light in Cornish's office still glowing. He peeped through a crack in the door to check it was simple neglect and that she had gone home for the day (inspectors *never* seemed to work past six). As he turned away, he heard her familiar Scottish accent.

'Pritesh? In here, please,' she called.

'Fuck off. What now?' he whispered, about turning and marching into her office. He resented nights - if she wanted a punch-up then so be it, he was feeling quite mercurial. She *was* working late.

Four blue paper cups were lined up in front of her waiting to be pinged away by a BB gun; behind them, an empty sandwich bag jumped an inch off her desk in the breeze from the office door as Sharma closed it.

'Evening Inspector. Late then?' he said. His voice remained steady, despite being on the front foot.

'Oh come on Pritesh, call me Diana. It's gone ten already' she smiled.

'Sorry, Diana. So...what gives?' he said, moving closer to her desk and waiting for her to gesture for him to sit down. Perhaps she wasn't going to kick-off after all.

'Take a seat,' she said, before he even reached the desk. 'And pay attention. Here's what I think you should do.'

FIFTY-NINE: HAMPER

'All I want to do is reconfirm that we are good to go?'

Perhaps Jason was wavering, a touch. Perhaps the pressure was getting to him after all, Clive thought.

'Jason, brother. We are good...tru-'

'NOT ONE SINGLE FUCK UP WILL HAMPER ANYTHING NOW WE'VE COME THIS FAR...OK?!'

It was those loud words that filled the room with tension and energy. Words Clive, Peter and Antoine cringed at. They found themselves in the boardroom, again. Antoine had literally stepped off the plane at City Airport sixty-five minutes prior.

They looked at Jason like he was an obsessed maniac, but none of them had the nuts to suggest he take a deep breath. It was do-or-die time, and they all knew it. He was becoming infatuated with the prospect of taking over STI – he clearly wholeheartedly believed it could make them all very rich. He also had a beef with Sean for poaching Tom so soon into his employment, the irony being that Tom's replacement was now pivotal in the scheme he'd devised. Maybe all of it had taken up so much of his energy recently that he didn't want any other result except a handsome victory. He was wired that way. They all were, but Jason just had an extra edge.

Clive broke the uncomfortable silence.

'Listen, Jason. The girls are briefed, ok? A million times! If we can't trust them now then we pull the plug. Right here right now.'

Clive was getting short at Jason's sudden lack of faith at the eleventh hour. It was unusual to see him like this. He went on nonetheless. 'The books are sweet thanks to your meeting with Mark on Friday, right? A new chair and a cut in the business...he'd have "signed a contract with his own blood" you said. Louis has done his bit, and you got a note from Rose on LinkedIn confirming all is good?'

Jason sighed and stared at the desk. 'I know. I just want to speak to each of them again, one more time. Check they're still clear on it all. Just got a weird feeling something's gonna fuck up.'

'For goodness sake. Antoine...get a discreet note to Stephanie and ask her to call this line from a pay phone,' said Clive, his patience surprisingly waning for a man who'd had to put up with Louis for twenty odd years.

*

Five minutes later and Stephanie – unaware she was on loudspeaker – told Antoine all was set and the plan had been gone through yesterday after work with Rose. They wanted her to explain it as she understood it, without knowing Clive and Jason were listening. She recited to them that Rose would take Sean to the pub, where they'd have a few drinks, and then once everyone had left the office, Stephanie would send a coded message to Rose informing her that the coast was clear for her to bring Sean back and do the role-play, during which Stephanie would stumble across them, having hidden around the corner under an analyst's desk, and film it for a few seconds before raising the alarm.

Sean would be powerless - no regular phone, of which all their WhatsApp and SMS messages to him had been deleted by Louis. The only ones left were the ones Sean sent to them, saying rude things or pictures of him naked. No evidence at all to suggest that he had been having consensual sex with both of them, just rude messages and pictures he'd sent. Nice, additional, undeniable evidence.

Then the rest was left to the men. Nothing more than Sean deserved.

Once Stephanie had recited the whole operation through the speakerphone, she signed off. A second later, all eyes were on Jason, who was much more at ease.

SIXTY: OVERTIME

'I must go home now, Pritesh,' Cornish said with a long sigh. Her eyes were black around the edges and she'd aged a decade since he'd seen her, which he liked.

'To recap, Colin has requested that – despite his doubts – we make an arrest as quickly as possible so we can make it known to the mainstream that we're on it, and it's under control before criticism of the Met gets challenging.'

She was rubbing her eyes, it was nearly midnight and she was in need of her bed. Sharma was not in such a state. He was thinking about his first break and what his wife had made for him to eat. He was on nights, yet somehow Cornish had persuaded him to make the arrest at a decent hour, no need to piss about with home visits. Apparently, surprise was better. Get to the offices around five or six – that would be ideal. Not many people about at that time, so if he went quietly, he'd be spared playing the main part in a very embarrassing show. Woodruff had said to make a quick and friendly arrest, then into the cop shop to trip him up and get him charged, bang to rights. The wheels were in motion. A high-profile arrest for racially motivated malicious communication, made even more poignant thanks to the recent horrendous trolling of a pair of teenagers who suffered in the last couple of months. Ones that ended in a mutual suicide streamed to Facebook live. With all the celebrities on the end of this latest, shocking campaign – one that the police described as a drunk and abusive evil troll - it promised to command a generous slice of media coverage and some much needed praise for Islington.

And if the esteemed Police Constable known as PC Pritesh Sharma was the one who busted it, then starting work a little early when he was on nights wasn't such a pain in the ass. His wife wouldn't dare say anything anyway.

SIXTY-ONE: PLAY

Rose stayed with me on the Sunday night, and I got up early to make some poached eggs and smoked salmon with brown bread. Fresh slices of lemon as well, naturally. It went down well and I made some fresh roasted Columbian coffee; the cobweb-covered Espresso machine getting a rare outing. She was reason enough to get it out of the cupboard and give it a blast. My efforts were truly appreciated and we sat quietly enjoying the food and coffee and the sun was just starting to shine outside. It felt nice, considering it was Monday morning and I had things to sort out – not least the hacker. I was close to saying something stupid out loud, but I settled on thoughtfully picking up Rose's phone and plugging it in to charge - she mentioned she was out of battery. And then I kissed her on the lips softly. Just a couple of little gestures like that was enough to show her how I was feeling, I think.

Something I've done umpteen times in the last fifteen years is sit opposite a whole host of girls who have stayed over and provided me with what I needed, enjoying my salmon and eggs and coffee, but I hardly ever enjoyed it relaxed. Usually, I'd just want to get it over with and boot them out, be left alone and go and tell myself off for being a dog. But Rose sharing it all with me, on a Monday morning after a lovely Sunday evening, was different. I was half tempted to tell her we'd take the day off and just hang out and stuff, maybe visit St Albans cathedral or do something that couples do, but I stopped myself; it was better to chill out and take it easy, try not to let it become all-consuming and smother her despite wanting to just let go. I felt that we were on the brink of it anyway. Just needed to know if she was on the same page as me, which I felt she was.

*

I called that Sharma again. Office hours as well. I even called the fucking main line to the police and asked for him, but the chav on the end of the line gave me a weird 0303 number to call and then politely told me to fuck off. What a bunch of twats. Seriously, they are just the Government's enforcers, aren't they? A handful of silly fat cunts bullied at school who think that enforcing rules for a fucking living and twenty grand a year is somehow doing the general public a favour - do *me* a favour, more like. The clowns spend all day driving around in a fucking white uniform, worrying about an indicator not blinking properly, yet they can't get themselves to Edmonton and stop a load of *gangstas* stabbing and shooting each other on a daily basis. Actually...fuck it. Let the stupid gangs all kill each other. Yeah, go police! Go and check brake lights and save the world!

*

So nothing on Monday; a quiet day and still no word from that copper, time to just crack on and let what will be will be. Oh, and a quick meeting with Hannah, Bruno and me. I'd asked Hannah to check on Bruno's Visa situation, and it turned out he was on a two-year jobbie, expiration in eighteen months - more than enough. But forgetful old Hannah had overlooked STI's company policy of a minimum of three-years on the Visa for anyone outside of the EU.

'Company policy, we like to keep our people here for the long term, develop them, Bruno. I'm sorry - it's as much annoying for me as I'm sure it is you. We'll pay you until the end of the month, but you're free to go now,' I said, with my palms raised apologetically. The look on his face was pleasurable, especially when I asked him if we could keep in touch, on Facebook, LinkedIn and *Twitter*. Silly cunt didn't react.

Once he'd left, I asked Darminder the Indian to let me see a list of websites Bruno had been using, specifically Twitter, but he hadn't. I got Darminder to double check cleared history as well, but he was squeaky clean. Must've done it from his iPad.

*

I then clocked off and went for the usual PWP's and got totally spanked – getting shot of Bruno was cause for celebration. Rose had said she was busy and we had our naughty little soiree/role-play planned for tomorrow in my office. Just a bit of careful planning and we were good to take our filth to the next level. She wasn't keen on it being filmed, though.

*

To avoid messing about and keeping Rose back unnecessarily, we agreed that we'd go to the pub for a couple first to loosen up. Rose didn't want to risk doing it with anyone around whatsoever, which allowed us an hour from about five in The Castle before we could slope off back up to the office and rock on. There was a buzz that hung in the pub, probably from the milder weather and the relief that the most depressing month of the year is gone and not coming back for another eleven months - I couldn't wait to get started. As we sat there, I couldn't take my mind off yanking up her skirt and bending her over my desk and going for it while she pretended to hate it all and tell me not to, a real buzz for her, which meant I would enjoy it, too. I'd never role-played something like that before and didn't think I ever would, but I would literally do anything to make this girl satisfied, and she knew it.

'Ok let's go. Now,' Rose ordered as she finished her glass of red. 'You better be ready to give it me.'

She was quick to get going. Oh boy was I in for a treat. I fucking was as well, and within a minute we'd left the pub and slipped back into the building and up to our floor, checking no one was around. There wasn't. Hallelujah!'

*

'Ok. It's simple. You and me in the office...you interview me, ask what I like in bed and then I don't quite understand,' said Rose as I loosened my tie and ushered us into my office. 'Then you get nasty and do me over your desk. Let me struggle, go along with it and all. Even slap me and stuff. Just be really *forceful*, ok?'

'Ok, simple enough. You better prepare yourself - I'm

gonna finish you,' I said, craning my neck and making sure there were no minions or any unwanted Mexican cleaners shuffling across the floor with a fucking hoover sprouting from their hand. There weren't. She went to the toilet and when she came back, the battle commenced.

We really did role-play out the whole thing prior to the sex. I was sat there with Rose opposite me, grilling her on stuff that she struggled to answer, gradually coaxing her into telling me what she liked having done to her. I made her put her hair in bunches while I pressed her on really easy questions until she got flustered and asked me if I would get her a water, which I did, and upon returning she was minus her blazer and had her legs wide open. Ready and inviting me to take part in her game.

'Why the fuck have you got your legs open, you bitch?'

I shouted in her face. She looked up at me while doing a bloody good job acting scared.

'I'm sorry?' she gasped.

I went for it.

'SORRY!? It's about time you learned a FUCKING lesson then isn't it?'

I screamed in her ear so she flinched, slamming shut my office door and unbuckling my belt, lifting her off her chair and forcing her down over my desk yanking up her skirt as her legs wriggled around, and she begged me to stop.

SIXTY-TWO: FILM

'See you tomorrow,' chirped Stephanie as Sean strode out of the office. Rose gave it five minutes before joining him in a secluded little spot in The Castle, away from any groups who might include STI employees.

Stephanie's job was to hang about for a while before production and marketing had eventually downed tools. In reality, she only had to sit at her desk and fiddle about on her PC for an hour or so. She was to drop *Mama* a message when the coast was clear, but it felt like the sands of time had gone on holiday as the clock on her PC appeared to reverse.

Finally, an hour passed. She hit the button, then went and hid around the corner from Sean's office under a desk where she peered out at the floor, feeling like she was playing a game of hide-and-seek. Five minutes later she heard the door swing open and the scuffle of shoes drawing nearer. Both voices talked furtively and got louder, and then she just waited, her arse became numb from the hard floor and she wanted to stand up and stretch her legs, but that would be suicide.

The office door opened and Sean walked back up the floor to the water cooler. Her phone vibrated with a message.

Give it 2 mins.

Conversation deleted, phone camera activated, adrenaline pumped.

They were all set.

SIXTY-THREE: STUMBLE

Pritesh Sharma left his three-bed semi in Wood Green at 3.30pm. The journey to the station would take less than forty, going against the traffic that was slowly chugging out of the city to the outer regions and beyond. His wife had prepared an early dinner, or was it a late lunch? Her man had to be well fed for his thirteen-hour shift.

His ritual of Heart FM on the way to work every day wasn't going to be displaced just because he was four hours early and on his way to make an arrest that would soon be all over the mainstream. He'd be a local hero for a few days. Stick that in your pipe, Woodruff. Heart FM was his own, special treat - until he was parked up at the station and in uniform, he wasn't working. A rebellious teen on his way to sixth form college in his first car, windows down an inch and music up just a notch too loud. There was a big softy inside him somewhere, despite the hard and disciplined upbringing he'd had.

'Hi Pritesh, you're in so early...you behind on your reports again?' asked Ryan, a brand new rookie, shirt just out of its pack.

'Nope got an arrest to make...duty calls,' replied Sharma, smugly.

Half-an-hour later he was in full uniform and armed with the necessary warrant. Going against Cornish's advice, he went round to Sean's home in Potters Bar, cursing his stupidity for not just going straight there from his own home, then even more so when no one came to the door. On went the flashing blue lights. He tore straight to the offices of STI. Thankfully the traffic wasn't that heavy, and he was parked up on Farringdon Road by half six. No explanation needed, but he did feel from their brief meeting last week that the guy wouldn't be too much of a headache and submit without fuss. In any case, he had the whole list of abusive tweets printed out for verification, and a copy of confirmation that they'd been sent from his handset. In theory, it would be a relatively straightforward arrest.

He got out of the car; a few bods standing in a bus stop eyed him up with interest, as was usual. Waiting for something juicy to happen.

'I need to speak to Sean Thomas of STI limited,' he said to the concierge, who didn't even sign him in.

As the lift doors opened he walked onto the floor, speaking to an imaginary sidekick. 'Probably not even here.'

SIXTY-FOUR: READY

Clive was nervously circling his pint of bitter waiting for the signal from Stephanie.

The script was rehearsed well enough. In the aftermath of Stephanie filming Sean 'raping' Rose, Clive would, by chance of course, walk in on both girls accusing Sean of rape with Rose point-blank categorically denying any such role-play had gone on while Stephanie threatened to call the police. It wouldn't be unusual for Clive to be there for whatever reason. He'd calm things down and a few minutes later Jason would appear with a written proposal to buy the company for a pittance. By then it wouldn't matter if Sean clocked on and worked out it was all engineered. The accounts sheet would appear with Mark, when Clive summoned him from the meeting room he was hiding in on one of the floors below, and that would be the justification for Jason to buy at such a small price, reasoning that what with the Twitter fiasco and then being caught in the act, the only solution for Sean to hang on to his liberty would be to play ball. It was blackmail, nothing else, and a very savage one at that. One *could* argue that it was nothing personal or just the way the business world worked. Dog eat dog. Strike a deal there and then and the video would be destroyed and nothing more would be said. Failure to cooperate would not be so wise; he'd end up in the slammer with a charge of rape and be forced to sell, regardless. Damage limitation and walk away with a couple of hundred grand in the bank, or risk losing everything he had, a few years at the hands of Her Majesty's pleasure, banged up for something he hadn't done, being released a few years later and coming out to fuck all and pushing fifty, if he made it out at all. Rapists don't tend to fare so well in prison.

*

'Relax will you. It's all going to plan. Keep your shit together,' Jason said. The roles had reversed. The tension was affecting them both - but it was Clive's turn to show it.

'Why she hasn't messaged yet...what's the holdup?'

wondered Clive. The words came out in a nervy, high-pitched dribble, like he was six and whining about not being allowed an ice cream.

'How on earth can you predict how long this is gonna take? You never know, Rose may be keeping it up for a while to make it more, erm, believable,' said Jason. 'Stephanie...she's ice cool. She's brutal. She'll be in touch any minute. Now drink your bloody pint before I do!'

Just then Clive's phone buzzed and a green banner appeared on his screen.

Clive picked up his pint and necked the whole lot, finishing with a gasp as his glass smacked onto the table. He stood up, nodded at Jason and walked out of the pub.

SIXTY-FIVE: STOP

'Wait a sec,' I said, pushing Rose down onto the desk. 'What's the safe word?'

'What?' Her eyes danced with confusion and her feet were wriggling about. I yanked down her tights.

'The *safe* word...in case you don't like it, and want me to stop. You can't exactly tell me to stop or shout *NO* if we're role-playing a *rape*.'

'It won't come to that though. Just do it, will you!'

She was edgy. I saw a real keenness in her to get going but I wanted to be sure that in case she didn't enjoy it, we at least had a code. I wasn't prepared to actually hurt her, after all.

'I know but...you know, just give me a word that you'll shout if you want me to stop...for real I mean.'

I ripped down her knickers and shoved two fingers straight into her. She was already moist, but she still let out a small yelp.

'*Pineapple*. I'll say that if I want you to stop. Hurry up and get on with it.'

Pineapple? Where the fuck did that come from - what kind of a safe word is that? I was expecting something like *vanilla* or *soap* or *kitten*, not a massive piece of tropical fruit more complex to peel than it is to finish a 49-square game of Sudoku.

Then I started. I tried to get into it.

'YOU'VE BEEN A FUCKING DIRTY LITTLE SLUT, HAVEN'T YOU?!'

I shouted at her and gripped around her neck with one hand, the other was on the ankle that I had bent up and over towards her ear. My grip was loose though, and I could tell it was going to be more her than me.

'No...n-n-n-no...please don't!' she squealed, sounding genuinely scared. I took my hands off her and pulled myself out of my trousers; my suit jacket still on and shirt hanging loose. I was still trying to force myself on her, to at least pretend I was, and try and please her with this bizarre game. But I really wasn't. I gave it another shot.

'DON'T WHAT?! DON'T DO THIS?' I screamed.

Her smooth legs were squirming away on the desk beneath me and the sound coming from her heels as they scratched against the wood of the desk was unpleasant, almost harrowing, but I managed to stay focused. It crossed my mind that she was really good at acting the part, and I tried to stop myself from thinking she'd done this before, but I couldn't, and it made me paranoid, which helped because I was having second thoughts already.

'Please...*please*, no, don't!' she cried.

'Too late BITCH! Let's see how you like this then,' I cried sliding into her, right hand helping me in as my left covered her mouth. All she could manage was a muffled wail, and I felt her breath through her nostrils on my hand as I began, her eyes wide in terror. She was really convincing but I was starting to flounder and felt off-colour about the whole thing.

'OH GOD,PLEASE STOP IT. YOU'RE HURTING ME....OHGODOHGODOHGOD!'

She properly screamed the second I took my hand away. It was not something I'd ever thought about – role-playing to this kind of extremity - but she was so into it. I went at her hard, and her fake tits jerked up and down and her nipples hit her chin, however, I couldn't shout at her anymore, or use force, and she was still pretending to struggle even though I wasn't really holding her down, and then it became just like a very passionate fuck, like one we've had before, to me anyway. I was close to coming and she was close to tears. I could feel her becoming looser and wetter, clearly aroused, so I tried to get back into character and half-heartedly told her to turn over, flipping her over with ease. A piece of chicken on a barbeque using tongs – that's how easy it was. She didn't put up much of a fight; just asked me to stop once or twice. I didn't know if that was the protocol and there would come a point where she gave up completely and we just had passionate sex or she would stop altogether because she saw something inside me that was unsettled, like she knew it felt weird and unnatural, stupid even. I was going to call it a day if she kept up the real struggling. I didn't care that she appeared to be enjoying it; I was battling with my own conscience and it was distracting me, making me feel uncomfortable. I was way out of my comfort zone. I wondered what she'd say, though, if I voiced my feelings. Then it all became too much as she went mad at me once again.

'STOP DON'T PLEASE! NO MORE, I HATE YOU!' she cried, trying to hit up me while lying face down, and clawing at bum with her arms stretched behind her. It continued to feel bizarre, in a bad way. I didn't like to see her like that.

'NOOOOOO! PLEASE ...STOP!' she screamed as I felt myself losing the will to continue. *I* was going to shout *Pineapple*. My hand lifted away from her and her mouth was open and I could see a puddle of her saliva where she'd been spluttering away in between shouting. I shook my head and slowed down and felt it changing from a role-play into just normal sex.

The whole rape thing was a terrible experience and something I knew I would never get turned on by. I felt ashamed that I'd given it the large and thought it would be fun; it was anything but. God knows what women who go through that for real must feel. I'd also let her down, I could tell. I kept on making love and felt like I was about to come. A minute later we were both just fucking on my desk and I wanted to just finish off normally so I held on for a bit longer and thought of the 1991 Spurs cup final winning lineup.

Spurs1991.

My Twitter password.

Stephanie knows it. I just remembered.

'FUCK!' I said, as soon as I realised it must have been her.

'What?' said Rose nervously, looking over to my office door. I turned my head to see what she was looking at.

Stephanie was standing there, pointing her phone at us.

'Ow about you stop what you're do-eeng, you sick fuck?'

She had been filming. Was she a pervert as well? Was I going to get a fucking threesome right here and now, was this all part of the plan and Rose's surprise to me?

I looked at Rose and then back at Stephanie, speechless, still with my pants down and Rose sobbing on my desk.

SIXTY-SIX: UNDER

Sharma walked onto the floor and took in the artificial light. It looked manufactured; like a scene from a film. Angry light lit up rows of computers that sat in silence opposite each other, just staring at one another, flickering softly in mute conversation, each one a different screensaver talking a different language.

Silence, except for the humming of the machines and the traffic outside on the road five stories down. And faint voices, somewhere.

It was twenty seconds or so before he heard the troubled shouts away to his right, then another five seconds until he was looking straight into the office at the end of the floor and witnessed Sean on top of a blonde girl over his desk. It didn't appear to be normal, not one bit, made even more strange by a dark haired girl who was standing with her back to him and filming it all. He'd walked into an amateur porn flick mid-production, and had no idea what to do. Unless it was something else?

The girl filming then walked into the office where it was all happening, clearly catching them by surprise. Sean turned around, startled at her entrance leaving the blonde girl on the desk shaking. It looked like maybe she'd been raped by Sean, and the other girl had caught him in the act and had the common sense and intuition to capture it on camera before alerting him there was a witness. Unless she was part of the rape, too, and wanted to film it for other reasons.

Sharma was now looking at making an arrest, maybe even two. And *two* charges. How good would that be? The police officer who busted a vile troll had also obtained a conviction for rape from the same man and possibly an accomplice. Catching him in the act. Stopping him the act, even. No one would know the true extent of Sharma's involvement, after all. His name would be golden in the force soon enough. All he had to do was get on with it and cuff the guy.

Stitched Up

As he ran over to the office to where it was all going on, he didn't see Clive emerge through the double doors, too.

*

'Woah there, chill for a minute. This isn't what it looks like,' said Sean as Sharma blasted through the doors of the office and held aloft his baton. 'It's all a misunderstanding. Rose will explain. Rose?'

'E fucking raped her. I have it 'ere on film. Look,' said Stephanie, thrusting her phone at Sharma.

'Keep hold of that for now, please,' said Sharma looking at her phone as if it was a used condom. 'Did you film it because you were witnessing a rape? Or were you part of it, too?'

'Non, er no, I just saw it now. Look.'

Stephanie showed Sharma a clip of about thirty seconds from her walking around the corner and then Sean and Rose on the desk, Rose trying to fend him off as she's bent over the desk, then Sean stopping and looking at the camera as Stephanie's voice tells him to stop what he's doing. That was enough for Sharma. Rose stayed silent, still sobbing. Then he made the arrest and read Sean his rights despite some struggles of being cuffed and his begging of Rose to explain.

Sharma radioed for a female PC for backup to come to the office and look after Rose; Stephanie would keep her company until then.

'Rose?!' Sean pleaded one last time before he was frog-marched out of his own office and down into the street. People were gawping as Sharma slammed the door and they sped away.

And Sean was crying. And he was beaten. All of a sudden he realised he'd been stitched up, again.

SIXTY-SEVEN: SPANNER

Clive played it well.

He did an about-turn as soon as he saw Sharma and the scenes in Sean's office. Hid in the toilets and then straight back out into the freezing cold. He saw Jason crossing the road over in his direction, on his way over to finish off Sean. Clive waited for Jason to reach him.

'Talk to me Clive, why aren't you up there?'

'It's not all bad. We just need to rethink our approach,' answered Clive.

'What happened?' Jason frowned and then blew into his hands to warm them up.

'So I got there but there was a *policeman* hovering around. Seems like he stumbled in on Sean and the girls. Carted him away in cuffs, I hid in the bogs and watched them leave,' said Clive, whispering and looking around. 'Once he's bailed we can make the move, be much easier to persuade him after he's tasted life in a prison cell, assuming he's on his way to one now. How the fuck would the police know?'

'Arresting him for trolling. How's the luck on that eh? Ok. Now let's go home. Good work, it'll all be worth it.

SIXTY-EIGHT: STATION

My heart was pounding. I'd only ever been in real handcuffs once before when I got nicked for drink driving at the age of 27. I was on my way round to some boiler called Helen's place - I think that's what her name was anyway. About 3 am and off my trolley, I sped through a red light and a fucking meat-wagon magically appeared out of thin air like a rabbit in a hat, flipping its lights on and busting me.

So here I was, fourteen years later and in a bloody Astra, speeding through Islington towards the cop shop where I'd be charged with rape and God knows what else.

*

When I got there they made me take off my watch and shoes and hand over any personal effects, which was thankfully only my wallet. I nearly fainted when I thought I may have a small amount of shovel hidden in there somewhere, but then realised that was a ridiculously stupid thought as no way would it have survived to the end of the day after a couple of large wines earlier on.

Then they ushered me into some back room to have my fingerprints and mug shot taken, then swabbed my knob, like I was in an STD clinic. The on-site doctor had a pair of rubber gloves on when he shoved what felt like a toothpick down my Jap's eye. Bad enough going to the clap clinic, let alone a fucking police station. Well anyway, I made a call to Chris straight after that, despite hardly being able to walk. Thankfully he answered. He always did.

'Sean, how are you?' answered Chris, cheerfully.

'Chris, listen carefully, you need to come and get me out of here.'

*

The cell was disgusting. It smelled of dust and wet dog and the tiny wooden bed had a blanket on it, all moth-eaten and dry and probably contaminated with so many diseases it could have jumped up and paced around the cell with me. In all the commotion, my nerves had got the better of me and I was bursting for a dump. I looked for a toilet but couldn't see anything, so I summoned to the cell some knucklehead sporting a white shirt and shaved head. It was only when I saw a walkie-talkie that I realised he was actually a police officer and not one of those bouncer type things that stand outside shopping centres pretending to be hard.

'Yes?' I think was its response.

'I need to use the toilet please, mate?' I managed to restrain myself from speaking like I was addressing a two-year-old, despite the thing on the other side of the door having a matching IQ. He looked at me like *I* was the cretin. The nerve. Perhaps I hadn't been clear - it was quite possible that anything more than "Tarzan hit Jane" would be too tall an order for him to process.

'The toilet? I need to go, mate,' I repeated, ensuring I spoke his language by using "mate" again. He pointed to something behind me.

'Over there.'

I turned around and saw nothing that resembled a toilet, just sort of a blue wooden cube about the same size as a box of multi-pack crisps.

'Eh, you wha-'

The cell window slammed shut.

I walked over to the box and peered down at it for a few seconds, lifting up its top with a fingernail to horrifically find that it *was* actually supposed to be somewhere to have a shit. Beneath me was a metal basin that looked like you'd end up in the pit of the fucking Sarlacc from Return of the Jedi if you fell down it, it was that fierce. Next to that was a basin closer in size to a thimble than something to wash your hands in, and a tap made of rock. This was going to be fun; I was strangely excited about how long fate would drag things out for and how long I could hold on. The curiosity didn't last, however.

A short, sharp, thrusting sensation hit me in the pelvic region and then surged round the back, hosing its way into my bum cheeks as a build-up of jacket potato and tuna from lunch gathered round and started swirling about and tapping at the exit hole; the familiar onset of a very aggressive crap was upon me as my arse entered *Strictly Come Dancing* and performed the conga. I regarded the 'toilet' once more, as if it was an undetonated bomb from World War Two, and carefully mapped out how things needed to be done to make use of this third world contraption that was taking up the corner of my cell. Off with the pants and relief, at last, I just made it, as well. A generous measure sprayed out of me and violently raided the bowl; the splashing sound was echoed to twice the volume as it bounced off the shiny metal and then I injected a good dose of comedy by throwing in a couple of proper rippers, so much so that I sniggered to myself. I had this image of the police thing on the other side of the door being distracted from trying to recite the alphabet or do his two times table, it was so deafening.

My pride in managing to alleviate myself from pebbledash under similar conditions to biblical times was short lived though. There was no bum paper. Anywhere. I looked around the whole cell, which bearing in mind was about ten square feet, didn't take me long. I could still feel small chunks of poo falling out of me and landing below with miniature splashes just about big enough to catch me on that bit that links my balls to my shitter.

What to do? Plan A would be to do a full-on provincial *third-worlder* and use my left hand, whereas plan B would involve removing an item of clothing such as my pants, or a sock, something I did do one time in Birmingham when I was out and wrecked in a pub toilet that had the dreaded *bare barrel*. I went with plan B seeing as I'd done it before – a prison cell is genetically similar to a dirty old, rundown, crapper in an old man's pub after all.

Next question: socks or pants? Seeing as the pigs had taken my shoes and given me some plimsolls to wear, I thought it safer to use my pants, so in record time I kicked off my trousers and removed a pair of Jack Jones boxers from Next and scrunched them up into a ball and then gave them a good tour of the havoc that was my arsehole. When I was satisfied it was clean enough, I placed them under the plastic mattress along the side of the cell and commended myself with a pat on the back, laughing at the thought of either some servant female PC tasked with cleaning the cells horrified expression, or the next inmate stretching out and putting his hands under the mattress to discover his fingers were probing half a pound of Sean's Tuesday night excitement.

When the cell door finally opened, the same caveman from earlier on ushered me out and led me back down to the front desk. Two people were waiting; one was Chris who was sat patiently holding a coffee, and the other was Rose. She turned away from me as soon as we made eye contact.

SIXTY-NINE: SPOT

That fucking dickhead who kept trying to buy the company last summer - Willey, and Clive, were sat in my office when I got in the next morning. It was only half seven, but my plan to grab all my stuff as early as possible and avoid bumping into anyone was instantly scuppered the moment I laid eyes on the pair of them sat there, like nothing was up. I needed to spend the day gathering as much evidence from my emails and any stored messages that had been saved on my devices - to build a clear picture around mine and Rose's relationship, and Stephanie's as well. I was still confused and numb from what had happened, and it frazzled my brain. Despite entertaining myself in the cell at Islington nick, it was no laughing matter. If there wasn't much by way of text messages and Rose maintained her story to the rozzers, with backup from Stephanie's video, then I was in for a proper fight. And one I would probably lose. No one could get out of that if the 'victim' stood firm in their testimony.

Concerned to find out if Clive found out about what had happened and why that Willey menace was skulking about, I went into my office and waved Clive out of *my* seat. I put my hard hat on.

'Gentlemen, I assume this isn't a social visit, but I am rather rushed today, so please be quick.'

Clive spoke first. 'Look, we know what happened with Rose. We can get you off the hook if you'll sit down and listen?'

What the fuck? How did they know; had word already got out? The past few days were fast becoming the collapse of a fucking cathedral.

'What?' I just about managed to say, despite my heart having travelled up to my mouth.

Clive went on. 'So, Stephanie has shown me the video, told me everything. Fair to say, Rose is traumatised. You'll be going inside for a few years.'

'Will I fuck. This is a stitch up Clive, you know it. You're in on it too, I bet' I said, calmer than I anticipated and still on my feet. Maybe I was tired. I gestured at Willey but didn't deviate from Clive. 'What the fuck is *he* doing here?'

'Allow me,' Jason said. 'Please, sit down.'

'Get on with it then, I've got a long day with my brief.'

Jason laughed at me when I said *brief*. Smug bastard. He sat forward and looked at me, a touch intimidating. I could feel my face warming and my pulse rising again. Happened almost every day, now. If I'd had a gun and a full bladder, I'd have shot him in the knee then pissed on his face.

'So, the last two offers to buy you out I've not made big enough,' said the smarmy cunt.

'What? Are you actually serious? They were a joke, pal,' I said.

'It wasn't a question Sean. I'm here to make you a third and final offer. One that if you accept will help preserve your freedom, and sanity.'

'Why's he here, then? It's nothing to do with Clive?' I asked.

'Well Sean you see, I, along with a couple of other silent partners, own a percentage of FFB. You do know that Clive is one of the founders of FFB, right? You did your due diligence when he stumped up a quarter-of-a-million investment? I have a say in all acquisitions. So it has *everything* to do with Clive,' replied Jason.

It was getting too weird. Clive, who injected a quarter of a million into my company, was working with Jason and now they're sat in front of me telling me they can save my bacon from the repercussions of a rape that I didn't do. Maybe Louis had spiked my *Tall* with acid, and this was a *really* bad trip.

'Go on. Tell me what it is and how this all works then cock, I mean Willey' I said.

Jason looked at me with appreciation. 'Very funny,' he smirked. 'Ok, so let's just say Rose would be willing to drop everything in the event you sell up. Got an offer here all ready to go, you just need to sign it.' He produced a contract and slid it over to me.

'By the way,' interrupted Clive, 'what the fuck is that hole in your desk all about?'

'Ask your son, pal. Anyway, like fuck Rose will. This is a massive stitch up and the police saw it all.'
,

Did these nuggets think I was fucking born yesterday? Jason slid another piece of paper to me. I picked it up and looked at the bottom to find Rose's signature. It was a signed statement retracting her allegation, saying it was mutual consent. I froze.

Rose - in on all this, too.

'This is blackmail! Rose, Stephanie, probably Louis too! You're all in on it you Mother *FUCKERS!*'

I was on my feet again, absolutely seething. I snatched up the other piece of paper and scanned over it. I looked at the offer to buy me out, reading it as one-and-a-half million, then realised I'd added a zero. I slid back into my seat laughing like a maniac.

'One fifty? Is there a missing zero? You are *joking* me, right?'

'No. We're deadly serious. I recommend you accept or face prison. Clive will assume full ownership of the business while you're incarcerated,' Jason said. Clive nodded. I looked at Clive who smiled a bit, and in that smile, I saw Louis.

Louis, my Twitter expert.

Twitter.

My Twitter.

Of course, that was nothing to do with Bruno. It was Louis and Stephanie.

In a split second the shroud that was covering my eyes lifted up and I could see clearly what it all was. Louis was in on it too. Fuck me who else? Was the *piece de resistance* going to be that cunt Bruno appearing around the corner and proceeding to smash me in the chops with his foot long weapon and then running off with Rose and taking my house from me? Probably.

I had to buy some time, appear calm. I gave a long, defeated sigh, waving the white flag. I guess if I could get a million from them I'd do it, to make this all go away; only two-fifty more than what he'd offered last time. But I wasn't going to give them that suggestion just yet. Things can change in a flash, after all, and I prayed that something would.

I waited for a minute.

No one spoke.

The tension was almost visible it was so heavy.

'Ok. Look, I need a day to work things out. Give me twenty-four hours to have the contract reviewed. The accounts will show a healthy balance sheet, so one-fifty won't fly, it will look far too hot, and you don't want a load of admin to wade through with Companies House. At least make me a sensible offer and I'll sell, really I will. I was going to look to sell in two years' time anyway.'

Jason shook his head. 'Your accounts are showing a puny profit margin on the balance sheet.'

'How would you know? The bottom line is pretty decent, actually, I can go and ge-'

Jason cut me off. 'Clive?'

Clive made a call on his mobile asking whoever was on the end of the line to come on up.

After two more minutes of silence and evil stares, Mark entered through the double doors of the sales floor and zoomed down into my office. Of course. Rose's mate she suggested I employ. It was clicking into place now.

Bastards.

SEVENTY: HOPE

A cup of tea warmed Rose's hands as she sat in The Spaniard's Inn. She was waiting impatiently, eager to get it over with, at the same time as not wanting to have this meeting. She yearned for something stronger, but figured if she didn't get something warm inside her right away, she would never be able to stop shivering; nerves and cold weather weren't the best mix. She had no idea how he was going to react to the news. Time would tell though. She tried to pass the time, playing around on her phone, scrolling aimlessly through her Facebook feed, or seeing who was tweeting about what, trending now, what tittle-tattle was the flavour of the month and so on. But the reality of it was that the only purpose it served was to give her something to look at rather than out of the window, where she would eventually see him pulling up. The die had been cast; it was out of her hands as to how it would go. She began to well up, wishing she could undo everything, wishing she could just wake up from the nightmare and it was day one at FFB and not STI.

But then that could never have happened either, she could never have had one without the other. She felt suffocated.

*

Jason agreed to give Sean twenty-four hours to go through the written offer with his legal team. Although Jason and Clive doubted very much that he had a whole team, he used that term. Mark had produced a copy of the financials from the last year; the bottom line showing poverty. Sean didn't look surprised when he looked at the numbers and saw that Mark had adjusted the figures to reflect a balance sheet that would be considered moribund, as opposed to the buoyant and fertile margin from a few weeks ago. Sean gathered his belongings and was out of the office before nine. They agreed to meet at seven the next morning at Smiths of Smithfield for breakfast, where Sean would hand over the signed papers.

*

Rose checked her watch again, as if it was going to tell her something different from the time displayed on her iPhone. Perhaps her text hadn't reached him; perhaps all of them were tied up in the meeting, or worse, someone had sprung them and it was all in a mess. He was fifteen late already. The noise of gravel dragging under some tyres interrupted the minefield of thoughts ricocheting around her head, and her heart skipped a beat as a black Audi A8 with darkened windows turned into the car park and stopped outside the pub's rear door. The driver got out and opened the passenger door. It was who she knew it would be, but he had company. Someone unmistakable, someone she could spot anywhere in the world.

*

Clive picked up the phone in Sean's office and went to dial out, but as quickly as he'd lifted the receiver, Jason slammed it back down.

'Any calls to tell Antoine the news let's do from our own phones, just to be safe.'

Beads of sweat formed on his upper lip, and he hadn't touched the croissant. Butterflies, Clive supposed.

'Of course. I'll send him a text and get him to call back.'

A minute later Antoine was on speaker, and they had a conversation led by Jason that lasted less than two minutes, Jason merely informing Antoine that the deal was nearly over the line. "One fifty parts and labour, no broken bones etc."

Next week they could make the announcement and begin on the plans to rebrand the business, blasting STI further into the solar energy business intelligence stratosphere.

Printing money. With a licence to.

*

Sean wheeled Mark into the pub. Both were wearing rain macs and both had faces that, despite taking a car to Hampstead, looked tired and weather-beaten. On top of that, Sean looked pissed off, Mark looked anxious.

'What is *he* doing here?' asked Rose, looking at Sean but

pointing at Mark.

'Cor blimey, no way to greet an old colleague is it? You get me a pint?' said Mark. His voice was precarious, not the usual confident cockney she was used to. She'd seldom seen him anything other than animated and full of rubbish.

'Here, take this and get me a large Rioja and whatever you and Rose want,' said Sean handing Mark his plastic. 'Contactless,' he said before Mark asked what the PIN was. He turned back to Rose. She had tears in her eyes.

'One question. Why?'

*

'Ok. Let me just see if I understand you correctly because I am thinking that somewhere along the last twenty-four, somebody has either spiked you or me, with acid. And I assure you Pritesh, all I've had is a camomile tea, made for me last night at home, by Graham.'

Cornish had removed her glasses after reading the report filed by Sharma in the early hours. He'd waited until she'd come in to explain what had happened with Sean and the arrest, and the subsequent release on bail. He'd also got a copy of everything Rose had said to PC Samantha Jacobsen, the officer who was on the scene straight after.

He remained silent, waiting for Cornish to unleash some more venom. He wasn't waiting long - fifteen seconds to be exact.

'Shall I tell you what all *this* means to me?' She held aloft the report for a good five seconds and stared at Sharma, before she dropped it down on her desk and it fell to the floor, just to put the boot in. She placed her head in her hands and sighed a long, frustrated, sigh.

'Pritesh, repeat after me: Semper in excremento sum, solum profunditas variat' said Cornish.

'Semper in excremento sum, solum profunditas variat ' repeated Sharma.

'Now, do you know what that means, Pritesh?'

'I'm afraid I don't Di- I mean Inspector,' replied Sharma.

'It's Latin for *I'm always in the shit, the depth of which does vary.*'

*

'So that's what we're going to do then. All of us, tomorrow. For now, let's stay here, lie low for a bit. Mark if you're clear, I'll order you a car.'

Five minutes later it was just Sean and Rose. Boy did they have some ground to cover. Rose was still pale and could have used a stiff drink to put some blush back into her cheeks. No longer the blooming Rose, she had turned into a shrinking violet. She stared at the cutlery that was on the table they were sat at, the red napkin had a pattern of dots scattered over it. Deep, red dots. From her tears.

SEVENTY-ONE: REVERSE

Still numb from the events of the last twenty-four hours - *twenty-four* - I left Clive and Jason and then walked through Smithfield's and past the Barbican to Moorgate. If there was ever a time I needed some fresh air to give clarity to my thoughts, then that time had arrived. I wanted to go home, sleep for an hour, eat something substantial and then get cracking on trying to work out what the fuck I had to do in all of this and clear myself. I'd been well and truly done over. Getting my head round it felt like someone was trying to untangle a pair of earphones after a few days in the coat pocket that was my brain. I did what anyone would do and worked my way backwards, almost getting run over just before the meat market.

So, Clive, the devious bastard, was in cahoots with Jason Willey to buy me out. His son Louis had hacked into my Twitter account with the help of Stephanie and set the ball rolling with the fifteen minutes of diabolical tweeting to alert the police.

But the whole 'rape' thing, where to begin? So many questions. How did the police know to come to the office at the exact planned moment, unless that copper Prit-stick or whatever his name is was in on it? Probably was, half the coppers in this city are as bent as a two bob bit. And then they got to Mark, how involved was he? From the start, or did they force him?

And then Rose. My dear, lovely Rose, how did they get to her, how did they know what the deal there was? Must have been Louis who told Clive then somehow they blackmailed her, as well. All of the theories were hurting my brain and it was tiring me out. And I'd lost her, at the worst time imaginable.

*

On the train home, I got a surprise. Something vibrated in my coat pocket. It was my second phone signalling it was out of juice. I'd picked it up from the office, along with my laptop and some other crap as I left Jason and Clive.

And it may have just saved the day.

May have.

When Rose had gone to the toilet before we started the game and the role-play, I positioned the phone behind the blinds in the office and hit record so it had a clear view of my desk. I knew she didn't want me to film it, the reason why she didn't want me to had become quite clear and had nothing to do with her being shy. I figured that if I did it on the sly, then I'd get a performance with no holds barred (unfortunately there were some *holes* barred) and I could happily beat-off over it whenever I wanted to. Literally ten seconds before she came back in, it was in position and the camera was rolling. Had I been slower off the mark, she'd have clocked it and made me switch it off, and I'd be snookered with a truckload of thorny, uphill ground ahead of me. But thankfully, luckily or miraculously, my timing was on-point, so the whole conversation about having the 'safe' word should be there, be audible at least. There was no initial struggle either, so that could really save my bacon from the pigs, too.

One big thing though: it all hinged on *if* it'd been caught on camera.

SEVENTY-TWO: S.O.S

'Go for the Eggs Benedict, I always have them.'

Jason and Clive were already sat at a long table in the middle of the ground floor of *Smiths of Smithfield*, or S.O.S as it's known. Clive was familiar with the place and recommending to Jason what to have. He used to love eating there before work, back in the days before semi-retirement.

'Ok, make that two, and bring us a large cafetiere and three cups, we have one more coming. Thanks,' said Jason to a waiter. The place was busy already, and the smell of breakfast filled the place: grilled meat, warm syrup, fresh coffee and comforting porridge. They blended in well - it was full of suits having breakfast before work. Just a few hundred yards in each direction, you had an untold amount of offices. The trendy conversions in Old Street and Clerkenwell, stuffy old units in Blackfriars and St Paul's, and the diverse selection of buildings in Farringdon. Even Hatton Garden.

'Are you *sure* you said seven, and not half-past? It's twenty-five past already,' asked Clive once they'd finished their food, and only a quarter of the cafetiere had survived.

'Relax, maybe he thought I said half past. Anyway we can swap these for Champagne flutes as soon as we're done. Little rat's got nowhere to run to now. From all I've been hearing he-'

Clive raised his hand and pointed over to the entrance. His expression went from relaxed and cocky into confusion.

Sean walked in and over to the table, accompanied with Rose, who was tailing Mark.

'Morning, hope you don't mind, but I thought seeing as Rose and Mark are so pivotal in all of this, I'd bring them along. Paperwork needs going over. Trust that's ok?'

Clive and Jason looked at each other, and then they both nodded.

'Waiter,' said Sean just as one appeared at the table.

Some alarm bells started to ring in Clive's head.

SEVENTY-THREE: TRUTH

The truth came out. It always does. But I still had no idea if it would be enough to get out of the mess I didn't deserve to be in.

As soon as I got in I charged my phone and waited patiently for that annoying minute where the Apple logo appears, and then it prompted me for the usual four-digits. I felt like someone had given me a line of Pablo Escobar's personal stash my heart was pumping so much. I grabbed a bottle of whisky and poured out a large measure and downed it. Thoughts ran through my mind, terrorising my ability to be level-headed. What if the video was there? How could I be sure it had captured the right words, and a clear documentation of what happened? If it did indeed then could I use it to blackmail *them* into buying me out, what would I do with a few million a couple of years ahead of schedule, etc.? What would life behind bars be like if it *wasn't* there, and I decided not to back down, but fight back?

Just as I was about to lose it, an email pinged up. It was from Mark, and the subject header had a phone number alongside a few words. *Sean if you get this message, please call me ASAP.*

He answered after one ring.

'Sean, mate listen. It's all a big scheme. Dangled some money in front of me, offered me a new top-of-the-range chair in exchange for fiddling the books. I'm so sorry.'

So he *was* in on it, too. Everyone was.

'Where are you now?' I asked.

'In a café, up on Hatton Garden. I haven't gone back to the office. I'm not sure I want to.'

'Don't move.' I hung up and ordered a car.

*

Mark's appetite had clearly not diminished in the morning's

drama. No surprise there, then. His nerves had held, and in front of him was an empty plate smeared in ketchup, egg yolk and grease, flanked by a side plate with the crusts of three slices of white toast. It looked good, I had to admit. I ordered the same – it was called *The Gut Buster* – and ignored my sky high stress levels.

'Mark, I need you to help me out here. What has gone on you won't believe but you have to tell me *everything you know*.'

*

On the way to Mark, choosing to take a luxury Audi that was going to be ferrying me about all day, I checked my videos. And there it was, the result I needed.

My beautiful, bastard, second phone had recorded the whole session, my arrest and all the trimmings, it remained running for ages, but I had what I needed. The conversation Rose and I had about getting ready, and around having a safe word, were both clearly audible. Crystal. Then her undoing her blouse and sitting in the chair with her legs open, and then the sex part, clearly showing it was a game. Furthermore, after I had been marched away by the policeman, Stephanie laughed and said to Rose about "how easy it was" and that they'd soon have their cars thanks to her uncle and his mates.

"The Motley Crew, I zink we ave to call them from now on, no?" was the last thing to be recorded before a young female PC entered the office and ushered them out.

*

'That's all I have Sean. They bribed me with company shares and a new chair if I made the numbers look bad. Clive put pressure on me, honest. Told me not to say anything to you, then when I didn't do it, he got me in the pub with Jason and they put a proverbial gun to my bonce. I didn't know what to do. I didn't realise they were going to fire you, I'm really sorry.'

'*Fire* me? You think they asked you to commit corporate fraud just to get rid?'

The puzzle became even more complex. Was Mark in on it,

or not?

'Well yeah, what else was it? I thought that me 'anding over the dodgy accounts was what they needed...' he trailed off and thought for a second. 'I thought it was weird when Rose was so keen to introduce me to you.'

Fuck, it was so hard to see clearly. What I had so far was that Mark was bribed to wangle the accounts, but didn't know the whole story, despite Rose introducing him to me and getting him a job, so surely she was in on it from earlier than Mark. Rose and Stephanie were, in my opinion working together, judging by the conversation they had after I was arrested. My head was spangled. I needed Mark onside. I had to get him to confess as much as possible. I fiddled about with my phone and hit the red button on the 'voice record' app and placed it on the table face down.

I gave Mark the whole story, including the Twitter hack. He was gobsmacked. Willey and Clive had clearly kept Mark in the dark about everything else. His jaw was on the table.

'Mark, will you tell me again, now, exactly what happened, regarding the accounts and the bribery? And the conversations you had. I don't deserve prison. No one does.'

Mark explained it all, again.

*

'Need me to make a statement?'

'Not sure, maybe, but why the change of heart? Why not get your shares and your new chair?' I wanted to know everything.

'You know guvnor when I saw you pack your things up, assuming you'd been given the old tin tack, I felt for ya. I'm in this chair cos of bad luck, nothing else. Not fate, not cos it was meant to be. Fuckin' downright bad effing luck.'

'And...?' I nodded for him to go on.

'And, well, no one deserves to be purposely fucked over like that. Bad luck, no one can control, you accept it and make the best of things like I've 'ad to do. But it's only bad luck that should be thrust upon ya, not some scheming, greedy fat cats, turning up tryin' to ruin lives and play God.'

He pointed to the arms on his wheelchair, and then prodded them. 'Being in this here makes me a bit more thoughtful about certain things, maybe not right away, but often after. Anyway, that's all it was. Sorry,' he said, remorsefully.

'Thanks, Mark. And apology accepted.'

He smiled. 'Need me to make a statement then, or what?'

'Won't be necessary,' I said as I turned over the phone to stop the recording. I had a text message from Rose, just seven words *call me if you get this pls*.

*

When Mark had left the Spaniards, having agreed the plan of action for the morning meeting with Willey and co, Rose and I had some talking to do. Rose was almost a reversal of what she had been in recent weeks: closed and nervy, flat and quiet. A shell.

'One question, why?'

She was looking down still. 'Why the whole rape thing? And why the written retraction, that's just bizarre. Why just *not* do it in the first place?'

I began with the question that I wanted to know the answer to the most. I knew why she'd allowed me to be framed with rape. That was fairly straightforward - greed. But why then go through with all of the unnecessary admin.

'*WHAT?* Written retraction? What in hells name are you talking about?' She was shocked to the core.

'Jason showed me a written statement from you, signed and dated. Kit and caboodle, he said it was ready to go, once I agreed to sell. You're telling me something different?'

'Damn right I am. Was it my signature?' asked Rose, incensed.

'No idea, I haven't memorised your signature.' I really

didn't have a clue if it was hers or not, so she could have been bluffing. I was paranoid now, beyond belief.

'Well, then that's fraud for starters. Fucking jokers. This is all wrong!' Tears filled up her eyes and climbed out of them and slid down her cheeks. Her eyes were puffy, and her eye makeup was smudged, and I was more attracted to her than I'd ever been before. Seeing her upset made me think how much I cared for her, it was bizarre. She looked up from the table, and stared at me, her eyes pleading with me to understand her. To forgive her.

'Sean, I'm sorry.'

It was the second time I'd had what sounded like a genuine and heartfelt apology, and, like the desperate smitten fool I still was, I grabbed it with open arms.

*

Rose answered all my questions. That chance meeting when I dropped Tom off at his brother's *wasn't* a chance meeting. That was where Stephanie came in, keeping in touch with Rose until the time was right for me to drop Tom home. Stephanie knew Tom would end up getting smashed at some point when we were all out, it was simply a matter of time as to when that was, Willey prepared to play the waiting game. Tom's heroics at the end of November sales month, coupled with a free bar, was too good an opportunity to pass up. It was all engineered. I felt a great deal of embarrassment when it transpired that the whole damn thing hinged on whether or not I looked at the letter from FFB which would begin the stalking. When she told me about that, I had dick-all by way of explanation except to admit that I was so bowled over by her when I first saw her by the front door, I had a *Carpe Diem* moment. She didn't know what *Carpe Diem* meant so I explained, and somewhere under that face of hers, I saw the surface of a smile.

FFB. Foster Fisher Baker. Clive Baker. That was all a massive *itchy beard* as well, that letter. A letter offering her a position to do a job that she could do at my place: it was the perfect bait for me to engage with her. She did actually go and do the interview anyway, to keep everything clean, authentic. Willey had said that if there were any repercussions then proof of Rose actually going to interview at FFB would add substance to any line of defence that they may need.

If something's too good to be true then it usually is. I'd do well to remember that in future. My offer of an informal chat, no strings, and then easing her into an interview to see what magic I could work was all too easy, in hindsight. It's the usual procedure I'd undertake nine times out of ten when a mega bird like Rose comes into the equation. The harder she pushed back, the more I was determined. When I'm involved, the chase is the thrill, usually. But her, nope, it was different. I told her so, as well. I told her that once I'd made it a mission to sleep with her, and had done, I decided there was more to it than just sex. She made me feel alive, feel young, and I figured that despite the eighteen years age gap, she was mature enough for me, mentally for sure. (When I told her that, I thanked my lucky stars she was definitely still physically youthful and nubile enough to keep me in a dizzy blur of mind-blowing sex for a good ten years.) I wanted to know if it was the same for her if she felt that connection, and she said she did. It was because of that which made her go to the cop shop and tell them what the real situation was, going on record to categorically deny there had been a rape. When the female copper asked why Stephanie had been there, she told them that she must have stumbled in on us and genuinely thought I was raping her and so filmed it for evidence. She protected Stephanie from that point-of-view, although I wanted revenge on that one. She told me that during the 'rape', she was flooded with guilt and that's why she started crying and it was too late to stop it. Then when Stephanie turned up, and the policeman too, she froze. She was worried and she couldn't think. Nothing. Blank.

So what about Louis? Why the hell did he almost ruin things with the fart machine prank? Again, it all boiled down to enriching the whole 'hard-to-get' element. It could never be so easy, could it? To just suddenly have a quick chat and Hey

Presto! she's working for me and got her legs wide open already. Where would the fun be in that? Answer: there is no fun in something that easy. The more I had to chase, the greater the prize was and then I would submit to what she wanted to do, further down the line. She had me wrapped around her little finger and that was the critical element of Jason's bizarre plan. Getting her to suggest a warped role-play which muggins here obliged to without a second thought.

Rose said that after the Christmas party she got a text from Stephanie late on informing her that she'd managed to get my four-digit passcode for the phone and password for Twitter, then distracted me in a meeting so Stephanie could swipe my phone to pass to Louis. It all clicked into place, almost.

How did Rose know Willey? Simple; it was Tom. Tom got her the job temping after he left Aspinall-Willey. Part of what I do involves poaching good people from other similar companies or those who have a similar sales process to ours, so when I nicked Tom from Aspinall-Willey he felt morally obliged to replace himself. With Rose. When she started at Aspinall-Willey, Jason obviously realised that she could be the weapon to release into the whole plan after I'd turned down his offer to buy me out and he'd made it a mission to pursue me. Rose could earn him the route to a takeover, if a nice enough carrot was dangled, like a brand new company car. Once she was in, of course, a stupid accountant like Mark would be the last piece in the jigsaw. Get him in for an interview with dumb old me, impress and voila, he's in charge of the numbers and persuaded to streamline them with the same promise of a new set of wheels. The stupid bastard had no clue as to the magnitude of it all and just took a bung.

But Jason underestimated one vital thing: *compassion*. Or maybe you could call it humanity, or moral fibre. Fuck it, call it whatever. He overlooked one thing: not everyone thinks like him, not everyone is as ruthless as him, and not everyone is always chasing a win.

Why did Rose U-turn? Compassion. Compassion blended

with her steadily growing feelings for me. She *did* have that said moral fibre. She *wasn't* the cunt that Jason or Clive or Stephanie proved themselves to be.

And Mark – he too let his conscience get the better of him and his moral fibre won over. His angel beat his devil.

*

When Rose had finished telling me all of this, I was ninety-nine percent sure she was telling the truth but I had to be one hundred, no less. I showed her the video to be sure she knew that even if she was still playing silly buggers, I held the ace. She remained calm and didn't seem to give a shit, which I took as a sign that she was giving me the whole, unedited version of truth.

'We'll have to edit out the end bit and watch it together, on your big screen sometime,' she said. And I knew she was on my wavelength as soon as she said it.

*

I dialled Islington nick and asked for PC Sharma, and when I got through I told him I was going to collect my phone. And give him an idea of who was behind the whole Twitter hack.

SEVENTY-FOUR: JOKE

Sean appeared to be beaten. He spoke slowly and in a higher pitch. Jason and Clive waited.

'So, we seem to have reached a solution. I'm willing to sell. I've spoken to Rose here and Mark, and it seems there is no real alternative. Mark's gone over the numbers and Rose has given me her word that there will be no implications from here on in, relating to the allegation of...you know.'

Sean couldn't bring himself to say it. 'That's what I needed to check on, gents. Make sure everything was covered off.'

Jason and Clive looked at one another. They wore a look that said *is he bluffing or is he for real?* A demi-frown and a small smirk across both their faces.

It was true. Sean was there to finalise things. He *was* willing to sell. Mark had been over the numbers and Rose had already promised Sean that was the end of it thanks to her interview with the police on Tuesday.

Jason went first. 'Ok, I think it's the best outcome for everyone. Wise move. So do you have the signed paperwork?'

'Sure, hold on a tick,' said Sean. 'Rose?'

Rose pulled out an envelope from her bag and handed it to Sean who opened it up, scanned over the three different documents and then handed them to Willey. And then he just sat there, waiting for the expressions of Clive and Jason to morph into a rage. Jason's mouth screwed up; his handsome, chiselled features went from Hollywood winner into guttersnipe loser. From a slick wolf to a dirty little sewer rat.

'Eh? Wha-what? Is...is..is this a FUCKING *joke*?' was all he could manage, like some other words in his brain were standing at the top of a ladder down to his mouth but too angry to take the first steps in case they stacked it and got jumbled up. His hands were trembling and his nostrils were frantically expanding and retracting a thousand times per second. It was quite funny to see, Rose thought.

'Oh, sorry, I almost forgot exhibit A. Have a quick look at this. You may need the volume up.'

Sean held up his phone. Both men watched the video of Sean and Rose, the realisation that it was taken from someone else other than Stephanie sunk in after five seconds. They shot Rose a sneer and then drew their attention back to the documents. Two of them were signed statements, one each from Rose and Mark, detailing the whole history of the goings on, describing how the whole stitch up had been orchestrated. Jason and Clive were mute, raging, as Sean looked on with a smug smile and hardly able to contain his excitement. He composed himself, however, and delivered a killer blow.

'So you see gents, I've checked with my legal *team*. What you've tried to pull off...phew...it'll see you struck off. Let's see...forcing Mark into corporate fraud, deception, blackmail, false accusations, wasting police resources, defamation, slander, pressurising female employees to have sex, Clive? A hell of a lot to get your heads around isn't it? Oh and not to mention racially, homophobic and extremely offensive malicious communication on Twitter. Yep, Louis fingerprints are all over my phone, by the way. Had to pop in to see PC Sharma last night with my solicitor. Tell Louis to expect a call from the police imminently, as I think they'll want to take some prints to close the case, Clive.'

All of the blood drained from Jason's face and Clive broke into a sweat.

'Now, I'd be grateful if you'd turn your attention to the third document,' continued Sean.

They looked at a copy of the offer letter they'd given to Sean twenty-four hours ago. There was only one small difference: the number had changed.

'Not so bad really,' said Clive.

'No, Clive. *Look*. It's five million, not five hundred grand. Read it again.'

They all fell silent. Clive concentrated hard.

'Give us a day to look over it, please,' said Jason after a minute.

But Sean wasn't playing.

'Seriously? Did those words actually just come out of your mouth, Jason? You were *so* desperate to buy me out that you went to fucking *extreme* lengths to stitch me up and get me to sell for peanuts, even send me inside. Really? Do you honestly think that there are any other alternatives here? I've got as much evidence as I need - right here - to drag you through a horrendous court case, win it, and then ruin you. You'll need a fucking good brief to keep yourselves out of Pentonville. And even if you did, then HMRC would want to investigate you when it's finished in court. Fuck knows what else they'll dig up if they get an anonymous tip as to your business ethics. Got an accountant's full statement right here citing the pair of you.'

It was not a bluff.

Clive spoke next. 'Listen, Sean. Am sure we can work something out here. Don't forget I have a stake in your company still.'

'I know, I'm not stupid. Far from it Clive, pity you for thinking I am. Five mill and all this noise goes away. You're happy, I'm happy and life is good. Look at the terms, dude. I'm bound to silence and all the other shit that goes with a takeover. I can't trade in business information for five years once I've sold. Pay me a little *something* over the odds and you can have it all. Everything - bells and whistles. Go and make hay, I couldn't give a flying fuck what you do once it's done.'

Sean finished his coffee and watched his words sink in. No one spoke for another thirty seconds, Jason and Clive just gawped at the offer, like it was a piece of toilet roll caked in excrement.

When neither of them spoke, Sean did again.

'Ok. Look...I'm going to make this *really* simple for you,' he said beginning to lose patience, 'you've got one hour to go away and confer. Use *my* office. I'll be up to see you at,' he looked at his watch, 'nine. You'll have it all signed and dated and then

I'm out of there for good. Communication to the staff can be managed by you. Oh and Mark here gets three month's pay, and that chair you promised him, and Rose gets three month's pay, too. I'll see you in an hour. Thanks for breakfast.'

Sean got up, dusted off the bread crumbs, as did Rose, who once she'd straightened out her skirt, grabbed Mark and reversed him away from the table.

The three of them strolled along to St Paul's for a coffee at Alchemy, where they sat down for an hour and enjoyed the best coffee in the city.

SEVENTY-FIVE: APOLOGY

'Islington Police issue statement of apology to local businessman Sean Thomas.'

The headline was simple enough; the rest of the article fairly straightforward and to the point. Cornish held up a copy of the offending publication that was the *Islington Gazette* and recited the headline like it was a question, goading Sharma into a response.

'I don't choose what those so-called *journalists* print, Diana,' he said.

'Inspector Cornish, please Pritesh. Today I am *Inspector Cornish*. Understand?' Her glasses were, as usual, steamed up from the hot drink she had on the go, although Sharma was beginning to wonder if they steamed up every time he was in her office.

'I do somehow marvel at how...at how...*blind* a police officer can be. I'm going to read you what the total sum of just *one* article has to say about us in this fiasco. Ready?'

He didn't dare say it. She took a sip of her drink and cleared her throat.

'Islington Police's Chief Inspector Colin Woodruff yesterday issued an apology over the wrongful arrest of local businessman Sean Thomas, CEO and owner of the Business Information firm STI Ltd. Mr Thomas was accused and arrested amid allegations he had tweeted homophobic and racist remarks from his Twitter account, targeting celebrities such as Damien Gold, Flame AKA Jade Smith's son Roman, Olympic medallist Tim Doyle and a host of other high-profile celebrities including members of the Great Britain Paralympic team. Mr Thomas, of Potters Bar, Hertfordshire, denied allegations and maintained his account had been hacked, despite a team lead by Woodruff making a formal arrest. Following a simple investigation, which seems to have been overlooked by the constabulary, Mr Thomas was found to be innocent. The plans to crack down on social media hate campaigns continues. The branch has been

scrutinised recently for an apparent lack of action on hateful social media, following the suicide of two teenagers in the past month, and this will do nothing to reassure the public of their protection from the sick individuals who hide behind social media aliases.'

'What else did you expect, Inspector? You backed me. Don't try and pin all of this on me. To be honest, shame on you for hiding behind Woodruff and letting me take the flak.'

'Oh, I'm not. There's more. You also walked in on some kind of bizarre love triangle role-play and decided to arrest this Thomas chap as well, without taking down any sensible possibilities. Imagine that? Forget the Twitter thing, let's just cuff him up and stick him in a cell, and accuse him of rape until the girl comes clean and says it was just a bit of fun. Why didn't you at least question *her* instead of believing the perverted German lass filming it?'

'French, Inspector,' he corrected her.

'I don't care if she was from Tasmania! Pritesh you just don't think, do you? You don't think like the rest of us. Colin wants to see you first thing Monday when he's back. That's all.'

Sharma couldn't get out of there quick enough. He was just through the door when Cornish shouted him back.

'Oh Pritesh, there's no cleaner in today. So you can go and clean out those few cells. And I mean clean. Under the mattresses, round the basins, the toilet seats. EVERYWHERE!'

And as quickly as it had presented itself, PC Pritesh Sharma's promotion had slipped away into the rotten, soiled underpants of his false nemesis.

SEVENTY-SIX: FUTURE
June 2019, various locations

So it all ended well for me, and I guess for the clowns at FFB and Aspinall-Whatever who tried, and failed, to stitch me up.

Before the money hit my bank account, I quickly set up another company to use as a vehicle to continue trading in the business intelligence space, despite being bound by the agreement that I wouldn't operate in the area. The five million I got for STI went into the bank account of STD Ltd - Sean Thomas Distribution Ltd - which now operates as an importer of translated trade publications from around the world, distributing them to libraries all over the UK, for a very small profit. Rose does some sales, Mark does the accounts, and I have a few other minnows dotted about doing stuff like marketing and HR, the usual – not social media, yet. We're doing well, and it's allowed me to purchase a start-up firm in the business intelligence space, exploiting a loophole in the contract made with Willey and co., and it's a company that is going to be focusing on *recycled* energy intelligence. It's the next big thing; solar energy is *so* last year. And when the time comes, Willey and his mob are gonna come knocking on my door again, but I expect a sensible and above board offer this time around. No honey-traps, no office jokers to prank the shit out of me, and certainly no dodgy accountants.

I'm on holiday at the moment, spending a few weeks away from my new flat in Hampstead. It's just me and Rose, in my Spanish villa, the place is called Mijas (mee-has), and it's close enough to Marbella if a night out is needed, but far enough away to avoid bumping into the entire cast of TOWIE, or Made in Chelsea or whatever else the place seems to attract i.e. a bunch of fame hungry, plastic orange dickheads, who think that the meaning of life is being on reality TV.

Back to the villa: when you walk into it, it has this Moroccan palace feeling to it. I opted for the smallest one - called *Villa Maria* - on the exclusive development of six. Five beds, four bathrooms, pool, tennis court and hot tub/Jacuzzi and outdoor bar area, balconies all over the show and a fucking stunning view out onto the most beautiful golf course I've ever seen. I spend a few weeks here every year – STD Ltd runs itself very well in my absence. I'm familiar to all the locals as well, and even wave at Sergio Garcia and Rafa Cabera-Bello when they're walking up and about to tee off on the seventh. One day soon I'll trot over and get a photo, and then I'll have a round when they're playing, and share a cold one afterwards in the clubhouse and discuss where it all went wrong for Tiger. Well, one can but dream.

Rose loves the place too, her folks have been out to visit when we're there, and despite being closer to her father in age than I am to her, they seem to have accepted me. They appreciate that she's looked after and doesn't want for anything, yet still works and contributes to the company. She's a director, of course, and in the summer we're off to the Maldives where I'm going to propose. Bit cliché I know, but it's time someone made a decent man of me. All that messing about, womanising and battering the gear and booze on a Monday night had to stop. The escapades with Willey and co and their fun and games made me see some light and realise that, when something is about to be snatched away from you, it's important to fight for it, and be true to yourself. So yeah, everything's cool now. Life is really good, and I've got a good tan.

Very occasionally when Rose isn't with me, I will dabble in a massage from one of the local brass houses up in the hills, just a hand job or maybe a cheeky bj, never the full package. Sonia usually gives me a discount, as well. What a Brucie!

What? Come on, I may have changed a lot, but hell, I haven't *totally* transformed.

*

'You're being counterproductive now, son. Enough of the jokes now.'

Hannah has just left the office and Clive is sat with Louis

after yet another disciplinary meeting. Louis, in his new found freedom of Chief Marketing Officer, had gone to the VP of Sales - aka Mo's - chair over lunchtime and poured two litres of water over the seat, so when Mo came back from lunch and sat down, his light grey suit became dark grey around his buttocks and chafed his skin. All afternoon. This, of course, caused a row - Mo calling Louis from his desk phone and irately lambasting him, Louis sniggering and apologising, and then walking over to observe how much of the black ink he'd smeared over the earpiece and mouthpiece had transferred onto Mo's mouth and ears. A fair amount, it turned out. The nail in the coffin was a mountain of Indonesian food being delivered up to the sales floor; the delivery man said the order was for *Mo the mad Muslim stocking up for Ramadan,* which sent the sales floor into hysterics.

Tom is still smashing the numbers, as well as into Stephanie, despite still being totally incapable of holding his drink. Stephanie has her car, thanks to Uncle Antoine taking pity on her. She fulfilled her side of the bargain after all, so she got looked after.

*

Lucy's relationship with Mark didn't last long. Mark opted to end things because she "wasn't really up for doing anything except watching Big Brother and getting takeaways."

Lucy now lives with another boiler called Nina, similar age and a total mental case who lives and breathes uppers, downers and round-the-corners. Together they make a right old pair of sad lonely old witches, holidaying once a year to somewhere awful like Kavos on Corfu, or Tenerife. Lucy was fired from her job as marketing manager for a chain of pubs after her manager caught her stealing a box of McCoy's and a litre of Jameson's. She's now working in Sainsbury's local until she finds something better, and her boss is "that black woman on the till."

*

PC Sharma resigned from the force shortly after the whole

Twitter/rape fiasco had quietened down. "Resign or be fired" was the precise term Woodruff used. He now works with a cousin in Birmingham, buying and selling electrical bits and pieces, and is much happier. He relocated up there last year, and his son has a little sister now. His wife still doesn't answer back.

*

Willey, Foster, Fisher and Baker are still at large, plotting the next takeover. Since acquiring STI Ltd, they've made healthy profits and taken big strides towards turning the company into a global leader, not just in intelligence around the solar energy markets, but other verticals, too. They were punished for their actions, but the punishment stopped as soon as five million left their account and hit Sean's. Safe to say they've learned from it; Jason doesn't have as much influence as he did before when they need to think creatively.

*

Woodruff retired a year ago and is doing some private detective work, charging the earth to spy on people's spouses with a telephoto lens. When he's not doing that, he sometimes does a bit of work as an extra on Eastenders, usually propping up the bar in The Queen Vic. His replacement at Islington is now Chief Inspector Diana Cornish.

*

Sean doesn't bear any grudges. There's no need to, after all. He's a changed man, and grateful he bumped into Rose that fateful November afternoon.

Who knows where he'd be now had he been just a minute later?

Acknowledgements

I would like to make a few small notes of thanks to some of the people who have helped me take the idea of writing Stitched Up through to realisation. Michael Terrence Publishing who have been extremely helpful throughout getting the original manuscript polished and ready to offer the general public.

I'd also like to thank various close friends who accepted the challenge to read either all or parts of the book and give genuine unbiased critique, without that I don't think I would have kept the faith. In no particular order: Matthew, Neil, Steve, Steve, Adam, James, Mo, Tony, John, Kara and Adam Gibson.

Also, a big thank you to everyone at The Cricketers Arms pub for allowing me to use their free Wi-Fi, drink their beer and hide away in one of their booths with the laptop, aiding my ability to write with freedom whenever cabin fever set in and I needed a change of scenery.

About D. A. MacCuish

D. A. MacCuish was born in Glasgow and grew up in Hertfordshire, before studying Hotel Management at Brighton University and graduating in 2000.

Since then, he has worked in Business Intelligence in the city and most recently set up and run his own recruitment business.

He lives in North London. He is a keen follower of football and golf, and plays both to a very questionable standard. When he's not doing that, he's spending time with his family, or reading.

Available worldwide from

Amazon

Printed in Great Britain
by Amazon